AROUSE ME

Club Genesis - Chicago, Book 4

USA Today Bestselling Author

Jenna Jacob

AROUSE
Me

USA Today Bestselling Author
JENNA JACOB

Arouse Me

Club Genesis – Chicago, Book 4

Jenna Jacob

Published by Jenna Jacob

Copyright 2023 Dream Words, LLC

Edited by: Raw Book Editing www.http://rawbookediting.com

ePub ISBN: 978-1-952111-44-0

Print ISBN: 978-1-952111-45-7

If you have purchased a copy of this eBook, thank you. Also, thank you for not sharing your copy of this book. This purchase allows you one legal copy for your own personal reading enjoyment on your personal computer or device. You do not have the rights to resell, distribute, print, or transfer this book, in whole or in part, to anyone, in any format, via methods either currently known or yet to be invented, or upload to a file sharing peer to peer program. It may not be re-sold or given away to other people. Such action is illegal and in violation of the U.S. Copyright Law. If you would like to share this book with another person, please purchase an additional copy for each recipient. If you're reading this book and did not purchase it, or it was not purchased for your use only, then please purchase your own copy. If you no longer want this book, you may not give your copy to someone else. Delete it from your computer. Thank you for respecting the hard work of this author.

This is a work of fiction. Names, places, characters and incidents are the product of the author's imagination and are fictitious. Any resemblance to actual persons, living or dead, events or establishments is solely coincidental.

Previously published as *Saving My Submission*.

He compelled the surrender I didn't want to give…

I'm **Mellie Carson**—bold, ambitious, career-driven, independent woman. When I hook up with sexy-as-sin sculptor **Joshua Lars** for a one-night stand, he totally blindsides me. I never expected his skilled hands and commanding presence to awaken the forbidden desires hiding inside me. The passionate night we share reshapes my definition of pleasure.

To save my sanity, I try to forget him. But fate—and a killer—have other plans.

Determined to save my life, Joshua hides me away. Safely protected in his loving arms, he steals my heart while doing everything in his power to…*Arouse Me.*

Previously published as *Saving My Submission.*

Chapter One

Joshua Lars kissed my lips like he owned them. His capable hands —those of a famed master sculptor—swept over my shoulders, sending my red designer dress down my body, past my hips to spill like a puddle at my feet. Languid and thorough, he made love to my mouth as if I were a masterpiece he sought to mold.

As he unfastened my bra and tossed it to the floor, his intoxicating scent made me dizzy. I clung to him, trembling with anticipation, as he lashed his tongue up the column of my neck before devouring each pebbled peak and the aching flesh around them.

From the moment he'd pressed me up against the door of his studio and kissed me breathless until he'd lowered me onto his bed, Joshua's jade-colored eyes held a piercing command. And as his body hovered over mine, all sinewy and taut while his bicep muscles bunched and rippled, I quivered beneath his steely erection pressed against my belly.

As a shock of his wheat-colored hair fell over his brow, I reached up to brush it away, but he clasped my hand. Then, with a barely perceptible shake of his head, he raised my arms over my head and pinned my wrists to the mattress.

My pussy clenched.

My heart skipped.

His Dominant gesture stole my breath as the need to submit surged through my veins. I hadn't let a man command me for years. I wasn't about to start now.

I struggled to break free, but Joshua shook his head.

"Easy, Mellie. I'm not going to hurt you." His voice was smooth, like fine-aged brandy. "Tell me, little one, are you what I hope you are?"

His actions, his ragged whisper, put a chink in my armor and made the burning pulse of surrender rise higher. "What exactly is it that you hope I am?"

"Don't play innocent. You know what I'm talking about. Earlier tonight, while you were staring at my sub statue, the glow on your face aroused my suspicion. But when you started to cry, it was as if you'd opened a window to your soul. I keep catching glimpses of your true nature, but it's elusive, like smoke. There and smoldering one second, then floating away on the wind the next. It's as if you're trying to deny your feelings."

What. The. Fuck? Out of all the men I'd been with—and there had been plenty—not one had ever sensed the sleeping submissive inside me. Yet, ninety minutes with the world-renowned artist Joshua Lars, and his Dominant radar saw right through the thick, sturdy walls I'd painstakingly constructed.

His lips brushed mine in a feathery-light kiss. "I'm dying to taste your surrender."

His words unnerved me. "I-I don't know what you mean," I lied. "Stop talking and fuck me."

To throw him off my submissive scent, I arched my hips and rubbed my pussy against his cock, aiming to coax him into a down-and-dirty, dazzling, one and done that I could handle. Diving into BDSM waters—especially with Joshua—would be like jumping off a cruise ship without a life vest. I didn't want or need to take my chances in those shark-infested waters again.

Lifting my head, I tried to force him to kiss me. He reared back with an arch of his brows. Disapproval lined his face. I'd never have the upper hand with the man, and it should have scared the hell out of me. Instead, it turned me on even more.

This is going to be tricky.

"Ah ah ah, play nice, pet. I won't allow you to top me. We're going to take the path that's got you so skittish, because it's the same one that has you wet and ready." He bent and nuzzled his lips close to my ear. "I can smell your cunt, little one. It makes my mouth water."

I didn't know what to say. He pinned me with a dissecting stare. His breath fluttered over my lips. Unable to look at him without wanting to melt in surrender, I cast my gaze to the golden patch of hair between his flat nipples. I couldn't risk him seeing those submissive parts of me I'd hidden.

"Yes, that's the one. My, my, what a gorgeous little thing you are."

His low, raspy praise sent lashes of fire dancing up my spine. It felt as if the devil himself had licked me with his scorching tongue.

Cinching both of my wrists into one hand, he skimmed his other down my body, pausing to roll each of my beaded nipples between his fingers and thumb. Shards of electricity shot south and gathered behind my already throbbing clit.

"Your safeword is *fantasy*, because that's what you are—a fantasy that's been plucked straight from my dreams."

Lord help me. The man had seduction down to a science. Combined with his potent Dominance, I didn't know whether to laugh, cry, or run for my life.

Desperate to keep this encounter as vanilla as possible, I scoffed. "What the hell is a safeword?"

Joshua narrowed his eyes. "Don't lie to me, pet. Lie to yourself all you want, but I've already seen everything I need to."

He bent and pressed his lips to mine with a kiss so explosive it stole my breath. Surrender, like a long-lost blanket, enveloped me, and for one brief moment I didn't care if he saw through my mask or not. The need to please him cracked my walls, and the stroke of his demanding tongue had my submission seeping through.

My mind was still spinning when I felt the cool tip of his latex-shrouded cock slide between my heated folds.

"Yes," I gasped, arching in willing compliance.

With a feral growl, Joshua thrust deep inside me as a cry of pleasure-mixed-pain tore from my throat. Blessedly endowed, he filled and stretched me with a captivating burn. Struggling to relax my passage, he withdrew, only to impale me once again. My packed pussy fluttered and rippled around his shaft. A low groan of delight rolled off his tongue and vibrated onto mine. Squeezing my wrists—almost to the point of pain—he emphasized his control, and it sent my heart soaring.

Joshua plunged in and out of my clutching cunt in a slow and steady rhythm. Arching to meet his thrusts, I held nothing back. The sounds of gasps, grunts, and slapping flesh filled the room. Tearing his mouth from mine, he gazed down at me. Sweat dotted his brow and his red, swollen lips glistened. The epitome of rugged beauty and command, Joshua drew me in even deeper with the fiery lust dancing in his eyes.

"Are you going to be a good girl and ask for it, little one? Beg nice and pretty for me?"

When I nodded sharply, he drove even deeper. Crying out, I wrapped my legs around his waist as every thick inch of him throbbed inside me. His glorious torture was sublime. Exhaling a savage hiss, he began dragging his bulbous crest over the sensitive bundle of nerves in a slow, decisive rhythm. As if orchestrating a symphony, the swell grew to a turbulent crescendo, sending lightning ricocheting through my cells. I cried out again, letting the sinful blaze burn me alive as he unleashed his potent sexual skills.

"Harder, Joshua. Please, fuck me harder!" I begged.

And he did. Hard…fast…and unrelenting, like a freight train thundering down a mountain slope. Joshua drove in frenzied thrusts as if his life depended on it. Sweat dripped from his face, mixing with mine as our harsh animalistic sounds echoed in the room.

Wedging a hand between us, Joshua strummed my clit with just the right amount of pressure. My moans turned to screams, morphing into keening pleas that he'd allow the swell to pull me under and annihilate my blistering need.

"Now," he bellowed. "Come for me, Mellie."

Right on cue, as if eight years had been but yesterday, I responded —like I'd been trained—and shattered at his command.

Rocked by the force of my powerful orgasm, dark spots formed behind my eyes. Pounding into my channel like a man possessed,

Joshua suddenly froze. Fixed deep inside me, he let out a deafening roar before pummeling my cunt in a torrent of erratic strokes; he followed me over.

Releasing my wrists, he dropped to his elbows. Panting, he pressed his face against my neck. Our coupled muscles twitched and pulsed until the sexual buzz faded. Easing from my pussy, Joshua collapsed to the bed alongside me. Both of us covered in a fine sheen of sweat, the heady scent of sex lay like a heavy blanket around us.

It took several long minutes before our ragged breaths slowed and evened out, and all the while I lay staring at Joshua. His eyes were closed, and a serene, sated expression lined his face. I wanted to pinch myself.

I just had sex with Joshua Lars.

Sex, my ass! The man fucked your brains out. And did a righteous job of it, too.

The little voice in my head was right. No lover before him had been capable of enticing an orgasm of *that* magnitude. Clearly, Joshua had more impressive talents besides gifted hands. Studying the sharp features of his handsome face, his rugged jaw line and the light blond scruff covering his chin, I smiled. His golden hair, now dark and wet, lay plastered to his head. Still, he looked like sin on a stick, and I'd have no trouble whatsoever taking him on for round two.

As if reading my mind, he opened his eyes. A quirky smile played over his lips. "Oh yeah, we definitely need to do that again, but give me a minute. I'm not as young as I used to be."

I laughed. "You're not the only one, Sir."

Sir? Sir? Where the fuck did that come from?

Joshua didn't bat an eye at my reply. Obviously, he was accustomed to being called 'Sir' by someone—maybe a whole lot of someones. The inward prick of jealousy surprised me, but I was more concerned at how easily the honorific 'Sir' had rolled off my tongue. Unnerved, I realized Joshua had picked the lock and opened the Pandora's Box of my submission. A knot of fear began to unravel, and a surge of panic-laced adrenaline exploded through my veins. I leapt from the bed as if it were on fire.

"Where are you going?" Shifting, he raised up on one elbow. A quizzical expression lined his face as he watched me race around the room.

"Bathroom," I replied curtly. Gathering up my dress, thong, purse, and shoes, I raced away.

"Wait," he called to me. "I thought we were going to—"

Before he could finish his sentence, I slammed the double doors of the bathroom shut and locked them. On shaky knees, I stepped into my dress, clutching the sink to steady myself. Catching a glimpse of my reflection in the mirror, I froze. My lips were red and swollen. My cheeks flushed in a 'just fucked glow.' Still taut, my dusky nipples tingled from all the attention Joshua had bestowed with his fingers and teeth. The elegant, coiffured bun I'd worn to his showing was now wild and disheveled in the vivid aftermath of how his urgent hands had snarled through my mane. Outwardly, I wore all the markings of a woman well satisfied, but gazing at my eyes, I could see the terror stamped within. A new, more potent wave of alarm slammed through me. I'd allowed Joshua Lars and his Dominant charm to touch me too deeply.

"Dammit, what the fuck are you doing? Get your shit together and get the hell out of here," I mumbled to my reflection in the mirror.

Stepping into my thong, I grabbed my purse and pulled out my cell phone. Scrolling an online search engine as I tugged the tiny scrap of material to my knees, I dialed the number of a local cab company. Tucking the phone against my shoulder, I fumbled through my beaded clutch, plucking out the invitation as a gruff man answered. Rattling off the address, I swiftly ended the call, shoved everything back in my purse, and finished yanking up the thong still abandoned at my knees.

A thunderous knock landed on the other side of the door. Jumping, I yelped in surprise.

"Mellie, open up," Joshua demanded.

"Just a sec," I called out, my voice cracking with anxiety.

"Mellie?" He pounded once again. "Don't make me break this fucking door down. We need to talk."

Talk? Oh hell, no. There was absolutely nothing I wanted to say to the man.

"Open. Up. Now."

I bit back a whimper. *Shit! Why did he have to use that imposing Dom voice on me?*

"Okay," I snapped. Cursing under my breath, I chided myself for letting him awaken my dormant submissive longings.

Slipping on my fiery red stilettos, I yanked the door open and instantly wished I'd kept the sucker shut. Joshua stared down at me, wearing nothing but his black tuxedo pants and a nipple-hardening scowl. His commanding mien nearly took me out at the knees.

When he opened his mouth to speak, I raised my hand and pushed past him, surprising him into silence.

"Thanks for a wonderful time, Joshua. I had fun." The tone of my voice was so dismissive I couldn't help but cringe inside. I couldn't even look at him. *Coward.* Plucking a business card from my purse, I held it out to him. "If you're ever in Phoenix, give me a call."

When he didn't take the card or utter a single word, I looked up at him. Both brows were arched in disbelief, and his eyes were steeped in 'Dominant censure.' Yes, the man had *that* look perfected, which further fueled the riot of panic inside me. He wasn't happy. The barbs of shame for displeasing him pricked at the sub inside me. She all but screamed to fall at his feet and beg his forgiveness—while the pragmatic parts of me wanted to slap him across the face for breathing life back into the woman I'd put to death.

"Really? You're actually going to tear out of here like your ass is on fire and not tell me what's wrong?"

"Nothing's wrong. It's time for me to go."

Liar.

A noise of disbelief rumbled in the back of his throat.

"I had fun. We got to burn off some stress, but it's late, and I'm tired. Besides, I need to get back to my sister's house. She'll worry."

"Worried, huh? Does she always treat you like you're a teenager?" he chuckled in disbelief.

I flashed him a sarcastic smirk and shook my head.

"You have a cell phone, right?"

"Of course."

"So, don't you find it ironic that it hasn't rung once since we came to the loft?" He cocked his head and stared into my eyes, delving far deeper than he had a right to. "Tell me what this is really about, little one."

"Stop calling me that," I hissed. "I'm not your little one. I'm no one's *little one*."

I tensed as Joshua clasped his hands on my shoulders in a gesture meant to calm. World War III raged inside me, and I had to force myself to stare at his face and not cast my eyes toward the floor.

Shit! His very touch seduced my submission and threatened to reduce my walls to dust. He was living, breathing kryptonite to my self-restraint, and it pissed me off.

Sucking in a shaky breath, I planted my fists on my hips. "Look, Joshua, the whole Dom/sub thing isn't for me."

"Okay. I can respect that. But that still doesn't explain why you're dressed and running out the door like…" He frowned. "Like…I'm a one-night stand."

Busted. While I had no intention of making a love connection with him or any other man, I'd established internal rules about one-night stands. Knowing I'd have to cope with the onslaught of guilt afterward, I usually kept my hormones in check, shying away from casual bed-hopping. Not the case with Joshua Lars. No, star struck, I'd tossed my principles out the window and bedded the man without a second thought about the consequences for my actions. Shame would come—probably in the morning, if not sooner—and I'd have to swim my way to the top of my remorse. But first, I needed to find a tactful way to get out of there without crushing Joshua's fragile male ego even more.

"It's not like that at all," I lied, *again*. "It's simply time for me to go before my sister files an Amber Alert," I replied with a forced chuckle.

Joshua's sour expression didn't change. Obviously, he didn't find my poor attempt at humor funny in the least.

"So you say, but I still don't buy it, my frightened little bird," Joshua challenged, stepping closer. "At least, let me drive you home."

"Frightened? That's crazy. I'm not the least bit afraid of you." Not *physically. Emotionally? You scare the beejeebers out of me.* "Really, I'm fine. I don't want to inconvenience you."

"It's not an inconvenience," he whispered, inching closer still. "Let me drive you home, Mellie."

"I-I Ah, I already called a cab."

His body tensed at my rejection. "I see. When do you go back to Phoenix? I'd like to see you again before you leave." His words were clipped and matter-of-fact.

"I'm…I'm not sure. Ah, maybe a week or two. Give me a call tomorrow. Maybe we can arrange it before I go."

Stepping back, I put some much-needed distance between us. It was either that or strip off my clothes, release the bulge beneath his straining zipper—*dammit, why did I have to look at his cock*—and wrap my body around him again. No. I couldn't afford to do that. He'd crawl so deep inside me I'd never want to leave. My only salvation was to bolt for the door. Get as far away from the intimidating artist as possible, and never go back.

"I will." He smirked. Striding toward me, he leaned in close. As his warm breath fluttered over my ear, I trembled. "You can run, Mellie, but you can't hide."

"Only children run away, Joshua. I'm not a child," I scoffed.

"No, you're definitely all woman. But you're definitely running away from what you truly are, and we both know it."

I opened my mouth to refute him, but snapped it shut. I'd lied enough to the man. "Good night, Joshua. I'll talk to you soon."

Spinning on my heel, I all but ran to the door. Wobbling down the stairs, trying not to fall, I raced outside, sucking the cool night air into my lungs. Peering up and down the street, goosebumps prickled my arms and anxiety pumped through my veins as I mentally willed the taxi to appear.

What the fuck?

Joshua had waved some Dominant magic wand and presto—every emotion I'd buried raged back to life in a fiery conflagration of confusion.

As a cab pulled around the corner, the sound of a slamming door behind me split the night. I jerked a glance over my shoulder to see Joshua striding toward me, the statue of the kneeling woman gripped in his hand. His unreadable expression disturbed me.

"You forgot something," he announced evenly as he thrust the delicate sculpture toward me.

"I'm sorry. I didn't mean to...I wasn't thinking...I..."

"No, you were too busy running for your life." He scowled.

"I-it's...a...so generous of you," I sputtered, taking the fragile piece from him. "Thank you so much for everything."

As I struggled to string a damn sentence together, a ghost of a smile tugged his lips.

"I'll be in touch with you *soon*, little one." Leaning in, he placed a chaste kiss on my cheek, then stood back, watching until I was safely inside the cab.

I gave him a little wave as the taxi pulled away, and it took every ounce of strength not to turn and look back. Four blocks later, my heart stopped pounding and my breath evened out.

Dammit, how the hell did you get yourself into such a cluster fucking mess?

"Prince Sheik Abbas," I murmured, staring down at the statue.

Six Days Earlier

Startled awake by my ringing cell phone, I sat straight up in bed. The first thought that blasted through my brain was the fear something dreadful had happened to my sister, Savannah. A rush of adrenaline shot through my system. My heart thundered in my ears. Blinking at the clock radio on my nightstand, the eerie green numbers illuminated three thirty-seven a.m. A whimper of terror seeped from my throat as I squirmed free of the twisted covers. Flipping on the bedside lamp, I squinted as I snatched up my cell phone.

"Hello," I answered fearfully.

"Meelee? It's Abbas calling. I have fantastic news."

My shoulders slumped and panic slowly melted from my veins when I realized it wasn't Nick or Dylan—my sister's Masters—on the other end of the line. There was only one man on the planet who butchered my name so brutally...the same man who had zero concept of time zones outside his native country of Dubai.

"Your Majesty. Do you have any idea what time it is in the U.S.?" I moaned.

"I do not think you understand what I am saying to you," he continued, ignoring my question. The lilt of his sensual velvet accent soothed my jagged nerves. "I have wonderful news to share, Meelee."

Scrubbing a hand up my forehead, brushing the hair from my eyes, I blinked several times, attempting to adjust to the bright light that filled my room.

"Yes, I'm listening, Abbas."

"Joshua Lars is back!"

Swinging my legs over the side of the bed, my heart skipped a beat as I sat up straight. Abbas had my undivided attention.

"Meelee, are you still there?"

"Yes, I'm here. Joshua Lars?" I repeated as a streak of anticipation rocked through me. "Where? When?"

"Sheecago. It will be his first exhibit in five years, Meelee. Is this not the best news I could give you? I want his art, Meelee. You will go for me and purchase them. Yes?"

"Of course," I replied absently. "An open exhibit? When? Do you know the date?"

"I have all the information you need. That is why I called." He all but purred in my ear.

"Why haven't I heard anything about this?" A flash of irritation ignited within.

"It is private. Joshua is only giving this treat to his special customers. And I, of course, am his special customer."

"Indeed, you are, Abbas. How do I get an invitation?"

"I will see that it is arranged for you. Now, listen carefully. You must buy it all for me, Mcclee."

I choked back a snort. "Surely, you realize they won't let me purchase *everything*, your Majesty. I don't know yet how many pieces he'll have up for sale."

"There are many pieces, Meelee. I have sources that tell me this.

Joshua has….how do you say? Ah…hibernating since the death of his wife and daughter." Abbas spoke softly, as if honoring the artist's loss.

"Which gallery in Chicago? And when?" Yanking open the drawer of my nightstand, I shoved my over-worked vibrator aside and snatched out a pad of paper and a pen.

"Christian Joyce Gallery. Thursday. Next Thursday, Meelee. At seven o'clock," he informed.

Christian, you little son of a bitch! That prick hadn't breathed a word of this to me. Oh, his frilly little princess ass was all mine!

"Thank you, Abbas. I actually know him. I'll call him when the gallery opens and make sure I'm put on his guest list. Unbelievable," I whispered, trying to wrap my head around the unprecedented news. "I'll start making arrangements right away. Is there a monetary ceiling you'd like me to stay under?"

"Oh, Meelee. Money is insignificant." For Abbas, it was. The man had more money than he could spend in ten lifetimes, and wouldn't that just suck? "No limit. Abbas will pay any price."

"I understand."

"My heart thanks you, Meelee."

"You're welcome, Abbas. I'll call you from the gallery with a total."

"No need. I took the pleasure and wired money to your account so you can purchase many treasures for me, Meelee. You will keep the rest. It is to show you many thanks."

I almost choked in astonishment. "Thank you, Abbas. That is overly generous of you."

"That will make me pleased. Now, one last question. When will you come to me and be one of my wives?"

I snorted. "We would fight day and night, Abbas. I don't like being told what to do. Besides, I'm lousy when it comes to sharing my man with others."

"But I would make you feel like my one and only, Meelee. You have a special place in my heart. It would be an honor to own you." His voice teemed with seduction.

I rolled my eyes and shook my head. Being part of a harem held as much appeal as a sardine milkshake. "Good night, Abbas. I'm going back to bed."

"Dream of me, Meelee."

"You know I will." I chuckled and hung up.

Wow! Joshua Lars is out of seclusion. I shook my head. This was going to knock the art world flat on its ass.

Climbing out of bed, I padded to the bathroom before making my way to my office to boot up my computer. Four hours and two pots of coffee later, I called Christian. With a saccharine sweet chastising, I busted his gay little balls for not informing me of Joshua's comeback. Christian was contrite in a whining-groveling sort of way. After vowing he'd never leave me in the lurch again, along with a promise to overnight an invitation, I accepted his apology and hung up.

Five minutes later, I had my airline ticket booked; however, finding a room proved more of a challenge than I'd expected. Every metro Chicago hotel was booked for some stupid festival. Squandering another two hours perusing design articles online, I finally picked up the phone.

"Sanna?"

"Mellie? Oh, how bizarre. I was just thinking of you."

I couldn't help but smile. My little sister had blossomed from a wallflower into a vibrant woman since falling in love with two men… her Masters. A pang of envy pierced my heart. Never in a million did I suspect that Savannah would be attracted to the BDSM lifestyle, but her total transformation proved she'd found her bliss. She was no longer a quiet, shy bookworm. Dylan and Nick had helped her break free of her chrysalis, and she'd blossomed into a stunning, submissive butterfly.

I *was* happy for her; happy her path hadn't ended in a fiery death, like mine.

"Uh-oh, what did I do now?" I teased.

"Nothing, dork. I just miss you. You're not packing to go anywhere soon, are you? I'd really like you to come to Chicago for a visit."

I sensed a hint of desperation in her voice. "What's wrong?"

"Nothing. I'm just…it's nothing."

"You're what?" My over-protective sister DNA zipped to high

alert. "Did Dylan and Nick do something to you, something they shouldn't have?"

"No. Heavens, no!" she shrieked. "I'm just missing you. After you broke up with Enrique, I thought you'd come for a visit, so we could drown your heartache in a gallon of ice cream. But you never came. You just got more wrapped up with work."

"I got swamped with clients. Besides, I was the one who called it off. There wasn't any heartache, it was mostly relief. He got way too serious. I told you that."

"Yeah, yeah, I know. But you were with him a long time—a lot longer than any of the others."

"Thanks," I grumbled sarcastically. "You make me sound like a bed-hopping bimbo."

"I didn't mean it like that, and you know it," Savannah scolded before her tone turned gentle. "I'm sorry, I'm just hyperemotional these days for some weird reason.

"Don't sweat it," I reassured. "So, tell me, what's *really* bothering you?"

"I don't know," she mumbled. "I have everything a girl could want. My life is beyond perfect. I just miss you and want to spend some quality time with my bestie."

"Well." I paused. "What are you doing this Tuesday at three fifty-five in the afternoon?"

"Nothing, why?"

"I could use a ride from the airport, oh, and a place to crash—if you think Dylan and Nick won't mind."

"Here? In Chicago?" She gasped.

"Yes," I giggled. "There's a private art showing Thursday night. I'm going for a client."

Savannah let out a scream so loud I had to yank the phone away from my ear. Not just one scream, but a whole bunch of them. Suddenly, I heard the thundering voices of Dylan and Nick demanding to know what was wrong. It took my excited sister several long seconds to explain why she was coming unglued.

"Mellie?" Nick's deep, authoritative voice sent a shiver up my

Four days later.

As promised, my sister and her men met me at the airport. When I stepped off the plane, Savannah rushed to my arms with a smile so wide I thought her face would split. I held her tight as we both swiped at our tears of joy. Emotions flooded through me. There was nothing more comforting than the unconditional love of my sister. We'd relied on each other for years after surviving the tragic death of our parents. It had been a heartbreaking time in our lives, but we drew strength from one another and grew to be more than sisters—we became best friends.

Guilt swamped me in an ugly veil as I held her in my arms. If I had been a stronger person, I wouldn't have left her and moved…err, rather, ran away to Phoenix. Tangled in my own turmoil, I'd convinced myself she was an adult capable of living independently after she'd graduated high school and enrolled in college. When in reality, staying in Kansas City, dodging phone calls from worried friends while trying to remain invisible to various lifestylers on the streets wore me down and ate at my self-confidence. My former hometown held too many memories—each one a slap in the face—reminding me I'd been a fool to believe the lies of a wannabe Dom and control freak.

It was pointless to wallow in guilt. I couldn't go back and erase Davis Walker—master manipulator—from my past, even if I'd wanted to. But oh, how I wanted to.

Pushing the depressing thoughts from my mind, I kissed Savannah on the cheek. After giving Dylan and Nick each a big hug, we retrieved my luggage, then headed to their house on the shore of Lake Michigan.

"Come on, let's grab some drinks and sit out on the deck," Savannah suggested after I'd unpacked my suitcases. "We can catch up on some gossip. Maybe I can sweet talk the guys into fixing us dinner."

"Sounds great." I nodded. "You know they're spoiling you rotten, right?"

"Yeah," she giggled. "But I spoil them right back."

Dylan and Nick possessed mad culinary skills. The men had no business being in construction. The two could make an even bigger fortune if they tossed off their hard hats for chef's hats and opened a five-star restaurant. They were that amazing.

As Savannah and I wound our way into the kitchen, I stopped and stared, like I always did. For a woman who could barely boil water, the extravagant room—with every top of the line appliance imaginable—simply overwhelmed.

"Every time I walk in here, I imagine myself having a nervous breakdown trying to heat up a can of soup."

Savannah laughed, then reached into the fridge and grabbed a couple of diet sodas. I followed her out to the deck. The summer sun warmed my skin, and a gentle breeze blew through my hair as we caught up on the latest gossip in our lives.

"And to think, you gave up living alone in that cramped, over-priced, two bedroom apartment for all this," I teased.

"I know, right? What was I thinking?" she laughed then reached out and clasped my hand. "Oh, Mel, it's so good to have you here. I've missed you so much." Her eyes filled with tears.

"Sanna, what's wrong? Tell me…"

"I don't know!" She threw up her hands and released a nervous chuckle before wiping her eyes. "I think I've got a wicked case of PMS going on."

"Ahh, okay. *That* I understand."

I sat up and leaned over, wrapping her in a tight hug. Boy was that the wrong thing to do. She didn't find comfort in my soothing actions, she simply broke down in a fit of gut-wrenching sobs.

Dylan and Nick stepped onto the porch wearing identical expressions of concern.

"Kitten?" Dylan softy whispered, as he knelt next to her chair.

"Hormones," I whispered to him with a knowing wink.

"Aww, princess," Nick purred as he bent in close, easing Savannah from my arms.

"I'm sorry for being such a hot mess, Masters," she sniffed.

A mischievous smile curled over Nick's lips. "We like it when you're a hot mess. We like it even more when we're the ones making you that way. Look at me."

Savannah raised her head and gazed up at him. The love that reflected in her red-rimmed eyes was blinding, and my heart nearly burst with happiness for her.

"We love you, precious. Raging hormones and all." Nick smiled as he brushed away her tears with the pads of his thumbs. "We want you to be happy, and if you're not, tell us and we'll fix it."

"I *am* happy, Master. I love you both so much," Savannah sighed as she flashed a look over her shoulder toward Dylan and me. "You make me feel like a princess."

"You *are* our princess, and we love you. So, put a smile on, kitten," Dylan urged, dancing his fingers up and down her arm. "Your sister's finally here. It's time for happiness instead of tears."

Savannah gave a resolute nod and forced a watery grin.

"Good girl," Nick praised before kissing her softly.

Good girl. A shiver slithered up my spine at his Dominant words. Being surrounded in an atmosphere of BDSM always played havoc with my head, and shoving my submissive longings down wasn't going to be a picnic. I'd find a way to cope. A few weeks of having the lifestyle slapping me in the face wouldn't kill me. Besides, spending time with my baby sister would be well worth it.

When Savannah finally regained her composure, Dylan and Nick grabbed a couple of beers and joined us on the deck. We sat and talked, laughed and teased. Dylan was as smart-assed as ever with his quick comebacks and taunting jabs, while Nick, the quieter one, enjoyed baiting his friend simply to rile him up. Both made it blatantly obvious they loved Savannah with every cell in their bodies. The maternal concern I'd harbored in regard to her relationship with the two men had been put to rest on my first visit. It was reassuring to see the three were still blissfully happy.

As the sun ebbed below the horizon, we drove to a quaint Italian restaurant called Maurizio's for dinner. I was surprised to see several familiar members from Club Genesis dining there as well. Shoving down the niggling urges within, I painted on a self-assured smile, inwardly drawing my armor tightly around me as Savannah re-introduced me to their friends.

Glancing toward the bar, I spied a hunk of a man—built like a lumberjack—smiling as he swaggered toward us. He zeroed in on me like a hawk circling a field mouse before extending his hand to me. Placing my fingers in his broad palm, an electric sizzle raced up my arm.

"Hello there, gorgeous. I'm Scotty. What's your name?"

"Mellie Carson," I replied, flashing him a daring smile. Never one to walk away from a challenge, I met his carnal stare with one of my own.

"Really?" he replied with a confident, wolfish grin.

Before I could counter with a sultry comeback, Nick whisked me toward the other side of the restaurant to a table where a smiling couple sat eating.

Nick introduced Tony and Leagh, the pending bride and groom who were to marry in a few short days. The man looked vaguely familiar as my mind flashed back to him sporting a tight black security T-shirt at the club. I recognized Leagh immediately. The first time I'd met her, she'd gone by the name Dahlia and had been with a much older Master named George. When Savannah phoned to tell me George had died, I remembered how heartbroken I'd been for poor Leagh. But watching her with her new Dom, I realized that not only had her heart healed, but she'd gone through a huge transformation. No longer sassy and brash, she projected a self-assured poise and serenity about her, all but glowing beneath Tony's tangible adoration.

A flicker of hope whizzed through me. Leagh had been given a second chance at happiness and submission. Could I, too, be that lucky?

Get real. Pining over power games won't make you happy. No, everything I needed I provided for myself. Not many women had the opportunity to make an obscene amount of money doing what they loved. Cultivating my own happiness was empowering, and I didn't need a man to do it. So what if I left dozens of short-term relationships in my wake? I lived my life without doling out promises, being tied to a collar, wedding ring, or marriage license. I took pride in the fact I'd orchestrated my life exactly how I wanted it to be, without apology. I had to stop wasting time allowing myself to fall victim to longings I couldn't afford to let resurface.

Your life is perfect, dammit!

We sat and ordered dinner. All through the meal, I caught Scotty checking me out, sizing me up, and luridly undressing me with his eyes. He didn't seem to give off a Dominant or submissive vibe, which was a relief. No, the man appeared to be a regular old vanilla guy and the exact distraction I needed to clear my head of BDSM thoughts.

Encouraged by his attention, I flashed him several suggestive smiles, even going so far as to run my tongue up and down the tines of my fork when no one else was watching. Scotty let out a long, tortured groan, shook his head, and turned away. I had to bite back a laugh. Toying with the poor, horny man was delightfully entertaining.

When dinner was done, Scotty approached the table with four small glasses of bright yellow liquor. Bestowing a bold and scandalous wink, he set one of the cordials down in front of me.

"Limoncello, in honor of your first—but hopefully not last—visit to Maurizio's."

I flashed him a coy smile. "Thank you. I'm flattered." As I lifted the glass to my lips, I noticed the phone number scrawled on the napkin he'd set beneath my drink.

"You're quite welcome," he smiled before bending close to my ear. "I get off work at two. If you're still awake, give me a call." Tapping his finger on the napkin, he flashed a wolfish grin.

"I might have to start drinking coffee," I countered in a sultry whisper.

"I hope you do." His reply sounded low and hungry.

Gazing at me for several long seconds, Scotty jerked his head, as if remembering we weren't alone. Embarrassment fluttered over his features before Scotty darted a glance around the table then cleared his throat.

"How about some dessert? We've got New York Cheesecake. Maybe some Crème brûlée, or a piece of our decadent chocolate mousse cake?"

I didn't miss the knowing smirk Dylan and Nick shared between themselves before the two declined dessert.

"Thanks, but I'm stuffed," I replied with a shake of my head.

"I'd love some," Savannah replied, grinning at me like a schoolgirl. "Cheesecake, please."

"You got it. I'll be right back." He nodded then turned and swaggered toward the kitchen. I couldn't help but stare at his tight ass or the way his well-worn jeans hugged him so perfectly.

"For crying out loud, Mel, you haven't been in town twenty-four hours, and already you're setting hearts on fire," Savannah teased.

"Trust me. It's not his heart that's on fire, unless it's slipped down between his legs. The only thing I'll be doing at two in the morning is snoring and drooling."

"That's an attractive picture," she snorted.

Scotty pushed past the swinging stainless steel doors carrying a thick slice of cheesecake. As he made his way to our table, I watched, appreciating the way the muscles on his arms rippled and bulged. No doubt the man spent hours at the gym honing his sculpted body. Savannah turned to see what I was staring at, then let out a smothered chuckle.

"Bet you five bucks you end up setting your alarm," she teased.

"Nah. He's a hottie, all right. But all I want tonight is sleep. Tomorrow? Well, who knows? I might need to come back here for lunch," I whispered as he drew close and placed a mountainous wedge of cheesecake in front of Savannah.

Chapter Two

Bright and early the next morning, Savannah bolted into my room and pounced on the bed.

"What the hell are you doing?" I groaned, trying to shake the sleep fog from my brain.

"Get up, lazy bones. We're going shopping!" she exclaimed with a wicked gleam in her eyes.

"Shopping for what?" I mumbled, rubbing mine.

"Nasty things, for Leagh's bachelorette party."

"I'm wide awake now. When's that happening, the party I mean?"

"Friday night at Maurizio's. We've reserved the back banquet room. No Doms allowed. It's gonna be subbies gone wild!" She waggled her eyebrows. "And Scotty's going to be our private bartender," she taunted in a singsong tone.

"So? What are you trying to do, play matchmaker now that you found love?" I teased.

"No, I'm not. But honestly, a blind man could see he wants you. He was practically drooling all over you," she giggled.

"Yeah, well, they all drool from time to time. Don't get me wrong. He'd be fun for a night or two, but that's it." I shook my head.

"How do you know?" she countered.

"Because they're *all* fun for a night or two, but after that..." I wrinkled my nose.

"I've always suspected you were allergic to monogamy."

"Yes, I am. It gives me hives that make me itch. Besides, you might be happy with two men slobbering all over you, but...gag me, I like my freedom. Now where's the coffee?" I asked, changing the subject as I bumped my hip against hers and climbed out of bed.

"Downstairs in the big, scary kitchen." Her voice wobbled in a creepy tone, and she made an evil face as she wiggled her fingers, like a wicked witch casting a spell.

"You're such a goof-ball," I laughed as I pulled on my robe and secured the sash. Flashing Sanna a mischievous grin, I stepped closer toward the door. "Last one to the kitchen gets to eat what's fixed."

Dashing out of the room, Savannah was hot on my heels. We both ran down the stairs like a herd of rampaging elephants, stopping when a fit of giggles hit us at the same time. We hadn't played that stupid game since she was in high school. Savannah would do almost anything to avoid eating what I cooked....or rather, burned. I had skills, but definitely not in the kitchen.

Dylan and Nick rounded the corner, staring up at us as if we'd lost our marbles while both Sanna and I laughed like a couple of loons. Nick held a phone against his ear and scowled. Dylan simply watched our antics with a goofy grin, shaking his head in disbelief at our crazy behavior.

"Shhh," I giggled, pressing a finger to my lips. "Nick's on the phone, and he looks like he's ready to spank your ass."

A devilish glint flashed in Savannah's eyes. Spinning around on the stair, she wiggled her backside, taunting the two men. "Here it is, baby. Come and get it. It's all yours."

Nick bit back a smile. Dylan's eyes flashed wide in surprise as he laughed. Still giggling, Sanna turned and blew a kiss to her Masters. Without missing a beat of his conversation, Nick reached behind his head. Pulling the leather strip that held his long, ebony hair free, his raven mane spilled down over his shoulders. Pinning Sanna with a disapproving expression, he nodded toward his feet in silent instruction.

Darting a nervous glance my way, she padded down the rest of the stairs. Once at the bottom, Nick motioned for her to turn around. A tiny 'oops' seeped from Sanna's lips. Wedging the phone between his shoulder and his ear, Nick took the leather strap and bound her wrists behind her back, then pointed her toward the kitchen.

"Not the rice, please," she whispered with a beseeching plea.

Nick swatted her ass. With a fierce scowl, he pointed more adamantly than before.

Joining the two men at the bottom of the stairs, I looked up at Dylan.

"Rice?" I whispered.

With a hungry smile poised on his lips, Dylan watched the sway of my sister's ass as she walked away. "Uh-huh."

"Do I even want to know?" I swallowed tightly.

"You've never been punished with rice?" Dylan asked.

I shook my head. "I'm not in the lifestyle. Not anymore."

My remark caught Dylan off-guard. He arched his brows and cocked his head, gazing into my eyes with a curious stare.

"You know, it's not a light switch you can turn off and on, Mellie. If the desire truly burns inside, it will catch fire no matter how hard you try to wish it away." Studying me intently, he frowned. "Something bad happened to you, didn't it? That's why you left the lifestyle."

His spot-on assessment crushed down on me like a ton of bricks. Dylan—the happy-go-lucky of the two—had seen right through me. Either he was psychic, or I had been more transparent than I thought. Either way, I felt naked and exposed. I quickly averted my gaze to keep him from gaining even more insight.

"I've worked through some bad shit, too. When you're ready, we'll swap stories. It might do you some good."

"I'll keep that in mind." I nodded, knowing damn good and well *that* day would never come. Then, like a big ol' puss-bucket, I turned and scurried away to find Savannah.

Unnerved by Dylan's keen assessment, my worries quickly changed focus when I found my sister nervously pacing in the kitchen.

Surely, they weren't going to punish her for our childish behavior, would they?

"I flippin' hate rice as a punishment."

Evidently, they would.

"Why can't they just spank my ass?" she moaned.

"Because you'd like it, precious," Nick announced with a devious chuckle as he and Dylan entered the room.

She jerked her head toward the two men. Regret lined her face. "I didn't mean to make you mad, Masters. Mel and I were just dorkin' around like we used to. You know…last one to the kitchen is a rotten egg kind of thing? Only, I didn't want to be the rotten egg because I'd have to eat what Mellie fixed, and well, Mellie's a lousy cook."

"Oh, the thundering herd of wildebeests isn't the issue at all, kitten," Dylan grinned. "It was the taunt and wiggle of your sexy backside that's gotten you into trouble."

"But I was just stating the obvious. It belongs to you two. I was simply acknowledging the fact," she said, trying to charm her way out.

I couldn't help but laugh. "You might as well take it like a woman. You're already busted, baby."

She turned, pinning me with a look as if I'd grown horns. "You're not helping!"

"I think you're beyond help, sis," I said with a chuckle.

"You're just as guilty as I am," she choked.

"Um, no, I'm not. I wasn't the one taunting your Masters."

Sanna stuck her tongue out at me, and I laughed even harder. Dylan and Nick turned their attention my way. Grabbing an empty mug, I cleared my throat, suddenly feeling like the third wheel at a motorcycle convention.

"I'm just going to get some coffee and get out of your hair," I mumbled. Staring at the handles and dials on the silver-plated appliance, I couldn't find anything that resembled the simple drip-style coffee maker I had at home. "Ah, if I can figure this fancy thing out, that is."

Without a word, Dylan sidled up beside me, hastily showed me which button to push and lever to pull. In a matter of seconds, I had a sweet, creamy, steaming cup in hand.

"I'll be, umm, up in the shower," I nervously announced. Flashing Savannah a clandestine wink of encouragement, I tiptoed toward the doorway.

"That's a wonderful idea, Mellie," Nick purred as he stepped in close to my sister, caressing a dark hand over her ass. "She'll be up when we're done here. It shouldn't take long."

Climbing the stairs, the sound of Nick's deep, placating voice wafted from the kitchen. I couldn't hear what he said, but his cadence was filled with love and compassion. A wistful smile tugged my lips before a pang of envy spiked inside.

Drying off after my shower, I wrapped my robe around me and padded into the bedroom. Savannah sat on the edge of my bed. Her cheeks were flushed in a rosy hue and her swollen lips bore a matching shade of crimson. Her eyes said it all. The look of a thoroughly satisfied woman reflected brightly.

"So, I guess you didn't get rice?" I snickered.

"Uh-uh," she replied on a dreamy sigh.

Lucky little wench, I chuckled inwardly.

"What the hell is rice punishment, anyway?"

"They sprinkle dry rice on the marble kitchen floor, then make me kneel on it. Sucks big ones, too."

Ouch! "I bet that hurts like hell."

"It does." She nodded with a frown.

"Yeah, but just think where you'd be without them, Sanna."

"Don't go there, Mel." She shook her head, then rose from the bed with a sheepish grin. "I need to go get cleaned up. Trevor and Julianna will be here soon. They're going to go with us. You don't mind, do you?"

"Of course not. They're fun, especially Trevor. Hey, is Julianna bringing the baby?"

"Nope, Mika is pulling daddy duty alone for the first time. It should be interesting." Her face wrinkled in a cringe. "Meet you downstairs."

An hour and a half later, Sanna, Julianna, Trevor, and I perused the aisles of a local adult toy store. Gazing at the plethora of vibrators, fuzzy handcuffs, and floggers, I couldn't help but wonder what one gave to a submissive bride-to-be that she hadn't seen or used? Was there something we could find so off-the-charts-kinky it would make Leagh blush? Doubtful.

"Hey, Mellie, can you grab that for me?" Trevor asked, nodding toward a display of rubber dildos while juggling an armful of latex toys and lube.

"Sure. Which one do you want?" I asked.

"That big double-headed sucker, right there," he replied as his gaze zeroed in on the huge rubber cylinder.

"What's Leagh going to do with this?" I asked, plucking it from the shelf.

"Oh, that's not for her. It's for me," Trevor replied as his cheeks blazed crimson.

"Okayyy. Guess that's what I get for asking," I chuckled.

Savannah let out a squeal from across the store. Trevor and I raced over to see what she'd found.

"This is *it*!" Sanna exclaimed. Struggling, she picked up the biggest butt plug I had ever seen. Its base was at least twenty inches in diameter and the tapered tip was as big as a soda can. The damn thing was heavy as hell from the way she strained to hold it in both arms.

"You're kidding, right?" I gasped. "That thing's big enough for an elephant."

"Lord, sister. I'm scared." Trevor's eyes were wide with fear. "If Daddy brought that mother home, I wouldn't even pack my bags. I'd just run out the door like the hounds of hell were nippin' at my heels."

"Why on earth would you want to buy her that?" I asked in disbelief.

"It's an inside joke. Trust me, she'll get it." Savannah winked.

"This can't be. No way is this thing made for human consumption. I mean, there's not an asshole on the planet that could stretch that much and still work the way it's supposed to. I'm just sayin'." Trevor shuddered.

"Hey, did you find the lube?"

"Yes." He nodded. "But if you insist on buying her that terrifying monster, she's going to need more, a *lot* more. Like a cement mixer of lube."

"She's not going to use it," Savannah laughed.

"No shit!" Trevor barked, still gazing at the plug in a combination of terror and shock.

"I think it'll make the perfect centerpiece for the party, don't you?" Savannah preened.

"Centerpiece? Oh, *now* I understand. You scared me," Trevor sighed in relief before a mischievous twinkle danced in his eyes. "I think we should shove a sparkler in the tip and light that sucker up!"

"That's a perfect idea," Sanna squealed.

"I found the penis sippers," Julianna sang out as she hurried toward us waving a handful of plastic cock-tipped straws in the air. "Oh, and I also found this lovely, albeit tacky, bridal veil. It's got a real imitation rhinestone tiara. She'll be so excited. Plus, get this. The veil lights up with flashing neon dicks. They'll see her coming a mile away."

"Oh, I want one of those," Trevor giggled.

"Two rows over on the left," Julianna pointed with a chuckle. Blinking, she stared slack-jawed at the massive plug.

"It's the centerpiece," I laughed.

"I'm speechless," Julianna gulped.

After doing damage to our credit cards at the toy store, we stopped for lunch at a Mexican restaurant. I suggested a pitcher of margaritas and was adamantly shot down. Not only was Julianna breastfeeding, but I learned my sister, Trevor, and Leagh had recently spent a memorable afternoon at Maurizio's consuming copious amounts of wine. Evidently, the three got so wasted their Doms had to fetch them from the *ladies'* room. I'd have paid money to be a fly on the wall that night.

Savannah wrinkled her nose. "It wasn't pretty."

After lunch, we decided to go window-shopping—which of course, turned into power shopping and I soon discovered my sister had grown into quite the shoe whore. I had no room to talk, especially after finding a pair of sinfully sexy red satin designer stilettos. Perfect for the red backless gown I intended to wear to Joshua Lars' gala the following night.

Julianna was first to throw in the towel, not because she was tired of shopping, but Mika had called her cell phone. Once she heard her baby squalling in the background, motherhood superseded shopping.

"Tristan won't have a thing to do with the bottle of breast milk I left. I swear it's like I've given birth to a clone of Mika. Neither one of them are truly satisfied unless they've got my tit in their mouth," she laughed.

We quickly said our goodbyes and drove home, then Savannah and I spent the rest of the day wrapping Leagh's gifts. When our task was done, we sat out on the deck sipping wine while Dylan and Nick prepared dinner.

"Mel, do you ever think about living somewhere besides Phoenix?"

"Sometimes, but not often," I replied. "Why?"

"I just wish you lived closer. I know the winters here scare you. After Mom and Dad's accident, I understand you wanting to move someplace without ice and snow. It's just that the fear doesn't have to control you. You can grow past it. I did. I know you can too. Besides, I know it's selfish, but I miss you. I mean, all the time."

Guilt tingled at the tips of my toes and crawled up my body like a cold, slippery eel. I'd used the death of our parents to spin a web of lies, concocting an excuse of being afraid of ice and snow to run away like a spineless wimp.

"My first winter here, the three of us went out to dinner, but before we could get back home, the weather turned horrible. The road was a sheet of ice. It took all the strength I had not to have a full-blown panic attack. I told them I was scared, and do you know what they did?"

I shook my head, still unable to look her in the eyes.

"They comforted me…reassured me. They actually talked me off the ledge, and ever since that day, I've been fine. They helped me conquer my fear. I don't have a phobia about dying the way Mom and Dad did anymore."

Sweet Savannah, trying so hard to sort out my life. What would she do…what would she say if she ever found out I'd lied to her? I'd kept my dirty, little secret from the one person on the planet who I loved more than life. If I ripped open the lid and spilled my guts, it would scald her to the core, but dammit, I couldn't keep hurting her this way. I had to tell her the truth.

"That's not the reason I left Kansas City," I mumbled.

Sanna set her glass down and stared at me with a shocked expression. Her gaze all but burned my skin. "Then why did you leave?"

"I had to get away from someone."

"Me?" she whispered, her words slathered in rejection.

"Hell, no!" I shook my head as her words stabbed my heart. Did she honestly think I left because of her? "No! No! Not you. It was because of a guy."

"Who?" she gasped. "Did someone hurt you?"

"Physically? No. Emotionally? He crushed me," I confessed on a shameful whisper.

"Tell me who, Mel. Tell me right now," Savannah demanded.

"You don't know him. He was a Dom I met at a club in Kansas City. He called himself 'Chain Master'," I scoffed derisively. "He was my Master for nine months."

"What did he do to you?" Her voice quivered, and tears filled her eyes.

"Why are you crying?" I asked, choking back the emotion clogging my throat.

"Because whatever he did must have been horrific and vile if it made you leave your home and me."

My walls within crumbled, and tears spilled down my cheeks. Savannah knelt in front of my chair and held me as I sobbed. "I'm so sorry. I had no business leaving you alone when you were so young. You must think I'm the most selfish bitch on the planet."

"No. I don't think that at all. Stop that. I turned out just fine," Sanna declared as she held me tight, rocking me in her arms. "You're scaring me, Mel. Please tell me what happened."

I didn't know where to start, but as the memories flooded through me, along with the slick, ugly revulsion I fought for months after, I sucked in a deep breath and closed my eyes. "I met Davis right before your senior year of high school. I found the club not long after I moved back home, after Mom and Dad…anyway, Master walked in one night and swept me off my feet. He was suave and sophisticated; well, he wore the persona. Supposedly, he'd been a well-respected member of a club on the east coast."

"Didn't anyone do a background check on him?" Sanna asked.

"Oh, I'm sure he was vetted like everyone else. He was liked by many in the club. I thought he was the real deal until he uncollared me like he did."

Pausing for a moment, I stared at my sister. Worry etched her face and her eyes brimmed with anguish. I didn't want to tell her the gory details, but I'd opened the lid on the keg of shit. I couldn't close it again until I'd confessed everything. Staring off at the horizon, the fateful night came rushing back in full living color. Every sight, sound, and smell filled my brain.

"I walked into the club one night, anxious to see him. He sat at a small table in the back of the social area with a young redheaded girl. She was giggling and batting her big blue eyes at him like he was a damn god or something. A hush fell over the crowd, and everyone stared as if they knew something I didn't. It's funny, I always thought they were my friends, but no one ever pulled me aside to tell me what my Master had really been up to."

"What had he been doing, Mel?"

"He'd been scening with her, dominating and fucking her behind my back." I shrugged. "I know a Dom playing with another sub isn't a big deal, but the fact that he never told me about her…wasn't honest with me was like a knife to the heart. I trusted him, believed in him… in us. I should have known something was up; things between us had started getting strained. I'd chalked it up to him being stressed out about work, so I just focused more on pampering him and trying to make him happy. I was such an idiot."

"Stop saying that. It's not your fault the bastard lied to you and your so-called friends didn't bother to tell you what he'd been up to, either. How the hell were you supposed to know?"

"I shouldn't have ever trusted him, but hindsight is always twenty-twenty, right?" I scoffed. "Anyway, I walked up to the table. He looked up at me like he'd seen a ghost. His shock turned to anger instantly, and he looked down at his watch and started barking questions at me. *'Why didn't you tell me you were coming to the club early, bunny?*

You're supposed to tell me where you're at and what you're doing. Or did my rules escape your tiny little brain? I don't appreciate you sneaking in and checking up on me, slut. That shows a real lack of trust on your part.'

"We both knew I'd busted him, but he tried to gaslight me and blame me, to save face look like some bad-ass Dom in front of his fuck toy and the other members. He totally stunned me. I had no idea what to say to him, because he'd never verbally berated me before. The whole room was thick with tension, and that's when the redhead asked if she could leave the table. She actually asked *his* permission," I scoffed. "I wanted to knock her teeth straight down her throat."

"You should have, Mel. Dammit," Sanna groused.

"Suddenly, he flipped off his anger and turned to the girl, smiling with a stupid, fake syrupy grin, took her hand and escorted her to the bar, leaving me standing there like an invisible, dumb, deaf mute."

"What a douche bag."

"Mega douche bag," I agreed. "My heart pounded in my chest, and I stood there fighting back tears. Hell, I didn't know what to do, so I turned and started walking toward the door. He yelled at me from the back of the room in a hateful tone. *'Where do you think you're going, whore?'* The club fell deathly silent, and I froze. Everyone turned and stared at me, waiting to see what I was going to do. Then Master ordered me to strip and get my ass up against the cross, that I needed to be taught a lesson. I should have just kept on walking, but I wanted to prove he didn't need the other woman. I was also afraid the members would think less of me as a sub if I challenged him. So, I did what he ordered me to do."

"Oh, Mel. You should have told him to fuck off, or at least kicked him in the nuts and walked out. Wasn't there a DM or an owner around? Someone to protect you?"

"No, I wore his collar, and I didn't use a safeword to stop it. I should have, but…" I took a long sip of wine and sucked in a deep breath. "He stormed up to the cross, dragging his flavor of the month behind him, sat her down and told her to watch a real Dom in action." I let out a humorless laugh. "If I'd been braver, I would have turned and asked him if he knew any *real* Doms, or how long I'd have to wait until one arrived."

"That's the Mellie that should have been there with you, sis."

"I was still trying to play by the rules of the lifestyle, Sanna. Not just to represent him in a good light, but myself as well."

"I know, I get that, but once he'd turned into a raging asshat, no one would blame you for tossing the rules out the window."

"Maybe…maybe not. It doesn't matter now."

"Tell me the rest," Sanna whispered with a nod of courage.

"He cuffed me to the cross and fired up my ass, fast and hard. I tried not to cry out. I wanted him to see I was a better sub than the other girl, but the pain got too intense. I couldn't take anymore, so I called out my safeword. The DM came up then and asked me if I was fine. Master scolded him and told him. *'Of course, she's fine. I know what the hell I'm doing.'* Then he laughed and told me I was useless and pathetic. When he uncuffed me, he didn't so much as give me a hug. He just threw my clothes at me and ordered me to get dressed. After I put my clothes back on, he told me to kneel, so I did. That's when he took off my collar. He told me I didn't deserve it anymore and that he'd grown tired of fucking the same worthless cunt night after night. He said I was nothing more than a waste of his precious time."

"Good grief. I can't believe he put you through all that," Sanna sniffed as tears slipped down her cheeks.

"He taunted me and told me if I wanted his collar back, I'd have to beg for it. I finally told him I didn't want it back. With a shrug, he turned and instructed the redhead to kneel at his feet. She jumped right out of her chair, giggling like a moron. I mean, honestly, she'd just witnessed how callous and cruel the man could be. Didn't she realize he'd do the very same thing to her eventually?"

"Don't feel sorry for her. She deserves everything she gets from that asshole," Sanna spat. Anger had replaced her tears.

"He fastened *my* collar around her neck and kissed her in front of the entire club. Everyone was looking at us with either absolute shock or pity in their eyes. The pity flipped some inner demon inside me, and I went off. I tapped the son of a bitch on the shoulder and when he turned around, I slapped him right across the face. I told him he was a worthless piece of shit and I hoped he rotted in hell. Everyone gasped, but I didn't care. I lifted my chin and walked the fuck out, and I never went back."

"Good for you, Mel. I bet that felt ubër empowering."

"It did, for a couple of days, but then I kept running into people from the club, and none of them even asked how I was doing. They just looked at me like I was a lost puppy. The amount of pity in their eyes was devastating. It seemed everywhere I went, someone or something reminded me of the whole damn mess. I couldn't escape it, so I did the cowardly thing. I ran away."

Savannah downed her wine and stood. Fuming, she paced back and forth along the wooden deck, clenching and unclenching her fists. I'd never seen her so angry in my life.

"If I ever get my hands on that motherfucker, I'm going to rip his dick off and shove it down his damn throat!"

"Kitten!" Dylan growled.

Sanna and I jumped and turned. Dylan glared at my sister as if she'd lost her mind.

"Sorry, Master, but…ohhhh, I'm so pissed right now I can't see straight. Give me a pass on my language or toss out the rice, because right now, I really don't give a shit. I'm so far from any semblance of submission it's not even funny," she railed, planting her hands on her hips and tossing her nose in the air defiantly.

"I can see that," Dylan hissed, his lips drawing in a tight line.

I placed my palm on his hard chest. "Please don't punish her," I begged. "She's upset because someone hurt me, and I let him."

I felt the tension leave Dylan's body. His features instantly softened. "I see. Okay, then here's what I'll do. I'm going to forget I interrupted this conversation and the unladylike words pouring out of your mouth, kitten." He narrowed his eyes, pinning her with a look of warning. "Just don't mistake my generosity for weakness, pet. Understood?"

"Never, Master."

With a hint of a smile, Dylan walked back into the house. Savannah spun on her heel, facing me once again. Anger hummed off her curvy frame in a palpable buzz.

"What kind of fucking player does that to his own sub?" she railed.

"That's exactly what he was…a player. But I was too young and stupid to see though his finely crafted veil of bullshit."

"You weren't stupid, Mel. You might have been a bit naïve, but you've never been stupid. Besides, it's a Master's duty to protect his sub, not toss her under the bus when a new piece of pussy walks through the door."

"I know, but I should have never given that bastard the power to hurt me or make me believe the only way I could hold on to my sanity was to get as far away from him as I could. Please, you have to believe that I never *wanted* to leave you. Back then, I simply didn't think I had any other option than to get as far away from Davis and the awful memories as I could."

"I believe you, Mel, but please tell me you haven't been beating yourself up all these years for moving away?"

My throat closed off with a sob as I nodded.

"Mellie, Mellie. My sweet Mellie," Sanna choked through her tears as she wrapped her arms around me.

"Dammit, Sanna, I'm so sorry. If I could go back and change things, I'd do it in a heartbeat," I cried. "I'm so sorry I never told you the truth."

"Me too," she whispered on a defeated sigh.

Clutching her tighter, I apologized over and over while mourning the precious time I'd selfishly stolen from the two of us. After several long, emotional minutes, Savannah pulled away and wiped her tears.

"Okay, I have a solution to this problem. While I hire a hit man to take out Master Asswipe, you sell your house in Phoenix and move here," she announced with a watery smile.

I choked out a sobbing laugh and sniffed.

Smoothing back my hair, she looked into my eyes. "I understand now why you were always so tense at Genesis, and why you never wanted to scene with any of the *real* Dominants there."

I nodded with a frown. "I'm sorry I never told you the truth, sis."

"No. Don't go there," she warned, narrowing her red-rimmed eyes. "We'll only start bawling again. Besides, I've already forgiven you. You're my sister. I love you."

"I love you, too. So, so much," I sniffed.

She poured us each another glass of wine, then we leaned against the railing of the deck and stared out at the lake. "Do you miss it... submission, I mean?"

"Not until I come here and spend time with you three," I softly confessed.

"Oh, Mel," Savannah groaned. "I'm sorry."

"Don't be. You have no idea how happy I am that you found those two wonderfully Dominant men. And I'm even more ecstatic that you let them into your heart and your life."

A slight blush rose on her cheeks.

"Do you know how proud I am that you've come out of hiding and have spread your wings? Or what a fucking gorgeous woman you've become?" I asked with a broad smile.

"Stop," she giggled, shaking her head.

"No. I'm not going to stop. Since you found those two, you simply glow. You're so full of life and so illuminating. Hell, you walk into the room and it's blinding...you're blindingly beautiful, baby. And you did that all on your own."

"Not on my own," she argued with a sappy smile. "I can say the exact same of you, and don't you dare deny it. Honesty, last night Scotty was all but humping the damn table to get to you. Men are naturally drawn to you, like a lighthouse in pea green fog. So, if you're going to blow smoke up my ass, you damn well better bend over, too."

I couldn't help but laugh. She'd always had a feisty side...like a little tornado. For years, she'd hidden it away, but it was back for the world to see. For a split second, I almost felt sorry for her two Doms. No, they knew exactly how to handle my spitfire sister, and they handled her with perfection.

As if sensing the coast was clear, Dylan and Nick joined us, announcing dinner was ready. Both men wrapped a protective arm around Sanna as we walked inside. Watching the special bond they shared, her question echoed in my brain: *'Do you miss it...submission, I mean?'*

Yes, Sanna I do, with every beat of my heart, but that's one secret I'll keep to myself.

Throughout the scrumptious dinner, I felt as if a great weight had been lifted off my shoulders. The food tasted richer, laughter sounded sweeter, and the outpouring of love between my sister and her Masters didn't scrape my heart as deeply.

When the meal was done, Dylan turned to me, his expression bordering on concern.

"We're going to take Savannah to the club for a bit this evening. You're more than welcome to join us if you'd like."

Darting a glance at my sister, I smiled as she nibbled her bottom lip.

"Thank you for the invitation, Dylan, but I think I'll stay here and take care of some work I've been neglecting."

"Very well." He nodded with a hint of understanding. "We hope to have a chance to talk to you soon."

With a quick nod, I cast my eyes to my empty plate. Dylan's message was loud and clear. Both men would know my story by the end of the night. The rules of submission were cut and dry; Savannah was not allowed to keep any secrets from her Masters. I didn't take her having to spill my story as a betrayal of confidence. Sharing everything with her Masters was necessary for them to maintain open, honest communication in their relationship. Besides, the cat was out of the bag, and with it, the realization it was time to bury the wounds Davis Walker aka 'Chain Master' had inflicted.

Present Day

I woke with butterflies swirling in my stomach and a hum of excitement pumping through my veins. It was crazy for me to feel so giddy. I'd been to hundreds of gallery showings, yet this one had me on pins and needles. I was going to meet the man. The legend. The. Joshua. Lars.

I'd seen pictures of him years ago after the tragic death of his wife and daughter. He was strikingly handsome. Tall with defined, masculine features, but in the photos his green eyes had appeared haunted—they had every right to be. The death of his wife, Victoria, and four-year-old daughter, Camille, rocked the art scene—hard. Victoria had been driving with little Camille to surprise Joshua at one of his local exhibitions. The weather was brutal. Caught in a massive downpour, the car had been swept away by flash flood waters. Search and rescue teams had discovered the vehicle and their bodies the next day. Joshua Lars went into seclusion and hadn't come out...until tonight.

My heart ached for him. I knew firsthand the hell of healing enough to rejoin the living. There are no words to describe the void left inside when a loved one is ripped from your life, or the struggle to gain closure when you didn't get a chance to say goodbye. But losing a child, I couldn't image surviving something like *that*.

Shaking my head, I cleared the morose thoughts from my mind before wandering down to the kitchen in need of a caffeine infusion. The room was empty, and I stood in front of the intimidating coffee machine wearing a frown as I tried to remember what buttons to push to make a cup of coffee.

"Technology, you're a pain in my ass."

I managed to brew a cup, but it was black and bitter as tar. Digging through the cabinets, I spied a container of sugar behind a box of rice. Holding the weapon of Savannah's most feared punishment, I couldn't help but grin. Lifting up onto my toes, I reached for the sugar.

"Can I help you?"

In the quiet room, Nick's deep voice vibrated through me like a sonic boom. With a startled yelp, I launched the box of rice into the air. It landed with a thud spilling out all over the marble floor.

"Dammit, Nick, you scared me half to death!" I shrieked as he laughed.

"I'm sorry, Mel. I thought you heard me come in."

"Well, obviously, I didn't," I huffed as I dropped to my knees to scoop up the mess.

That was about the time Dylan and Savannah entered the kitchen as well. My sister's eyes nearly bugged out of her skull.

"Mel, what did you do?" she gasped in an accusatory tone before turning a beseeching gaze Nick's way. "Honestly, Master, you can't punish her. She's not in the lifestyle anymore."

The tall Native American pinned Sanna with a look of disbelief. "I wasn't attempting to punish her. I accidentally scared her, and she dropped the box of rice, precious."

"Oh," Savannah murmured on a quiet rush of air. "Oops."

"But since it's already laid out so nice and pretty, would you like a few moments to kneel on it, pet? Maybe think about why you assumed I'd dole out punishment on anyone other than you?" Nick's brows arched and a ghost of a smirk played over his lips.

"Oh, no, thank you, Master. I'm fine. I…" she stammered.

Both men laughed, and I bit back a grin while a wry smile spread over Sanna's mouth.

"Where's the broom?" I asked, flashing my sister a playful smile.

The rest of the day dragged on and on, and even though I had my sister and her Masters to keep me company, I was antsy and unfocused. After an early dinner outside on the deck, I raced to my room to get ready for the gallery event. Primping far more than usual, I wondered if Joshua would show up for the gala with some svelte, blonde model on his arm.

Hell, he could be married again for all you know. And why on earth are you entertaining sophomoric notions about him in the first place?

"You're certifiable, Mel," I scolded my reflection in the mirror. "Go buy Abbas his art and get your ass back home."

With one last look, I smoothed my hands over the silky fabric, sucked in a deep breath, and snatched up my red beaded clutch. Watching me from the foyer as I made down the staircase wearing a pair of vampy red stilettos, Savannah's eyes grew wide.

"You look gorgeous," she cooed. "Like you just stepped off a Paris runway."

I chuckled. "I wouldn't go that far, sis, but thank you."

Nick joined Sanna and issued a long, low whistle. "I guess we won't be waiting up for you tonight, Mellie. Just try not to break whoever ends up dragging you to his lair."

"Oh, for the love of…I'm not going to bed some stranger. Give me a break," I replied, rolling my eyes.

"Wanna bet?" Nick chuckled. "Come on, we'll drop you off at the gallery. It's right down the street from the club. Our little smart-ass here needs a gentle reminder that it's not nice to question her Masters." Nick issued a sideways glance at Sanna and smirked.

"I can call a taxi."

"Nonsense. It's on the way," he insisted. "But you might need to grab a cab home. I'm not sure how long we're going to be handing down our discipline."

He wore a quirky grin as he watched Sanna's nervous expression. It was obvious Nick loved to pull her chain just to watch her squirm.

"The club's open already?" I asked.

"No. We have the code to get in. We'll be busy in our private room for quite some time," Nick explained as we joined Dylan in the garage.

"Holy shit!" Dylan grinned. "You look amazing, Mellie."

"Thank you." I giggled, feeling the heat rise on my cheeks.

Dylan reached into his pocket then palmed a stack of condoms in my hand. "You'll need these tonight. Trust me."

"The hell I will," I gasped, trying to give them back to him.

"Keep 'em. Just in case." He winked.

I quickly shoved the foil packets into my purse with an exasperated sigh.

"Oh, before I forget," Savannah announced as she handed me a piece of paper. "It's the alarm code, in case we're not here when you get back. Are you sure you can find a way home? I hate the thought of dropping you off and just leaving you there."

"Nice try, kitten," Dylan chuckled. "Mellie's a grown woman with a cell phone. I'm one hundred percent convinced she's capable of calling a cab."

Savannah pouted, and I giggled. She might like to think she had both men wrapped around her little finger, but they were more than capable of keeping her in line. Each time I observed the by-play between the three, I became more confident she'd found her happy ever after.

"I think you're just looking for a reason to spank me," she grumbled.

"Who said anything about spanking, pet?" Nick arched a brow.

"But now that you mention it, with a slathering of contempt, we might just have to accommodate your wishes and give you a few with the motherfucker."

Sanna groaned and opened her mouth to argue but wisely snapped it shut. I didn't know what the motherfucker was, but obviously, it wasn't my sister's favorite toy.

The entire ride downtown, Sanna fidgeted while Dylan and Nick taunted her with various implements they intended to use on her. They were giving her a royal mind fuck, but I knew while I tended to vanilla business, my sister would be drowning in submissive bliss. I thought it ironic that we'd somehow switched places over the years.

Standing in line outside the gallery, I watched Nick drive away. The butterflies I'd tried to calm all day came fluttering back to life with a vengeance. Inwardly scolding myself for my immaturity, I inhaled a deep breath and thanked the elderly man who held the door for me. Stepping inside the foyer, I scanned the crowd, wondering what eye-scalding eclectic outfit Christian would be sporting for such a grand occasion. The man had a penchant for anything neon and wore it proudly. Spotting him immediately, I smiled while his spiked bleached white hair tipped in neon orange assaulted my eyes.

"Mellie," Christian squealed as he rushed toward me wearing a subdued black tux with tails. With a dainty hug, he air-kissed my cheeks then stepped back. "You look stunning."

"Thank you, Christian. You're looking handsomely formal this evening."

"It's a special night," he announced with a shiver of excitement.

"Yes, indeed, it is. Is Joshua Lars here?" I asked, trying to keep my tone as blasé as possible.

"No. Not yet. He'll be arriving later." Turning his head, Christian tossed his nose in the air with a dramatic lift. "Come. You've got to see all these incredible pieces."

Following him into the gallery, my mouth fell open. The enormous room showcased dozens of phenomenal works, both large and small. Each piece was painstakingly displayed beneath a network of lights designed to highlight the intricate detail of Joshua's amazing talent.

Awestruck, I stood in one spot turning slowly, attempting to absorb the vast splendor before me.

Guests mingled, their murmured voices buzzing like bees in a hive. A life-size piece in the center of the room drew me like a magnet. Edging closer, I stood enamored at the breathtaking harem girl. Wrapped in scarves that appeared to flow on an invisible wind, she stood poised on tiptoe as if in mid-dance. A mischievous glint seemed to reflect in her eyes, leaving the impression that a seductive smile lay hidden beneath the veil draped over the lower half of her face. The piece was so stunning it nearly took my breath away.

Abbas would kill for this piece.

Turning, I locked gazes with Christian who'd been watching me with a boyish grin, and I gave him a slight nod. Laughing, he scurried away, returning moments later with a black leather folio tucked under his arm. Over the next hour and a half, I procured eight exquisite pieces for Abbas.

Christian disappeared to process the financial transaction, and I wandered the gallery one last time, eyeing the pieces I'd chosen for Abbas. I lifted a flute of champagne from the tray of a passing waiter and stepped to the back of the gallery, indulging myself with a private toast for a job well done. Raising my glass, I spied a piece of art tucked away in the corner that I'd somehow missed. Stepping closer, I stopped. Frozen in shock, I stared at the piece, totally mesmerized.

Situated on a tall pedestal was the tiny figure of a naked woman, kneeling. Her face was upturned toward the heavens; her long slender neck banded in a wide metal collar. My breath caught in my lungs as I stared at her hands resting on her splayed thighs—palms up—her pose undeniably submissive.

Tears burned the backs of my eyes and my heartbeat quickened. The statue called to me in a way so powerful and primitive, I couldn't stop staring. How had the man managed to transform a lump of clay into such a powerful reflection of submission? The enthralling piece of art seemed to have been crafted as a tribute from the heart.

The intricate details were so painstakingly exact that meticulous tears clung to slivers of her eyelashes. So realistic, I could clearly see the lines on her palms and whorls carved into each fingertip. Even the pads of her heels had been etched like the living. Long hair fell in soft curls over her slender shoulders and cascaded down her back, kissing the apex of her ass.

Studying her oval face, her prominent cheekbones, narrow nose, and full lips bore a disturbing resemblance to my own. A shiver slithered up my spine. The longer I studied the piece, the more convinced I became; she wasn't gazing toward the sky. No, the girl was focused on the face of some unseen Master—seeking approval, pleading for Dominance, or begging his mercy.

Entranced by the lifelike figure, memories bubbled to the surface, igniting a blistering fire of longing and neglect. Seduced by the smoky images filling my mind, I could see myself—through the eyes of an unknown voyeur—kneeling before the man who once held my heart, mind, and soul. Lost in reminiscence, the ghostly sound of my own submissive voice resonated in my ears, while sheltered surrender warmed my empty soul. My days had been bound to unfulfilling duties and tasks, but my nights, oh, my nights had been spent liberated in the bliss of submission. Every cell in my body ached to re-live that glorious feeling…for one more night.

The sensation of hot tears sliding down my cheeks brought me back to the present. Quickly brushing them away, I lifted the champagne to my lips with a trembling hand. The bubbly liquid fizzed over my tongue, and I swallowed tightly, unable to look away from the work of art.

"She's quite beautiful, isn't she?" a deep voice asked in a smooth, velvet whisper.

Even the stranger's question didn't lure my gaze away. I absently nodded. "Yes," I murmured.

"She speaks a language you seem to understand. I've watched you stare at her for over half an hour," the whiskey-voiced man noted. "Tell me, why the tears?"

His question finally broke the statue's spell, and I jerked my head toward the stranger. Startled, I found myself gazing into the same striking green eyes from the article about the tragedy that befell Joshua Lars. No longer haunted with pain, the artist's eyes held something far scarier…awareness.

Chapter Three

Joshua Lars—the Joshua Lars—stared at me like a hungry wolf evaluating a lone rabbit miles from the safety of its burrow.

"Oh!" I gasped, extending my hand to him. "Mr. Lars, it's an honor."

A modest smile tugged his sensual lips, and my heart tripped over itself as it skittered in my chest. "Please, call me Joshua. And trust me, Mellie, the pleasure is all mine."

He knew my name? No doubt he spied my surprise as a warm chuckle rolled from the back of his throat, sending a streak of arousal igniting within me.

"Abbas has quite a penchant for my work. I made it a point to find out about the woman he'd sent on his behalf."

"Oh." I nodded, stunned Joshua would bother with such mundane details.

"You never answered my question, Mellie," he reminded me.

Joshua stepped close into my personal space. I glanced back at the alluring woman, trying to ignore the decadent heat emanating from his long, lean body. Quickly averting my gaze—for fear the sub statue might pull me beneath her spell again—only to be snared by Joshua's intense appraisal.

"Actually, I'm a bit embarrassed by my reaction to the piece. I was brought to tears by the sheer beauty and detail of your work," I fibbed.

"I see." His expression suddenly turned somber. "My mistake. I thought perhaps she'd swayed you on some other level."

"Oh? What level is that?" I feigned confusion.

"It's not important," he replied with a wave of his hand. "Listen, I was just on my way outside to get some air and I'd like some company. Are you up for that?"

I swallowed tightly. "Yes. Thank you, I'd be honored." I smiled, then tucked my purse beneath my arm, gripping my champagne glass to keep it from shaking.

"Come." He smiled.

His word sounded like a command, and I hesitated as he extended his elbow. He arched an inquisitive brow as I forced my hand to grasp the crook of his arm. His muscles were strong and sturdy, and I instantly wondered how they'd feel against my naked flesh while in bed beneath him.

Joshua led me through the gallery and out the back door. Without a word, we walked down a stone pathway surrounded by fragrant rose bushes that did little to soothe my frazzled nerves. Though the gentle breeze from the night air was a welcome change from the bustling, stuffy gallery teeming with prospective buyers, it, too, didn't help calm me. Nervous energy zipped through me with a level of anxiety so foreign I didn't know how to sort or suppress it.

Seated on a padded bench beneath the stars, I glanced at the foliage surrounding the courtyard, slowly sipping my champagne. I could feel Joshua's intense, hot gaze piercing through me, producing awkward and unsure emotions that were so out of character for me that I tipped back the glass and drained the contents in one big gulp. Placing the flute down, I glanced over at him. He smiled, and I all but melted.

"It's a beautiful night," I blurted out nervously. "The roses smell so sweet."

"Yes," he murmured, staring at me for a disturbingly long time.

Darting my gaze away from him, I felt awkwardly unsure and perplexed.

Get a grip. What the hell is wrong with you? You act like you're never talked to a damn man before. Yeah, yeah, it's Joshua Lars, big deal. Grow a set and snap out of it.

Gathering my courage while trying to wrap my head around the fact that I was with one of the most talented artists of the twenty-first century, I turned to face him. It was time to nip this ridiculous sophomoric crush shit in the bud.

"Why are you staring at me?"

"I'm memorizing every gorgeous contour of your face. I'm going to capture your beauty in clay." He skimmed a single finger up my cheek, sending a tremor of excitement rippling through me. "You're so damn beautiful. I can already feel you coming to life beneath my fingers."

Images of dissolving beneath his masterful hands flickered through my brain. The erotic visuals, coupled with the champagne, melted all my inhibitions away. Acting on impulse, I leaned in and kissed him. Joshua started but didn't pull back. Instead, he cupped a hand around my nape, laid siege to my mouth, and stripped away my attempt at control. He brushed his tongue over the seam of my lips, enticing me to yield beneath the kiss. Opening, I let him in as a voice inside from long ago sighed a contented '*yes.*'

Joshua sucked in an energized breath so deep it stole the air from my lungs. Empowered by my surrender, his kiss turned urgent and demanding. Our tongues dueled in a frantic dance as he slid his hand from my neck and palmed my aching breast. Swallowing my soft moans, he gently brushed a thumb over my turgid nipple. Gripping his tuxedo jacket in my fists, I held on as he ate at me like a ravenous animal.

Abruptly Joshua pulled back. In the moonlight, I saw the weight of desire blazing in his eyes.

"I want you in my bed, Mellie," he whispered in a raspy, edgy rumble.

Jerking his head upright, he blinked, seemingly startled by his confession. Joshua scrubbed a hand through his golden hair and exhaled a deep sigh. "Dammit, you must think I'm a bastard. One kiss and—"

"No," I blurted out. "You're not. Take me to bed."

What the hell are you doing? You don't even know this guy. He's not even asked you out to dinner, and you're going to fuck him? You know what's going to happen after. Right? Shame, remorse, and guilt. Tons and tons of guilt. Remember what happened the first time you thought you could handle a one-night stand? For the love of...don't be stupid and set yourself up for that mental shit-storm again.

A sensual smile tugged one corner of his mouth, effectively wiping away the reprimanding voice in my head, and all my rationale. Leaping from the bench as if he'd just won a trip to Tahiti, he clasped his hand in mine. Pulling me to my feet, Joshua all but dragged me across the stone walkway and back inside the gallery.

Bending close to my ear, his warm breath had me biting back a moan. "I have to mingle for a few minutes. Don't leave."

"I won't," I murmured, turning to gaze into his twinkling green eyes.

"Good girl," he whispered. Flashing me a quick wink, he hurried away.

My pussy fluttered at his praise, and I swallowed the lump of lust lodged in my throat.

You're really going to do it, aren't you? You're going to wish you hadn't when you're crying and beating yourself up, feeling like a ten-cent whore, again.

Lifting a flute of champagne off the tray of a passing waiter, I downed its contents in two gulps. I wasn't aiming to get drunk; I simply needed some liquid courage and hoped it would silence the righteous voice screaming in my head.

Meandering toward the back of the gallery, I caught Joshua glancing my way while he chatted with his fans. It was impossible to miss the lustful flicker in his eyes or the knowing smile adorning his erotic mouth. Anticipation had those damn butterflies dipping and swooping in a gut-churning free-fall. Turning away from his enticing glimpses, I once again found myself staring at the alluring woman on her knees. Just as before, she held me hostage while my tattered and bruised submission stirred to life.

"You please me, girl, and make me happy." The familiar voice

from long ago echoed in my head, dragging with it the warmth of pleasing a Master.

Squeezing my eyes shut, I clenched my jaw as my body grew taut. *No. He wasn't a Master, he was a fake, and you were a fool to believe his lies.* Even as I tried to convince myself the submission I'd experienced was a farce, I couldn't deny the contentment yielding had brought to my soul. I couldn't rationalize away how utterly complete I'd been beneath the command of a Dom. Even one who was a son of a bitch and had little regard for a collar. Master wasn't all bad. There were moments when his command had been simply divine, and something special blossomed inside me…or at least, I'd thought so at the time.

I missed my submission. Even admitting there was a missing part inside me, I knew I could never allow myself to sink back to such a vulnerable position again. It would be emotional suicide. I had to drive away the beguiling memories—slam the lid down tight, and seal them away—fast. This was definitely not the time or place to toss my yearnings into some emotional blender and start whipping up dysfunctional submissive smoothies.

Opening my eyes, I had every intention of suppressing my inner submissive, but all that was shot to hell the instant I gazed at the imploring expression on the figurine's face. I'd been that woman, haunted by the same compulsion to please reflected on her beautifully etched face. Yearning for that fulfillment sliced deep, opening me up with a raw and unforgiving blade.

No matter how desperately I wanted to deny it, Joshua's mannerisms conveyed his Dominance. I'd have to be deaf, dumb, and blind not to notice. Like a slippery eel, apprehension slithered within. I'd successfully hidden my real desires when he'd questioned me about my reaction to the statue. But what if he got past my defenses? Would he expect me to kneel at his feet and hand over my control so he could mold me into a perfect statue? Then what? Dangle me like a puppet until a younger, inexperienced submissive blipped his radar? How long would it be until he snipped the threads and set me free, only to sink his talented hands into the flesh of another to sculpt and mold *her* into a flawless sub?

No more champagne for you, chicky. You've known the man a whole five minutes. If he expects you to hand over your control without trust, he's nothing but another big, fat fucking player. Besides, none of it matters. All you're going to do is have a nice, hot tumble in the sack with him. That's it. No Dom/sub nothing! So get a grip and for the love of...Stop torturing yourself looking at the damn sculpture!

Snapping my head up, I found Joshua staring at me with a gaze so intent I suddenly worried I'd let my mask slip. My cheeks grew warm, and I began to mentally draw up my crumbling shield. My only saving grace was that the man couldn't read my mind. Quickly pulling bold and brazen Mellie to the surface, I flashed him a seductive smile. I had no intention of letting him see how quickly he unraveled me.

Seduction, not *submission.*

Joshua inched closer toward me, never missing a beat of conversation with the crowd of people pressing in around him. Hyperaware his methodical movements were aimed in my direction, the room felt hotter. My nipples ached, my pussy wept, and all I could think about was begging him put out the five-alarm fire he ignited within me.

I couldn't stop staring at the curve of his lips or the memory of how his fervent kiss had possessed me. Watching the unconscious sweep of his hands as he talked, I studied each long finger before dropping my gaze to his feet. I couldn't help it. I was curious. I'd spent enough horizontal time in the sheets to know the old adage; *big hands, big feet...big cock* was true, and Joshua Lars had a massive cock hidden beneath his pants. My palms itched to caress, grip, and stroke it to life. Subconsciously, I slid my tongue over my teeth, hungry for a taste.

"You must be extremely proud." A deep-voiced man shook me from my sexual musings.

Turning, I peered over my shoulder and was startled to find a stunning piece of eye-candy

beside me. Dressed in a gray suit, his dark eyes matched his coffee-colored hair and the well-manicured scruff adorning his chiseled face.

"I beg your pardon?" I asked, confused by his remark.

"I said you must be extremely proud. Joshua captured you

impeccably in this decisive piece of erotica." The man nodded toward the statue.

"Oh!" I blinked. "No. That's not me."

He cocked his head as if trying to decide if I was telling a lie. Darting several glances between the sculpture and me, he pursed his lips in a frown. "She bears an uncanny resemblance of you."

"Coincidence, I guess." I shrugged.

"Hmmm," he grunted in disbelief. "That's *some* coincidence, and a quite a pity."

"Why do you say that?"

"Because I think you'd look stunning on your knees before me," he quipped with a wicked smirk.

My mouth fell open in absolute shock.

"Ah, Ian. Glad you could make it, man," Joshua announced as he slapped the other man on the shoulder with a broad smile, joining our conversation.

Snapping my jaw shut, I welcomed his interruption. Joshua had left me speechless.

"You know I wouldn't miss this," Ian chuckled.

"Melinda Carson, Ian Stone. Ian, Melinda," Joshua introduced.

"Not Melinda." I cringed. "Please call me Mellie."

"Mellie, I'm enchanted," Ian replied with a wolfish grin. Lifting my hand to his lips, he brushed a kiss over my skin.

"Back off, bro," Joshua warned. An unmistakable tone of jealousy resonated in his voice.

"Seriously?" Ian asked, arching his brows. "I should have known." Turning, he pinned me with an accusatory stare. "I almost believed you when you said you weren't the model for the statue."

"I'm not," I gasped.

As if putting the pieces of our conversation together, Joshua peered down at the kneeling woman, then turned and studied me with a razor-sharp gaze. "That's truly amazing."

"What?" I asked as a rush of anxiety rippled through me.

"She looks just like you," Joshua affirmed.

"No, she doesn't."

"Yes, she does," both men chuckled in unison.

"It's fate and can only mean one thing," Joshua marveled as he plucked the statue from its stand.

"What?"

"She's yours," he insisted, thrusting the delicate woman into my hands.

The unexpected weight of the piece surprised me. I clutched it tight, praying it wouldn't slip through my fingers and splinter over the glossy hardwood floor. "I can't possibly accept this. It's too much, honestly."

"I don't believe it," Ian gasped. "I just witnessed history in the making. Mellie, you're the first woman I've ever heard say 'no' to the great and powerful Joshua Lars."

Ian let out a loud laugh.

"Bite me, bro," Joshua drawled in a low, sarcastic whisper. "Don't believe him, Mellie. Ian's a habitual liar."

"I think you're both just trying to rattle my chain." I grinned.

"Oh, so you like chains, do you, princess?" Ian winked.

"No," I lied with a roll of my eyes. "Are you two brothers or something?"

"No, we met, ahhh," Ian stuttered. "Through some mutual friends a few years back."

"He's my brother from another mother," Joshua smirked, then quickly sobered. "Hey, we're going to sneak out of this soirée and grab a drink or something. I'll see you this weekend."

"You need a co-pilot to help pour the drinks?" Ian asked cryptically. I couldn't miss his hopeful expression.

"Not tonight, bro. I'm flying solo," Joshua replied with a shake of his head.

I felt my brows furrow. Seriously? Was I reading the gist of their conversation right? Was Ian asking to be a third in our pre-arranged sexcapade? My heart skipped a beat and a rush of arousal flooded my thong. *Holy crap! They share women?* The thought made my aching clit throb even more.

"Fuck, my luck sucks," Ian groused with a grin as he slapped Joshua on the back. "Don't do anything I wouldn't enjoy. It was a pleasure meeting you, Mellie. Oh, and if Joshua disappoints, give me a call."

"Prick," Joshua mumbled under his breath before wrapping his fingers around my elbow and gently pulling me to his side.

"I doubt you'll be hearing from me, but it was nice meeting you, Ian," I giggled as Joshua led me away.

"You'll have to excuse him. He doesn't have much of a filter," Joshua whispered in my ear.

"It's okay. I don't shock easily," I reassured him.

He winked, then ushered me toward the door leading to the rose garden. But before we could make our escape, our plans were thwarted by a group of adoring fans that converged around us. Joshua's smile was warm, his voice calm and collected, but his fingers gripped my elbow tighter as a palpable tension vibrated between us. I wondered if being thrown back into the limelight made him uncomfortable, or if he was simply as anxious to get naked and start fucking as I was.

Christian chose that moment to make a toast. I almost laughed when Joshua issued a barely perceptible growl from the back of his throat. It was comforting to know I wasn't the only one anxious to leave—or suffering raging hormone syndrome.

Like a quintessential gentleman, Joshua thanked Christian and his fans for their steadfast support and announced his hiatus was over. After Joshua promised to have additional exhibitions in the near future, the guests seemed placated enough for us to finally slip out the back door.

As soon as we stepped outside, Joshua spun me against his chest and crashed his lips down against mine in a hot and desperate kiss. Gripping my purse in one hand and the stunning work he'd given me in the other, I whimpered at my inability to slide my hands inside his tux jacket to feel the ridges and planes of his body. When he pressed his heated shaft against my sweltering pussy, I quickly gauged the size of his massive erection. The man might very well kill me, but oh hell yes, what a way to go.

His tongue swept inside my mouth, and passion erupted like a volcano. Squirming, Joshua trailed his tongue in a deviant path from my mouth, along my jaw, and down the column of my neck.

"I'm two seconds away from laying you on the ground and driving into your soft body, Mellie. We need to get out of here."

"Where are we going?" I asked in a breathless whisper.

"Next door. My studio. I own the loft. It's where I live," he mumbled against my skin.

"What are we waiting for?" I asked with a lustful laugh.

"My lips don't want to be apart from your sweet flesh that long."

When he sunk his teeth into the lobe of my ear, I purred, "Take me here, or take me there. Right now, I don't really care. But dammit, stop torturing me. I need to feel you."

A low chuckle vibrated in his chest. "Sassy little minx, aren't you?" Raising his head, he stared into my eyes. "I can fix that. Come on."

Tucking his arm around my waist, he pulled me to his side before lifting my feet off the ground and racing past the padded bench.

"Here, you carry this," I instructed, handing him the sculpture. "My hands are shaking so bad, I'm afraid I'm going to drop her."

"Why are your hands shaking, Mellie?" he asked with a taunting grin as he grasped the figurine from my hands.

"Oh, I don't know, maybe because you've got my blood thundering in my ears and my knees so weak, it's a good thing my feet aren't touching the ground or I'd fall off these damn stilettos," I laughed.

"Are you wet and throbbing for me?" The gruff, hungry tone in his voice sent a shiver down my spine.

"Do you really need to ask?" I challenged.

Stopping abruptly, he narrowed his eyes and silently studied me for several long seconds. I'd suspected he was a Dominant, but his stern, disapproving expression thoroughly confirmed it. Every fiber in my being implored me to remain strong, but I wilted under his compelling gaze and cast my eyes toward the ground.

"I asked because I wanted to hear it from your own lips, little one."

Little one. If there'd been a shred of doubt still rolling around in my head, his term of endearment annihilated it on the spot.

Joshua Lars. Accomplished artist. Sizzling hottie. Fucking Dominant. You're toast, woman.

"When I ask you a question, I expect an honest answer, not a flippant response. Don't get me wrong, Mellie. Your spirit is enchanting, but now isn't the time or place for it. Do you understand?"

He chastises like a damn Dominant, too. You need to fake a headache and get your ass back to Savannah's. Call it self-preservation, survival, or downright fear, but you're not ready for the games he wants to play with you.

Before I could answer, he kissed me with a blood-pumping, panty-melting fury so strong it obliterated the voice in my head. Drowning beneath the warm, soft texture of his lips and the heated breath between us, I brazenly reached up and smoothed my palm over his cheek.

Hesitantly, Joshua pulled away. His nostrils flared, and an impatient groan rolled off his tongue before he raced us toward a plain, three-story warehouse.

"It's not much on the outside, but inside isn't too bad," he explained as he tugged a set of keys from his pocket and unlocked a sturdy metal door.

Stepping through the portal, I scoffed inwardly at his remark. Designed in a bold Avant Garde style, the spacious open floor plan with its partially rounded walls and sharp geometric accents blended in appealing contrast. His décor looked nothing like I'd imagined it might be. He'd merged several of his own works with glass and metal creations. From a design perspective, it shouldn't have worked, but it did, beautifully. Brightly colored furnishings and decorative vases in red and burgundy hues generated a soothing atmosphere. Joshua Lars was a high caliber artist through and through.

"This is incredible," I whispered, trying to absorb the details of his lavish surroundings.

"I'll take you on the grand tour later. Right now there's only one room I want to see you in…my bedroom."

With an invitation so honest and seductive, how could I refuse? With a provocative smile, I nodded. "Lead the way."

"Oh, I fully intend to," he chuckled.

His double entendre was clear. Setting the sculpture on a table, Joshua took my hand and led me up a wide staircase. Once we reached the landing, he pulled me against his chest and pressed me against a door before dissolving me beneath soft, seductive kisses. Blazing with impatience, I yearned for more…much, much more. The slow, methodical tempo of his masterful mouth confined me to the fringes of madness. Joshua seemed in no hurry to seize the bubbling lust within me.

When he sunk his teeth into my bottom lip and tugged, I couldn't keep my frustration in check a second longer. I cried out in a suffering wail, impatiently palming the doorknob next to my hip. Twisting the cool metal, I discovered it was locked.

"That leads to my studio." He smirked, reveling in my eagerness. "We're definitely not playing in there, little one."

"Stop stalling, Joshua. Take me to your bed. I'm dying," I begged.

"Surely, you don't think I'm finished warming you up yet? Do you?"

"Warmed up?" I scoffed. "I'm ready to go up in flames here."

"Good. I'm glad I'm not the only one," he murmured with a grin so lethal my knees wobbled.

Scooping me off my feet, Joshua carried me down the hall. As we breached an open doorway, he flipped on the lights. Sweeping a gaze over the wide-open loft, I locked my sight on a massive four-poster bed poised atop a red and gold Persian rug in the center of the room. Tall windows covered in ecru gauze lined the perimeter of the room, and a set of open double doors led to a spacious cream and gold tiled bathroom.

Dark cherry furnishings combined with the chocolate and burgundy comforter, and matching accent pillows, lent a bold, masculine impression. The room screamed of power, command, and Dominance.

Darting a glance toward the gleaming armoire, I caught myself wondering if a plethora of BDSM toys were hidden behind the ornately carved doors.

Stop it! You're here for good old-fashioned vanilla sex. That's it!

Joshua laid me down on the bed with a wolfish grin, then stood. "Now where were we?"

Peeking up at him beneath dark lashes, I watched as he stripped off his jacket and tugged at his tie.

"I've pictured you here, in my bed like this, all damn night," he confessed in a hoarse whisper.

Swallowing tightly, I stared at his nimble fingers as he worked the buttons on his shirt open before peeling away the fabric. His sinewy muscles bunched and flexed as I gazed at his tall, lean body. Drinking in the sight of his broad shoulders, defined pecs and biceps, I danced a gaze down to his washboard abs. A trail of ash-colored hair disappeared beneath the waistband of his trousers, stirring the demand inside me to see where it ended.

Sitting up, I reached for his belt and drew the leather strap back through its buckle. Once freed, my trembling fingers released the button of his trousers as Joshua yanked the belt from the loops and set it on the bed.

"We might need this later," he smirked. His smoky green eyes studied my reaction like a hawk.

A ripple of delight slithered through my veins. The thought of taking his spankings made my neglected submissive within stir to life. When he stroked one broad knuckle down my cheek, I closed my eyes and nuzzled my face against his finger, savoring the warmth of his touch.

"Release my cock and taste me, little one. I can't hold back any longer. I plan on making this good for you, but I need to take the edge off first."

Yes. Yes. I couldn't wait to see, feel, and taste that glorious cock straining beneath his zipper.

As I reached for the metal clasp, Joshua wrapped his hand around my wrist. "Careful, girl. I go commando. I have a feeling I'm already wearing an imprint of my zipper, but the only teeth I want to feel on my cock are yours."

I shook with a silent chuckle and nodded. Dipping my hand past the waistband of his trousers, I shielded his throbbing erection with my palm. Big was an understatement. Slowly easing the zipper down over my knuckles, he watched and smiled as he toed off his shoes.

"So protective and gentle and nice," Joshua praised.

His cock sprang free, and I sucked in a quivering breath as my heart skidded in a staccato of delight. Gazing at his long thickness, a glistening pearl of pre-come swelled on the broad crest, calling to all my carnal desires. As he kicked off his trousers, I stared at each glorious inch of his shaft. Although I had a semi-muted gag reflex, I knew I'd never be able to take all of him down my throat; he was too damn big.

Sliding from the bed, I settled on my knees. I'd assumed the same posture a thousand times before in a strictly vanilla context. This time, however, I couldn't ignore the implications of my submissive posture. But once I opened my mouth and Joshua pressed past my lips, the taste of his salty essence quieted the disturbing undercurrents rippling within me. An absolute rightness encompassed me all the way to my core.

Fueled by his groans and hisses, I poured my heart into each bob of my head, yearning to bring him as much pleasure as possible. Sucking and licking his distended veins, I nibbled and gently scraped my teeth over his length before once again swallowing as much as I could manage. My pussy wept and my clit throbbed; even my nipples ached. I worshiped his cock as if it were the only one on the planet.

"Such a lovely sight you are down on your knees before me, Mellie, and your mouth is exactly as sinful as I suspected."

His guttural praise echoed in my ears and sent me soaring with the need to please. Reaching up, I cupped his balls and gently massaged them as I feasted on his cock.

Joshua let out a growl. Gripping a fist into my coiffured bun, he set a quick and rapid pace. Lunging in and out of my mouth, he tilted my head back, driving in deeper as I stared up into his erotic eyes. Lust and need chiseled his handsome face, and his lips pressed together in a tight line. He looked rugged, determined, and pleased. A heart-melting reflection of a Dom in control—not only of himself but of me, as well.

"Fucking beautiful," he murmured.

Cinching another hand in my hair, he solidified his control—not only of himself, but of me as well—and began driving his cock to the back of my throat.

Stuffed full of his massive shaft, I swallowed, compressing my throat around the bulbous tip. Pulling back slightly, Joshua let out a feral roar as hot streams of come spurted over my tongue and exploded down my throat. Swallowing frantically, I greedily captured every drop.

After several long moments, he eased from my mouth. Lifting me off the floor, he sat me on the edge of the bed. Wrapping his broad hands around my calves, Joshua pressed me backward until my shoulders settled onto the mattress before kneeling alongside the bed. I couldn't help but smile at the devilish glint in his eyes. I knew what he was preparing to do, and my body went lax in anticipation of his skillful mouth devouring my pussy.

Lifting the hem of my dress, Joshua paused to slide a hungry gaze over my flesh. The approval and adoration reflecting in his eyes made me tingle. I wasn't accustomed to lovers bestowing such reverence. All the other men I'd been with were more focused on the deed. Not so with Joshua. Something about him was different from all the others, even my former Master. I didn't know if it was the dizzying lust Joshua conjured, or his subtle command, that unnerved me most. Pushing the questions from my mind, the only fear I wanted keeping me poised on the bed—flat on my back with my legs spread wide—was the fear of missing a single second of what he had in store for me.

"The scent of your cunt is mouthwatering, Mellie," he murmured.

Hooking his fingers around the thin lace at my hips, he stared into my eyes as he eased the skimpy thong down my legs. Arching my hips to hurry his progress, Joshua chuckled and shook his head.

"It's not funny, Joshua. Stop torturing me and lick my pussy."

"Who said anything about licking your pussy, little one? Although I must admit, it smells quite delicious. And such a pretty shade of pink with it so wet and glistening. It's hard to resist driving my tongue deep inside you to suck out all that hot, spicy nectar, little one."

Lord, the man was going to make me come just by talking. Not only was his voice deep and erotic, his words painted lewd, panoramic pictures in my head. I could almost feel my cream spilling over his chin as he ate me to oblivion.

"Why are you torturing me like this?" I implored as I lifted my head from the mattress.

"This isn't torture." He smirked with a crooked grin. "But I could do that if you'd like me to. Tie you to my bed and make you suffer all night long. Is that what you need, little one?"

"No," I cried in a breathy whisper. *Liar.*

"Then tell me what you need, Mellie," he murmured as he brushed his lips along the inside of my thighs.

"Your mouth on my cunt," I hissed.

"Cunt, is it? Hmmm, such a vulgar word from a classy woman."

"I'm not a lady in bed, Joshua. If you can't handle that—"

"Good. I want a lady on my arm, but a nasty, dirty girl between the sheets. No inhibitions allowed."

"I'll be as filthy as you want, just as long as you lick my cunt, fuck me hard, and make me come."

"Oh, you're going to come all right, gorgeous. You'll come on my tongue until I'm ready for you to come over my cock…all night long."

"Then stop talking and do it," I demanded.

Joshua threw his head back and laughed. "Mellie, Mellie. You told me to take the lead, and I fully intend to. But you don't get to take back the reins after you've handed them over to me. And. that's exactly how you like it, no matter how hard you try to deny it. You're mine now, little one. Mine to do all the wicked things I'm fucking aching to do to you."

Just when I thought I couldn't get any hotter, Joshua's words cranked up the heat, enveloping me in a new and blistering inferno of arousal.

"Lay back for me, Mellie. Close your eyes and let me feast on that sweet submissive you're hiding inside."

"But I'm not a submissss…Ohhhhhh. Oh, hell. Yessss…Joshua."

Before I could finish my sentence, he fastened his mouth over my pussy and sucked. Licking and stabbing with his tongue, he devoured me with a mind-blowing skill I'd never experienced. My release swelled in a flash of white-hot lightning, sizzling through my veins and frying the synapses in my brain. His lips, tongue, and teeth seared me from the inside out, and when he concentrated his talents on my clit, I bucked and whimpered, wanting to both quench the fire and prolong the bliss. Sucking the throbbing nub between his lips, he slid two long fingers deep inside me. Writhing and panting, I arched my hips from the bed when his wiggling digits found my hidden bundle of nerves. Burnishing his fingers against my sweet spot, he scraped his teeth over my distended clit, driving me to the brink of ecstasy. Teetering precariously on the edge, I ground my pussy against his face and fingers.

"Joshua. Pleaseee," I screamed.

"What a good girl, asking so nicely," he murmured against my cunt. "Give it to me, Mellie. I want it all, and I want it now."

Demand and euphoria coalesced into an arc of static fire, vibrating from the top of my head to the tips of my toes. Joshua squeezed another finger inside my clutching cunt as he lapped at my clit. I threw back my head and screamed as the crushing orgasm splintered through me like an atom bomb. Powerful contractions seized his fingers within my tunnel as I exploded in a stormy fire of ecstasy.

Joshua rode the torrent with me, gliding his fingers through my quivering tissue while circling my hyper-sensitized nub with his tongue. Even as rapture receded, he didn't stop stroking my core or lapping my nectar. A consummate lover, like no other, Joshua took his time as he eased me down with subtle caresses and tender praises.

My body still hummed in a blissful languid heat when Joshua rose to his feet and extended his hand. Helping me from the bed, he wrapped me in his arms, keeping me steady and safe. Leaning in, he kissed me, stroking his lips over mine as if he'd known them forever. Sweeping his hands—the capable hands of a master sculptor—over my shoulders, he sent the red designer dress I wore to puddle at my feet. Languid and thorough, he made me feel as if I were a masterpiece he sought to mold. In one fluid movement, he unfastened my bra and tossed it to the floor while the intoxicating scent of his flesh made my head swim. Raking his tongue down the column of my neck, I trembled in anticipation of what erotic magic he had in store for me next.

Chapter Four

As the taxi pulled to a stop in front of the house Savannah shared with her Masters, I shook the vivid memories from my mind. Lights illuminated several windows, and I knew I was the last to arrive back home. Steeped in Joshua's masculine scent, I paid the driver, clutched the submissive statue to my chest, and hurried toward the house. Reaching for the door, I let out a cry of surprise when it opened wide. Sanna blinked at my tousled exterior and grinned.

"Oh my. Looks like somebody had a fun night," she giggled.

"Hush," I admonished with an uneasy hiss.

Dylan sauntered up behind Sanna. He took one look at me and grinned like a Cheshire cat. "Good thing you took the condoms after all, huh, Mel?"

Their ridiculous gloating made me feel as if I had the words *"Freshly Fucked"* tattooed across my forehead.

"So, who was the lucky guy?" Sanna pressed, still giggling. "And what is that in your arms?"

"None of your business," I snapped, then looked down at the delicate work of art. "It's a gift."

"Oohhh, let me look," Sanna demanded, prying the statue from my grip. "Holy cow. This is beautiful. Look at it, Master. Isn't she most gorgeous thing you've ever seen?"

A look of awe lit her face as she studied the kneeling woman, rotating her slowly and taking in all the intricate details. No doubt my reaction had been much the same at the gallery; no wonder Joshua saw through my façade so easily. "Joshua Lars made this, didn't he?"

"Yes." I nodded, anxious to snatch the statue back and race upstairs. I didn't want to answer questions about the art, my appearance, or anything related to Joshua.

"Good grief. How much did this thing cost you?"

"Nothing. He gave it to me."

"He's the guy you had sex with, isn't he?" Savannah pressed with a knowing grin.

"Sanna. I already told you, I don't want to talk about it. Give me that," I ordered as I snatched the woman from her hands. "I'm going to bed."

"Hmmm, it must have been disappointing. You're grouchy." She pouted.

I closed my eyes and issued a heavy sigh. *Disappointing? No. Mind-blowing? Yes, and then some.*

"Come on, Mel. You and I always compare, you know…" Sanna flashed a guilty look Dylan's way as his brows arched up high and his blue eyes grew wide.

"Compare notes? Do you now, kitten?"

"No," she whimpered with a nervous chuckle. "We don't compare. We just talk about…oh hell."

"Language, precious," Nick warned as he stepped into the foyer. Cocking his head, he glanced at the figurine in my hands. "What do you have there?"

"It's one of Joshua Lars' sculptures, Master. Isn't it beautiful? He gave it to Mellie, but I still can't get her to tell me what she gave *him*."

Nick smirked as he took in my disheveled state. "I'd say a very memorable night."

"That's what I think, too," Sanna replied in a conspiratory whisper.

"This is quite stunning," Nick nodded as he, too, admired the kneeling woman. "The man is obviously talented."

You have no idea.

"So, you're really not going to spill the beans, even to me, your only sister?" Sanna asked, her bottom lip sticking out in a dramatic pout.

"Stop pestering her, kitten," Dylan chided. "If she wants you to know, she'll tell you."

"Yes, Sir."

I felt guilty keeping the details of my night from Sanna, but I needed to sort the barrage of emotions pinging through me. Sort them, dissect them, and then put them away. Something had happened inside his magnificent loft. Something that had the potential to haunt me the rest of my life.

"I'm sorry, Sanna. I'll tell you all about it tomorrow. Right now, I just want to take a shower and climb into bed."

She studied me in microscopic appraisal, then frowned. "Are you okay?"

"Yes, of course. I'm just wiped out," I replied before planting a reassuring kiss on her cheek. "Let me get some sleep. I promise we'll talk in the morning."

"Okay, but if you need me, I'm always here for you, sis."

"I know, and I love you for it."

Feeling as if I didn't deserve her unconditional love, didn't stop me from gathering it around me. Raw and confused, her devotion soothed the craggy edges of my jagged nerves.

Sanna still wore a skeptical expression as I said my goodnights then climbed the stairs. I couldn't fault her for being concerned. Even before she found Dylan and Nick, I'd always confided in my sister. But my encounter with Joshua left me feeling defensive, as if talking about what we'd shared might somehow sully its sanctity. That alone had me perplexed. I hadn't expected a one-night stand would leave me feeling so damn fragile. I should have been choking on guilt and shame and finding ways to forgive myself instead of hoarding and savoring the memories. Sanna would want answers for my unusual demeanor, but then, so did I. Hopefully by morning, I would have it sorted out.

"Why are you obsessing over him?" I groused as I stripped off my clothes and climbed into the shower. "You had a fabulous fuck. Get over it."

As the hot water washed Joshua's scent from my skin, a pang of regret slid through me. The thought of erasing him from my skin dismayed me, and the emptiness that accompanied it was alarming. I'd never pined for a man before, at least not to this degree. The bizarre sensation made me prickly and on edge.

No matter how hard I tried to compartmentalize the aftereffects of my night with Joshua, I couldn't stop tossing and turning. Visuals of the incredible ways he'd unraveled me spooled through my brain, and the more I tried to push them away, the brighter and bolder they became. I'd washed away his scent, yet I could still smell his skin. Even brushing my teeth couldn't erase the taste of his slick come branded on my tongue. My lips still tingled from his toe-curling kisses, and his deep, rich voice refused to stop echoing in my ears. The man was like a ghost, fixated on haunting my psyche.

Glancing at the clock, I groaned. Four thirty in the morning, and I was no closer to sleep than I'd been when I crawled into bed two hours earlier. Tugging the extra pillow from behind my head, I wrapped my arms around the firm foam cushion and closed my eyes. Giving in to my foolish fantasies, I imagined clinging to Joshua's rugged body, and finally drifted off to sleep.

The soft snick of the door woke me, and when I opened my eyes, I saw Savannah approaching the bed. A weak smile tugged one side of her mouth as she nibbled her bottom lip; a clear indication she was worried. Tossing back the covers, I patted the mattress and turned on my side. Without a word, she pounced into the bed beside me.

"You worry too much, baby," I whispered. Combing my fingers through her hair—an act of reassurance I used to do when we were young—I placed a light kiss on her forehead.

Savannah had been just sixteen when our parents died. When I finally arrived home from college, after getting the heart-breaking news, she and I had climbed into our parents' bed and held each other as we cried. I felt the same need to ease her troubled mind as I did back then.

"You've never shut me out like that before, Mel. I can't help it."

"I wasn't trying to shut you out, baby. I just needed some time to sort it out is all."

"Was it Joshua?"

"Yes."

"So, what happened? Was it something bad?"

"No. Totally the opposite," I confessed.

She rose on her elbow and looked down at me as a sly grin lit up her face. "He matters to you, doesn't he?"

"Oh please," I scoffed. "It was one night. One night I'll never forget."

Dammit, I needed to shut my mouth. If I gave her the tiniest crumb, she'd want the whole slice of bread.

"It happens like that, you know?"

"What happens?"

"Love," she giggled.

I grabbed the pseudo-Joshua-pillow next to me and smacked her with it. "I'm not in love, Sanna, geezzz."

"How do you know? You always run away before you get the chance to find out."

"Zing. Ouch. You nasty little brat," I groused, hitting her with the heavy foam a second time.

With a squeal, she snatched it from my hands and hit me back.

"Uncle," I laughed when she brought the pillow back for another blow.

"You're such a girl," Sanna drawled with a grin.

"Thank you," I laughed. "What time is it? Did I miss breakfast?"

"Uh, yeah. It's one o'clock in the afternoon, sleeping beauty. Oh, there's plenty of food in the kitchen if you're hungry. But that's not why I came up to roust your lazy ass out of bed. We need to get to Maurizio's at three to set up the decorations."

"Decorations? That's right. The bachelorette party is tonight, isn't it?"

"Yep. How much time do you need to get ready?"

"Not long if you'll give me some privacy." I grinned.

"I bet Scotty will be happy to see you," she taunted as she rolled out of bed.

"Out," I growled and pointed to the door.

"You're such a party pooper now that you're in love."

I gasped. "Shut the...I am *not* in love. Now get out of here before I hit you with the pillow again."

Sanna laughed as she left the room. I could still hear her giggling as she made her way down the hall.

"Brat," I grumbled as I climbed out of bed.

Reaching for my phone, a flutter of excitement rolled in my belly. It was juvenile and sophomoric, but I couldn't keep from hoping Joshua might have left me a text.

"You're a fool for wishing," I mumbled as I tossed the phone onto the bed and stalked toward the bathroom.

Sanna and I were the first to arrive at Maurizio's. When Scotty spied me, he puffed out his sculpted chest just a little and swaggered out from behind the bar. My not-so-subtle sister waggled her eyebrows at me, grinning like a fool. I wanted to smack her.

"Hey, Mellie. It's good to see you again." He smiled, stepping close inside my personal space. "I guess sleep won out the other night, huh?"

"It did. I'm sorry. I've been traveling too much lately. I think it caught up with me," I replied, pursing my lips in sorrowful apology.

"Maybe after the party, you can join me up at the bar so we can talk or have a drink."

His hopeful expression made it impossible for me to shoot down his offer. "I'll see what I can do," I hedged with a light smile.

One drink wouldn't kill me. Besides, I needed something to occupy my brain cells to keep them off a certain artist who still hadn't called. What if Scotty wanted more than conversation? No thanks. The thought of any man besides Joshua touching me sent an icy chill of revulsion through my veins. The prickly, edgy sensation was back.

"Come on, Mel. Let's start setting up. The party's back here," Sanna called, motioning me toward a room off the back of the restaurant.

"Let me know if you need anything," Smiling, Scotty took my hand and lifted it to his lips, placing a sweet kiss on it. Then he winked. "Anything at all."

His kiss left an itchy burn on my hand, as if millions of ants crawled under my skin.

"Will do." I nodded, flashing a quick smile.

Steering toward the opening Savannah had disappeared through, I frowned.

Why all of a sudden are hunky, desirable men off the menu? Surely, you're not delusional enough to think Joshua is ever going to call, are you?

Wanting to prove the voice in my head wrong, I tugged my phone from my pocket and checked my messages. Nothing. Maybe Joshua wasn't ever going to call. That thought made my stomach turn in a sick sort of way. Shoving my phone away, I stepped into the large, lackluster room and groaned. It needed a lot of work. Thankfully, my inner designer diva roared to the surface—ready to turn the dull room into a dazzling bachelorette utopia—and shoved my foolish hopes of Joshua away.

Inhaling a deep breath, I started helping Sanna sort out the decorations.

Julianna and Trevor arrived, their arms draped with shopping bags and their hands loaded with boxes. Sanna and I rushed to help lighten their burden.

"There's more in the car," Trevor smiled. "I'll be right back."

"Do you need some help?" I offered.

"Yes, please. We have a shit-ton of stuff." He grinned.

As Trevor and I made our way through the restaurant, I felt Scotty's eyes on me. Trying to focus on Trevor's excited ramblings, I couldn't shake the awkward sensation Scotty's attention evoked. It was perplexing. Rarely did I shun the interest of a sexy, hot man. What was wrong with me?

"How'd your art thingy go last night?" Trevor asked, opening the back hatch of a big, black Escalade.

"It went great. Thank you." Steering the conversation from more questions, I chuckled and tipped my head to the bags and boxes packed inside the vehicle. "Are we decorating the whole damn city?"

"Just about," he giggled. Lifting a box, he issued a loud grunt.

"This is that damn elephant butt plug thing. Why on earth did Savannah want to buy this enormous, scary thing in the first place?"

"I have no idea," I chuckled. "But you're right. It is frightening and then some."

"I'm just glad Daddy never got to see it. He definitely doesn't need any help thinking up ways to push my limits, that's for sure."

"I don't think you have to worry, Trevor. That thing wasn't made for humans…at least, I hope not."

"I should say not! That damn thing would stretch your sphincter to the point of no return. I mean, think about it. You'd have to wear diapers the rest of your life because your shit would just fall out."

I started laughing so hard I almost dropped the supplies. "I don't want to think about it. It will scar me for life."

"It already *has* me." He shuddered and blanched.

After two more trips, the SUV had finally been unloaded. By then, half a dozen subs from the club had arrived, bringing balloons and a humongous penis sheet cake. I was excited when I discovered Julianna had brought several bolts of burgundy and cream fabric. After Trevor borrowed a couple ladders from Scotty, I draped and tacked the material from the rafters.

In between tasks, I snuck a couple more glances at my cell phone, hoping for a text, but there was no communication from Joshua. Inwardly chiding myself for behaving like an adolescent teen, I decided to simply turn the damn thing off and be done with it. So I did, at least for a little while.

Someone let out a squeal as a group of subs clustered around Trevor while he hung a poster of a male fitness model on the wall. Either he or Julianna had printed '*Pin The Junk On The Dom*' at the top of the image, and it was then I noticed the poor man's cock had been photo shopped out of the picture. I could only imagine what pictures had been designed to pin on the poster.

Laughter was plenty, and the submissive stories swapped were educational, but with them the pangs of longing surfaced, along with the memories of submission Joshua had brought to life inside me. Rubbing my palm over the phone in my pocket, I resisted the urge.

Savannah delegated duties while orchestrating the controlled chaos.

While Trevor and a few of the subs hung streamers, I slipped out to use the ladies' room.

Once finished, I washed my hands and begrudgingly turned on my phone to check for messages and frowned. Deciding to put the device on vibrate, I shoved it back in my pocket before pulling open the door.

Scotty stood, leaning against the wall in the narrow corridor, wearing a seductive grin. I yelped in surprise as a shot of adrenaline spiked within me.

"Sorry, gorgeous. I didn't mean to startle you."

"You did," I gasped, placing a palm on my chest, trying to steady my breathing.

"I just needed to know," he murmured before stepping forward. Extending his arm, Scotty placed his open hand on the wall, trapping me in before leaning in close.

"Know what?" A wave of claustrophobia stilled the air in my lungs.

"If you taste as good as you look," he murmured.

Before I could duck beneath his arm and make an escape, his lips latched onto mine. *Ewww. No.* Tensing, I placed my hands on his chest and pushed him back.

"Scotty…I can't do this," I gasped as heat rose on my cheeks. "I'm…"

"Whoa. Damn, Mellie, I…" he stammered, clearly embarrassed. "I didn't mean to come on like a horny schoolboy. I thought…"

"It's not you, Scotty. It's me. I'm not looking for…"

"Yeah, I can see that now. I'm sorry, Mellie. I totally misread your body language the other night. Shit. My apologies."

"No apology necessary, Scotty. I…it's just that things have changed."

"Wow. That sure didn't take long." He issued a soft chuckle, then lowered his arm. "But then, I'm not surprised. You're a beautiful woman. Who's the lucky man?"

"Ah, it's not important," I stammered. "If you'll please excuse me, I need to get back."

Scurrying away like a coward, I raced back toward the party room. I'd never turned tail and run from a man in my life…well, except for Joshua—and Scotty now, too. Something was wrong. Terribly wrong.

Dammit, Joshua. If you've ruined me for other men, I'm going to hunt you down and cut off that massive, amazing cock of yours. Shit, this can't be happening to me. It just can't. Son of a bitch!

I raced back into the room, frazzled and panicked. Savannah blinked as a look of worry swiftly fixed over her face.

Raising my palm in surrender, I shook my head. She issued a heavy sigh, rolling her eyes and shrugging before plucking several tubes of lube from one of the boxes.

Guilt sluiced through me. Aside from Davis Walker's crushing humiliation, I hadn't kept many secrets from my sister. Yet over the past twenty-four hours, I'd unintentionally walled her out from my emotions.

No more. After all you two have been through, you can't shut her out.

I decided that after the party, I would sit my sister down and have a nice long heart-to-heart. Hopefully, she would help me figure out how I'd gotten so twisted up over a simple romp in the sack with a man I barely knew. So, why didn't it feel simple? And where was the fallout of guilt for my shameful behavior? When was that ugliness going to show up? Everything after my encounter with Joshua felt wrong. Not in a bad way, but in a pull your hair out and scream like a crazy woman sort of way. It was pointless to waste my brain cells on a man I'd probably never hear from again.

A few hours later, the room looked festive and bright. All the guests had arrived, all except Leagh. With one last item on our to-do-list, Savannah struggled to lift the massive butt plug out of the box before heaving it onto the table.

"The pièce de résistance, and centerpiece for our guest of honor," Sanna laughed with a sweep of her hand. "May I present: '*Monster Plug from Hell.*'"

The room fell utterly silent, Seconds later screams of laughter erupted as Trevor helped Sanna center the massive slab of latex on the table. Julianna and I helped the other two slather the colossal plug with lube then stood back and giggled as Trevor flipped the button on the penis strobe veil and placed the tiara in front of the grotesque, glistening centerpiece. He let out a shrill laugh as he pulled a two-foot sparkler from one of the boxes.

"May I have a drumroll, please?" he asked the laughing crowd of subs.

Sanna, Julianna, and I started tapping our fingers on the wooden table as Trevor took a bow, then slammed the metal end of the sparkler into the top of the plug. Cheers and applause filled the room as Trevor took another dramatic bow, cracking up with laughter. His giddiness was contagious as even more laughter filled the room.

"Oh, shit, they're here!" a young, woman cried as a look of terror marred her beautiful features.

"They? Who do you mean *they*, Ebony?" Julianna frowned.

"Tony and Leagh and—oh hell, I think all our Doms are here too," Ebony choked with a wide-eyed, worried expression.

"Fuck! Errr, I mean crap. Hide that thing," Trevor screeched, pointing to the gargantuan plug.

"Where? Where the fuck do you suggest I hide it?" Savannah yelped.

"I don't know," Trevor wailed in panic.

"Well, I'm sure as hell not going to sit on it," I laughed. "Just light it, and we'll surprise them all."

"Are you crazy?" Trevor shrieked. "If Daddy sees that…Oh, hell. I don't want to wear diapers the rest of my life."

"Get real, Trev. Drake would never use that thing on you," Sanna laughed.

"Now," Julianna ordered in a loud whisper. "Light it now, Trev."

With shaky hands, he ignited the sparkler. It flickered to life right as Leagh and Tony crossed the threshold. She jumped when we called out '*surprise!*' then her shocked expression quickly transformed into a look of pure delight as a parade of Doms flowed in behind the couple.

Tony grinned and squeezed his bride-to-be as the arriving party turned their attention to the sputtering sparks shooting from the giant butt plug.

"What the fuck? Where the hell did you all find that? Plugs-r-us?" Tony laughed.

"Don't get any ideas, Master. That thing is not getting anywhere *near* my parts," Leagh laughed.

"Or mine either," Trevor cried, casting a terrified look at Drake.

"That's just...holy mother of..." Mika murmured, gazing at the shimmering centerpiece. "That thing's scary as fuck."

"I know," Trevor howled, still pinning Drake with a fearful gaze.

"What are you worried about, boy? I'd never use that on you. The damn thing would kill you," Drake laughed.

"Thank you, Daddy. Thank you so much," Trevor exhaled a sigh of relief.

As the sparkler burned down, the hot embers landed on the lube-covered plug, and without warning, the whole damn thing burst into flames. Black smoke rolled off the blazing plastic setting off a high-pitched squeal from the smoke alarms.

"No. Oh, shit," Savannah, cried. "Do something, Trevor."

"What the fuck do you want *me* to do?" Trevor cried.

"Watch your mouth, boy," Drake thundered. "You better hope to all that's holy you didn't have anything to do with this, or your ass is mine."

"But Master..." Trevor began.

"Everybody out," Tony screamed. Gripping Leagh's arm, he pulled her to the doorway. "Wait for me outside, angel. I'll be right there."

"Don't you dare make me a widow before the wedding, Sir," she scolded.

"Never gonna happen," Tony laughed, then kissed her hard. "And don't talk to me in that tone, girl, or you won't like our wedding night." With a firm swat on her ass, he sent Leagh on her way.

The other Doms gathered up their subs and raced out the door. Only a handful of us remained, trying to decide how to put out the fire. The acrid smoke burned my lungs, but I refused to leave Sanna's side.

"Did you have a hand in this, boy?" Drake demanded. His face clouded over like a wicked storm.

"It was an accident, Daddy. I swear." Tears welled in Trevor's eyes as he flitted his gaze between the flickering plug and his pissed-off Master.

"We need a fire extinguisher," Julianna yelled over the bleating alarms. "We've got to put this thing out before it ruins the whole party."

Scotty tore into the room, wide-eyed and mouth agape. "What the fuck did you do back here?"

"Get an extinguisher," Nick barked.

With a panicked stutter step, Scotty bolted back out of the room.

"Grab an edge, guys. Let's try to snuff this sucker out," Tony instructed, pinching a corner of the tablecloth in his fingers.

Drake, Dylan, Nick, and Mika lifted the linen, but once the fabric came in contact with the lube, it ignited the cloth like a match to kindling. Forced to stop their efforts, they dropped the fabric and stepped back.

"Was there alcohol in that lube?" Mika thundered.

"I-I don't know, Master." Julianna cringed. Digging through one of the boxes, she lifted out an empty container of lube. Coughing, she scanned the ingredients. "You've got to be shitting me. What idiot puts alcohol in lube?"

"You've earned ten swats with the rubber paddle for your language, girl." Mika glared.

Julianna coughed again and frowned. I suspected the rubber paddle wasn't pleasant.

Scotty burst back through the doorway carrying a big, red fire extinguisher. Breaking the seal, he aimed the rubber nozzle at the flaming plug, spraying thick white foam over the bubbling goo. But it wasn't enough to put the fire out. The flames continued to dance, higher than before, in a macabre dance. The biting stench of burning rubber permeated the room, making it hard for all of us to breathe.

"We've got to get out of here," Dylan hollered, pointing toward the door.

In the distance, the sound of sirens grew louder as Julianna grabbed the cake off the gift table. Trevor peeled the poster from the wall as he and Drake snagged up several of Leagh's gifts. Following their lead, the rest of us plucked up the presents before racing out the door.

Savannah, Julianna, Trevor, and I made our way outside, coughing and wiping our eyes.

"We're up shit creek without any paddles," Trevor whispered in a nervous hiss. "Hell, we don't even have a fucking boat."

"Come on, Trev. It's not that bad. It was an accident," I said, trying to reassure him. "They're not going to punish you guys for an accident."

"Yes, they are," Trevor, Julianna, and Savannah chimed in together.

"Have I mentioned that I fucking hate rice?" Sanna groused.

"You're going to hate eating soap just as much, kitten," Dylan barked from behind us.

She squeezed her eyes shut and groaned at being busted.

"Hurry it up, you four. We've all breathed enough of this shit into our lungs. Get your butts outside for some fresh air," Nick ordered.

His tone was firm, but he sounded more concerned about our health than taking us over his knee. Even in all the chaos and destruction of the party, I couldn't stop envisioning myself poised over Joshua's knee while his big, broad hand slapped my ass.

You just won't give it up, will you? Dream all you want, but it's never going to happen.

Once outside, Julianna opened the back of the Escalade, and we filled it with Leagh's presents and cake. The fire department pulled up and several men rushed inside the building as I stood with Sanna and the other subs, huddled in a circle.

Several firefighters paraded out of the building unable to hide their smiles. Some were even outright laughing. As a couple of them passed by us on their way to the pumper truck, I caught a snippet of their conversation.

"I've been on a lot of calls, but I've never been to the scene of a raging butt plug inferno before," one of the men said with a chuckle as he unbuttoned his long yellow coat.

"I'm so sorry, Leagh. This was supposed to be fun, not a flippin' catastrophe," Sanna moaned with tears in her eyes.

"Are you kidding?" Leagh grinned. "How many brides can say that a butt plug caught fire at her bachelorette party?"

Sanna let out a wail as tears spilled down her cheeks. Laughing, Leagh hugged my sister tight and shushed her.

"Come on, Savannah. Don't cry. I thought the plug made an

awesome centerpiece. Besides, it holds a special meaning between you and me, doesn't it?"

"Yes," Sanna sniffed. "That's why I got it. I knew you'd understand."

"Well, I will tomorrow night. Tony plans to deflower my ass in front of everyone at the club." Leagh cringed. "And I'm scared shitless. Pardon the pun."

"Tony's been doing the training on you, right?" Sanna wiped her tears. Her forlorn tone vanished, replaced by a serious, mothering tenor. Leagh nodded. "Then don't be scared. Tony would walk through glass barefoot before he hurt you, sweetheart."

Filled with a sense of pride, I couldn't help but admire the way Sanna eased Leagh's fears. Not only had my sister totally embraced every aspect of the lifestyle, but she also took on the onus of teaching and sharing her knowledge with other subs. Glancing back at Dylan and Nick, gratitude flooded my veins. If not for their love, Sanna would still be lost, closed off, void of the incredible gifts they so freely gave her. My throat tightened with emotion as I realized my baby sister had come full circle; she was finally whole.

Scotty marched over to where we stood, his face an angry thunder cloud.

"Who's going to pay for fixing my restaurant?" Fury blazed in his eyes as he pinned an accusatory gaze over the four of us responsible for the accident.

"Easy, Scotty," Dylan warned. Clenching his jaw, he moved in, toe-to-toe with the livid owner. Nick, Mika, and Drake stepped up alongside him. Shoulder-to-shoulder, the Doms formed an imposing barrier between the enraged man and us. "Nick and I will have a crew here first thing in the morning, man. No matter what it costs, we'll make sure it's better than before."

"You're damn right it will," Scotty barked before turning on his heel and storming away.

Dylan snarled at the owner's parting words.

"You can't blame him," Nick chuckled, trying to lighten the mood.

"Wow, he is *pissed*," Sanna whispered as she watched the Doms filter back to where they'd stood before Scotty appeared.

"Yeah, I know. What part of 'accident' doesn't the male population around here seem to understand?" I asked, darting a gaze at the stoic faced Doms watching the commotion of the firefighters.

"It's not that..." Julianna began.

"Oh, I know all about the whole sub code of conduct. But it wasn't like you guys purposefully started a fire to make your Masters look bad. Even in the middle of all the pandemonium you guys represented them as best you could. Sure, there were a few accidental curse words—which is totally understandable if you ask me, but all in all, you didn't do anything to disrespect any of them."

"You're preaching to the choir, sister," Trevor chimed in. "But trust me. They'll still find a way to make sure we learn a lesson."

"What bigger lesson is there than not to mix sparklers with alcohol-based lube?" I laughed.

"None, but they're still going to drive home the fact that we fucked up...most likely over our asses with big motherfucking paddles," Julianna whispered with a pensive pout.

Mika let out a low growl. "That's twenty now, girl. Clean up your language, or I'll add twenty more to it."

Julianna cringed and nodded.

Before the fire department had even left, a handful of workers from Dylan and Nick's company showed up ready to repair the damaged restaurant. Deciding a change of venue was needed, we drove to Tony and Leagh's house, intent on enjoying the party there. Once the presents and cake had been situated, the Doms left us alone to spend the evening at Tony's bachelor party. Before they left, we were banned from using lighters or matches for the rest of the evening.

Decades had passed since I'd been made to feel like a child. At first, I resented the hell out of us being talked down to, but I realized the Doms were simply setting limits for their subs. I wondered how I'd feel if Joshua were the one laying down rules for me to follow. Would I be miffed and filled with contempt? Did I still have it in me to bend and supplicate, or would that stubborn, independent streak of mine be my submissive demise?

You're never going to find out, so stop running stupid scenarios through your head.

The fact that Joshua hadn't bothered to call stung. Trailing a fingertip over the phone in my pocket, I swallowed my disappointment.

Gathered around Leagh in her living room, we watched as she opened her gifts. I forced myself to focus on the party and not a certain artist who'd thrown me off-kilter. With each present she unwrapped, Leagh squealed with delight and laughed hysterically at some of the more risqué presents. The rocky start at Maurizio's didn't dampen our spirits one bit. Sipping my margarita through the tacky penis straw, I realized I hadn't laughed so hard in years. It was an absolute joy to be around so many people who were truly happy in their own skin. Suddenly missing my lifestyle friends back in Kansas City, I reminded myself that it was another lifetime ago.

Trevor became our "Slave boy of Ceremony" for the kink games. With dramatic flair and smart-assed one liners, he passed around several tubes of red lipstick. He then instructed us to paint our lips for our first game, 'Deep throat the banana.'

A pretty, redheaded sub named Tiffany won the contest when she took the entire banana down her throat. With a collective cheer, we clapped at her deep-throating skill as her cheeks blushed bright red.

"Now we know why Master Brax is always wearing a smile," Julianna laughed.

After a lot of ribbing, Tiffany preened. "I can't help it if I have talents," she giggled.

Trevor pulled out a blindfold and held up several cardboard cutouts of penises. Dragging one toward his mouth, he licked the image and sighed dreamily.

"You ladies ready to 'Pin The Junk on The Dom?'"

"Only if you're done giving it a blow job," Leagh laughed.

"I'm not sure yet, sis. This one looks pretty damn tasty." Trevor smirked.

"Oh, I'm telling Drake on you," Julianna threatened with a laugh.

"No, you're not, or you're going to have to find yourself another babysitter, sister," Trevor warned with an impish grin.

"You're right, I'm not," she agreed.

Trevor passed out the penis pictures before blindfolding Leagh.

After he spun her around and pointed her in the direction of the poster he'd rescued from Maurizio's, Leagh rubbed her hand over the paper and stuck the penis on his chin. The whole room started laughing, and when she pulled off her blindfold she screamed.

"That's where it *should* be," she laughed. "And we all know it."

Suddenly, there was a loud knock at the door. Leagh was still giggling as she ran to answer it. Tilting my head, I peered into the foyer. Two police officers stood on the porch. Leagh let out a thin cry of fear and crumpled to the floor.

Julianna's face turned white as she raced to Leagh's side. Looking up at the officer with a pained expression, Julianna sucked in a quick breath. "James? W-what's happened? Is Tony all right?"

"Fuck," James hissed. "Nothing's happened to him, I swear. It's not what you think. Leagh, honey—"

"James? What's going on? What's happened?" Julianna's tone was sharp as she wrapped her arms around a visibly distraught Leagh.

"Nothing. I swear," he repeated before kneeling and cupping his hand beneath Leagh's chin. "Honey, I'm sorry. I didn't mean to scare you. Tony is perfectly fine. He and the guys are playing poker over at Dylan and Nick's place."

Listening to the exchange, I instantly saw red. Whatever reason the two officers had for being there had wound up inadvertently scaring the crap out of Leagh. After losing her first Master so unexpectedly, two officers showing up on her porch had led Leagh to the worst possible conclusion: something horrible had happened to Tony.

Bolting from the couch, I rushed to the door and pinned an angry gaze on the officer, James.

"If Tony hasn't been in any kind of accident, what the fuck are you doing here then?" I planted my hands on my hips and glared at the kneeling officer named James, seething with a rage I hadn't felt in years.

Blinking up at me, he stood. Wearing a look of confusion, James shook his head. "Who are you?"

"I'm Savannah's sister, Mellie. Who the hell are you? Are you even a real cop? Did you come over to scare the hell out of Leagh for shits and giggles?"

Suddenly, Sanna appeared at my side, tugging on my arm. "Mel," she whispered tersely.

"Stop it," I hissed, jerking from her grasp. "You've got some nerve, you know that? Do you have any idea what she's been through? What the fuck is wrong with you? You're an asshole, you know that?"

"I thought this was a subbie party. I take it you don't hang out with these ladies on a regular basis, do you, girl?" James smirked as he squared his shoulders and spread his legs. Everything about the man screamed 'Dominant.'

"No, I don't, and just for the record, I'm nobody's *girl*," I spat. "What you've done to Leagh is careless and cruel."

"Mellie, stop," Sanna begged. "James is a switch at the club."

"I don't bottom anymore, sweetheart," James corrected. "Arianna and I are still friends, we've just both gone over to the Dom side."

"Oh, wow," Julianna murmured.

James frowned. Visibly worried, he knelt in front of Leagh once again. "Hey, Tony is alive and perfectly fine. Do you hear what I'm saying?"

"He's not hurt? He's not dead?" Leagh asked in a quivering voice filled with fear.

James issued a heavy sigh and shook his head. "No, sweetheart, he's one hundred percent fine. I volunteered to come by with Officer Hung here to make sure things don't get too out of control," he replied, jerking a thumb at the officer standing behind him.

Julianna looked up at the other cop and laughed. "Officer Hung, huh? Cute."

The pieces fell into place, quickly. The cop with James was a stripper. "Oh, for the love of…someone should have hired Commander Cock Choker instead of a damn cop," I scolded.

"I'll be sure to let the guilty party know the policeman was a bad choice." James shot me a mischievous grin. "I think 'Ball Gag Green Beret' would be the perfect stripper for *your* bachelorette party."

I couldn't help but snort. "Save your money. I'm never getting married. Look, I'm sorry for being so harsh and insulting, but…"

"It takes more than that to insult me, pretty lady." James grinned. "I still think you need a ball gag, though. You'd look stunning in one."

Even though I was still irked at James for frightening Leagh, I regretted ripping into him so vehemently.

"You're here to spy on us too, aren't you, James?" Julianna asked, cocking her head and watching his reaction closely. "Yep, you're here to make sure we behave like proper submissives, right?"

A guilty grin tugged his lips as he winked. "Now, would I do that sort of thing?"

"In a heartbeat." Turning her attention back to Leagh, Julianna and I helped the girl to her feet.

"Come on, baby. Tony's perfectly fine. Officer *Hung* here has a present for you…in his pants," Julianna explained with a giggle.

"Oh hell, he's a fucking stripper?" Leagh gasped. "Who got me a stripper?"

"I think Tony did. Come on, sugar. It's time for you to sit in the hot seat," Julianna laughed.

Suddenly, as if a light had gone off in her head, Leagh scowled and pinned James with a look of suspicion. "Tony's got a female stripper at his party, doesn't he?" she hissed, wagging a finger in James' face.

"How the hell would I know? I'm here with you."

"Oh, that's a convenient excuse now, isn't it?" she spat. "Fine. I'll get the details out of him one way or another. Oh, and one more thing. You do not have permission to record any of this…um, I mean, please, Sir, don't record this for me?"

"Tony will have a good time breaking you of giving orders, Leagh. And I'm personally going to enjoy the hell out of watching him do it, too." James smirked. "I may not have *your* permission, but I do have Tony's." James laughed and slid his cell phone out of his pocket.

"Oh, shit," Leagh moaned.

Trevor set an empty chair in the middle of the room with a giggle, as Julianna and I led Leagh back into the living room. James and Officer Hung—complete with a 1980s boom box—followed behind us. The subs surrounded Leagh in a big circle, laughing and taunting her as loud dance music echoed off the walls.

Officer Hung wiggled his hips in Leagh's face, gyrating in sexual suggestion before peeling off his clothes. Laughing, Leagh pointedly gazed at James' cell phone as he recorded every bump and grind.

"Thank you, Master. But just for the record, I'd rather have a lap dance from you. Hurry home and strip for me, please? I'll pay you with something special."

Casting a glance up at the muscular man, he stroked his night stick with hard, jerking movements. Leagh squealed, then looked back at James. "Okay, so maybe this once, I'll manage to enjoy another man dancing for me. Thank you, Sir. Thank you so much."

Several subs pulled out their phones to record every shimmy and shake. Trevor all but drooled as he watched the buff dancer. When the stripper tore away his pants, wearing only a bright blue thong with a massive bulge, the whole room went wild. Screams, whistles, and cheers thundered as I stood back, laughing at the raucous bunch.

Julianna kissed Leagh on the cheek, then placed a wad of money in her hand.

"See what he'll give you for tips," Julianna giggled.

"Oh, lord. I think I'm going to pass out," Trevor exclaimed as he grabbed a stack of napkins and began wiping the perspiration from his forehead.

When Leagh was done carefully tucking money into the dancer's grinding g-string, he scooped out the bills and shimmied out of his thong, wearing nothing but a nice tan and a hard, thick erection.

"Oh, sweet mother of big, beautiful boners," Trevor whimpered. "If I ever get married, I hope Daddy sends this guy to *my* bachelorette party. Look at that cock. It's breathtaking. I bet that monster's at least eight inches."

"Eight and a half, Goldilocks," the dancer replied before blowing Trevor a kiss.

Joshua's cock is bigger and far more talented. As soon as the thought entered my head, heat rushed to my cheeks and blood pooled behind my clit. Sliding my phone from my pocket, I quickly glanced at the empty screen. With a silent curse, I shoved it back in my pocket, convinced I'd clearly lost my mind.

"Get over here, Mellie, and get in this chair," Leagh demanded. "You're the only one who won't get into trouble. Come on. Get nasty with this big ol' cock."

Laughing along with Leagh, I shook my head. "He's all yours. Enjoy him as best you can."

Trevor whooped and hollered when the dancer began twerking his cock in Leagh's face. "Kiss it. Kiss it. Kiss it," Trevor chanted.

"Hell, no," she screeched. Her eyes grew wide, and she blushed. "*You* kiss it."

The dancer turned, pinning Trevor with a knowing stare. "Would you like a taste, darling?"

Trevor turned bright red. Blond hair whipped his face as he backed way, adamantly shaking his head. "No way. I love my Daddy. I'm not doing anything to screw that up."

"Pity." The stripper pouted. When the music faded, the naked man bent and kissed Leagh on the cheek. "Have a fun party, and happy wedding night."

James escorted Officer Hung to the foyer, waiting patiently as the man redressed. Raising a hand to wave goodbye, James continued to hold the door open, and as all the Doms paraded back in, a hush fell over the room.

"Mind if I take a look at your phone, James?" Tony grinned as he held out his hand.

"No. Don't," Leagh blurted before hiding her face in her hands.

"What's wrong, angel? You haven't been a bad girl, have you?" Tony taunted. "You know what I do to bad girls, don't you?"

"Aarrgghh," she groaned. "No, I was a perfect angel, for the most part. You set me up, didn't you, Sir?"

"Indeed, I did, princess. Indeed I did," he laughed.

"And what about you, boy?" Drake pinned Trevor with a suspicious grin. "You look awfully guilty. Is there something you need to tell me?"

Trevor raced across the room and wrapped Drake in a desperate hug. "I might have said a few things I shouldn't have, but I was good. I swear, Daddy. But now that you're here, I really…realllyyyy want to be bad with you…right now."

Drake laughed as he bent and slanted his mouth over Trevor's in a rough and hungry kiss. "I like you primed and ready for me, sweet boy."

"Oh, I am, Daddy. I'm sooo, sooo ready."

"Yes, I know. I can feel your hard cock on my thigh," Drake laughed. "Keep it that way. I have plans for it, and you, tonight, my love."

"Thank heavens," Trevor whimpered.

"Oh, Leagh," Tony howled. "My, my, angel. You got a face full didn't you?"

She gave him a playful pout and nodded. "But as you can plainly see, I was your perfect little angel tonight, Master."

Tony laughed and pulled her to his chest. "I'm proud of you, baby." He beamed, then kissed her long and passionately.

Claimed subs paired up with their owners, and I tried not to notice the pangs of envy within me, but they chaffed. Painting on a happy smile, I visited and mingled, wishing Joshua were a part of the Genesis family. Did he know about the club? Surely, living down the street and being a Dom of his caliber, he had to know of its existence. Maybe, like me, he'd become disenchanted and left the community. Or maybe he was a natural-born Dom who didn't know there were others like him outside his artistic bubble. Wishing and hoping for fairy tales seemed a fruitless waste of time. I desperately wanted to see him again but refused to seek him out like a pathetic fan girl, or, God forbid, a crazy stalker. I had to devise a way to banish him from my brain, drive out thoughts of the incredible night we'd spent, and find my resilient equilibrium again.

That sounds all good and fine, yet here you are...still obsessing about him. Why?

Taking a sip of margarita through my penis straw, I frowned. *Because he touched something inside, and no matter how hard I try, I can't wipe it away. At least, not yet.*

"Are you ready to head out?" Nick asked. A quizzical look wrinkled one brow. "What's got you so deep in thought, Mellie?"

"Nothing. Yes, of course." I smiled, trying to deflect his concern. "I'm good to go whenever you guys are ready."

After kisses and hugs and lots of good nights, we climbed into Nick's big red truck and headed home. The silence was deafening, and I caught Nick's concerned gaze in the rear-view mirror more than once.

"Okay, enough," Sanna announced as she squirmed in her seat and turned to face me. "What's going on, Mel? Spill it, and don't tell me nothing's wrong. I know you."

"Easy, kitten," Dylan instructed.

"It's called tough love, Master. And she needs it," Sanna explained as she continued to probe me with a stern gaze. "Out with it, chicky-pooh."

"Fine," I huffed. "I had a wonderful time last night. More earth shattering than I'd expected. It's rocked me a bit, but I'll be fine. I just need to get it into perspective."

"Tell me what happened with Scotty, before the fire, I mean," she pressed.

"Nothing. Absolutely nothing. And nothing is ever going to happen with him. Okay?"

"That's quite an about turn from the other night," Nick interjected.

"I know," I sighed. "That's another thing that's got me stumped. He kissed me—Scotty, I mean—and it was like kissing a brother. It felt awkward and gross."

"So, the man from last night, why do you think he's left such an impression?" Dylan asked.

I knew exactly why Joshua had unnerved me so, but I wasn't sure I wanted to confess it to the world.

"Don't stall, Mellie," Dylan coaxed. "Don't try to analyze it, just spit it out."

"Because he was a Dom."

"Who was he?" Nick asked.

"Joshua Lars," Savannah offered.

"The artist who created your statue?"

"Yes." I nodded to Nick's arched brows reflecting in the mirror.

"By the look of his work, I'd say he most definitely is a Dominant," Dylan chimed in. "And it's dredging up old feeling in you, isn't it?"

"Yes," I whispered in a dejected tone.

"Don't make it sound as if it's a death sentence, girl," Dylan chuckled. "I told you the other day, it's not a light switch you can turn off and on. Your true desires will come out no matter how hard you try to wish them away. I think you're finding that out, aren't you?"

"Yes, but it doesn't change the fact I can't allow myself to go back to the woman I was…the submissive, I mean. I just can't."

"Can't or won't?" Nick challenged.

"Both. It's too much of a risk. I can't put myself through that again, and I won't."

"So, what do you propose to do about it? Obviously running from your desires isn't working. You've not tried to stand and face your fears yet. Where does that leave you?"

Nick's eyes twinkled. The man was actually smiling as he figuratively backed my ass into the corner.

"It leaves me exactly here, coping with it until I get back home. I can shove it under the carpet, like I always do, and go on about my life."

"Okay, but if Scotty didn't flip your switch after Joshua, what makes you think some other—"

"Don't go there," I cut Sanna off. "I've already thought it."

"And?"

"And, I don't know. It's only been a day. Give me some time to put it behind me, okay? I'll work him out of my system…eventually."

"You hope," Dylan smirked.

"I will," I argued defiantly.

"Look, I'm not finding fault with anything about your life, Mel, but you have a history of running away when things get too intense," Sanna interjected.

"Like you don't?" I challenged.

"Not anymore," she bragged.

"I'm happy for you," I scorned, immediately wishing I could take the sarcasm out of my reply.

"I know you are. You already told me and meant it." She waved her hand at the growing tension between us. "Have you ever sat down and asked yourself why you won't get close to anyone besides me?"

"No, Doctor Phil, I haven't."

"Stop being pissy with me. I'm trying to help you," Sanna huffed.

"I know why. It's the same reason I closed myself off from my own life, Mel. You're afraid of loving someone and losing them."

The air left my lungs in a rush. Tears prickled my eyes, and my heart felt as if she'd punched through my chest and yanked it out.

"It's okay to let someone in. It's okay to take a chance because it's so worth it. I could keel over and die tomorrow, but I'd go happy. I have these two incredible, wonderful men in my life who fill me full of all the things I'd missed out on by being afraid. Listen to me and believe me. The joys outweigh the risks by so much, it's incomprehensible."

Tears slid down my cheeks as Sanna scrambled over the bench seat and wrapped me in her arms. "It's okay, sis. You have so much love inside your heart. You have to stop wasting it all on me."

"It's not a waste," I sniffed.

"No, but you've got so much more to share. Give it to someone who deserves you. Someone who understands your needs, even when you don't. You knew long before I did that a Dom would complete you and fulfill the longings buried deep inside you. So, you picked the wrong one the first time. You might even pick the wrong one the second time, but somewhere along the way, you're going to pick the right one. Just imagine how wonderful your life will be. You're not a quitter, Mel. You don't walk away from a job until it's totally perfect. You didn't bat an eye at moving back home to finish raising me when Mom and Dad died. So, why are you letting your fears make you quit and cheat you out of a chance at happiness?"

Chapter Five

When I woke the next morning, my eyes felt like they'd been dipped in kitty litter. After a second night of tossing and turning while residual images of Joshua filled my head, I couldn't stop thinking about all the things Savannah had said. The two combined proved to make sleep an elusive indulgence.

Of all the questions that spooled in my brain, one in particular continued to stump me. When and how had my little sister found such profound enlightenment? Finally, it dawned on me. "When she found her Masters, of course," I whispered aloud.

I tried to close my eyes and get some sleep, but it was useless. Dragging myself out of bed at nine o'clock, I shuffled to the bathroom and climbed into the shower. Leagh and Tony's wedding was at three. Even though Julianna and Trevor were her bridesmaids, Leagh wanted extra reinforcements to prepare for her big day and had asked if Sanna and I would come early to help her get ready. I was strangely excited to be a part of it all. Usually, I avoided weddings, but after spending so much time with Leagh and the rest of the gang from Genesis, I was actually looking forward to it.

When I stepped out of the shower, I found a hot cup of coffee sitting on the vanity. *Sanna.* A smile spread over my face as I quickly dried, donned my robe, and opened the door. A pensive look lined my sister's face as she sat on my bed.

"Hey. I'm sorry if I was too hard on you last night. I know you're a big girl and live your life exactly the way you want. I had no business sticking my nose in it."

"Oh, baby," I groaned. "You have every right to stick your nose in. You're my sister, and you're worried. I get that. You have no idea how many nights I spent worrying and wondering if I'd done the best I could to raise you, to prepare you for the big bad world out there."

"You did." Sanna smiled. "I just needed a little help breaking out of my cocoon. Thankfully, I found the two men who could get the job done."

"Yes, you did." I grinned. "I'm sorry about my snarky comments last night. I am happy for you."

"I know you are, and I know you were lashing out because, well…I was attacking you. I'm sorry for doing that to you. I just want you to be happy. Honestly, that's all I've ever wanted. So, whether you're with someone or alone, as long as you're happy, then I'm happy for you."

"I *am* happy. I'm just a little screwed up at the moment because of a certain *man*. But don't worry. I'll be back to my old self soon. I promise."

Savannah gave a resolute nod, then hugged me tight. "We need to be at the church at one. The guys are going to fix breakfast, so come down when you can."

"I will, and thank you for the coffee, baby. I love you."

"I love you too." A broad smile spread over her lips as she scurried out of the room.

Three and a half hours later, I stood staring at the two dresses draped across the bed. Vacillating between the designer, tea-length, cranberry twist, silk chiffon strapless, or the designer, knee-length, champagne chiffon halter, I couldn't decide.

There was a soft knock at my door, and I let out an indecisive sigh. "Come in," I called, too distracted to glance over my shoulder.

"Oh, Mel, you're not dressed yet?" Sanna gasped.

Spinning around, I looked at my sister and gasped. The knee-length, strapless, royal blue, chiffon dress hugged her curves and made her eyes pop and her skin glow. She looked like she'd just stepped from a fairy tale.

"Oh, wow," I whispered. "Sanna, you look…damn! You look *stunning*."

She couldn't hide her proud smile. "Hurry up. The guys are looking at their watches and pacing a hole in the floor. They sent me up to fetch you."

"Okay, hang on. I need you to help me with the zipper."

Snatching the cranberry silk off the bed, I stepped into it, adjusting my boobs as Sanna zipped me up. With one last glance in the mirror, I snagged my clutch, hooked the straps of my gold-heeled sandals around my fingers, and rushed from the room.

When we arrived at the church, Dylan and Nick took off to find Tony while Sanna and I discovered Leagh in the bride's room with pandemonium in full swing. She looked frazzled beyond sanity and fighting back tears as a short, pretty Italian woman tugged at the neckline of her wedding gown. Three younger, dark-haired women looked on wearing various expressions of annoyance as they watched the older woman attempt to conceal Leagh's cleavage.

"I've got it, Alisa. Really," Leagh snapped, brushing the woman's hands away. "I'm afraid this is as good as it's going to get."

"Oh, honey. I'm sorry. I'm not trying to be a prude, but Tony's grandma is going to be here. She's from a different generation," Alisa began with a pained expression. "I think your breasts are beautiful…not that I spend my days staring at your…oh, dear."

"Ma," a younger woman with dark hair and big brown eyes hissed. "Just stop. Leave poor Leagh alone. If Gramma Rose can't remember what it was like to have a set of perky tits, that's her problem. She'll just have to get over it."

I bit my lips together to keep from laughing.

"I suppose you're right." Alisa exhaled heavily. "I just don't want to hear…oh, never mind. I think she's getting senile, anyway. She probably won't even remember the ceremony after a couple of drinks at the reception."

"Exactly, so give it a rest, Ma," another one of the girls chimed in.

"What can we help you with, Leagh?" Sanna asked. Swooping in to give the bride a hug, she accidentally-on-purpose nudged the overly anxious Alisa out of the way.

"I don't know. I think I need a bigger dress." The look of mortification on Leagh's face was heartbreaking.

"No, you don't, sugar. You look like a fairy tale bride; breathtakingly stunning," Sanna reassured her.

"Oh, I'm sorry. I haven't introduced you all." Turning toward the four dark-haired ladies, Leagh extended her hand. "These are my friends, Savannah, and her sister Mellie Carson. Sanna and Mellie, this is Alisa Delvaggio, Tony's mom, and his sisters, Anna, Sofia, and Maria."

"It's a pleasure to meet you," Sanna and I replied in unison.

"How's Tony holding up?" I asked, hoping it might prod the nervous mom out of the room so we could try to calm Leagh down.

"Oh, dear, I'm not sure." Alisa wrung her hands as she flashed a worried look toward her daughters.

"Maybe we should go check on him, Ma," Sofia urged as she flashed me a look of gratitude. "Leagh's got plenty of help now. We need to get out of her hair so she can finish getting ready."

"Yes. Yes, that's a good idea. Let's go check on your brother." Alisa nodded.

Like a mother hen, she gathered up her daughters before leading a parade out the door.

"Good luck," Sanna called.

Maria, the last in line, paused and glanced over her shoulder.

"We don't need luck, we need Prozac," she announced, rolling her eyes. "You look gorgeous, Leagh. My brother's eyes are going to pop out of his head, and his tongue's going to hit the floor. Don't worry about Gramma Rose. She's half blind, anyway."

The young girl grinned, winked, and blew a kiss before closing the door behind her. I rushed over and quickly engaged the lock.

"Thank you, Mellie. You just saved my life." Leagh let out a loud sigh and slumped down on a fluffy couch in the massive dressing room.

"You're doing fine, Leagh. Just try to relax," Sanna comforted her as she eyed a big tray of finger sandwiches, fruits, and cheese. "Have you eaten today?"

Leagh shook her head.

"Okay, we need to get some protein in you."

"I can't. My stomach is rolling so badly, I'm afraid I'll barf all over Tony's Italian dress shoes."

"No, you're not. Listen to me. Just close your eyes and take some deep breaths. Relax and think of the night Tony proposed to you. Go back to that romantic beach and how he got down on one knee in the sand. Come on. Think back on how it amazing it was, just like you told me," Sanna urged.

I put together several plates of food while Sanna helped Leagh out of her dress before we started applying her make-up and talking the nervous bride down off the ledge. Taming Leagh's anxiety, my sister reminded her about the butt plug fire, the twerking stripper, and what a lucky man Tony was to take her hand in marriage. Coaxing Leagh to eat some food, the girl downed two full plates and asked for another. The bride-to-be had actually relaxed until a knock came from the door, and her anxiety spiked again.

"I love Alisa, I really do, but *please* don't let her back in here," Leagh whispered in a desperate plea.

"I won't," I mouthed before I cracked open the door and peered through the tiny gap. Smiling, I swung it open wide as Julianna and Trevor rushed in, both wearing broad smiles and dressed to the nines. Closing the door behind them, I locked it once again.

"Thank goodness. I was getting worried that you two weren't going to show," Leagh groaned.

"Bitch, please," Trevor chastised with a grin. "I think you need some liquid calm."

Untucking his arm, he pulled a bottle of champagne from his tuxedo jacket.

"Yes, I do." Leagh nodded emphatically. "Lots and lots of champagne. Hell, just give me the bottle."

"No way," Trevor giggled. "If I get you drunk before the wedding, Drake will have my balls dangling from his rear-view mirror. You get *one* glass, then I'm going to have to cocktail block you."

"Make it a big one then, please," Leagh begged.

"Why is the door locked? Are you expecting more cop strippers or something?" Julianna laughed.

"No. No more strippers. I can barely function as it is. We're keeping Tony's mom, Alisa, out. I know that sounds really bad, and I love her to pieces, but she's making me crazy today."

Sanna found some plastic cups as Trevor popped the cork with a squeal. They filled the cups and passed them around.

"Oh, honey," Julianna moaned. "Come on, drink up. You need to jump start your Zen. You're getting married to the man of your dreams."

"Yes, I am." Leagh nodded with conviction then downed her glass. Grabbing the bottle from Trevor, she took a long swig, then handed it back to him. "Let's do this."

"That a girl," Sanna giggled. "Come on, gang. It's time to work our magic."

As Sanna, Julianna and I began primping Leagh for her big day, Trevor stepped toward the door.

"I vow to keep everyone out of the sacred beautification room, with the exception of our Masters," Trevor declared with a solemn salute.

In less than two hours, we'd transformed not only Leagh's outward beauty, but calmed her inward anxiety, thanks to several pep talks and a couple more swigs of champagne. When we were through, we helped her back into her bridal gown. Leagh looked every bit the quintessential 'blushing bride', and when she checked herself in the mirror, a smile so bright spread across her lips, it rivaled the sun.

Trevor wiped a tear from the corner of his eye as he stared at her. "Oh, sis. You look stunning."

"Don't cry, Trev. You'll get me started. Then the girls will have to redo my face, and there's not enough time for a major overhaul."

"I'm sorry, love. It's just that you look…amazing. All but one thing." He pouted.

"What? What thing?" Sanna scrutinized Leagh's hair and make-up as she nibbled her lip.

Trevor reached into his breast pocket and pulled out the flashing penis veil from the adult toy store. With a flick of his wrist, the netting unfurled. He then pushed a button on the imitation rhinestone encrusted tiara, and the penises started pulsating in neon colors of green, red, orange, and purple.

Leagh snorted in surprise as we all started howling.

Trevor placed the plastic tiara on her head, careful not to mess up her hair, then issued a satisfied sigh. "There. You are now a complete and perfectly breathtaking, kinky bride."

"You are so bad," Leagh giggled.

"The one we bought for your bachelorette party perished in the fire. But being the awesomely, fantabulous friend *I* am—" Trevor preened, with a snap of his wrist. "—I decided to raid my own wedding stash. No self-respecting tawdry bride would even *think* of walking down the aisle without one."

"Is that so?" Leagh laughed as she dashed back to the mirror.

Unbeknownst to us, the phallic symbols were motion activated. Once we'd discovered the added feature, Leagh raced around the room as the strobe of cocks throbbed. We were laughing so hard, we had to blot away our tears.

"Stop. Stop," Julianna begged. "My cheeks and stomach hurt."

"That's just wrong on so many levels," Sanna chortled.

"I know it is," Leagh snorted. "I bet Gramma Rose wouldn't pay one bit of attention to my boobs if I danced down the aisle wearing this."

Roaring with laughter once again, Trevor shook his head, barely able to speak. "If you try to wear that damn thing, you won't sit for a month. Tony will paddle your ass till it's black and blue."

"I know. But it would be so worth it."

"Yes, but poor Gramma Rose's false teeth might fall on the floor. That wouldn't be good," I warned.

"True." Leagh pouted, before a mischievous flicker lit up her eyes. "I'll just save it for our wedding night."

Trevor snorted. "By the time Tony's done with you at the club, you won't even know your own name, let alone have the energy to put that thing on your head."

Leagh's eyes grew wide with fear, and just as she opened her mouth to reply, a loud knock filled the room.

"Oh shit," she hissed. Snatching the tiara from her head, she shoved it back at Trevor. "Hide that."

"You mean, you're not going to wear it?" Trevor teased as he quickly tucked it back in his jacket and unlocked the door.

Dylan and Nick stepped through the portal, still looking like bookends out of GQ magazine. Suspicion furrowed their brows as they studied us.

"What trouble are you wild ones cooking up now?" Nick asked.

"Nothing, Master." Sanna smiled ever so sweetly.

"Right." Dylan rolled his eyes and shook his head. "You five look as guilty as a fox in a hen house. You didn't start another fire, did you?"

"Honestly, Master," Sanna chastised with a peevish scowl.

"Kitten." Dylan's tone dipped in warning, making it clear he didn't appreciate her sass.

"I think you just earned an attitude adjustment tonight, precious," Nick announced with a conspiratory grin.

"You bet your sweet ass you did," Dylan chuckled as Sanna frowned.

"Come on, you two, it's time for us to take our seats," Nick announced.

Both men stepped in close to Leagh. "You look like an angel. Tony's a lucky bastard,"

Dylan praised.

"Our happiest blessings to you both," Nick added with a grin.

"Thank you, Sir,." Leagh whispered, softly.

Sanna and I hugged our partners in crime before following Dylan and Nick to the chapel. Stopping at a pew close to the front of the church, Nick stopped and tapped a man wearing a dark suit on the shoulder. When he stood and turned, I couldn't help but smile. It was James, the cop I'd railed on the night before. He floated an approving gaze over my body, and I issued an inward curse. I didn't want his attention. I wanted Joshua's. That was nothing more than a hopeless pipe dream. The man *still* hadn't called; he wasn't going to.

"It's good to see you again, Mellie." James grinned.

"Likewise." I smiled as an awkward pall settled between us.

James sidled down the pew, making room for us to sit, and I exhaled a sigh of relief for not having to sit next to him. He seemed nice enough. I simply wasn't attracted to him, and I didn't want to encourage him, especially after the inner conflict of Scotty's kiss.

A buzz of excitement filled the air as the ushers hastily seated guests. Soft organ music filled the ornate sanctuary as people packed the pews. Sanna and I bided our time, whispering and giggling, wondering if Leagh would shock the crowd and wear the tacky penis veil. Evidently, we were getting a little too carried away, because Nick flashed a stern glare in our direction. Of course, that only made us giggle harder. He narrowed his eyes and shook his head. I was afraid our bad habit of feeding off one another would wind up getting Sanna into trouble, so I quietly shushed her and bit my lips.

I watched an usher escort Alisa to the front pew with Tony's handsome father following behind her.

When the organ fell silent, anticipation spiked. Tony and the priest appeared from behind the nave, looking calm and cool. The groom smiled at his family before locking his gaze to the back of the church, as if mentally calling Leagh to join him. The organ blared with dramatic music as both Sanna and I wiggled in our seats, staring toward the back of the room. Drake and Trevor appeared arm in arm, wearing stunningly tailored tuxes. Drake's dark charcoal gray ensemble accented his beautiful eyes, while Trevor's deep burgundy color seemed to make his pale skin glow.

Following the two men were Mika and Julianna, linked arm in arm. The dungeon owner wore the same gray sophisticated tux as Drake, while Julianna wore a luxurious, strapless flowing, burgundy, ruched chiffon gown. Their fashions were lavishly chic, but it was their dazzling smiles—even Drake, who rarely ever wore one—that cast each in an almost ethereal hue.

At the altar, Mika, Drake, and Tony shared a private chuckle as Julianna and Trevor stared at the doorway, waiting for Leagh to appear. As the chords of *'The Wedding March'* echoed through the A-framed interior, I joined the rest of the crowd and stood.

Turning to watch Leagh walk down the aisle, I noticed one lone guest facing the front of the church. His gaze locked with mine. A startled cry fluttered over my lips as Joshua Lars' twinkling green eyes snared me like a hunter's trap. My heart clutched. My knees nearly buckled, and I wanted to pinch myself to make sure I wasn't dreaming. Unable to avert my gaze, I stood mesmerized by the fiery lust shimmering in his sexy eyes. Once again, his bewildering ability to see deep inside my soul, rocked me to the core.

My entire body shook. My heart thundered in my ears, and my mouth felt as dry as a desert. The room began to spin. I placed my hand on the back of the pew to keep from sliding to the floor. Trying to keep my hammering heart in place while struggling to draw air into my lungs, I placed a palm on my chest and issued a tiny whimper.

Amused by my astonished reaction, a brazen smile crawled across his lips—lips that had unraveled me to the bone—before he flashed me a devilish grin. Drinking in the sight of him, every minute detail of our night together rushed through my mind, bringing with it an onslaught of arousal. My nipples tightened, and my pussy wept. The physical ache to be beneath his naked body, filled with his massive cock stretching me with that amazing silken burn, stole my breath. Tearing from his gaze, I bent to whisper in Sanna's ear.

"What the fuck is Joshua Lars doing here?" I hissed.

"What? Where?" Sanna blinked as she scanned the crowd.

"Right there," I choked, nodding in his direction. Scared to lock gazes with the man for fear I'd never break free, I looked at my sister, hoping she'd see the man staring at me.

"That's not Joshua Lars, that's Master Stephen," she whispered with a frown.

"No, *that* is Joshua Lars," I spat.

"Are you kidding? Oh, my," she replied, seemingly surprised. Tugging Nick's sleeve, she arched on her tiptoes and whispered in his ear.

Taking his attention off Leagh, Nick and Joshua exchanged nods, then Nick bent and softly said something to Sanna.

Fighting the urge to look at Joshua and failing miserably, I watched his shoulders shake with a silent chuckle.

Sanna's breath warmed my ear as she leaned in. "Yeah, that's him all right. Damn. I had no idea Master Stephen was Joshua Lars."

"Nick did," I grumbled in a terse whisper. "Why didn't he tell me?"

"Don't be mad at him, Mel. You know the rules. Anonymity is a sacred thing among lifestylers."

"I know, but...Shit. I am so screwed," I hissed under my breath.

"Not yet. But I'd say the way he's undressing you with his eyes, you could have another shot at it," Sanna whispered, then giggled.

So stunned I couldn't even think of a witty comeback to Sanna's jab, the blurring white figure of Leagh making her way down the aisle briefly obscured my view of Joshua. Thankfully, it was long enough to sever the magnetic hold he had over me.

Vaguely aware of people around me turning to face the front of the church, my feet remained frozen in place. Sanna elbowed me in the side, and I almost tripped, readjusting myself in the narrow pew.

When Leagh reached the altar, the priest stepped up to the microphone and invited us to take our seats. His words registered in my brain, but my body wouldn't seem to obey. With a tiny giggle, Sanna cupped my elbow and pulled me down next to her in the pew.

"You've got it bad, sweetie. Really, really bad," she whispered in a giddy tone. "He's an impressive Master, by the way."

Like I hadn't already figured that out?

"Does he have a sub?" I murmured.

"Not anymore. He released the one he had a few months ago."

My heart sank as a combination of anger and grief burned in me. What were the odds of me attracting another *player* who got his jollies off slapping Velcro collars around subs' necks? Why did they always seem to sniff me out? *Joshua Lars was really Master Stephen in disguise.* My brain swirled in shock and dread, while unwelcome desire zipped through my girl parts like a bumblebee on crack.

Drawing in a deep breath, I forced myself to focus on the priest's words as he instructed Leagh and Tony to join hands. All the while, Joshua's heated gaze seared into the back of my head, making it impossible to concentrate on anything but him. *The fucking rat bastard.*

I needed to stop him from driving me insane. He was forbidden fruit. Not only was he a friend of Sanna and her Masters, but a Dom with little regard for the gift of submission or the sanctity of a collar.

No matter how badly my body ached for one more night with the man, drowning in his commanding lovemaking skills wasn't enough to warrant self-inflicted emotional harm. I needed to box up my lofty fantasies of submission and slap on a shiny new lock—one that couldn't be picked quite so easily again—and drive him out of my psyche.

The harder I tried to ignore him, the hotter his gaze seemed to grow. Clenching my jaw, I squared my shoulders. If he wanted to watch me, fine. Let the man get his jollies however he chose. I didn't have to participate in his stupid cat-and-mouse game. I may not have known Tony and Leagh well, but I was there to celebrate their union, not get sidetracked obsessing over some wannabe Dom and our one-night stand.

I spent a whole thirty-seven seconds mentally browbeating myself before I caved. Glancing over my shoulder, I discovered Joshua's fiery stare had not been a figment of my imagination. He remained zeroed in on me with those gorgeous green eyes and a toe-curling gaze.

His hungry stare flipped some masochistic switch in my brain. I could feel the warm texture of his lips, taste the tart bead that swelled on his cock, and smell his masculine scent, as sure as if he'd been hard-wired inside my brain…my body.

My growing arousal sparked an electrical current that literally hummed in my ears. The man hadn't so much as touched me, yet he had the power to draw me to him, like a moth to a flame. I had to put a stop to it all. Once and for all, I had to exorcize the demon known as Joshua Lars. Problem being, I had no idea how.

The priest cleared his throat. Snapping my head toward the sound, I swallowed tightly. "Dearly beloved," he began. "We are gathered here today…"

To watch Mellie Carson lose her ever-loving mind.

I closed my eyes and drew in a ragged breath. The forty-five minute ceremony seemed to drag on for hours. The nuptials were beautiful and heartwarming, yet I couldn't focus on anything except Joshua's incessant stare. Well, that and calculating how long it would take me to jump from the pew, dash out of the church, and race back to Sanna's to hide away in the safety of my room. There were only two obstacles in my way: I couldn't run three seconds in my five-inch heels, plus I didn't have a car to get me back to the house. It was a hell of a long walk in stilettos, which I probably wouldn't achieve without breaking an ankle. Nope, running away wasn't an option. I'd have to stay and face the music—which pissed me the hell off.

"You may kiss the bride," the priest instructed, pulling me from my ruminations.

Tony cupped Leagh's cheeks in his hands and bestowed her with a commanding, potent kiss. A shiver rippled through me. Joshua had kissed me in that exact manner, and I could still feel the heat of his lips.

Aarrgghh.

"Ladies and gentlemen," the priest cried out as he raised his hands, "It is my privilege to introduce to you, Mr. and Mrs. Anthony Delvaggio."

Tony and Leagh's faces beamed in absolute bliss. For a few glorious moments, joy for their happiness drowned out the chaos swimming inside me. Tony wrapped a protective arm around Leagh's waist, then bounded down the stairs, escorting her toward the back of the church. The rest of the wedding party followed behind, all wearing happy, broad smiles as they joined the bride and groom in the receiving line.

The guests began to spill into the aisles toward the church's foyer. The passage quickly became so choked there was no place for us to go, so we remained in our seats, waiting for the steady line to shorten.

When it came our turn to get in line, I stood, but froze like a statue, unable to move. I had assumed Joshua would follow the other guests in his pew, but he didn't. He lingered in the aisle, paying no attention to the people going ahead of him. Joshua's focus was on one thing—and one thing only—me.

"Come on, Mel, move," Sanna urged, prodding me to move. "We're not going to find a good table at the reception if we don't get through the line."

I swallowed tightly and stumbled from the narrow passage, cracking my ankle on the edge of the kneeling bench beneath the pew. Biting back a curse—because I knew swearing in church was frowned upon—I hobbled on one foot as I reached down and massaged the zinger.

Sanna, Nick, Dylan, and James stepped into the aisle as well.

"You okay?" James asked in concern.

"Yes, I'm fine. Just clumsy is all."

"You can lean on me if you need to," James offered with a broad smile.

"Thanks, but really, I'm fine," I assured him, hoping I wouldn't embarrass myself further.

Peeking over Dylan's shoulder, I saw Joshua working his way against the flow of guests and heading our direction. Extending his hand, he and the other Doms exchanged hellos. Two sets of eyes were intently watching James, Joshua, and me.

For the love of...can this possibly get any more awkward?

"It's good to see you, Master Stephen," Sanna said with an impish grin.

"It's a pleasure to see you, as well, little one." Joshua briefly turned his attention on my sister and smiled. Then, like clockwork, his stare landed right back on me. "What a delightful surprise to see you again, Mellie. I take it Savannah, is the sister you spoke of the other night?"

"Ah, yes."

"You two know each other already?" James questioned with an arch of his brows.

"Yes, we met the night before last." Joshua nodded.

"What a coincidence. We met last night," the other man replied with an assessing smirk.

"Yes, but I saw her first," Joshua added with suave self-assurance.

Oh, good grief. Their posturing had all the markings of an ensuing pissing match. I wasn't having any of it. If cussing wasn't welcome in church, peeing on the pews to mark their territory wouldn't be either.

"I guess what really matters most is that we've all been introduced, right?" I snapped my mouth shut before I slipped and reminded them I wasn't some toy in their sandbox to fight over.

"May I accompany you to the reception?" Joshua asked with an intrepid smile.

"Hell, yes," Nick replied. "Please, join us."

My body tensed. *Dammit, Nick. He was asking* me, *not you.* By then, the damage was done. I couldn't un-invite Joshua without looking like a heinous bitch.

"You're going to join us too, aren't you, James?" Nick inquired.

I wanted to kick him in the shins.

"I appreciate the offer, man. But I promised I'd save Arianna a seat. She missed the ceremony because of work, but she's coming to the reception." Turning a solemn expression toward Joshua, James gave something that resembled a ceding nod. "I guess I'll see you guys downstairs."

With a wave, James circumvented the crowd and took a route out of the chapel via the front of the church and through an uncongested door. As we waited to congratulate both Tony and Leagh, I had time to calculate how many hours I'd be forced to sit at a table with Joshua, deflecting his charismatic advances. I wanted to throw up. Even more unnerving was the steady sexual throbbing in my core. Joshua slid in next to me. A few minutes later, he wrapped his arm around my waist, and I tensed. Out of the corner of my eye, I saw him turn a confused frown my way as he intently studied me.

Do you honestly want to shun him?

My brain cried out in a resounding 'Yes,' while my body churned in a desperate 'No.'

As we reached the back of the church, Sanna sucked in a little gasp. Wobbling with a stutter step, she gripped Nick's hand. Turning an angry look toward her Masters, she huffed. "What in heaven's name is *she* doing here?"

Craning my neck to see who'd ruffled Sanna's ire, I spied a curvy blonde staring at Joshua with a worried expression. This time, he tensed, then turned toward me, his face lined in concern, or maybe annoyance, I wasn't sure.

"I'll be down to join you shortly," he announced in a bitter tone.

In four firm strides, he ate up the distance between the pensive blonde and us. Wrapping his hand around the woman's elbow, Joshua led her to a corner of the chapel. Leaning in close, the woman wilted into the crevice as Joshua's tall body shrouded her from view.

Studying his body language closely, it wasn't difficult to put the puzzle pieces together. The blonde had to be his former submissive. He clenched and unclenched his fists, finally jamming his hands into his pants pockets. Joshua's reaction left no doubt: he was *not* happy to see the woman. Dying to ask Sanna a million and a half questions, I discovered she was now wedged between Nick and Dylan as the line tapered to single-file near the open doorway. I'd have to wait until I had my sister alone. Nearly to the portal, I caught a glimpse of the girl, all but cowering in the corner. Tears brimmed in her eyes as she adamantly shook her head.

"No," she cried out in a heartfelt sob.

Don't do that to yourself. He's nothing but a callous prick who doesn't deserve your gifts. Don't grovel for the bastard. Let him go and find a real Dom.

Nick glanced toward the woman's cry and issued a scowl. Dylan simply rolled his eyes before ushering me out of the chapel. After giving our best to the bride and groom, we followed several others downstairs to the reception hall.

The room was chilly, but the temperature wasn't to blame for my throbbing, beaded nipples. No, the man upstairs dealing with the teary-eyed blondE was responsible for that. Focusing on the interior of the lush hall with its hues of cream and burgundy, I smiled at its simple elegance. Offsetting colored linens covered dozens of round tables. Fragrant centerpieces of white calla lilies and roses surrounded by purple hydrangeas lent a classic, formal flair to the room. No buffet tables had been erected, so I knew dinner would be served in several courses. Great. I hadn't calculated the time that would take in my mental equation upstairs. Near the dance floor, members of a five-piece orchestra tuned their instruments as guests situated themselves at the numerous tables.

"This looks like a good spot." Dylan smiled. "We're close to the bride and groom's table and near the dance floor."

"You two are going to dance with me, right?" Sanna turned an expectant look to both her men.

"Of course, kitten," Dylan chuckled.

"Indeed, we are. Have you ever known us to turn down a chance to hold you close, precious?" Nick teased.

"Aww, Thank you, Sirs." She beamed.

Half-listening to their continued conversation, I couldn't keep from checking out the doors as more guests entered the reception. Curiosity was killing me. Would Joshua appear alone, or would the blonde be latched to his arm?

"What do you think, Mel?" Sanna asked.

"Huh?" I blinked. "Think about what?"

"We were talking about the club. You know, after the reception. Tony and Leagh's collaring ceremony? We talked about it. Remember? You're still coming with us, right?"

"Oh, yeah," I absently replied.

Joshua would be at the club. *I'd* be at the club. Shit. I needed to back pedal...fast.

"Um, I mean, maybe."

"Melllll," Sanna moaned. "You can't change your mind. You already said you'd go, twice even. Please don't back out on me now."

"Sanna." Nick frowned with a warning. "If she's not comfortable..."

"Sorry, Master," she sighed dejectedly.

"No, I'm sorry, sis," I replied, forcing a smile. "Yes. I'm going to the club with you."

Her eyes lit up as a wide grin spread on her lips. "Yesssss," she hissed, giving a tiny fist pump.

"Thanks for saving me a seat." Joshua smiled as he pulled out the white wooden chair and eased in beside me.

What the hell? There were four other chairs across the table he could have plopped his Dom-playing ass into, but oh, no...he had to choose that one, right? Shit.

"Everything all right?" Nick asked with a cautious expression.

"Yeah, fine," Joshua replied with a curt nod.

"It was a beautiful wedding, don't you think?" Savannah asked, rushing to expunge the sudden tension in the air.

"The only bride more beautiful will be you, kitten." Dylan winked as he leaned over and placed a tender kiss on Sanna's lips.

"Oh, Master," Sanna gushed.

Jenna Jacob

"I don't know," Joshua began. "I think Mellie would make a stunning bride as well."

"Who? Me?" I gasped. He nodded, and I couldn't help but laugh. "Oh, no. No. Marriage is not in my life plan. Not at all."

"Really?" Joshua looked shocked. "Why not?"

"She's allergic to monogamy," Sanna snickered.

"I am not." I scowled at my sister. "The typical wifely mold doesn't fit me. I have a business to run, and I travel all the time. What kind of husband wants a wife who's never home? I wouldn't even attempt a relationship. It would be next to impossible."

"Nothing's impossible," Joshua replied with a shrewd grin.

Thankfully, a roar of cheers and applause interrupted the awkward conversation. Tony and Leagh entered the hall, waving to the crowd as they hurried to the long, oblong table at the front of the room. We stood and clapped in celebration while the rest of the wedding party joined the bride and groom.

After helping Leagh arrange the train of her dress, Tony picked up a microphone and tapped the mesh-covered end, cringing as a scream of feedback squealed from the speakers.

"Oops. Thank you all for coming to share this special day with us."

"Wouldn't miss it for the world, son. It's about damn time," Tony's dad cried out from the table next to us, drawing a collective round of laughter.

"I was waiting for the perfect woman, Dad, like you did." Tony flashed his father a grin before turning a love-struck gaze on Leagh. "And luckily, I found her."

He bent and kissed his bride, then straightened and smirked. "Let's eat." Tony grinned before taking his seat beside Leagh.

A bevy of servers converged around the tables, filling glasses with water and wine, and serving the first of several courses. Throughout the commotion, Joshua's hot stare kept me riding a rollercoaster of anxiety. I desperately wanted to ask why he hadn't called. Instead, I popped a crusty piece of bread into my mouth. No matter how I tried to arrange the words in my head, they ended up sounding like a love-sick fool. It didn't matter—not now—not since I'd discovered he was nothing more than a well-polished player.

Taking a sip of water, I swallowed down the sweet yeasty dough. "So, I assume I should call you Stephen from now on?"

"Master Stephen," he corrected with a mischievous twinkle in his eyes.

"Of course," I replied dryly. "Master."

"Do you have a problem with that, little one?" he pressed.

Clenching my teeth together, I exhaled a long, quiet sigh. "Nope," I replied with a sarcastic pop of my lips.

"I think maybe you do," he smirked before lifting a glass of wine to his lips and taking a long swallow. "I'll make you a deal, Mellie. You call me Master Stephen for the rest of the day and when I pick you up for dinner tomorrow night, you can call me by my first name."

Dinner? With him? Oh, hell no. Not in this lifetime.

A date with the man was entirely out of the question. It was bad enough I had to sit by him at the reception. No way would I volunteer to be tangled like a fat fly in his web of deceit.

"I'd rather call you Master Stephen without *any* strings attached," I snapped with a forced smile.

You'd like to call him a whole lot of things, and not a one would be ladylike.

"Either way, we're having dinner tomorrow night, little one. Just you and me," he pressed with a jovial wink.

"I'm sure you'll be having dinner at some point tomorrow night, but rest assured, it *won't* be with me," I challenged with a sarcastic sneer.

"Ah-hem," Sanna cleared her throat and shot me a scowl. "I need to use the ladies' room. Why don't you come with me?"

My sister's ploy to get me alone and scold me was as veiled as a Mack truck. She could lecture me all she wanted. I wasn't going to shuck off my armor and wilt like a hothouse flower for Sanna, her Masters, Joshua, or anyone.

"You go ahead. I'm eating right now," I replied with a stern glare.

"But I need your help to um…zip my dress back up," she stammered, blatantly grasping at straws.

Denying my sister any kind of help would make me look like a cold-hearted shrew.

"Fine," I spat.

Dropping the fork on my plate with a clatter, I stood and followed her into the bathroom.

Once through the door, Sanna checked the two stalls, making sure they were empty before she spun on me like a feisty tornado. Slamming her fists on her hips, she frowned.

"Just what the hell crawled up your ass? Stephen just asked you out on a date, and you're acting like a total bitch. I've never seen you treat anyone so rudely. What the fuck is going on?"

"Nothing," I barked.

Shooting me a look that screamed 'bullshit', Sanna arched her brows.

"We're not discussing this. Pee and let's get back to the table, so I can get this craptastic day over with."

"I don't have to pee. I brought you in here to talk."

"Sanna," I began in a tone of warning. "I'm not discussing this. Drop it."

"Oh yes, you are." She glowered. "We're not leaving this bathroom until you tell me why you're being so mean to him. What did he do to you?"

"Nothing."

"Nothing? I don't believe you."

I let out a long-suffering groan, my shoulders slumping. "He didn't do anything, he did *every*thing."

"Talk to me, Mel. Help me understand why you're so upset." Desperation resonated in her voice as she grasped my hand.

"I can't do it. I can't let him in any further. Shit, he's already so deep inside me, I don't know how to get him out," I cried. "It's never been like this with anyone else. How do I get him the hell out of my head?"

"Oh honey." The starch instantly left her body. "You don't have to push him away. Hell, the way he looks at you gives me chills. It's a good thing. Why can't you just enjoy the time you have with him while you're here?"

"Because he's already ruined me for other men. But that's beside the point. Don't you understand?" I implored. "Why would I want to get mixed up with another wannabe Dom? That's fucking insane."

Savannah blinked, and her jaw fell open. "A wannabe? Who the hell told you he was a player? Master Stephen isn't a player."

"You did," I argued.

"Me? I never said he was a player. What the hell are you talking about?"

"You told me he released his sub. Was she the woman upstairs? The blonde? Was that his former sub?"

"Yes, but hold on. I *never* said Master Stephen was a player, ever." She gaped. "He's a well-respected Dom in our community."

"Well, maybe not in so many words, but he obviously has a fine collection of Velcro collars."

"Have you lost your fucking mind, Mel? He does not," she snapped. "He never...it wasn't a Velcro collar. He tried to teach her about submission. Carnation is a...well, she's a lot of things, mostly a bitch and a drama queen. But trust me. Stephen did all he could to set her on the right path. She didn't. He tried to...shit."

"Spit it out, Sanna. I can take it."

Sanna closed her eyes and held out her palms. "Okay. Listen to me. Carnation wasn't really a sub. She just pretended to be one. At the club, she was more concerned about performing to the crowd than anything Stephen tried to teach her. He never gave up on her. He was tenacious. Hell, the man has the patience of a saint. He's even more stubborn than my Masters, and that's saying a lot. But nothing he tried to teach her worked, because Carnation wasn't in the lifestyle for the right reasons. After trying and trying and trying, he finally released her. It was the only choice he had. Dammit, Mel, do you hear what I'm saying? Carnation is really one horrific bitch."

"Yes, I hear you. But why did he collar her to begin with if she's such a bitch?"

"I asked Julianna the same thing a while back. She told me that a couple years ago Stephen and Carnation started scening together. It was no secret she needed direction, so he offered her his training collar. *That's* the collar he removed. He never formally collared her because she never earned it. She just wanted to flaunt the fact she had a Master to all the un-owned subs."

As Sanna explained it all, a heavy cloak of humiliation weighed on me. I'd thought horrible things about the man. Made a total ass of myself in front of him and Sanna's Masters. I owed them all an apology, but I owed Joshua an even bigger one. But what if he took my capitulation as a sign of submission? How could I make amends without him storming through my defenses harder than he already had?

"A few months ago, Carnation got pissed at Leagh and verbally tore into her like a raving lunatic, right in front of Stephen. He released her, but soon after, she dumped a soda over Leagh's head in front of all the members at the club. Drake tossed Carnation's ass to the curb, and Mika rescinded her membership, and that's the last we saw of her, until today. I don't know what she was doing upstairs, but obviously, Stephen handled it, because she's gone."

"Gone, for how long though?" I wondered aloud.

"Forever, I hope," Sanna replied with a sour expression. Suddenly, she blinked and tried to bite back a grin. "You're jealous of that heifer. Holy shit. I've never seen you jealous of anyone before, Mel."

"I am not jealous," I lied.

"Oh, Mel, shut up. It's me you're talking to. Remember?" Sanna chided. "You really need to go to dinner with him. What's the worst that could happen? You'd have a good time?"

"No. The worst that could happen is falling deeper under his spell and doing something stupid, like submit to him."

"Maybe you should. Don't you think it's time you put the past behind you and give it a try with someone new?"

I glared at my sister, wanting to debate her suggestion, but I couldn't. The gnawing desire to feel whole again was all but eating me up inside.

"First, I have to apologize to him," I pouted. "He might not even want to take me out now."

"Yes, he will, but you definitely need to say you're sorry." She giggled. "Dressing down a Dom is…well, you know. You might already be in some serious trouble. He might just have to spank you."

Spank me with those incredible hands of his? The submissive inside me stretched with an ancient burn. My brain protested, but I blocked out the screams and nodded.

With a squeal of delight, Sanna hugged me tight. "Good. Let's go back."

I mentally practiced my apology the whole way back to the table. Joshua smiled and stood, holding my chair like a classic gentleman, I took a seat and stared at my plate filled with rich Italian food. My stomach pitched, and I swallowed back the urge to vomit.

Turning to face him, I raised my head and timidly gazed into Joshua's compassionate eyes.

"I'm sorry for my disrespectful behavior. I was inexcusably rude to you. My attitude was totally out of line and uncalled for. I truly am sorry. If your offer for dinner still stands, I'd like to accept, Sir."

A slow, sensual smile spread over his lips. Drawing my trembling hand to his mouth, he pressed a soft kiss over my skin. Warmth enveloped me, like a calming blanket of bliss.

"Apology accepted, little one, and yes, the offer of dinner still stands." A wolfish smile tugged at his lips. "I know the sub inside you is timid and shy. I'd like to know why. But I'm a patient man. Besides, I've coaxed her out before, and I damn well plan to do it again."

"I remember," I whispered. And dammit, if I didn't get my libido under control, he'd be coaxing her out again before the night was through.

Leaning in closer, his warm breath made me shiver. "Trust me, Mellie. We'll take this nice and slow, but I need you to be open and honest with me, okay?"

Would he? Would he really take it slow, not push and demand more than I could give?

You'll never know unless you try. Question is, do you want to try?

"Yes. I mean, I will."

Sanna and her Masters watched our exchange. My sister wore a cheeky little grin, but Dylan and Nick looked smug and guilty. Sanna had clearly had no idea Stephen and Joshua were one and the same, but Nick certainly did. I suspected Dylan had known, too. Once I got the two men alone, I planned to bombard them with a whole lot of uncomfortable questions and make sure they never played me again.

The orchestra began playing, and soft, romantic music filled the air as we ate. The Doms talked and laughed while I picked at my chicken parmesan. Without warning, Joshua suddenly leaned in close. His masculine, erotic scent wafted over me and I nearly dropped my fork.

"By the way, dinner's at my place tomorrow night, little one. I'll pick you up at seven."

Chapter Six

"I thought we were going out for dinner," I whispered as unwelcome panic clawed up my spine.

"Oh no, little one." The words rolled off his tongue in a slow, seductive purr. "I'm a greedy bastard. I'm keeping you all to myself, at least for tomorrow night. I don't want to share the sight of you with another man."

"Oh," I whispered as visions of the night we'd spent together tangled through my head.

"Will you do something for me?"

Was he asking for something simple, like passing the butter, or something far more difficult, like a submissive task? This was what I'd been afraid of…that he'd assume my apology, or acceptance of his dinner invitation, meant I was ready to plunge headfirst into submission. He was in for a rude awakening.

"I don't know. It depends on what it is," I challenged with a wary glance.

"Hmmm, you're not ready yet. Let me rethink this. We'll talk about it over dinner tomorrow night."

The man was smooth, no doubt about it. I had a feeling he'd purposefully piqued my curiosity, but wild horses wouldn't drag a single question about his request out of me. If I was going to venture down the submissive road again, I planned to take it at my own pace—whether it be like a rabbit or a snail. I wasn't about to leap into the fire simply because he fanned the enticing flames.

"Make no mistake about it, Mellie. I'm on a mission. I'm going to peel back the layers you're hiding behind, one by one. And when I think you're ready, I intend to bring you face to face with the beautiful submissive inside you. Let you see how fucking gorgeous she is so that you'll never think of hiding her away again."

I swallowed tightly. He wanted to strip me bare and revive my dormant desires. The thought of emotionally exposing myself sent a rush of panic through my system. Strangely, the tingling sensation also held a level of excitement. My inner sub began emerging from her slumber. I couldn't see a way to keep her imprisoned when everything about the man called to her. It pained me to acknowledge I didn't possess the willpower to refuse the freedom Joshua's Dominance offered. It was too strong, too compelling, too tempting.

Could I give Joshua the power to dominate me for the rest of my stay in Chicago? While the idea stirred a level of unease, it also brought me an unexpected feeling of peace.

Still, I wasn't a fool. Setting my submission free would be a costly gamble. I'd lose a piece of my heart, and in the end, pay a very high price. My head and my heart were at war. Internally weighing the pros and cons of such a daunting decision, I couldn't emphatically choose yes or no, at least not there on the spot. I needed more time, but my visit would end before Joshua and I could foster the level of trust necessary to enter a power exchange...or could we? I still wasn't convinced it was what I truly wanted.

Right, the voice in my head scoffed.

"That wasn't meant to scare you, little one. I'm simply being honest and voicing my desires. Well, some of them, at least." Joshua smiled, but I didn't. He pursed his lips and issued a thoughtful hum. "Stop analyzing it, Mellie. Let's just take one step at a time. Can you do that?"

"Yes, I think I can." I nodded.

"Good, now let's kick back and enjoy the party. What do you say?"

"I say that's a wonderful idea." A smile curled my lips, and Joshua grinned.

Sitting at the table, we talked, ate, drank and laughed. Julianna and Mika gave poignant speeches as they toasted the bride and groom before the happy couple made their way to the dance floor. They looked stupidly in love with one another, and I couldn't help but smile.

Watching Tony's father float Leagh across the wooden floor while her groom danced with his mother, bittersweet tears stung the backs of my eyes. Someday, Sanna would be in the exact same place, but there would be no father to hold her and share one last precious dance as guardian of her world. No mother for either Dylan or Nick to sway with the soft music, vowing to keep her little girl happy, healthy, and protected.

Stealing a glance Savannah's way, I watched her dab a tear from her cheek. I knew our thoughts had traveled down the same path. I'd done my best to provide for her when we were orphaned, but the inability to bring back the center of our lives was a void neither of us could ever replace.

Dylan bent and kissed away her tears before cupping her chin. Holding her in a sublime, cherished gaze, he smiled. "I love you, kitten." His words were softly spoken yet suffused with such riotous emotion I had to look away.

It wasn't jealousy that pricked my heart, but a never-ending longing that rushed to the surface and caught me off-guard. The chances that I'd find love like Sanna's grew slimmer each day. Joshua drew a circle over the back of my hand with his fingertips. Turning, I stared into his eyes. A tender smile softened his handsome features.

"You'll never have to worry, Mellie. Savannah will always be thoroughly loved," Joshua murmured in my ear.

"Yes, I know." I smiled with a secure nod.

"What about you, though? Is there a part of you that aches to be loved the same way?"

His question took me aback. My knee-jerk reaction was to lie through my teeth, but I'd promised him honestly.

"Of course. All girls dream of being Cinderella and finding her handsome prince, but girls grow into women, and reality conquers childish fantasies."

"Ouch." Joshua chuckled, clutching his hand to his chest in mock injury.

"What?" I laughed. "It's true. We grow up and kiss what we believe to be Prince Charming, only to discover we've been making out with a toad covered in warts."

Joshua shook his head. His eyes twinkled with delight. Gliding his hand to the nape of my neck, he pulled me in close. "I may not have a castle or ride a white horse, but you already know I don't have warts. Come on, my cynical gorgeous beauty. Let's dance."

He stood and extended his hand. A ripple of delight zipped through me as I slid my fingers into his palm. Drawing me tight against his toned body, I closed my eyes as Joshua guided me over the dance floor. Clearing the fears and worries that had cluttered my brain, I let the sure command of his palm at the small of my back and the decadent heat that leached beneath his dark suit consume me. It was enough…more than enough.

"You haven't asked why I didn't call you yesterday. Were you not curious?"

"Oh no, I was very curious."

"Then why didn't you ask me?"

Quirking one brow, I shrugged.

"Should I start keeping a list of punishments?" he asked in a soft, serene tone. I wondered if I'd heard him correctly.

"Punishments? What for?" I blinked in surprise.

"Communication, little one. I expect simple, honest communication."

Joshua wanted to flex his Dominant muscles. Fine, but I had no intention of rolling over to show him my underbelly, at least not yet.

"Well, since we've not had five minutes alone to even talk about the weather, I don't think it's fair you want to punish me for not blurting out such a personal question in front of everyone at the table."

"You're such a sassy thing," he chuckled.

"I prefer to call it playful."

"Playfully telling me what you think I should do as a Dominant, huh?" He smirked.

"Uh, yeah," I answered incredulously.

He scowled. "Since you've not accepted what I'm offering, I'll let your cheeky retort slide. Just be aware, once you decide to give me your submission, you can bet your sexy ass that I *will* keep lists…lots and lots of them."

A rush of heat washed through me, followed by a quiver of anticipation. Should I dare tell him I looked forward to it? No, not yet. It was still too soon.

"So, my slate is clean?" I asked with an impish grin. He shook his head. "I'm not misunderstanding things, in regard to punishments you *think* I've earned. Do I get to plead my case or am I guilty without due process?"

Joshua threw his head back and laughed. "You're going to have a red ass twenty-four-seven. You know that, right?"

I couldn't help but giggle.

"Okay, since I don't want you to think I'm a heartless bastard…"

"Just a greedy one," I reminded with a grin.

"Indeed," he chuckled. "I'll give you one last chance to ask why I didn't call you. Then we'll be starting with a clean slate. But, fair warning, I'm not usually this generous, so don't expect an offer like this again."

"I expect a lot of things from you, Josh…err, Master Stephen, but leniency isn't one of them." I smirked.

"Oh really?" His brows arched with intrigue. "Like what?"

"Like keeping me on my toes and walking the straight and narrow."

"Pretty much." He nodded. "Now stop evading and ask your question, girl."

"Okay, okay," I conceded. "Why didn't you call me Friday?"

"Nice, little one. Direct and to the point. I like that." He stroked my cheek, and damn if I didn't want to close my eyes and nuzzle his hand. "I got a phone call from Nick after you'd gone to bed last Thursday. He called to congratulate me on the opening."

"He did, did he?" I drawled in a derisive tone.

"You can't imagine my surprise when I discovered that Mellie Carson was the sexy older sister of his darling submissive, Savannah."

"That rat bast—"

"Ah, ah, little one. Watch your language. At least he didn't call taunting that the most beautiful woman in the world was curled up in a bed under his roof. Nick doesn't have a malicious bone in his body."

"No, just a couple of underhanded ones, it seems."

"Now that's a possibility," Joshua laughed.

"I'm sure Nick's revelation was completely unexpected, but it still doesn't explain why you didn't call," I reminded with a playful tug on his tie.

"What? And spoil the look on your face when you turned to watch Leagh walk down the aisle and saw me instead?"

"You're evil," I scolded with a mock growl. "These past two days I couldn't…"

"Couldn't what?"

"Ugh. I don't want to say it." I cringed.

Pulling me in closer, Joshua dipped his mouth to my neck. He swirled the tip of his tongue in a lurid path to my ear, and I quivered. "Tell me, girl," he murmured in a penetrating demand that vibrated all the way to my toes.

"I-I couldn't stop," I stuttered as he continued to dance his tongue in a lurid waltz down my neck and along my jaw.

"Keep going." Motivating me beneath an onslaught of sensual sensations, he inched his palm to the base of my spine and pressed me against his steely erection.

"Ahhh," I moaned shamelessly. "Couldn't stop thinking about you."

"Good girl." Slanting his lips over mine, he delved in deep with a sweep of his tongue.

Threading his fingers through my hair, Joshua clutched me to his mouth. Opening wider, I exhaled on a tiny whimper.

When someone bumped into us, Joshua raised his head.

"Get a room," Dylan chuckled with a goofy grin.

"Marvelous idea," Joshua agreed with a feral grin.

"No. Not yet," Sanna scolded. "You promised to come to the club tonight, Mel."

Joshua's eyes widened. "Oh, you did? Fantastic. That'll work for me."

The grin fell from my face as anxiety wormed its way in. Floating us toward the back of the dance floor, near the orchestra, Joshua placed his fingers beneath my chin. Gazing into my eyes, his expression grew serious.

"Settle down, Mellie. Nothing's going to happen at Genesis that you don't consent to. So, erase that flicker of fear from those beautiful brown eyes of yours for me, little one."

I slowly nodded as the panic bled from my veins.

"I want a verbal answer, Mellie." His tone bore absolute command.

"Yes."

"Good. Now where were we?" he asked. A mischievous grin crawled across his face before he sobered and claimed my lips in a panty-melting kiss. I clung to him. The strength of his toned body and the feel of his masterful hands wrapped around my nape and pressed against my spine, combined with the smooth glide of his tongue, vanquished the last of my fears.

"How is it I never saw you at the club before when I've been there with Sanna and the guys?" I asked.

"I don't know. I definitely would have remembered seeing you, that's for sure," he murmured with a wolfish little smile.

We danced, talked, and kissed for hours, stopping only to watch Tony and Leagh cut the cake, toss the bouquet, and sling the garter. The short times I was free of his embrace, I felt an uncomfortable, foreign void inside. I wasn't sure what to make of it, but I didn't like it.

Standing outside the church, we tossed bird seed as Tony and Leagh raced to their car. A strange sadness that my time with Joshua was almost over seeped into my core. Even though we'd be seeing each other again in an hour or so at the club, this carefree easiness between us would probably vanish. I'd be on edge, as usual, and he'd likely be suffused in a dazzling Dominant headspace. I questioned whether or not I'd be strong enough to keep from falling into his bed. My greater fear was ending up falling at his feet.

Yes, please.

My inner sub had grown stronger, and so did my inclination to let her take over. I needed to find a way to hold on to my self-restraint and keep my wits about me.

Slinging his arm around my waist, Joshua broke my mental pondering and escorted me to Nick's truck. As the others climbed inside, Joshua pushed me up against the door. Burying his face against my neck, he sunk his teeth into the tender flesh with a low growl.

"I'll see you at you the club, little one. Wear something skimpy for me. Something I can easily bite away."

A tremor of need shook my body, and my throat tightened. I couldn't even answer him. I simply nodded before he cupped his hands around my cheeks and kissed me hard. Pulling away, Joshua opened the back passenger door.

"Soon, little one," he promised. Fire flickered in his erotic eyes, and I bit back a moan.

On our way back to the house, Sanna and her Masters discussed the wedding and upcoming collaring ceremony. I zoned out, reveling in the words Joshua had whispered in my ear, each luscious stroke of his tongue, and every passionate kiss that stole my breath.

It suddenly dawned on me that I'd already given him the power to hurt me. When? How? I didn't remember making a conscious decision. Panic swelled as the little voice inside my head took control.

Go with it and see what happens. He might never let you down, if you'd give him half a chance. Stop assuming the worst when it comes to men. For once, follow your heart, not your head. See what happens. It's not like you'll die if he breaks your heart.

I knew giving him my submission wasn't going to kill me—at least not physically. But could it really be that simple? How the hell was I supposed to trust a man I barely knew?

You'll never know unless you try. Stop being such a wuss. Pathetic isn't in your vocabulary when it comes to business. Let him in, for crying out loud. Loosen the reins on your submission for a week or so. You know you'll enjoy it.

The battle within wasn't going to end in a peaceful truce, and I knew it. Yes, I could give some of my power to Joshua. When it was over, I might end up dispensing a ton of self-induced ass kicking, but I'd give it a shot. The greedy sub side of me giggled with glee while I tried to wrap my head around having just made the most insane decision of my life.

Once back at the house, we piled out of the truck. Dylan chased Sanna inside, playfully swatting her ass as she squealed and giggled, while Nick hung back. His face was tinged with traces of guilt. I'd never seen Nick wear anything akin to remorse, and he didn't wear it well; in fact, he looked like hell.

"Mel, I need to talk to you for a minute." He was nervous, and I had a pretty good idea of what he wanted to say.

"Sure," I replied.

"I don't know what you and Stephen, err, Joshua, talked about on the dance floor, but I need to tell you something."

"He told me you called him, Nick. I'm not mad about it, but I'm disappointed you didn't tell me you knew who he was the night I came home from the opening."

"I didn't realize how attached you'd gotten to him until last night. If I'd known he'd touched you so deeply, I wouldn't have called him, because I'd never purposefully hurt your feelings, sweetheart. I'm sorry, Mellie."

"You didn't hurt my feelings. I just feel like I've been played by you both."

"It wasn't like that, Mel, honest. Joshua wanted to surprise you at the wedding today. I didn't think there'd be any harm in that, but that wasn't my decision to make. It was yours."

"I accept your apology, Nick." Extending my index finger, I poked his rock-solid chest. "But I'm not going to forget that I spent two days wondering why he hadn't called. *That,* Mr. Nick Masters, is your fault."

"Shit," Nick grumbled.

"Oh, lighten up. I'm not mad. I forgive you."

"You do, huh?" Nick chuckled. "What made you decide to do that?"

"Joshua's kiss… It was all worth it then," I replied on a dreamy sigh.

"That must have been some kiss." He grinned.

"It was amazing," I laughed.

"Then I'd say he's doing a fine job," Nick chuckled. He draped his thick arm across my shoulders, and we walked inside the house.

An hour later, we sat at a table inside Club Genesis, surrounded by friends. The excitement in the air was contagious. Drake, Trevor, Mika, and Julianna had joined us. I couldn't stop laughing at the things coming out of Trevor's mouth. The young man had absolutely no filter whatsoever. Even the stern looks Drake shot his way didn't slow the young man down one bit.

Glancing at the thick velvet curtain, I nervously tugged on the corset and short black leather skirt Sanna had let me borrow. Feeling nearly naked, I feared my boobs would spill from the ivory lace corset with every breath. Checking my make-up and hair in the small mirror inside my clutch, I exhaled a nervous breath. As I tucked it away, my cell phone vibrated.

My heart fluttered, and a smile tugged my lips when I read Joshua's message.

Look toward the bar, my beautiful vixen.

Snapping my head up, I skimmed the members clustered around the bar. Slightly to the left of the crowd, Joshua stood in the alcove that led to the private rooms. My body quivered as the surrounding conversations lost all meaning. Friends and members melted from view as I watched the tall, handsome Dom with piercing green eyes stride toward the table.

Drawn to his possessive aura, I wanted to bolt from my chair and rush to his arms, but I tempered my urges and focused on his slow, deliberate gait. Checking my billowing breasts once more, I stopped myself from tugging the fabric. Joshua wouldn't like it if I tried to cover myself from his view.

Lord, I'd already began to think like a sub.

I swallowed the ball of unease rising in my throat as he approached the table.

"Do you have room for one more?" Joshua asked, giving Mika a slap on the back.

"Stephen," Mika announced cheerfully as both men shook hands. "Of course. Grab a chair and join us."

"Don't mind if I do," he smiled. Sliding a chair in next to mine, Joshua sat down.

A smile curled one side of his mouth as he gazed at my overflowing breasts. Raising his eyes, he shot me an animalistic look of approval.

"Good evening, Master Stephen." I smiled demurely.

"It's always a good evening when I sit next to a beautiful woman whose breasts taunt me to ravage them endlessly."

Heat crawled up my face, and my nipples tingled in agreement.

"No offense, Master Stephen," Trevor began. "But from my vantage point at the reception, you've already decimated Mellie from the neck up. It might be time to move on down for a while."

"Boy," Drake bellowed with a scowl.

"What, Master?" Trevor gasped. "It's the truth."

"How would you like to spend the night cuffed to the bar naked with a fat ball gag shoved in your mouth?" Drake scolded.

"No, Daddy. Please. Not that," Trevor begged in a mournful plea.

"Apologize to Stephen, boy."

"I'm sorry if I offended you, Master Stephen," Trevor contritely offered before casting his eyes downward.

"Thank you, boy, but you've only stated the truth. No harm done," Joshua softly laughed.

"Thank you, Master Stephen," Trevor respectfully replied.

"Can I have your attention, please?" Standing at the front of the room next to a tall, padded table, Tony spoke into a silver microphone. Immediately, a hush fell over the dungeon. "Thank you. As you know, I will be formally collaring my wife and sub Leagh this evening. We'll get that fun started in just a little bit, but first, there's a bit of punishment that needs to be dealt with before we begin the ceremony."

"What did Leagh do to piss him off already?" Trevor whispered with a groan.

"Last night at Maurizio's…"

"Oh shit," I blurted out, flashing a look of concern first at Sanna, then Julianna and Trevor; each wore a look that mimicked my outburst.

"I don't like that kind of language, little one." Joshua frowned.

Duly chastised, I cringed. "Sorry," I mumbled.

"There was an incident involving several of our subs, mine included," Tony continued. "We Doms have spoken and have come to a mutual agreement. The guilty parties must be punished en masse."

"Oh, Sanna," I whispered as I shot an imploring look her Masters' way. "It was an accident."

"Shhh," Nick instructed with a stern shake of his head.

I pinched my lips together and issued a heavy sigh as I reached beneath the table and gripped Sanna's hand in support.

"I need the following subs to come to up with their owner's please: Leagh, Emerald, Trevor, Savannah, and our one un-owned girl, Mellie."

"Me?" I squeaked as my eyes grew wide and my knees trembled.

Mika, Drake, Nick and Dylan all leapt from their chairs as if they couldn't wait to rush to the front of the dungeon. Julianna—known as Emerald at the club—slowly rose to her feet, as did Trevor and Sanna. Dylan cleared his throat and arched his brow as he extended his hand toward me. Freaked out and dumbfounded, I stared at it for a long moment.

"I'll protect you, Mellie." Reinforcing his words, Dylan issued a tender smile.

"So, you were part of the blazing butt-plug of destruction as well, little one?" Joshua chuckled.

I issued him a slight nod before rising on rubbery knees. Taking Dylan's hand, he led me toward the scening area. Glancing back, I spied Joshua following close behind.

A wave of relief washed over me. He'd be nearby if I needed him.

Leagh joined Tony. Trepidation replaced the happy smile she'd worn all day.

Lined up in a row like criminals before a firing squad, we exchanged pensive glances with one another.

"Remove any clothing that covers your asses," Tony instructed with a wolfish grin.

"Sanna," I whispered in a tone of pure panic.

"You don't have to take off your thong," she whispered in

reassurance. "Masters won't let anything bad happen to you, and neither will I. You don't even have to do this. I'll take your punishment for you if you need me to."

Her fervent declaration melted away my fears and filled me with determination. I wasn't about to let Sanna take my portion of the blame, even though the whole damn thing had been a fucking accident —which none of the Doms seemed to give a shit about. Wanting to howl in outrage, I jumped when Mika slipped his hand around my elbow and led me away from the others.

Compassion and understanding shimmered in his unique amber eyes.

"In my club, all acts are strictly consensual, Mellie. If you're unwilling to participate in the punishment, you can forego the little spanking we've planned and work behind the bar for an hour. The choice is yours."

"I understand, Sir. Thank you," I replied. "I find it ridiculous that any of us are being punished for an *accident*. But since our fate has been decided, I'd prefer to take my punishment alongside the others, if it's all the same."

"As you wish." Mika flashed an intimidating scowl. "Drop your skirt, feisty one, and go stand next to your sister."

Closing my eyes, I slid the soft leather off my hips, placing both it and my purse with the other subs' clothing on a low table. My heart hammered in my chest as I watched Drake cinch a meaty hand in Trevor's hair before marching him to the tall table.

"Bend over, boy," Drake instructed with a tone that brooked no argument.

"You're next, my blushing bride," Tony chuckled as he helped Leagh into position.

One by one, they lined up and bent over.

"Emerald, you're next, my beautiful slave." Mika grinned.

"Honestly, Master, I'd like to communicate with you, but you're not listening. The company is to blame, not us. You should write a letter telling them the dangers of putting alcohol in lube. Not only is it a fire hazard, but it can also dry out and damage tender tissue," Julianna protested.

Mika flashed a stern frown, then swatted her on the ass before forcibly bending her over the table. "Your objection has been duly noted, my sassy little wench. Now, not another word or I'll add orgasm denial to your punishment. Am I clear?"

Julianna pinched her lips together and nodded vigorously.

"Kitten." Dylan patted the foam surface and crooked his finger at Savannah.

"Good luck," I whispered to my sister.

"You too," she mumbled back.

"Mellie," Dylan called to me as Nick moved in behind my sister's proffered ass.

Sucking in a deep breath, I squared my shoulders and marched to the table to join my partners in crime.

"Would you prefer me or Nick to hand down your punishment?" he asked.

What? Hell, no. I couldn't stand the idea of Sanna taking extra punishment because I'd chickened out, but the thought of Dylan or Nick's hands on my ass felt so grossly incestuous I had no other choice. Not to mention they expected me to pick one of them? That was so not happening.

"Um," My stomach roiled as I darted a frantic glance first to Dylan, then to Mika. Swallowing tightly, I sucked in a deep breath. "Mika, Sir—"

"I'll do it," Joshua volunteered, stepping forward wearing a serious but gentle expression. "That is, of course, with your consent, Mellie?"

Relief and gratitude careened through me. "Yes, thank you, Master Stephen."

Before I lowered myself to the table, I watched Joshua move in close to my bare backside. Dylan sidled up next to him and leaned in close.

"Don't you dare hurt her," he threatened Joshua in a low growl.

"What? Slow down, Dylan. I have no intention of... What the hell have I ever done to make you think—"

"It's not you," Dylan hissed. "Mellie's been...Listen, she's fragile. This is the first time she's...shit. It's not my story to tell, it's hers. Just go easy on her, okay?"

"I give you my word." Joshua's vow teemed with conviction.

Great, he'd want to know all about my embarrassing past. I wasn't sure I could bring myself to tell him so soon. A new kind of panic pricked. I jumped when Joshua pressed his strong hand against the small of my back. Leaning over my body, his delicious heat surrounded me.

"Can you give me a little piece of your trust?"

His hot breath caressed my ear. "Yes, Sir."

"Thank you, sweetheart. I'll treat it like priceless gold." Placing a soft kiss on my shoulder, he stood. The loss of his body heat left me feeling brutally barren.

"Four subs. Four swats. And Mellie shall receive an obligatory four as well," Tony announced in wicked glee. "Drake, you have the honor of first punishment, my friend."

"My pleasure," he chuckled. Then, in a raspy growl, he commanded Trevor to count.

The sound of Drake's angry paw meeting Trevor's ass reverberated in my ears. The bench we four lay across jerked beneath the power of the Dom's blow.

"One, Master," Trevor cried out in a howl of pain.

Fear gripped me in an icy hold. I wasn't a pain slut by any stretch of the imagination. I couldn't handle what Trevor was being subjected to. I wouldn't last past the first slap.

Snapping my head toward Sanna, I stared into my sister's chocolate brown eyes, desperately trying to temper my panic.

"Trevor likes pain. Drake's doing it hard, so Trev won't enjoy it. We're not going to get spanked that hard, I promise," she whispered softly.

"No talking, precious," Nick admonished.

Sanna's explanation slightly eased my fears. Still, the longing to bolt from the table and run from the club rode me hard. I'd given Joshua a vow of trust. If I took it back now, it would be the same as confessing I couldn't place my faith in him.

"Two, Master," Trevor's voice cracked.

The young man wailed inconsolably before he choked out the last number, and my heart broke for all he'd endured. Drake let out a heavy sigh, then scooped his crying sub into his burly arms, clutching him tightly to his chest. Trailing kisses over Trevor's mouth, Drake captured the young man's lips and drank in his mournful sobs. As I watched the poignant exchange, I gained a new understanding of their relationship. Tears stung my eyes at the sheer beauty of it.

"Your turn, my beautiful bride." Tony announced before landing a quick succession of loud slaps over Leagh's ass.

I didn't understand why Leagh was being punished. She had nothing to do with the chain of events leading up to the fire. Maybe Tony decided she'd been guilty by association in some screwy Dominant-Caveman way. I smartly kept my opinion to myself, even though it made absolutely no sense to me at all.

Even before Tony had gathered his new bride in his arms, Mika sank his fingers into Julianna's red, springy curls.

"Let this serve as a reminder," Mika warned, aligning a sharp slap across her backside. Julianna let out a yelp. "Always." *Slap.* "Read." *Slap.* "The ingredients." *Slap.*

"Yes, Masterrrr," she keened through clenched teeth.

Mika pulled her to his chest, smoothing back the riot of ringlets from her face.

"My precious girl. You make me proud." Mika's smile reflected the depth of honor Julianna had brought him. Leaning close in an ardent rush, he kissed her ruthlessly.

"Ah, my naughty Savannah," Nick began in a tone imbued with regret. "Tell me, love…whose idea was it to purchase the elephant-sized butt plug that caught on fire?"

"It was mine, Master."

"I see," he chuckled. "Was there a particular reason you wanted such a scary slab of rubber for the centerpiece of your little soirée?"

"Yes, Sir. I bought it for Leagh as a joke."

"Ironic, none of you seem to be laughing now, are you?"

"No, Master," Sanna closed her eyes as her chin quivered.

Nick's questions bordered on humiliation. I was getting madder by the second knowing his interrogation was far worse than any physical punishment he could inflict on her.

"I'm sorry for embarrassing you and Master Dylan, Sir."

"You're never an embarrassment, kitten," Dylan corrected. "You light up our days and nights."

A contented smile curled on her lips as each of her Doms landed two firm swats on her ass. I issued a sigh of relief for Savannah as both Doms covered her with their big bodies and lifted her from the table. Trailing kisses over her lips, jaw, and neck, they whispered praises as they led her away. Dylan stopped before they got very far, watching Joshua closely, like a concerned big brother.

I was next. Trembling with apprehension, I closed my eyes as Joshua pressed his wide chest against my back. When he leaned in close to my ear, his heated breath fluttered down my neck making me quake harder.

"If you get scared, use your safeword for me. Do you remember it, little one?"

"Yes, Sir. Fantasy."

"Good girl," he praised.

As he stood, taking every ounce of soothing warm with him. I squeezed my eyes shut, and held my breath...bracing for the impact of pain. Instead of spanking me, Joshua skimmed his wide palm over my flesh. I released the air burning my lungs with a grateful sigh. Caressing my ass, he brushed the hair from my face with his other hand before trailing his knuckles down my cheek.

"Open for me, little one," he instructed, dancing his fingertips over my lips.

Open, what? Legs? Mouth?

My hesitation earned a quick slap to my left butt cheek that stung with a delicious little burn. He tapped his fingers against my lips. I took a chance and opened my mouth. Joshua leaned in, whispering his approval as he slid a finger onto my tongue.

"Show me, little one. Remind me how your silky, hot mouth felt wrapped around my cock."

With a tiny whimper I sucked, licked, and nibbled, exactly as I'd done to his ample erection a few nights before. Joshua landed another quick slap, slightly harder than the first. I couldn't help but moan.

"You're not as fragile as they think, are you, gorgeous girl?"

Shaking my head slightly, I worshiped his finger as if it were his shaft, swirling my tongue around him and sucking hard.

"I think it's time to let you feel a little fire with the next one. You'd like that, wouldn't you, little one?" He traced the tip of his tongue over the shell of my ear, and I moaned in agreement.

The smack of his hand echoed in my ears as a sweet burn flowed up my spine and ebbed down my legs. Seemingly weightless, I floated on the liberating sensations.

"Give it to her, Stephen. She likes it harder than that." The malevolent voice of Davis Walker—my former Master—thundered in my ears and instantly shattered the euphoric splendor.

Bolting upright from the table, I whipped my neck toward the direction of his voice. There, standing among a sea of curious faces, Davis smiled. Only I could see past his mask, see the contempt glistening in his cold, heartless eyes. Bile rose in my throat. Every graceless emotion—embarrassment, degradation, rage, and fear—galloped through me, leaving a trail of slimy disgust. Trembling like a leaf, I flashed a glance toward Sanna. I needed a lifeline to pull me in from the choppy, volatile water I was drowning in. Meshed between her Masters, my sister's confused frown creased her brow. Both Dylan and Nick volleyed their attention between Joshua and my former Master.

"It's been a long time, bunny. I've missed you." Davis addressed me in the club name he'd given me. The sound of it after so many years made my blood run cold. He flashed me a smile I found repulsive and vile as he took a step toward me.

Inching back, Joshua put his arms around me, reinforcing his presence. Davis smirked as if pleased to see my overt fear.

Sliding his attention back to Joshua, he nodded. "Don't let me interrupt, Stephen. I'm thoroughly enjoying the show, but there's one thing I need to know, does her ass still feel as soft as cotton? I imagine it does. I've never forgotten the feel of her flesh. Go on, slap her again, hard. I can't tell you how much I've missed hearing her lusty cries."

"Then don't," Joshua commanded in a tone colder than stone. Turning his back on Davis, he shot Mika a look of controlled fury as his arms remained cinched around me in a protective hold. "She's done here."

"Yes, indeed." Mika nodded as his hulking body seemed to expand. "Master Kerr, I need a word with you upstairs, please."

It wasn't a question—it was an order.

Joshua gripped my quaking body against him tighter. Even the heat pouring off him did nothing to stop my nervous tremors.

"I've got you, Mellie. Relax, baby. You're safe. Totally safe."

"Seriously?" Incredulity wrinkled Davis' face. "Come on, Mika, I was just giving Stephen some pointers, that's all."

"I don't believe he asked for any. Stephen needs no help in any Dominant fashion, not from you, me, or anyone," Mika countered, his tone dripping with contempt. "We can do this here, or in private. I really don't give a fuck. But we *are* going to have a conversation, Kerr."

"Oh, for the love of…fine. Fuck it. Let's go," Davis spat.

Before turning to follow the club owner, Walker turned and pinned me with a contemptuous look. Riddled with insecurities, I dropped my gaze as Drake rushed past the back of the padded table. Peeking up, I watched the three men round the archway to the hall of private rooms.

"Are you all right?" Joshua whispered as his narrow eyes delved into mine.

"Yeah." I nodded, still shaking uncontrollably.

"Okay, folks. Show's over," Tony announced through the mic. "If you'll all sit back and relax for a bit, we'll begin the ceremony shortly."

"Mel?" Sanna asked in a quivering voice ripe with fear. I turned my head. Panic etched my sister's face. "Was that…him?"

"Yes." I nodded, grateful the members were gravitating toward their seats.

"What's he doing here?"

"I don't know. I don't know how he found me, or if he was even looking." The combination of shock, anger, and fear had tears threatening to spring forth. I blinked them away as Sanna bent and handed me my skirt, but my fingers trembled so badly it slipped back to the floor.

"Here, let me help you."

I clung to Joshua's chest as Sanna picked up the garment then waited. When I turned, Joshua's hands supported my waist, and I stepped inside the opening before she pulled it up around my waist. Everything and everyone around me seemed to move at the speed of light. My muddled brain made it difficult to focus on anything other than the all-encompassing bewilderment surrounding me.

Scattered thoughts flitted through my brain, like buying a lottery ticket. I felt the odds of Davis showing up the first time I dipped my toes into the submission waters had to be so outlandishly high, I should try my luck on something far less frightening. What the hell was Davis Walker doing at Genesis in the first place? Was he visiting, or was he a member? But why would Mika allow a player like Davis inside his club? Dizzied by the barrage of questions, I braced my hand on the spanking bench and drew in a deep breath.

"Stephen. Why don't you let us take Mellie to our room? She can sit down for a bit, in private, and relax," Nick suggested.

"I'd like to take her, if you don't mind."

"Of course." Nick nodded.

"Wait," I protested through chattering teeth. "We'll miss the collaring ceremony."

"No, we won't," Sanna assured me before racing off toward Trevor. The two exchanged words, then she kissed his cheek and rushed back.

"It's all set. Trevor will come get us before it starts. Come on, sis. You're as pale as a sheet. You look like you've seen a ghost."

"I have," I mumbled.

Trevor reached out and squeezed my hand as we passed. "Don't worry, sis. Mika's got this under control. And if Kerr needs his ass kicked, Daddy will be happy to do it. He's way pissed."

"Thanksss." I shivered, forcing a tight smile.

"Come on, little one. You need a warm blanket and a stiff drink," Joshua murmured. He held me tight against his side as we followed Sanna and her Masters down the long hallway.

"I'll be back in a few," Dylan announced as Nick unlocked the door. There was a far-away look in Dylan's usual jovial eyes. The man looked downright scary.

"Don't call me to bail your ass out of jail, bro," Nick warned with a derisive smirk.

"I won't be the one going to jail," Dylan assured him before marching toward an open doorway near the end of the hall.

Once inside the private room, Sanna sought shelter in Nick's arms. Her face clouded in worry. "What's he going to do, Master?"

"Nothing, precious. Dylan will be fine. I was only teasing him. He's mad, but he'll get over it. Don't worry, love."

Joshua tugged a blanket from the foot of the bed, shook it open, and wrapped it around me. "Sit down and try to get warm," he directed.

"I'm not cold, I'm just…I don't know. Maybe shocked is a better word," I explained as I plopped down on the bed.

In unison, Sanna and Joshua each took a seat beside me, enveloping me in their arms. My sister gave me a reassuring smile, but it didn't reach her eyes. She was worried about me.

"Really, I'm fine, sis. I'm not made of china." Reaching out, I held her hand.

"I know, but he scared you. I want to kick his fu…" She stopped short and peeked up at Nick.

"Dylan's taking care of that for you, precious," Nick laughed as he handed Joshua a glass of amber liquid.

I blanched. "He is?"

"Well, that all depends. Mika's going to handle it, but I know Dylan. He'll offer to bury the body." Nick smiled.

"I'd gladly help with that," Joshua groused as he took a gulp from the glass.

"Umm, that was supposed to be for Mellie, bro," Nick chuckled. "Oh, what the hell. You probably need it as much as she does."

"Just testing it for her, man," Joshua smiled. Holding the glass to my lips, his warm breath caressed my cheek. "It's strong, so take little sips. Okay?"

The pungent odor of alcohol wafted up my nose. I took a swallow and almost spit it out. Whatever was in the glass tasted like sweaty gym socks soaked in kerosene, and it burned like acid. I sputtered and coughed then wrinkled my nose.

"That's nasty."

"You're not a Scotch girl, I take it?" he chuckled.

"No. Do you have a margarita or cosmopolitan?"

"Not tonight, little one. Tomorrow. I'll let you have both, if you'd like."

"Oh, so you're going to ply me with alcohol and take advantage of me?" I teased, trying to lighten the mood.

"I don't think he'll have to get you drunk to do that," Sanna giggled.

"Sanna," I gasped. "I can't believe you said that."

"What?" She grinned. It was a welcome change in her demeanor.

"That was some display of control out there, Stephen. I'm not sure how you kept from knocking that bastard on his ass."

"You have no idea," Joshua assured her. Turning toward me, he caressed my cheek with his hand. "My first responsibility is to protect Mellie. But I plan to have a talk with Kerr very soon."

"I appreciate that." I smiled. "I would have happily kicked his ass if there weren't so many Doms in line ahead of me," I teased.

Joshua cracked a small smile, but I could tell something heavy weighed on his mind. "Will you tell me about your history with Kerr?"

I knew Joshua's curiosity would lead to questions; I simply hadn't expected it to be so soon.

"Yes, but I'd like some information first, okay?"

"Of course. Just don't attempt to sidetrack me, little one. It won't work."

"I won't," I replied solemnly. "How long has Master Kerr been a member of Genesis?"

"About, what would you say, Nick? Maybe six months or so?"

"About that." Nick nodded.

"He must live here in Chicago now," I mused aloud.

"Yes. He's told several of us that his job transferred him here, and he was happy to find our community," Nick informed me.

"Has he done anything…"

"You mean, has he repeated his old behavior?" Nick prompted.

"Yes." I nodded.

"No. He's not collared anyone. Kerr scenes with a lot of subs, but he hasn't set his sights on a particular girl yet. At least not that I know of."

"He uses them like paper towels. I get the impression he likes to show off to the other members, like someone else I know," Joshua groused with a sour expression. "He's always shown respect and honored the code until tonight when he shit all over it."

"Do you think Mika will rescind his membership?" Sanna asked as she nibbled her bottom lip.

"I don't know, precious," Nick replied.

"You don't think Mika will let Kerr hurt Dylan, do you?" she whispered.

Nick chortled. "It's not Dylan you need to worry about, precious. Stop worrying. Mika will keep him from killing Kerr."

My head swam with images of bloodied faces and broken knuckles. Surely, Dylan wouldn't risk assault charges for me, would he?

Joshua tipped back the glass and downed the Scotch. He picked up my hand and placed a tender kiss in my palm. "Tell me your secrets, little one," he whispered.

The compassion swimming in his beautiful green eyes gave me the courage to spill the embarrassing saga of Davis's uncollaring. I skimmed over the details of running away and leaving Sanna to fend for herself. There were some things too raw to share with anyone but my sister. Joshua absorbed my disconcerting story without a question or comment. When I was done, he gathered me into his arms.

"He never deserved you or your gifts, little one."

I closed my eyes and inhaled his scent, drank in his warmth, and thanked the heavens that my truths hadn't turned Joshua away.

Still wrapped in his arms, I realized I'd been a pawn in Davis Walker's game. Not only had he shown his true colors to the people of my former club, but the members of Genesis now, too. The embarrassment I'd hauled around like an anvil around my neck had never been mine to begin with. *I* wasn't a reflection of Davis's ineptness; he was responsible for that, all on his own. He was an asshole and a player, and probably always would be.

Yes, I'd been naïve to believe his lies, but I'd been a bigger fool to give him the power to toss aside the passion and fulfillment of my submission. Eight years denying my desires was long enough. No more.

"He won't bother you again, little one," Joshua vowed.

Sanna jutted out her chin. "No, he won't, 'cause I'll cut off his—"

"Stand down, precious. Pull your claws back in. If any Dom needs to be dealt with, *we'll* handle it. You stay in your place for Dylan and me. Got it?"

"Yes, Sir." Sanna pouted.

There was a soft tap on the door. Nick opened it, and Trevor bounded in wearing a huge smile.

"It's almost time," he announced. Then he zeroed in on me. "Are you doing okay?"

"I'm good as gold," I assured him.

"Good. We've saved you some seats. Oh, and just so you know, Mika asked Monster…errr I mean, Master Kerr to leave," Trevor made a funny 'ooops' face and laughed. "You hold your head high, girly-girl, and prance that sexy lil' ass of yours out to the dungeon. It's partayyyy time."

"I love you, Trevor," I laughed.

He blew me a kiss. "It's mutual, dahhhling. Come on, they're about ready to start." With a squeal of excitement, Trevor skipped out the door.

I squared my shoulders and raised my chin as we paraded back inside the dungeon. Of course, Joshua's arm banded around my waist bolstered my self-assurance, but I'd decided Davis Walker no longer had the power to unhinge me ever again.

Drake, Trevor, and Dylan sat in the front row. Dylan wore no visible signs of a fight—thank goodness—just a smug, confident smile poised on his lips. Once seated, Joshua slipped his arm around my shoulder, and I settled in against him.

Moments later, Mika stepped onto a raised platform at the front of the room and placed a fluffy red pillow on the floor. Facing the crowd, he placed his hands behind his back, spread his legs in an imposing Dom stance, and stared toward the back of the room.

Chapter Seven

Twisting in my chair, I watched Julianna and Leagh enter the back of the dungeon through the velvet curtain. Julianna carried a gold tray that held a wide silver band. Tony joined Mika on the platform, each focused keenly on their women dressed in matching burgundy silk gowns.

The smiles they'd worn at the wedding had been replaced by serious expressions, underscoring the significance of the event. Even the felt weighted in authority, and envy pulsed in my veins.

Julianna and Leagh stepped up to the platform, assuming positions strikingly reminiscent of the wedding.

"You look exquisite, angel," Tony praised as he reached up and stroked Leagh's cheek.

"Thank you, Master. You look incredibly handsome, as always."

Leaning in, he pressed a kiss to her forehead before pulling away. His expression fell sober. "Tonight is the last time I will ever *ask* you to kneel before me."

Leagh's breath rushed out on a ragged quiver, and her whole body visibly shook. She lowered her head and sank to her knees on the pillow at Tony's feet. With grace and beauty, she spread her legs and rested her open palms on her thighs.

Tony's chest expanded as he drank in her submissive splendor. "Raise your head and look at me, sub."

She obeyed his command, and they stared at one another for a long moment, enveloped in a private bubble of love. With a resolute nod, Tony took one step forward then cupped his hands and placed his open palms against Leagh's lips.

"With these hands, I promise to mold you. Caress and soothe you in times of harmony and in strife. Punish you, when necessary, and soar you to the heavens, time and again. Never will you be alone, for I will always be by your side, treasuring your gifts and providing your fulfillment. You are my love. My slave. My slut. My angel. For all the days of my life, I vow to hold and protect you in the palm of my hands."

Tony's deep, heartfelt vow echoed through the dungeon. Tears swelled in my eyes, and Leagh's shoulders shook in silent sobs. Struggling to hold back my own emotions, I had to fight even harder when I spied Sanna's flowing tears.

Removing his hands, Tony stepped back. "I give you all I am, girl. Is there something you wish to give me?"

Leagh nodded ever so subtly, sniffed, and inhaled a deep breath.

"I ache to give you my heart, mind, body, and soul to shape beneath your Masterful hands. To yield to your Dominant commands. Immerse you in all the love I possess and fulfill your every fantasy. Ease your burdens and bring you joy, both day and night. Live my life as the embodiment of your command, to represent you in a golden light of devotion and honor. I vow to kneel at your feet, stand by your side, and follow where you lead. All that I am, all that I'll ever be, is yours. I beg your collar, Master. Please, grant me the precious gift my heart desires and make me whole."

I held back a sob as a tear slid down my cheek.

Leagh had put voice to all the longings trapped inside me, and the floodgates burst open. The onslaught of submissive desires exploding inside left me raw…exposed. There was no place for me to hide.

Joshua issued a murmured sound of understanding and squeezed my shoulder, drawing me closer to his side.

Julianna bowed her head in respect as she stepped up and presented

Tony with the golden tray. He lifted the silver collar and bent to one knee before Leagh.

"I accept your gifts. Your love. Your commitment. I bind you to me, now and forever, my beautiful slave." Clicking the metal fastener in place, Tony slid his fingers under her chin and tipped her head up slightly, then gazed into her eyes with a look of pure possession.

"You are mine," Tony proclaimed in a beastly roar.

Lifting her from the floor, he devoured Leagh beneath a blistering kiss. A collective sigh of appreciation fluttered through the crowd. There was no thunderous applause or rowdy cheers, simply a potent sense of respect permeating the air.

I ached to feel the completeness their ceremony conveyed. Joshua leaned over and tenderly sipped the moisture from my cheeks when I was unable to hold back my tears.

"It's time you unlocked the cage and set her free, little one," he whispered in my ear.

I sucked in a shaky breath and nodded. Did I possess the strength to perform such a feat?

Mika turned and walked from the platform. In proper submissive etiquette, Julianna fell in behind her Master, leaving Tony and Leagh to revel in their bond. Without disturbing them, James ascended the stage, hauling a small spanking bench and table. Dressed in a tight black T-shirt with the word 'Security' emblazoned over his muscular chest, he arranged the furniture then set a black silk bag atop the table. Smiling at the kissing couple, James left the stage.

When Tony finally ended his claim of Leagh's mouth, she spied the equipment. Her blissful expression transformed into a look of panic.

"Remove the items from the bag, angel," Tony instructed with a wicked grin.

She hesitated for the briefest second before resolution replaced apprehension. Her mind might have coerced her to obey, but her hands trembled as she removed a tube of lube--proof her body wanted to rebel at the task. Reaching in again, Leagh removed a bright pink butt plug. Her cheeks blazed in a crimson blush.

"Now that's what I'm talking about," Trevor whispered with glee.

"Shhh," Drake admonished with an angry scowl.

Snuggling in deep against his Master's chest, Trevor's pretty blue eyes sparkled in longing.

"Thank you, angel." Scalpel sharp, Tony studied Leagh's reactions closely. No doubt he knew her anxiety at publicly performing the ritual. "Off with the dress, and there'd better not be a scrap of anything beneath it, my love."

Her face burned a deeper red as she tugged the silky fabric off over her head, and placed the dress in Tony's waiting hand.

Her pale skin glowed beneath the harsh lights, and her nipples grew dark and tight.

"Do you know what I have planned for you, angel?"

"Yes, Master."

"What?"

"You plan to claim me."

"Indeed, I do. Claim you how?"

Leagh's eyes widened before she cast them toward the floor. "The way a Master claims his slave, Sir."

"Stalling is not a wise choice, my beauty. Say it." Tony's command turned harsh.

"You plan to claim my ass, Master."

"Yes," he softened. "I've been hard for months dreaming about this day."

Tony patted the padded spanking bench in silent instruction. Leagh slowly positioned herself upon the apparatus and closed her eyes.

Tony smirked. "Turn your head toward the crowd, girl, and look at the sea of faces watching and waiting to witness the precious gift you intend to give me."

She sucked in a ragged breath and did as Tony bid. Homing in on Sanna, her stare never wavered. My sister issued a tight but reassuring smile and nodded in support of her friend. "You'll be fine," she mouthed in encouragement.

Tony wore a grin from ear to ear as he slowly smoothed a palm over Leagh's butt cheeks. "So soft. So silky…so mine," he triumphed before bringing his hand down with a hard slap.

Leagh jumped with a start before a dreamy expression spread over her face.

"I own your heart, body, and soul. Now bend over, angel. The heady offer of your virgin ass is too hard to resist. And granting this gift for all to witness is a potent declaration of your bravery and reinforces the vows you just made to me. This leap of faith proves your word is as solid as the metal around your neck. Thank you, angel. You make me proud."

"Thank you, Master."

"Ahh, but you've also given me your mind, haven't you, love?"

"Yes, Master."

"You know I'm especially fond of crawling inside your mind, don't you, my love?"

"Yes, Master." Her brows furrowed ever so slightly.

"Then it probably comes as no surprise that there's still a sadistic bastard running around loose inside my head, does it, angel?" Tony chuckled. "Do you understand what that means?"

"No, Sir." Leagh swallowed tightly, her face lined in a pensive expression.

"It means I fully intend to claim your virgin ass, alone in the privacy of our own little room."

Talk about a mammoth mind fuck. Tony was *a sadistic bastard, a huge one.*

Leagh closed her eyes and exhaled a huge sigh of relief. No doubt elated she'd not have to perform such an intimate act in a room full of people. Suddenly, her lids flew open. Her expression hardened. Drawing her lips in a tight thin line, she shot a glance over her shoulder, pinning Tony with a look of a slow and certain death.

Tony arched his brows and wagged his finger. "Ah, ah, ah, my saucy slave. You promised to be the embodiment of my control and to represent me in a golden light of devotion and honor, did you not?"

I wasn't sure if Leagh was going to scream, cry, or slap the wicked smirk off Tony's face. Grappling to find her submissive place, Leagh's expression softened as she nodded.

"Good girl. I plan to hold you to that whether I'm fucking your luscious, hot body, or your pretty little mind, my love."

"I understand, Master." She shook her head and smirked. "This is what I get for falling in love with a shrink."

"A shrink *and* a sadist, angel," Tony added. Turning toward the crowd, he pulled a small note from his pocket. "Let's see. Get married. Check. Collar my girl. Check. Claim her virgin…ah, fuck yes."

The entire dungeon exploded with laughter. Even Leagh giggled. With a mischievous grin, Tony plucked her off the spanking bench and tossed her over his shoulder like a caveman. Leagh yelped as Tony turned and faced the crowd.

"If you all will excuse us, seems I have one last item on my to-do list."

With a wave to the crowd, he raced from the platform and hurried toward the private rooms.

A buzz filled the air as guests clustered in conversation, while some milled toward the bar. Several Doms and employees began rearranging the dungeon for play.

Sanna sidled next to me while her Doms and Joshua gathered in a circle, talking and laughing.

"That was so beautiful," she gushed. "I didn't think I was ever going to stop bawling."

"It was absolutely gorgeous," I agreed.

Trevor squeezed past us, plying Drake with a hopeful expression. "Do you have a '*to-do*' list, Daddy?"

"I do. But you'll have to find it, boy." The big Dom smirked. "I'll give you a hint. It's not in my pocket, but it *is* in my pants."

Trevor squealed and nearly crawled up his Master's body.

Drake shook his head. "Why do you act so deprived, like I never play with you, boy?"

"It's not that at *all*, Daddy. I can't help it. I'm totally addicted to your big, fat—"

"Boy," Drake thundered. "To our room. Now!"

Laughing, Sanna and I watched Trevor wriggle with excitement as Drake led him away.

Joshua, Dylan, and Nick were still clustered together, engaged in an extremely serious conversation.

"Wonder what those three are plotting?" I chuckled.

"I don't know, but it looks pretty intense. Maybe they're planning to take over the world."

"I'd like it better if they were plotting to put some sated smiles on a couple of sisters' faces. All this wedding and collaring shit's made me horny as hell," I grumbled.

"Me, too," Sanna whimpered, eyeing the butt plug and lube sitting untouched on the small table.

"I know what you want, you dirty little monkey," I teased with a laugh.

"Damn straight, I do." she grinned.

We were both laughing when Joshua came up behind me and slid his arm around my waist. I jumped with a start. "Come with me," he murmured in my ear.

"Ah, I guess I'll see you later, Sanna," I squeaked as he whisked me away.

My stomach began fluttering the moment I realized Joshua was heading toward the hall.

"I've been dying all day to get you alone," he murmured.

"To do what?" I asked with an impish grin.

"Well, to talk, of course. Why else would I want you alone?" He grinned.

"Talk, huh?"

"Or whatever," he smirked with a wave of his hand.

"I'd prefer whatever over talking, in case you're wondering…err, Sir." I flashed him a sultry smile.

"Sir? I like where this is going, but save that look until I get the damn door unlocked, would you, girl?" he groused, digging through his pocket for the key. "Because if you don't, I'm going to lay you out in the middle of the hall here and fuck you seven ways to Sunday. I somehow think you'd be a bit mortified giving such a display."

"So, you're an exhibitionist? That kind of turns me on a little." I couldn't stop toying with him. His impatient and harried mien was…cute.

He pulled out his keys and drew his palm over my ass. "You're still one swat short, little one. Don't forget."

"Trust me. I haven't, Sir," I purred in a vampish kitten-soft voice.

"Fuck," he cursed, trying to jam the key into the lock. I swallowed down a giggle. Mr. Cool, Calm, and Collected was unraveling wildly.

"I'll never force you to do anything, little one. But if you don't stop taunting the beast within me, I'll make sure you wind up begging me to stop."

He inhaled a deep breath, unlocked the door, and practically dragged me inside. Slamming it shut behind us, he pressed me up against the cool wooden surface. His long fingers tangled in my hair, and his mouth seized mine in a frenzied rush to own. Tossing my clutch to the floor, I wrapped my arms around his neck, giving back just as good as I got.

He drove me insane, stripped my inhibitions, and set my whole body ablaze.

Lips locked in a passionate duel of tongues, our impatient fingers tore at each other's clothing. Slowed as he tried to set my corset free, Joshua issued a few colorful curses before we were both naked and tumbling into his bed.

Skimming his lips down the column of my neck, he nipped and licked, ramping me up with his gifted mouth. Dipping lower, he latched onto my nipple and sucked the aching bud in deep. I arched, crying out at the blissful sting racing beneath my flesh.

"You've been driving me out of my fucking mind all night, wanting to taste these sweet berries," he grumbled against my skin. "I should spank your ass for wearing that damn sexy corset and teasing me like you did."

"Spank Sanna, it's hers," I giggled. "Oh, wait, what am I saying? No. I mean yes, spank me, Joshua. Spank me."

Suddenly, he lifted from my body. A scowl knitted his brow. "What did you call me?"

A wave of despair slammed me, far harsher than a mere slip of the tongue should have. *Where was this shit storm of shame coming from?* Granted, I'd started to submit, but not a level lofty enough to elicit such remorse.

"Stephen, Sir." My voice quivered, and tears stung my eyes.

"Easy, Mellie. It was nothing more than a reminder. I certainly didn't mean to toss you to the four corners under a landslide of rejection."

I was unnerved by his uncanny intuition. He knew exactly how to pluck me off the ledge of panic and wrap me in a cloak of safety. Joshua seemed almost psychic when it came to my emotions. I'd read about that kind of thing in romance novels, but never thought for a second it could really exist—until now.

"I know. I'm sorry. I overreacted."

But why? Why did you? I had no answer to give the enquiring voice inside my head.

"I'm not upset. But don't internalize those things. Share them with me, or I'll spank your ass for that, too."

Still struggling to fathom why disappointing him had put me in such a tailspin, walls of protection shot up around me. Painting on a sassy smile, I deflected his instruction with humor.

"I think you're looking for excuses to spank me, Sir."

"I think you're wishing I'd shut up and do it," he laughed.

"Me? Think that? Why, I never..." Glancing around the ceiling, I whistled in feigned innocence. As long as I kept things light and breezy, I might just survive this test of submission.

"Right. Okay, little one. Let's get this ironed out. Do you still trust me?"

"We're not talking spankings anymore, are we?" I asked.

"Nope."

"Trust you with what?" I taunted, attempting to steer him from delving too deep into serious waters.

"If you even have to ask, then I think you need some time to think about it. I'll give you ten minutes."

Joshua rolled out of bed. I blinked and sputtered, but he silenced me when he held a finger to his lips. Biting my tongue, I watched him open a dresser drawer, slip on a pair of sweatpants, grab his keys, and walk right out the door.

Stunned and chaffed, I stared at the closed door. The son of a bitch had left me; put me in a Dominant version of 'time-out.' I fumed. Couldn't he tell I was pulling his chain? The man obviously had no sense of humor.

He's trying to teach you a lesson, and you know it.

"Yeah, yeah," I scoffed aloud to the voice in my head. I knew exactly what lesson he wanted to teach me. It was time for me to shit or get off the pot, and Joshua was bent on maneuvering me exactly where he wanted me...at the fork in the road.

"So, what's it going to be?" I asked myself aloud. "You going to stay and fight, or wimp out and take a hike?"

Exhaling a heavy sigh, I closed my eyes. Staying on my safe path had been easy. Lonely at times, but I made my own comfort. Relying on myself to find happiness and comfort wasn't always easy, or ideal. So what if I had a bad habit of satisfying my needs with a slew of short, but intense relationships? I'd never claimed to be a nun.

Yet, on the other hand, the morsels of submission Joshua placed on my tongue tasted sweet and creamy, like chocolate; I could easily become addicted. The new path might assuage my ache for submission, but I'd have to change my attitude...a lot. I'd have to stop getting my back up when he issued commands. And on top of all that, I'd have to temper my mouth and not allow my stupid knee-jerk reactions to rule my tongue. The modifications expected sent my head reeling. The challenge would be huge.

A slight smirk tugged at my lips. I never sidestepped a challenge. I'd definitely keep him on his toes, and I didn't have to worry about him trying to collar or claim me for any long-term Dom/sub relationship. A few days of fun and fulfillment might last me another eight years, or it could very well break the seal and release a submissive nympho. It was a fifty-fifty shot. I could either take a chance, or take a hike.

The key clattered in the doorknob. Joshua entered and pinned me with a stern gaze.

What's it going to be? Safety or Scamper?

"I trust you, Sir."

"Good." Skimming off his sweatpants, he stood in the center of the room. His cock was hard, thick, and ready, drawing me like a magnet to steel...hot, velvety steel. "Kneel before me, little one."

I blinked in confusion. That was it? No conversation? No demand for an apology? Didn't he want to know what I'd thought about while he was gone?

"Mellie?" He arched one brow. "I don't like to repeat myself."

"I know." I nodded and rushed from the bed. "I mean, no Dominant does, Sir."

Kneeling in proper submission fashion, I closed my eyes. The temptation of his bobbing cock so close to my mouth felt like torture. Saliva pooled, and I wanted to suck him in deep and hard, slide my tongue over his glistening crest and feel the pulse of his thick throbbing veins again.

"Simply stunning." The approval in his voice calmed me. "I think it's time we fed your inner sub. She's all but starving, little one."

What an ironic choice of words. I thought on an inward chuckle. *I vote we let the sub go hungry a little longer and feed my mouth and my pussy first.*

"Raise your head and look at me, Mellie."

Eyes. Look at his eyes. Don't stare at his cock.

Letting my brain have its way for a few torturous moments, I skimmed a gaze up his body and tipped my head back, locking onto his shimmering green pools.

"You're doing excellent, sweet one." He smiled. "I asked you to do me a favor at the reception, but I could see you weren't ready. I think maybe now you are. I wanted you to make me a list, but I'm going to switch your assignment around, make it an oral test instead."

I moaned out a tortured scoff.

"Is there a problem, girl?" He narrowed his eyes.

"No, I mean, yes, but I'll suffer through it."

He chuckled. "There'll be no suffering unless I'm the one inflicting the pain. Tell me."

"Oral test? Your cock all hard and ready. I..."

With a hearty laugh, he shook his head. "I enjoy the way your mind works. Okay, let me rephrase. I want you to give me a list of hard... errr, rather unacceptable limits...verbally."

Joshua seemed to enjoy my suffering way too much. *Smart-ass.*

"Hard limits, okay. No breath play, skat, snuff. No shaving my head or eyebrows."

"Shaving your...? Oh, of course. Subs that claim they have no limits, I understand. Please continue."

I nodded. "Um, no children, animals, daddy/daughter or diaper stuff. To each their own, but age play isn't my kink. Forced prostitution, permanent marks...hmmm. I can't think of any more off the top of my head."

"That's a well-thought-out list, little one. Very nice, but let me ask you about some specific limits. Raise a finger for a mild limit, or if it's something you've not tried and might like to, and we'll discuss those individually. I'll assume no signal means you're okay with it. Do you understand?"

"Yes, Sir." I nodded.

"Then let's begin. Anal play, including sex and plugs. Bondage. Floggers. Paddles. Clothespins. Cock worship...hmmm, I think I already know the answer to that one now, don't I, little one?" I smiled and nodded. "Fisting. Gags. Humiliation."

I raised my finger.

"Humiliation doesn't put me in a good Dom headspace either. But if you needed it, I would see to it. Let's carry on. Clamps on clit and nipples. Play piercing."

Again, I held up a finger.

"You've had it and don't like it?"

"No, Sir. I've never done it."

"I'll make note of that. TENs units. Violet Wand. Ménage."

Slowly, I raised my finger. Joshua studied me for a long time.

"You've never experienced two lovers at once?"

"No, Sir."

"Tell me your feelings about it."

My mind zipped back to the night of his opening and the comments his friend Ian had made. "The idea both arouses and intrigues me, but..."

"Continue." His face was unreadable. His eyes like placid pools of ocean water. I couldn't tell what he was thinking, and I didn't like it. "It is something you fantasize about?"

"Yes, Sir," I whispered and cast my eyes toward the floor.

"That's nothing to be embarrassed about, little one."

"I can't help it, Sir. I've not shared my fantasies before. It's...awkward."

"I understand, but you're doing fine. I'm extremely grateful for your honesty."

"You've shared women before, haven't you?"

"Yes. I have. It's a remarkable experience."

"With Ian?"

"Lately, yes." He pondered for a moment. "Answer me honestly, Mellie. How would you feel if I wanted to share you with Ian?"

Heat flooded my face. My body screamed, *'fan-fucking-tastic'*. His friend was hands-down hot. But my brain flipped into hyper-analytical-overdrive, and a tide of insecurities swamped me.

"I'm torn, Sir. I think the bodily experience would be, like you said, incredible. But the emotional side of it...I'm not sure. I don't have sex with someone I don't feel a connect—"

I stopped in mid-sentence. *Feel a connection with.* From the very start, I'd tried to convince myself that Joshua was nothing more than a scratch to my itch. Nothing more than a one-night stand. Though I'd only had one in my life, the guilt after made me feel dirty and cheap. But that hadn't happened with Joshua. Puzzled that remorse hadn't swallowed me whole, I'd convinced myself that obsessing over him so fiercely was the reason the ugly self-reproach had never materialized.

It hadn't been his dominant nature that scared the crap out of me that first night. He'd connected with me, touched something deep inside that I'd never realized. He'd somehow linked with me on some strange and primitive level I didn't understand. It hadn't been about bedding the famous artist, or flirting with the fringes of submission. No, it ran much deeper, and subconsciously, I knew. That's why I ran.

Keeping men an arm's length away, I never had to worry about giving them a piece of my heart. The notion that Joshua had chipped off a fragment of mine, without my knowledge—like a thief in the night—sent panic slamming through me with a red-hot shot of adrenaline.

"I've got to go." Launching up from the floor like a rocket, Joshua reared back. The look of shock and confusion on his face surely mirrored my own.

"Whoa. Hold on," he declared as he grabbed my arm and spun me to face him. "Take a deep breath. Close your eyes and focus on my voice. You've hit an internal trigger, and from the looks of it, a big one."

Panting as panic consumed me, I shook my head. "I can't."

In a voice so calm I wanted to scream, Joshua placed his hand over my eyes and pulled me against his naked body. His turgid cock throbbed against my belly, and his arm banded around my waist scorched me. "Breathe with me, Mellie. Nice and slow. Breath in, now let it out. Again. In and out."

Keeping time with his steady rhythm, I wrestled the bristling barbs of fear biting within.

"It's okay. Everything is fine. I've got you." The deep timber of his soothing voice sent a shiver down my spine. "It's this crazy connection we share, right?"

How the fuck did he know that? Maybe he was a freaking psychic.

I nodded slightly as panic and confusion took on a whole new meaning. Sliding his hand from my eyes, his features were drawn in concern. He seemed as unhinged about it as me, and for that, I was grateful. I didn't want to be the only one spazzing out over this weird vibe we shared.

"I feel it too, that incredible draw, like a fiber that's connecting us to each other. I felt it the first time I saw you at the gallery and how emotional you got staring at the sculpture I gave you. In some bizarre way, she's you. Or the embodiment of you. I know that sounds totally insane, but I swear, I'm not crazy. Whatever this is…whatever it means, we'll sort it out. But running away from it and from me? That isn't an option. I won't allow it, Mellie."

He'd actually felt it. What did it mean?

"Look, I'm sorry I panicked. I'm confused. I think you've ruined me."

"Ruined you? How?" He blinked, shocked by my claim.

"After that first night with Scott, I didn't understand how…Oh hell, I'm screwing this all up."

"You were with Scotty? Scotty from Maurizio's?"

"Yes…I mean, no. I didn't want to be with him…he wanted…"

A knowing grin tugged the corners of his mouth. "You did what I did, didn't you?"

All the tension fell from my face. "I don't know. What did you do?"

"Last night, I was supposed to be with the guys at Tony's bachelor party, but I bowed out. You knocked me clean off plumb the night before. I'd been seeing someone for a few weeks, so I called her. I thought I could..." He gave a sheepish shrug. "Fuck you out of my system."

Boy, that sounded familiar.

"But sitting with her at dinner, I couldn't stop comparing her to you. The shape of her face wasn't right. Her eyes were the wrong color. Her laugh sounded like fighting chickens. I faked a headache and cut the night short. When I got home, I lay in bed—the bed we'd shared—and relived every single second I'd had you with me."

"But you knew who I was. You knew how to find me. Why didn't you just come to the house?"

"For the same reason you ran away from me, Mellie. You scared the shit out of me." His face fell; he looked lost. "What happened with Scotty?"

"Nothing. I didn't try to have sex with him," I assured. "He kissed me at the bachelorette party, and it felt so wrong I wanted to gag. I shoved him off me and told him no. He wasn't being a jerk or anything. In fact, he apologized. It didn't make sense. I mean, you'd done something to me. Okay, look, I met Scotty the night before and, I can't lie. I probably would have gone to bed with him eventually. But after being with you, I couldn't stand the thought of being with him. What the hell did you do to me? None of this makes sense."

Joshua chuckled. "No, it doesn't. It's a strange and wonderful feeling, isn't it?"

"Yes, but..." A sense of foreboding landed in my gut. "But you and me...it's never going to work. You know that, right?"

He didn't answer, just clenched his jaw.

"It can't, Joshua. I live in Phoenix. I have a company to run. I can't just close up shop and shuck off my responsibilities for some crazy-assed connection we don't even understand. Seriously, it might just be the right combination of hormones and pheromones."

"I know." He nodded. Disappointment flickered in his eyes. I felt the same hollow ache inside. "After what you said at the wedding reception, I tried to rationalize away my attraction to you. But when I'm with you, all rationale goes straight out the window. I want you, Mellie...want you for as many days as I can have you."

"I want you too," I sighed. "I haven't felt this ridiculous since high school."

"Look. We don't have to figure this out right now. Not tomorrow or the next day. Things happen for a reason, and while we don't know what that reason is yet, let's just relax and let it happen. It'll reveal itself in time."

"And you don't think all this is a little insane?" I asked, arching a brow at his passive acceptance.

"Oh, it's as crazy as a shithouse rat, but..." He shrugged. "Instead of trying to analyze the piss out of it, let's just see where it takes us."

"Where it takes us?" I gasped. "I feel like I bought a one-way ticket on a runaway freight train. I know where it's going to take us."

"No, you suspect. Look, instead of freaking out, try to take comfort in the fact that I'm on the damn thing too. If it goes down in flames, I'll be right there beside you, okay?"

The inevitable end to this surreal bliss plowed through me. I wrapped my arms around his neck and held on. Willingly jumping on board, I knew I was in for a hell of a ride. I just hoped in the end it would all be worth it.

Without a word, Joshua picked me up and carried me to his bed. I tried to sort out my stormy emotions as he silently held me in his arms. I'd only known the man a few short days, but the instant attraction we shared was outrageous.

Trying to pacify all the riotous emotions, I worked on convincing myself that once I returned home and settled into a regular routine, the craziness would pass. But all that did was bring a stab to my heart with a well-honed blade. I didn't want this to end. I wanted what I couldn't have...Joshua.

The day had been a rollercoaster of emotions, but in a way, our conversation felt cathartic. At least we shared the same mystified emotions, and lying in Joshua's arms as he threaded his fingers through my hair felt better than right. It felt like perfection.

The fringes of sleep tried to pull me under, but Joshua's soft lips drew me back to the surface.

"Make love to me," I whispered on a wistful sigh.

"How could I refuse such a lovely request?" he murmured.

Inching his lean body over mine, I moaned at the feel of his hot, soft skin. Our bodies meshed together, and strangely, it felt more profound than the first time. His kisses were slower, more passionate; his touches teemed in adoration. The methodical way he unraveled me was the complete opposite from our rush to rut a few short days ago.

"Mmmm, yesssssss," I purred as his long, sure fingers toyed with my folds.

"You're so soft, and silky, and so fucking wet. Oh, the things I want to do to you, Mellie."

Joshua's words came out raspy and low. Driving his fingers deep inside, he sent my desire spiraling high and hard.

"Pleaseee," I whimpered. "Do anything you want."

A roguish fire flickered in his eyes. "Anything?"

"Yess," I hissed. My frustration clawed deep.

"Be careful what you ask for, girl."

"I'm not asking. I'm begging."

Easing his fingers out my pussy, he stared at the glistening juice on his digits. Drawing his hand to his mouth, he licked them clean, savoring the flavor as if it were the finest nectar in the world. Feeling coveted and treasured, I was rattled to the bone.

Joshua dragged his broad thumbs over my nipples. "I want to lose myself in you, little one. It's been a long time since I've craved a woman as much as I do you."

His confession pressed in on me from all sides. A blistering torrent of emotions suffused my heart. I'd never hungered for a man the way I did him. It was all-consuming.

"Take me. Please?"

Bending low, he granted my request, claiming me in a ravenous kiss as he took control. Floating his lips and tongue down my body in whisper-soft strokes, he edged closer to my needy cleft. My belly rippled as the muscles twitched beneath his sensual indulgence.

Repositioning himself between my legs, Joshua parted them with gentle persuasion, then closed his eyes and inhaled a deep breath. A slow smile of gratitude curled his lips. Gazing upon my sex, I knew what he planned to do, and I couldn't help but rock my hips, impatient to feel his tongue on my sex.

Sliding a hungry stare over my body, his expression was tight, rugged, and ruthless, totally incongruent to the calming stroke of his fingertips up and down my inner thighs.

"So anxious. So needy. So fucking gorgeous," Joshua lauded before leaning low.

His warm breath spilled over my pussy, and I twitched. Placing a wide palm low on my belly, he held me to the bed before swiping his tongue between my folds. As he groaned in delight, my whole body quivered. With long and deliberate strokes, Joshua lapped my pussy, scraping his teeth over my clit, while methodically driving me out of my mind. He was in no hurry, seemingly content to drive me up the mountain of ecstasy one agonizing stroke at a time.

"I could stay here all night long, drinking in your sweet, slick juice, little one. You taste so warm and tart, it makes me dizzy."

Floating on a cloud of surreal splendor, Joshua sailed me even higher when he inched his fingers back inside me. Curling and circling, he beckoned the growing fire as he crept deeper still. He pinpointed that secret bundle of nerves, and I whimpered as he stroked the screaming tissue. Writhing and moaning, I ground my pussy against his mouth and hand. Circling my clit with his tongue, he purposefully prolonged the exquisite agony, and the maddening torture was glorious. I didn't want it to end.

"Your cunt is sweltering," he murmured against my folds. "And the way your silky tunnel sucks at my fingers…it feels incredible, baby. Fucking incredible. My cock's so jealous right now."

Each raspy syllable vibrated straight up my spine.

"Please," I begged. "I need…"

"You need what, little one? Tell me."

Even as he asked the question, his tongue didn't stop dancing its taunting trail alongside my clit.

"I need to come, Sir. Please." The desperation in my voice was shocking, even to my own ears.

"Yes, I know you do." Joshua increased the tempo of his coaxing stroke. "You're going to give it to me, because I demand it from you, little one. And I want it. Now. Right now. Come for me, girl," he commanded in a harsh roar.

Latching my throbbing clit between his lips, Joshua sucked. The pool of blood behind the tender nub seemed to expand, and the muscles in my legs tightened and trembled. I tried to arch from the bed, but he held me down with his powerful hand.

His wicked fingers strummed.

His ravenous mouth consumed.

A sizzling ball of electricity shot through my limbs, collided with my brain, and slammed down my spine. Shards of light exploded behind my eyes, and I threw my head back, screaming to the heavens as I shattered all over his face.

Contracting, my tunnel sucked at his fingers in brutal spasms. Still, Joshua didn't relent. He continued licking my clit while his fingers churned in silent demand for more.

"Again," he bellowed. "I want to drink you in, possess every drop of you, girl."

Another wave started cresting over the one still annihilating me. Helpless, I swirled in the eye of the cyclone as Joshua drove me up, fast and hard. Streaking to the crest once more, I fisted my hands in his hair, holding on for dear life, and sailed over the edge. Shrieking, the convulsing explosion obliterated every cell in my body.

Boneless, panting, and spent, I felt Joshua crawl up from between my thighs. Lifting my heavy eyelids, I watched as he smiled and licked my offering from his lips before wiping his chin on the back of his hand. A sated smile curled one side of my mouth as he brushed strands of sweat-soaked hair from my face.

"You're so fucking amazing," he praised, gazing at me as if I were the most beautiful creature on the planet.

"No," I choked out on a hoarse whisper. "You're the amazing one. The things you do to me…"

"I've only just begun to unravel you, little one."

A twinkle of delight danced in his eyes as an aftershock rippled through me. Oh yes, he'd unraveled me, all right. I just prayed that his masterful hands could weave me back together when we were through.

I managed to lift one limp arm and drape it around his shoulder before pulling his mouth to mine. Tasting my essence on his tongue, Joshua bathed me in a poignant kiss so brimmed with emotion, tears burned the backs of my eyes.

Careful. You're in over your head.

As if challenging my internal warning, I moaned and fell deeper into his kiss. Shifting his weight, Joshua positioned his body over mine. The heat of his steely erection pressed against my stomach, igniting fires I thought had been extinguished.

His unique sexual magic left me utterly amazed. He'd taken me from quenched to parched with just a kiss and the touch of his body. I was unaccustomed to such unrelenting pleasure; Joshua stoked an insatiable side I didn't know existed. But I knew one thing: I'd never get my fill of the man.

"Whatever this is…whatever it means, we'll sort it out."

His reassuring words sang in my brain as he palmed a condom from the nightstand. I put my pondering to rest as he sheathed his angry shaft.

"Fuck. You test my control, little one. The need to be gentle and not hurt you battles with my demand to consume you," he hissed through clenched teeth. Stroking his thick shaft as if trying to soothe its ache, he edged in, aligning the wide crest with my swollen folds.

"Don't be gentle. I won't break. I need to feel all of you again."

He lunged inside me, fast and hard. That unforgettable burn flared through my core and rippled like a bubbling brook. Joshua stilled, and I held my breath, struggling to relax my quivering passage and accept his glorious invasion.

"Fuck, girl. You're strangling me," he growled.

"I'm not trying to," I gasped, closing my eyes to focus past the exquisite sting.

"It's okay. I'm not complaining. Trust me. I'm going to stay right here until you relax and give me room to move in that pretty pussy of yours."

I tried to widen my thighs, but it only served to stretch my searing flesh further. I hissed and bit back a curse.

"Easy, baby. There's no rush," he whispered.

Circling my nipples with his tongue, he flicked the hard tips. I moaned and pressed my lower back into the mattress, then drew up my legs and wrapped them around his narrow hips. The pain had lessened even as Joshua wedged in deeper. I closed my eyes, enveloped in sensations too wonderful for words.

He slanted his mouth over mine, and we became fused together in every way possible. I wasn't sure where I ended and Joshua began until he started slowly rocking in and out of me and the universe seemed to settle into an unfathomable rightness.

As he devoured me in fervid kisses, I moaned in a carnal melody of delight. With his long, languid strokes, he seemed as if he were struggling to hold back. A part of me felt cheated. I didn't want him censoring a single need or emotion, not when he demanded I give him *my* all. Watching the growing toll play across his face, I dipped my chin and swiped my tongue over his flat nipple. His body grew even more rigid as a growling curse rolled off his tongue. Determined to find the key to releasing the beast he held caged, a wicked idea slid though my brain.

"Harder, Master Stephen," I whispered. "Use me. Use me hard. I need…I want… Please, let me please you, Master."

"Fuck," he roared.

A streak of something wild flashed in his eyes. Joshua clenched his teeth and began to drive into my cunt like a man possessed.

Inside, I cheered. *This* is what I wanted…For him to shuck off his kid gloves and unleash his animalistic desires. Wild and untamed, Joshua claimed me in a frenzy of thrusts, grunts, and growls. Pounding into me, I realized neither Joshua nor his alter ego Master Stephen had allowed their inhibitions to run free for a very long time.

An unexpected wave of submission swelled, swallowing me whole. Stripped of my resolve to never unfurl my surrender, I floated like a bird toward the heavens. Surrounded in the surreal, white peace, I tried to claw my way back to reality, but the hold of completeness was too strong. Serenity saturated my pores, seeped into my bones, and left me feeling small and fragile…breakable, and so very frail.

"You're fucking perfect," he spat. His tone held an icy, savage edge, and damn, if it didn't turn me on even more.

"Take me, all of me, Master Stephen," I cried. "Use me hard. I'm yours."

There was no need to bait Joshua's beast further, but I couldn't stop myself. My submissive pleas nurtured us both. Freed, he feasted on my acquiescence, ruthless and feral, as I willingly fed him the pieces of my resurrected submission.

"When I tell you to come, girl, come hard for me. It's mine," he hissed.

Jerking back, he yanked me onto his thighs. Pinching my waist in a grip so tight I'd be wearing his bruises for weeks, Joshua hurtled me up and down his cock. Burnishing my clit against the root of his shaft, the swell of release burned. Clawing at his back, I held tight to his body… to my orgasm, and to what shards of sanity hadn't slipped through my grasp.

A fierce expression etched his face.

Narrowing his eyes, he delved deep into my soul, and in that one precious moment in time, he owned me. Remnants of my independence vanished like smoke. Losing myself so freely, I waited for the toll of pain to pierce my heart, but it didn't. Instead, an unequivocal liberation consumed me—all because of his command.

"Give it to me now, girl," he insisted. "Come for me. Now. Fucking come hard!"

As if I were a bird, Joshua snipped my wings, and I plummeted into a swirling abyss of pleasure. I closed my eyes to savor our mingling screams, and the feel of his cock jerking and sputtering as he spilled his hot seed into the latex barrier.

He gripped me to his chest, and my pussy compressed around his shaft, gnawing with spontaneous spasms. His drumming heart pounded against my cheek. Sweat-soaked, we clung to each other, holding tight long after our breathing evened out and the rippling quivers of pleasure faded.

He was unusually quiet. In fact, Joshua hadn't uttered a single word since he'd ordered me to come. Silently, he lifted me off his cock and stood.

"I'll go get a shower started for us,"

"That's okay. I'll grab one back at Sanna's place."

He froze as if I'd cast a spell on him. Turning slowly, he pinned me with an angry scowl. "No. You're staying the night here. With me. In my bed."

Without another word, he stormed into the bathroom. I watched as he flushed the soiled condom down the toilet, then twisted the knobs inside the shower.

My inner sub bowed her head in compliance, while the sovereign woman I feared had been lost bristled at his callous directive.

"Joshua, I'd like—"

"So, it's back to Joshua again now, is it?" Standing in the doorway of the bathroom, he arched an arrogant brow.

What the hell?

Undaunted, I raised my chin; all semblance of submission disappeared without a trace. "I'd like to discuss the fact you want me to spend the night with you."

"No, you're searching for an excuse to run from me again. It's fucking written all over your face," he spat.

"What is wrong with you?" My tone was combative, but I didn't give a shit. He was acting like a pompous prick, and I aimed to find out why. "I'm not running, but it sure seems as if you are. You're not even listening to me. You're shutting me out behind an impenetrable wall of Dominance. I didn't give you my submission to toss in the garbage like a pile of dog shit. Why are you being so callous and rude?"

"Is that why you've decided to lock the sub back in her cage?" he countered with an angry sneer.

"I asked you first." My reply sounded stupid and childish, but he'd backed me into a corner. Right or wrong, I came out fighting. It was my nature.

He lowered his jaw and flashed me a condescending smirk as if to say, *'Really? That's the best you can do?'*

Blinded by a red haze of rage, I leapt from the bed and gathered up my purse and clothes. "You know what? It doesn't matter. You're going to think exactly what you want to regardless of anything I try to say. But just for your information, I wasn't questioning the great and powerful *Master*. I was trying to *communicate* with you. But you've got your bad-ass Dom persona slathered on so thick you can't see past your own fucking ego."

Storming out the door, I slammed it behind me. Naked as a jaybird, I nearly collided with James as he walked down the hall.

"Whoa," he declared in stunned surprise.

Anger oozed from my every pore. James' expression immediately softened with concern. He didn't say a word. He simply wrapped his hand around my elbow in a tender show of compassion and drew me to his side.

"Come on," he whispered softly. "Let's get you someplace quiet."

The door to Joshua's room opened with a bang. Wearing nothing but his pants and a pissed-off glare, he stepped into the hallway. Zeroing in on James' hand clasped at my elbow, Joshua's nostrils flared.

Chapter Eight

"We need to talk, Mellie." Although he'd kept his voice low, it was rife with fury. I could feel his anger bubbling below the surface, even though he kept it in check.

"Call me tomorrow, Sir. I think we both need some time to cool off."

I hadn't intended for my tone to sound so arctic, but I couldn't take it back. Joshua closed his eyes briefly and inhaled a deep, irate breath.

"Fine. Expect a call from me in the morning, but for now, come inside and get dressed."

I didn't have a clue where James planned to take me, but I knew going back inside the room with Joshua would be catastrophic. We were both seething; it would be like tossing a match to gasoline.

"No, thank you. James is taking me someplace private so I can dress, Sir." At least, I hoped he was. And why the hell was I still calling Joshua Sir? *Dammit.*

He turned toward James. "Exactly where do you plan on taking her? Surely not your *own* private room, I hope." His words were slathered in jealous suspicion.

What the fuck had crawled up his ass? He'd gone from a

compassionate, understanding knight on a white horse to a full-fledged son of a bitch in the blink of an eye.

"No. I'm taking her to Dylan and Nick's room. They're sitting at the bar with Savannah. Mellie will have privacy there." James' tone was matter-of-fact. I admired the man for not letting Joshua bait him with ridiculous innuendos.

"I appreciate your concern." Joshua looked as if he'd rather cut off his left nut than choke out an ounce of gratitude to James.

Both men glanced my way. Awkwardness scraped like nails on a chalkboard. "I'll talk to you tomorrow," I snapped.

I had no intention of answering my phone *if and when* he called. There was nothing Joshua could do or say to take back the hurt he'd inflicted.

For a split second, the same haunting sadness I'd seen in the photo after his wife and daughter died settled in his eyes. A sudden pang of guilt sliced through me. But before I could open my mouth to say anything, Joshua turned, walked inside his room, and closed the door.

James didn't ask a word, simply led me down the hall to Dylan and Nick's room while a torrent of questions whirled in my brain.

Was Joshua still struggling with the loss of his family?

Of course, he was. You of all people should know the unrelenting hurt never goes away. The best you can do is survive the emptiness one day at a time.

"Do you need to file a formal report?" James asked as he turned the key and opened the door.

"What?"

"A formal report about Stephen? Do I need to get Mika down here?"

"No, of course not. Master Stephen didn't do… You honestly think he'd…" I couldn't believe James would insinuate such a thing. "He's the last person in this club who would ever do something non-consensual. We had an argument. It wasn't even lifestyle related."

"Don't get all riled up and in my face. I'm just doing my job, girl."

"Our friendship is new, but Stephen…err, Master Stephen is an outstanding Dominant."

Just not at the moment.

"I know. But even so, you're upset. I need to know if he crossed a line. Look, I'll let your sister and her Masters know where you are."

"No," I barked. "I'll join them at the bar in a few minutes. Just don't say anything to anyone, all right?"

"All right. All right. Calm your horses. Are you always this high strung?" James frowned.

I shot him a pained expression. "Look. Thank you for your help, okay?" It was a half-assed show of gratitude, but I was all talked out. With a sad sigh, I closed the door in his face.

Fuming, I threw on my clothes...well, everything except the stupid corset. No matter how hard I tried to attach the metal busks, the damn things kept coming undone. Too frustrated to deal with it, I tossed the garment aside and began to pace.

I had no idea what I'd done to enrage Joshua. Maybe it wasn't *me* that tripped his trigger. Maybe it was self-inflicted. Pondering the time between our mind-blowing orgasms to his icy silent withdraw, I grew increasingly convinced his mood shift had nothing to do with me, and everything to do with his late wife.

It would be an ironic and fatal combination if both of us suffered from the same fear of attachment. No, he was too confident, too successful, too much like me. *Shit.* We probably wore identical masks, but simply couldn't see them. Or chose to ignore them. I knew well how to align smoke and mirrors to hide my soul; I'd been doing it for years. Did Joshua possess the same knack to keep people from crawling inside too deep, as well?

Sanna's confession swirled in my brain. She'd closed herself off after the death of our parents. Dammit, she'd hit the nail on the head when she accused me of being afraid to love for fear of losing someone. I wasn't afraid to fall in love; I was terrified. Maybe Joshua was too. The similarities between us weighed like a medicine ball in my gut. He was right about one thing—we definitely needed to talk.

I'd learned two important rules that day; never pick a fight with a Dominant until you know what ghosts are rattling around in his closet, and never try to put on a corset alone.

As I made my way toward the dungeon, my boobs peeked out from beneath the skewed top. Pausing outside Joshua's door, indecision held me in a stranglehold. Should I leave him alone, or should I reach out to him? If he was battling demons from his past, I could lend him a shoulder. After all, I had experience with the emotional fallout, not to mention it was a compassionate thing to do.

Raising a fist to knock, I stopped. All I had were suppositions. I lacked the pieces of the puzzle to his sudden snarky, sullen mood. *Maybe if you'd tried a little harder to find out what was bothering him instead of arguing with him, you'd have the info you needed.* The sub inside picked a stellar moment to raise her head. I exhaled a perturbed sigh. I owed him an apology, but dammit, he owed me one too. That or an explanation. It wasn't too much to ask.

Sucking in a fortifying breath, I closed my eyes and knocked.

"It's open," Joshua barked from beyond the door.

From his tone, I surmised he hadn't sweetened up much. I gave serious thought to walking away. My luck, he'd open the door and see me ding-dong-ditching like a six-year-old. It was bad enough feeling so ridiculously awkward, like I did back in high school; my insecurities left the same bitter residue on my tongue as they had back then.

Gripping the handle, I turned the knob and opened the door. Joshua sat on the edge of his bed, legs spread, shoulders slumped, and a glass of that nasty amber Scotch in his glass. Still naked from the waist up, he raised his head, issued a heavy sigh, then glanced back at his drink.

"I'm sorry I disturbed you. All this can wait until tomorrow," I backpedaled, instantly regretting my decision to help him.

"No, it can't, Mellie. Come in and close the door, please."

Swallowing tightly, I did as he asked before making my way to where he sat. Joshua put the glass down and stood. Taking in the state of my corset, a tiny smile pulled at the side of his mouth.

"Come here."

I wanted to rush to his arms, feel his lean body against mine. Hear him tell me in that calm, reassuring voice everything was going to be all right. But this wasn't Disneyland. No amount of magic pixie dust could float our excess baggage to the heavens.

When I slowly stepped toward him, he reached up and began to align the steel busks on the corset.

"I'm sorry I lost control earlier," he began. "I don't expect you to excuse my behavior, and I'm not ready to dissect it with you, yet. I need time to sort it out. But I had no right to be cruel and inconsiderate. I'm truly sorry I was such a prick to you, Mellie."

Every word he said came from his heart. It pained me to see him drowning in remorse.

"Was it something I said? Something I did?"

"No. Not directly. You were perfect. Stunning. You gave me something I hadn't experienced for a very long time. Your gift was precious, little one. Please don't doubt that. I'm sorry I made you think it was you. It wasn't. It was me. There're things I need to…"

"I'm the one who should be apologizing. My stupid knee-jerk reaction spoiled everything. I didn't mean to let Mouthy-Mellie take over. I should have bitten my tongue."

Joshua shook his head. "No, little one. I don't want a woman who's afraid to speak her mind. I'm truly humbled at the submission you gave me. I'll cherish it…always."

Dread rose from the pit of my stomach, expanding and thickening in my throat. His speech sounded like a preamble to 'goodbye'.

"But I've not earned the submission you graciously gave me, at least not yet. After learning about your past with Kerr, I understand why submission is so hard for you. You've slipped on a pair of shoes you discovered in the back of your closet. They feel funny, their fit isn't quite yet comfortable, and won't be until you've had a chance to break them back in."

I nodded and wanted to smile at his analogy. Using shoes instead of car parts was…sweet of him. "I didn't mean to upset you or call you names, they just slipped out."

"*You* didn't upset me. There's no need to apologize for calling me names I earned. You didn't bring this on, Mellie. I did."

"Please, tell me what happened?" I sounded desperate in a pathetic, nagging sort of way, that I inwardly cringed. Somewhere inside was a grown, confident woman, but at the moment, the cowardly bitch was hiding.

Joshua shook his head then leaned in and pressed his lips to my forehead.

"Your true nature calls for you to fix this, smooth things over and make me happy, to take care of me, my problems, and my issues." He shook his head. "But they're not yours to fix. I have to sort my shit out on my own."

"I understand." I really didn't, but I had no idea what else to say. I issued a slight nod and a weak smile. "Well, I guess I'll go join Sanna at the bar."

At least with my sister, my footing was sure and sturdy. I didn't have to worry about falling through the cracks and landing on my ass.

"You don't have to go if you don't want to. I'd like it if you stayed. I know I've treated you poorly and made you uncomfortable, but if you can find it in your heart, I'd like the chance to redeem myself."

"I'd like to, but I'm afraid if I stay, you won't be able to sort out the things you need to."

"Probably not, but the distraction would be a welcome relief from the…" He scrubbed a hand through his hair and let out a soft sigh. "Stay, Mellie."

He wasn't asking me to help him sort his emotions. No, this was a cry for help. He wanted me to stay and chase away the demons so he wouldn't spend the rest of the night reliving the past. I recognized the underlying anguish in his request. Sanna and I had shared the same unspoken language for years. We could talk for hours about surface things; it comforted and kept us from delving too deeply into grief. But every once in a while, the darkness descended and having someone beside you brought the light you desperately needed.

"Okay," I whispered.

A broad smile spread over his lips and my heart did a little flip-flop in my chest. Joshua ordered a pizza, and we sat on his bed, drinking soda and watching a rom-com. The movie was about a girl who lost her memory every night, and a man determined to make her fall back in love with him every day.

I almost envied her. What a blessing it would be to wake up each morning *alone* without retaining a single memory of the incredible time I spent with Joshua. Even the couple bumps in the road we'd encountered didn't take the happiness we'd shared away. But movies weren't real life. No, real life came with laughter, love, and whole lot of heartbreak. Joshua would leave my heart deeply scored, it was inevitable. But I wasn't going to dwell on the end. I wanted to enjoy what time we had left.

After the pizza had been devoured and the movie ended, Joshua turned to me. A hint of apprehension marred his expression. "Can we try this again, little one?"

"Try what?"

"The shower?"

I smiled and nodded. "I'd like that. Yes."

He stood and held out his hand. That familiar calm, reassurance emanated from him, and I knew the tormented Joshua had retreated.

The bathroom filled with steam as he shucked off his pants. Standing behind me, he loosened the ties of the corset as he trailed endearing kisses over my shoulder. I closed my eyes and lolled my head to the side. Reaching back, I cupped his nape, drifting away on wings of delight. Once inside the small enclosure, he pulled me beneath the spray and pressed his lips to mine. It was the start of a slow, languid seduction.

Sliding his soap-slick hands over my entire body, he cupped my cheeks. In his eyes, I saw regret and shame. "I never want to hurt you again, little one."

I pressed my finger against his lips. "Let's not make promises we can't keep. We need to stay in the here and now."

"Don't fool yourself, little one. We both know it'll never be enough," he whispered, then kissed me.

I met his passion with a burst of my own. Joshua pressed inside me with tender indulgence. Never before had a more heart-melting or benevolent lover carried me away. The tempo of his gliding cock never altered, the intensity of his kiss never lessened, and beneath the compelling rhythm of his thrusts, and the fiery stroke of his tongue, I shattered. There was no Dominance, no submission, only the muffled cries of a woman and man lost in splendor.

Joshua's body tensed as he followed me over on a groan. Held tight in his arms, I let the spray fall on my face. We'd never have forever. But this was one moment I'd never forget. I hoped as time passed, and his taste faded from my lips, he'd remember this solitary moment of perfection, too.

Long minutes later, Joshua raised his head and inched back. "Mellie, we didn't use…"

"I know. I'm clean, and I'm on the pill."

He nodded soberly. "I've never forgotten to glove up before."

"I'm glad you did. Feeling your release was beautiful," I shyly confessed.

A wicked smile curved his lips. "Beautiful can't even come close to describing the way you felt. I might have to forget to use them again, and again, and…"

"Hold up, there. I might have to rest a bit in between. I'm not as young as I used to be," I teased.

"That's my line, girl," he laughed, then kissed me again.

Joshua turned off the water. Drying me first and then himself, he led me back to bed. Just as he reached up to turn off the light, a light knock came at his door. With a curse, he climbed out of bed, slipped his sweatpants back on, and opened it.

James bit back a grin as he spied me in Joshua's bed. "I need to talk to you for a minute," James said as he nodded toward the hall.

"I'll be right back," Joshua promised before stepping out and closing the door.

After twenty minutes, I realized Joshua's perception of 'be right back' and mine were on different time zones. The longer I waited, the more curious I became. Climbing from the bed, I rifled through his closet and found a black silk robe. Cinching the belt around my waist, I tiptoed to the door and pressed my ear against the wood. Nothing but silence greeted me.

Turning the knob, I peeked around the door, glancing up and down the long corridor. Joshua was nowhere in sight; in fact, the club was empty from what I could tell. There were no sounds of smacking flesh echoing from the dungeon. Even the lights were dimmed, as if the place had closed up hours ago.

Suddenly, the sound of heavy footsteps echoed from an open archway to my right, followed by deep male voices. I held my breath, straining to hear their conversation.

"Do you think she's telling the truth?"

The voice sounded like James, but I wasn't certain.

"No," Joshua replied emphatically. His tone teemed with disgust. "I don't believe a word that bitch says anymore, and neither should Mika."

"Wait at the bar. I'll go back upstairs and help him keep an eye on her until the unit arrives. You'll need to file a vandalism report."

By then, I knew James was the man talking to Joshua.

"No problem. I'm going to check on Mellie first."

Their voices grew louder. I knew any second they'd round the corner and catch me eavesdropping. Closing the door quietly, I scurried back across the room, tossed the robe in the closet, and jumped back into bed. As the key jingled in the lock, I yanked the covers around me and sat up as Joshua walked in the door.

"Is everything all right?"

"No, unfortunately not. Someone slashed my tires."

"What? Who would do such a thing?"

"Ah," he hesitated and scrubbed a hand through his hair. "My former sub is upstairs in Mika's office as we speak."

"She slashed your tires?"

"Well, she claims she didn't, but I parked so far back in the lot, my car was out of camera range so there's no video proof. James just happened to be taking out the trash and saw a figure by my car. He went to investigate and hauled her upstairs. She claims she didn't even notice the tires were flat. But she was the only one around."

"What was she doing waiting by your car?"

"She said she was waiting for me to come out so we could talk again."

"She was the blonde at the wedding today, right?"

"Yeah," he replied on a heavy sigh.

I wanted to ask if she was coming around to see if he'd take her back. But I didn't. I wanted him to volunteer the reason, to share a part of himself with me. He didn't, and it chafed.

"Do you believe her?"

"No." There was a distant harshness in his reply that told me he'd been burned far deeper by the woman than Sanna had revealed.

"So, now what happens, with her, I mean?"

"The cops are on their way. They'll question her. I'll fill out a report and call my insurance company in the morning."

"Is there anything I can do?"

"No. I need to wait for the police in the bar."

"I'll wait with you, if you'd like."

"I'd rather you didn't. I don't want to risk her seeing us together. It's not safe for you."

His desire to shield me from the girl frightened me a little. "Is she an axe murderer or something?"

Joshua smiled for the first time since he'd entered the room. "I don't think so. But she's territorial, to an unstable degree. She thought for a time I was playing around with Leagh. That's what ultimately led to me releasing her."

"I see. Okay, well, I can catch a cab back to Sanna's place if you'd like," I announced, tossing off the covers.

"What I'd like is to wake up with you in my arms, Mellie," he whispered softly as he eased down on the edge of the bed and tucked the sheets back around me. "I'll be back as quickly as I can."

"I'll be here." I smiled.

He bent and placed a quick, chaste kiss on my lips. "Get some sleep. I'll try not to wake you when I get back."

As he left, he turned off the lights. Tugging at the blanket, I snuggled his pillow. The clock on the nightstand bathed the room in an eerie blue glow. Breathing in his rugged scent lingering on the pillow, I drifted off to sleep.

I didn't hear him come back to bed, but when I woke the next morning, he was laying on his side facing me, snoring softly. Even though the cloudy fog of slumber enveloped my brain, he looked beautiful. Rumpled sandy blond hair dusted his forehead, and I stared at the tiny lines around his eyes as I'd done before. Drinking in the golden scruff adorning his face and the fullness of his erotic lips, I longed to trace my fingertips over every inch of his face. Instead, I closed my eyes and branded his peaceful image to memory.

Glancing at the clock, I saw it was almost noon. My stomach rumbled, and I was dying for a steaming cup of coffee, but I nuzzled in against Joshua and exhaled a blissful sigh. The enchantment was severed by the sound of my cell phone. Joshua woke with a start. Bolting upright in bed at the unfamiliar sound, he scrubbed a hand over his face as I scurried to retrieve my phone.

"Hello?"

"Mellie? Hayes here. I'm sorry if I'm disturbing you. I know you're out of town. I got your automated e-mail message." Hayes Brockman, a rich oil tycoon with more money than sense, prattled on in my ear. He and his wife Dixie had sold their home in Corpus Christie years ago and bought a castle in northern England. Every six months or so, Dixie grew tired of the décor, and Hayes would hire me for another one of her never-ending projects.

"It's good to hear your voice. How are you and Dixie doing?"

"Not too good, actually. She's got a bee in her bonnet and wants the dining hall gussied up again. Problem is, we've got Lord and Lady Galbraith of Northshire scheduled for some pomp and circumstance shin-dig in three weeks."

"Three weeks?" I choked.

Joshua frowned as he watched and listened.

"Yeah, yeah. I know. I tried telling Dixie you wouldn't have time, but dagnabbit, she put on the saddest puppy dogs eyes, I couldn't take it. Besides, you know how she gets once she sets her mind on something. So, I promised her I'd call and see if there's a way you can move heaven and earth and work your magic to get us fixed up in time."

I glanced back at Joshua, now sitting on the edge of the bed, naked. His eyes were vacant, and his expression looked so bleak, my heart clutched.

No. No. Not yet. My head screamed as a wave of despair reached up from my gut and squeezed my heart. I closed my eyes and sucked in a deep breath.

"Of course. I'll catch a flight tomorrow. I'll call you from New York with my arrival information."

Hayes let out one of his infamous hog calls and thanked me profusely. When I hung up, I swallowed the lump of grief clogging my throat. Forcing a weak smile, I walked to the bed, straddled his legs, and crawled onto Joshua's lap.

"Duty calls," I murmured softly. "I have to leave for London in the morning."

Sliding my arms over his shoulders, I nuzzled his chest. He banded me in a desperate grip, and I fought to hold back my tears.

"I'm sorry," I choked.

"Shhh," Joshua soothed. "Just let me hold you, little one."

The grief resonating in his tone was more than I could bear. Enveloped in his sheltering arms, I mourned the days and nights we wouldn't share. The bittersweet taste of submission would be gone, replaced with the pain of severing our newfound connection too damn soon.

"It's only three weeks, right?"

I nodded gloomily.

"Then go do what you need to and come back to me when you're done."

Before I could open my mouth, Joshua tipped my chin, cupped my cheeks. and pressed his lips to mine. His kiss held more than passion, much, much more. There was adoration, devotion, and promise on his tongue as he rolled me beneath him.

Just as he'd done in the shower, Joshua set a leisurely pace, trailing kisses down my throat, over my chest, and lower still, to my breasts. He laved, sucked, and scraped his teeth over my pebbled nipples, and I cried out.

Repositioning his body, Joshua straddled my chest. Gripping my hair in a firm but subdued hold, he coaxed my mouth to his shaft. Guiding my mane with his fist, he dictated the tempo and depth of each slick caress. His body tensed and relaxed as I worshiped his cock, and all the while, he murmured praise and encouragement. Working my lips up and down his shaft as he allowed, I basked in the submissive glory he granted.

"Enough. I'm going to come down your sinful throat if you don't stop," he cautioned with a hoarse cry as he pulled from my mouth. Capturing my wrists in one talented hand, he raised my arms above my head. "Keep them there and open your legs for me, gorgeous."

The affection reflecting in his brilliant eyes made me feel more adored than his words. I complied with a wistful sigh, and Joshua fed inch after sweet, burning inch inside me. My pussy was sore, but I didn't care. This might be our last time together. I had no intention of refusing him, not for anything in the world.

With one hand wrapped around my wrist, he feathered the fingers of his other hand over my clit, fully seating himself inside my quivering passage. Locked in his gaze, covered by his rugged body, and filled with his turgid shaft, I ached to stay in this exact moment until the end of time.

"Remember, Mellie. When you're across the pond and alone in your bed at night, remember my hunger, remember my claim. You belong to me." As he ended his declaration with a snarl, I shuddered.

Dragging his wide crest over my G-spot, demand sizzled and hissed. "Yours, yes," I murmured, lost in a mist of pure pleasure.

He issued a roar, half feral and hungry, the other half fraught in something that sounded like torment, then he bent and captured my mouth with his. I yielded to his thrusting tongue and his driving hips. One minute insistent and frenzied, the next so slow and velvety it nearly brought me to tears.

Swirling in a vapor of emotional highs and lows, I clung to his glistening body, riding each crest as it built and blazed. Blocking out whatever tomorrow might bring, I seized each glorious second he bathed me in sweet, sublime splendor.

Holding back my release as the pressure built and throbbed, I stared into his fiery gaze, watching as he summoned the strength to hold back, one painstaking second at a time. A low grumble vibrated from deep in his chest, and Joshua sucked in a ragged breath. Shaking his head, refusing to concede to the blaze within, he kissed my nose and issued a melancholy smile.

"Come for me, little one," he whispered in a tone suffused in such reverence it nearly shattered my heart. "Look at me and come undone for me, precious girl."

Even as his image blurred, I stared at him as the force of my orgasm stole the air from my lungs.

"Mine," he declared as he released his hot seed, showering my clutching passage.

Collapsing onto his elbows, Joshua buried his face against my neck. His thundering heart reverberated against my chest as we clung to one another, panting and sweating. Clutching him in my arms, I felt as if the potent connection we shared was being severed in two with a rusty saw.

Long minutes passed, and neither of us said a word. We didn't have to. There was silent understanding as we gazed into each other's eyes. Begrudgingly, he eased off me, then cradled me in his arms and carried me into the bathroom. Joshua started the shower, then lowered me beneath the hot, silky spray. As his seed and virile scent washed down the drain, a sense of grief gripped my soul.

"After we're all cleaned up, I'll call us a cab and take you back to Dylan and Nick's place."

I smiled and kissed his soft lips. "I'd like that. Can you spend the day with me, if you don't have any other plans?"

"There's nothing in my life that can't be put on hold for a day, Mellie."

"Thank you, Sir."

He grinned, then pulled me in for another toe-curling kiss.

Sitting in the back of the taxi, I felt like I was taking the ride of shame. Joshua had given me a jacket to wear over my corset, but the short, black leather skirt gave me away. As he paid the cabbie, I rushed up and rang the bell.

Joshua joined me on the porch as Dylan opened the door. Sanna's Master looked surprised before a smug smile curled his lips.

"I'm sorry I didn't call ahead of time, Dylan. Joshua…err, Stephen, grrrr," I hissed. Both men smirked. "Master Stephen's car was vandalized at the club last night, and I got an emergency call from a client. I have to leave tomorrow."

Dylan frowned just as Sanna stepped in behind him.

"Tomorrow?" she cried. "No. You just got here. You can't go yet, Mel. You just can't."

Tears welled in her eyes, and her chin started to quiver. I was already hanging by an emotional thread, and my sister's disappointment tugged the fraying fiber. It took several seconds for me to choke down my own sadness.

"I know. I don't want to go, but I have to."

"What happened to your SUV, man?" Dylan asked, motioning us inside.

As soon as I hit the foyer, I hugged Sanna tight, grappling with my own bleak sadness.

"Tires got slashed. Carnation..." Joshua frowned.

"You've got to be shitting me." Dylan gaped.

"Nope. She swears she didn't do it, but she was the only one at the scene. Hell, when it comes to her, who knows what to believe?"

Wiping the tears from Sanna's cheeks, I forced a smile. "Don't cry. I hate seeing you sad."

"What was she doing there? Mika banned her ass," Dylan asked, darting a glance at his girl before trailing a sympathetic caress down her arm.

"What's going on?" Nick joined us in the foyer, his expression lined in concern.

"Let's go to the kitchen," Dylan suggested as he bent and kissed Sanna's head. "Come on, kitten. No more tears. She'll be back."

"Yes, she will." Joshua nodded with a confident smile.

"Who's going where?" Nick asked in confusion. "And why are you crying, precious?"

"Come on, bro. We'll explain it all," Dylan replied with a jerk of his head. "Who wants a beer?"

The five of us sat around the kitchen table, filling Nick in on the chain of events. Minutes turned into hours, and by then, we'd moved to the deck, laughing and swapping stories. Dylan and Nick decided to grill some chicken, so Sanna and I popped into the kitchen where she could prepare the side dishes.

"You don't want to leave him, do you?" she asked, with a probing stare.

"No. If it weren't Hayes and Dixie, I'd decline and suggest another designer. But they've been with me for years. I couldn't tell them no. Besides, it's a ridiculous amount of money to turn down."

"Is it enough money to keep you from missing him? He's going to miss you. You know that, right?"

"Yeah, I know. I'm going to miss him too, and you." I grinned, poking her in the arm.

"You really need to move up here, Mel." She pouted. "I don't mean to harp, but think about it. I mean, really think about it. Please? For me? And maybe even a little bit for him."

I stared out the window just as Joshua threw his head back, laughing at something Dylan had said. I was going to miss Joshua's laugh and the easy banter we shared. Not to mention, the way my body tingled when he looked at me with those decadent green eyes. Sobering, I hoped it might be easier for him to sort out his demons, if he could, without me around.

As if sensing my stare, he turned and smiled, warming me from the inside out. Yes, I was going to miss him far more than I had a right to. Saying goodbye was going to be brutal, but I wasn't ready to start shoring up my armor. We had the rest of the day, and hopefully, the night, to spend together. I could sleep on the plane and mend my heart. If I got lucky, I'd manage to wrap myself so thoroughly up with work that I wouldn't miss him.

Good luck with that, cupcake.

"Mel?" Sanna jabbed me with her elbow.

"Huh?"

"I said your name like five times. Where were you?" she asked, peeking over my shoulder with a snort. "Never mind. I know exactly where your mind was. And you called me a dirty little monkey."

"Well, we *are* cut from the same cloth," I reminded her with a laugh.

"That we are, sis. Hey, if you'll grab the salad dressing, I think we'll be set."

As I bent to retrieve the bottles, the sliding glass door opened, and all three men paraded in. Nick set a platter of sizzling chicken on the counter. A mouth-watering aroma of smoke and spices filled the room.

Joshua stepped up behind me, crowding in close, and leaned his mouth to my ear. "It's dangerous to bend over like that in front of me, little one. Need any help?"

I smiled and wiggled my ass against his crotch, then flashed him a lurid smile over my shoulder. "Not with this, but I could sure use some later."

"Minx," he chuckled before gliding his tongue over the shell of my ear. "Believe me, Dylan and Nick won't mind a bit if I lay you over the kitchen table and spank your ass."

"Is that all you want to do to it?" I smirked.

"Hell, no. I want to sink balls deep inside it." His expression looked animalistic. "By the way, you're not leaving until I've had *that* pleasure, little one."

The thought of Joshua's cock buried in my ass made my body tremble so violently I almost dropped the salad dressing.

"Easy," he laughed and slid the bottles from my fingers.

"Okay, no sex in the kitchen," Sanna called from the table.

"Why not, precious?" Nick smirked. "We have sex in the kitchen all the time."

Sanna gasped. Her face turned beet red. "Master," she choked.

"Well, we wipe the damn table and counters off when we're through," Dylan chuckled. "What's the big deal, kitten?"

She let out a low, mortified groan.

"Sanna," I giggled. "It's okay, sis. I know you have sex with two men at once. I'm not shocked or appalled. It's all good."

I sent her a knowing wink as Joshua held a chair for me. Sitting next to me, he grinned.

"I think it's safe to say there are no virgins here," Nick chuckled as he filled his salad bowl.

"Well, so much for the sacrifice we'd planned for later," Dylan quipped.

"And just where were you going to get a virgin?" Sanna laughed.

"We hadn't gotten that far yet." Dylan grinned, filling his bowl next. "We'd only gotten to tying you up and pretending you were a virgin."

I chuckled as I took a bite of a drumstick. The thought of losing this wonderful family, and the contentment I'd found with Joshua, hurt.

"I guess I'm going to have to give you a rain check," Joshua commented as he grazed his knuckles over my thigh beneath the table.

"Rain check?"

"Dinner tonight. It looks like we're having it here instead." He smiled.

It was hard to believe he'd only asked me out the day before. So much had happened so quickly, it suddenly seemed surreal.

"No worries," he declared. "We'll do it when you get back."

"You're coming back?" Sanna asked with elation.

"Yes, but I'm not sure when exactly."

"In three weeks." Joshua's statement sounded more like a question.

"That's fantastic," Sanna squealed.

"I-It might be a little bit longer than three weeks," I spluttered.

"Why?" Joshua pinned me with a wary frown.

"Well, I'll need to go back home sometime to pay my bills, check on the house, do laundry, re-pack...those sorts of things."

He issued a nod of understanding as his demeanor turned brittle and cold.

"I'll get things taken care of as soon as I can. Trust me. I'd rather be here in Chicago with you all than sitting in front of my computer at home."

"You booked your flight already, right?" Sanna asked.

"Yes. I logged onto my computer a little while ago. I leave for New York at eight in the morning."

"Do you need a ride to O'Hare?" Nick asked.

"No," Joshua interrupted as I snapped my mouth shut. "I'll take her."

The thought of having to say goodbye to him in a crowded airport full of strangers made my skin crawl. I didn't like farewells, and this one, I feared, would be exceptionally difficult. Instead of challenging the man at the dinner table, I bit my tongue and stifled my knee-jerk reaction. Later, when we were alone, I'd spill my guts and try to explain why I didn't want him to take me.

Suddenly, the smell of the food made my stomach swirl. I took a gulp of water, praying no one noticed my hands shaking, but of course, Joshua picked up on it right away.

"If you'll excuse us?" Joshua smiled as he stood and took my hand. Without another word, he led me out the back door toward the wooden railing overlooking Lake Michigan.

"What's wrong?" I asked as he watched a boat off in the distance.

"That's my question to you, little one. The minute I offered to take you to the airport you tensed and started shaking. I want to know why?"

"You didn't offer. You told me you were going to take me."

"Oh, so we're back to that again? Come on, Mellie, I thought we'd made some headway."

The man was nothing if not direct. I sucked in a deep breath and closed my eyes, aligning my thoughts. Turning to face him, I ran my fingertips along the crease of his brow.

"I'm not good at saying goodbye, Joshua."

"But we're not saying goodbye, Mellie. We're simply saying, see you soon."

Maybe. Maybe not.

"I need to warn you, my job goes in spurts. There are times when I'm flying from one side of the world to the next, not even sure what airport or city I'm landing in. It's hectic, and stressful. Usually, one phone call from a client leads to another. I don't know for sure that I'll be able to come back in three weeks."

"So, based on past experience, you're anticipating a slew of clients will call and book you up for what? Weeks? Months?"

"It's a possibility." I nodded.

"I see. Were you going to tell me all this? Were you going to wait and tell me in three weeks, or whenever you got your laundry done?"

That icy edge was back, and so was the impenetrable wall. There was no way in hell I was going to end this—whatever this was between us—in a nasty fight.

Pausing, I mentally smoothed my hackles down and put my temper in time-out.

"I'd planned to tell you once we were alone, *Sir*." My calm demeanor and stress of the honorific took the starch out of him. "I'm sorry you thought I was trying to keep details from you, Master Stephen."

A self-loathing smirk curled the side of his mouth, and he nodded. The man had a touchy Dom switch. I seemed to flip that sucker nearly every time I opened my mouth.

"So you'd rather Dylan, Nick, and Savannah take you to the airport in the morning?"

"No, Sir. I'd rather take a cab."

He cocked his head and stared at me. "That seems like a rather cold and impersonal way to leave your family."

"Yes, I suppose it is." I nodded.

Out of nowhere, tears filled my eyes and streamed down my cheeks. I knew I had to explain my visceral reaction, but I wasn't altogether sure I could speak. I tossed my head back in an attempt to stem the flow, and sniffed.

"If something should happen to me, and I never come back home, I don't want my sister's last memory of me to be waving goodbye in a throng of strange faces. I want her to remember my smile, my hug, the kiss I left on her cheek, and me saying, *'I'll see you soon'* before I climb into a cab and drive away."

Chapter Nine

Joshua wrapped his arms around me and held me lovingly. "Who did you lose that you never got a chance to say goodbye to, pet?"

"Our parents," I choked on a sad sob.

"Then, I'm staying here with you tonight. And in the morning, I'll stand on the porch, hold you in my arms, savor your kiss, and drink in your beautiful smile, and before you pull away in the cab, I'll tell you, *see you soon*, but make no mistake, I'll be here when you come back." He kissed my forehead, sealing his vow.

His acceptance of my fears was all but crushing. He took my hand and led me toward the lake. We walked for what seemed like miles as I told him about the death of my parents, about raising Savannah, and finally confessed the toll Davis Walker had claimed on my self-confidence.

We touched briefly on the tragic accident that claimed his wife and daughter, but he wasn't ready to share the hell he'd lived through after his loss. I suspected he was still living it to a degree, but then, weren't we both? You move on and live your life, but the emptiness left behind never goes away.

When we arrived back at the house, Sanna wore a sly, little smirk on her lips.

"Something came for you, Mel."

"What?"

Dragging me by the arm, she pulled me into the family room. "Good job," she whispered to Joshua.

"For what?" he asked in confusion.

A massive floral arrangement of yellow and white roses sat on the coffee table. It was teeming with huge, purple and pink day lilies, and surrounded in rich green foliage. I blinked, then smiled and turned toward Joshua.

"Oh my…they're gorgeous," I cried, rushing to his arms. "Thank you so much."

His body tensed, and I pulled away. "I didn't…I should have, but…"

"They're not from you?" I felt a bit awkward, but Joshua looked totally embarrassed.

"Then who are they from?" Sanna asked, her brow wrinkling in question.

I peeked through the arrangement and finally found the small envelope. Opening it, I read the card, and my stomach pitched. Dropping the printed card on the table, I turned to Sanna. "Toss them out," I instructed with a wave of my hand.

Joshua leaned in and plucked up the card. Reading, his features hardened.

"Who the hell are they from?" Sanna demanded, trying to peek over Joshua's shoulder.

"My dear Mellie," he began. "I wish to apologize for any heartache I caused you in the past. I've changed and am a different man now. I hope you'll give me the chance to prove it to you, bunny. Please accept these as a token of my sincere desire to rekindle what we once shared. I miss you. Call me. Davis." Joshua didn't bother to mask his sarcasm. "Oh look, he even left his phone number."

"What a pig," Sanna huffed.

"He can't be serious, can he?" Dylan thundered.

"Serious or not, he's a dead man," Joshua snarled.

"You can't kill him," I sighed. "Just maim and disfigure him, if you want. That's fine with me."

Sanna snatched up the heavy vase and held out her hand as Joshua crumpled up the card. Turning on her heel, she stormed out of the room toward the garage and the trash barrels.

"Does he have your number?" Joshua asked with concern. "Does he have a way to get in touch with you, Mellie?"

"No. I mean, I suppose he could find me through the internet. I'm easy to contact via my website. But if you're asking if I've ever gave him my number when I moved to Phoenix, no, I didn't."

Joshua tipped my chin with the tips of his fingers and gazed soberly into my eyes. "You let me know if he contacts you again. Understood?"

"I doubt he'll bother me, especially when I don't reach out and thank him for the flowers."

"That's not what I asked, little one." Joshua's lips flattened to a thin line. Trying not to scowl, I reminded myself he wasn't intentionally treating me like a five-year-old—his Dom-beast was roaring with the need to protect me. Still, it chaffed. I wasn't his sub, not in the *real* sense, but I sure ached for it.

"You will be the first to know." I smiled then arched a suspicious brow. "You're not going to kill him, are you?"

"Does it matter?" he challenged.

"Yes," I cried. The look of shock and jealousy that blossomed over Joshua's face was almost comical. "You'll end up in prison, and I can't cook to save my soul. There's no way I could bake you a cake with a file in it so you could escape."

A laugh tore from his lips. "Mellie. You're like a glass of ice water for a man who's been lost in the desert."

I closed my eyes as I clung to him, breathing in his masculine scent. "We've both been lost a long time, Sir."

"Yes," he replied in a whisper so soft I almost missed it.

As night fell, we all sat on the deck once again. A feeling of finality weighed in the air. My last night with both Sanna and Joshua, filled me with melancholy. I was torn between wanting to race to my room and curl up in Joshua's arms and spending a few more precious hours with Sanna warred within.

As if sensing my dilemma, Dylan stood. "It's time to go upstairs, kitten."

The look of disappointment on her face broke my heart. "Already?"

"Yes, love. Mellie and Stephen need some time alone. Besides, Nick and I would like some with you."

"Come on, precious. We'll turn that pout into some sensual screams," Nick teased before he picked her out of the chair and curled her in his arms.

With a giggle, Sanna blew me a kiss and waved. "See you in the morning."

"Sweet dreams…eventually," I laughed.

It wasn't long before Joshua linked his fingers with mine and led me inside. I directed him to my guest room where he closed and locked the door behind us.

After peeling off my clothes, he undressed. We spent hours making sweet, passionate love while I absorbed his blissful touch, warm breath, and every satisfied growl and moan. He tumbled me over the edge, time and again. Lubing up my ass, he worked his way inside my tiny opening with such patience and care before bestowing me the most sublime orgasms of my life. As he held me in his arms, I sobbed, overwhelmed by his tender mercy.

As dawn began to break, Joshua's arm lay slung around my waist as I faced him, watching him sleep. I brushed a strand of golden hair from his forehead. He opened his eyes and gave me a sleepy smile, another vivid image of him that I branded to my memories.

"Hey," he murmured. His voice was thick and deep and sent a shiver up my spine.

"Hey," I whispered. "I have to get up, take a shower, put myself together, and pack. Go back to sleep. I'll be quiet."

"Uh-uh." He shook his head. "I'm showering with you."

The gleam in his eyes and the wicked smirk curling his lips told me it would be a thoroughly enjoyable shower.

"You're going to make me miss my flight."

"Damn. You figured me out. And here I thought I was being all stealthy and suave."

I laughed and kissed him, then sobered. "I'm going to miss you," I whispered as I gazed into his eyes.

"Only for a little while," he assured. "Come on. Let's get you ready for work."

I washed every inch of his body, memorizing the feel of his hard, defined muscles. When I stroked my soap-slick fist around his cock, he let out a groan and begrudgingly pulled my hand away.

"You *will* miss your flight if you keep that up. Turn around," he instructed.

I closed my eyes as his strong hands spread luxurious bubbles over my flesh. I wasn't disappointed we didn't make love in the shower. It would have been rushed, taking away the memory of our incredible night before.

Stealing up behind me as I dried my hair, he pressed his chest against my back. His cock, hard and ready, settled between the cheeks of my ass. I groaned. Joshua snickered as he reached around me and placed a cup of sweet, creamy coffee on the vanity.

"You sure know how to spoil a girl," I quipped. Turning my head, I planted a quick kiss on his cheek.

"Oh, little one, I haven't begun to spoil you yet," he warned. "The guys are downstairs cooking a farewell feast. I think they're trying to bribe you into staying with food."

I laughed. "And we both know what you tried to bribe me with last night. Don't we?"

"That wasn't a bribe, sweetheart. That was just a precursor of what's to come."

Packing my suitcases, I took extra care as I wrapped the kneeling woman. Simply having a piece of Joshua with me lightened my spirit. I wasn't altogether sure if the sculpture would grant me solace or pain in the lonely nights ahead, but I'd soon find out.

Through breakfast, I had to keep reminding myself that I'd only be gone three weeks. It wasn't a lifetime. Soon, I'd be back to the loving arms of my sister and her Masters, and back to the sweet indulgence and command of the man who'd captured a piece of my heart. Those mental reminders were all that kept me from breaking down into a blubbering, snot-soaked mess at the table.

Standing on the porch after phoning for the cab, Sanna bravely swallowed back her tears. Both Dylan and Nick wrapped a supportive arm around her waist, as did Joshua to mine. The five of us bantered back and forth a bit, but the air weighed thick in a somber, doleful cloak.

When the taxi pulled into the circular drive, I fought the urge to run back inside and lock the door. Digging deep, I dredged up my courage and hugged both Dylan and Nick. I gave Sanna a kiss and held her tight, then turned to Joshua's waiting arms.

"I'm ready for my kiss and my hug, little one."

I swallowed back a sob and gripped his strong body, holding tight one last time. He brushed his hand over my hair as the sound of his thundering heart echoed in my ears.

Pulling back slightly, he captured my lips in one final passion-filled kiss.

Even when his lips left mine, I couldn't let go. Clinging to Joshua, I watched Dylan and Nick load my luggage.

"I'll see you soon," Joshua whispered.

When the cab driver opened the door, I sucked in a deep breath.

"Yes, I'll see you soon."

Squeezing Joshua tight one last time, I pried myself from his arms and rushed inside the taxi.

"I'll see you soon. I love you," Sanna called to me.

"See you soon, sis. Love you more," I replied in a quivering voice.

Forcing a smile, I waved as the cab pulled away. I only made it two houses before the tears I'd bravely tamped down rose to the surface.

Willing a calmness I didn't feel, I could smell Joshua's ghost in the cab. Dipping my head, I sniffed my blouse; his scent was all over me. It was going to be a brutal three weeks.

Stretched out in first class beneath a blanket and wearing sunglasses to hide my swollen eyes, I stared out the window. Paying little attention to the blue sky, I relived every precious second I'd spent with Joshua. Emptiness settled through my soul like a black hole eating the life out of me.

Halfway through the flight to Heathrow, I decided I'd wallowed in enough misery. It took a mighty crowbar, but I managed to pry my ass off the pity pot and started focusing on work. No matter how hard I tried, my thoughts inevitably wound their way back to the tall, sandy blond artist with the shimmering green eyes.

With an inward curse, I exhaled a heavy sigh and pounded away at my computer, prioritizing a sizable list to expedite the renovation of Hayes and Dixie's dining hall. Catching my last flight to Manchester-Birmingham, I was exhausted. When I landed, I was relieved to see the driver Hayes had sent to pick me up, and the short hour drive to Northshire was a piece of cake compared to the unending hours I'd spent in flight.

Hayes and Dixie met me at the door. They were both in their mid-seventies, and neither fit the stereotype of castle owners, not by any stretch of the imagination. Loud and gregarious, they dressed in comfy flannel shirts, blue jeans, and brown cowboy boots. They were serious, down-home country people without a refined bone in their bodies.

Unable to curb her excitement, Dixie chattered about all the changes she wanted made to the dining hall. She was more animated and full of life than I'd ever seen before. I followed her up the grand staircase, nodding in a sleep-deprived stupor as their somber-faced butler dragged my luggage behind him.

Leading me to one of the massive suites I'd redecorated on a previous trip, Dixie beamed with pride. It seemed a shame the only time I'd get to spend in the elegant room was when I tumbled into bed, exhausted from a long day of multi-tasking and overseeing a small army of workmen.

"You get your gear stowed, darlin', and I'll have some grub sent up to you. You look worn thin," Dixie fussed. "I'm sure you're half-starved by now."

I smiled. "Thank you. It has been a long day, but don't worry. I'll be good as new in the morning." *I hope.*

After dinner, I started to unpack. The inviting bed all but goaded me to lie down and float away into peaceful darkness. *Not yet,* I scolded inwardly. I still had clothes to put away. Once the sun came up, I'd have no time for anything except work.

When the last suitcase was empty, I carefully unwrapped Joshua's sub statue. Cradling her in my hands, the urge to repack my bags and fly home pressed hard. Longing for a man I'd known a whole five days was ridiculous, yet the ache within was real, and foreign, and unsettling. Lifting the statue to my lips, I placed a reverent kiss on her head, in honor of the Master who'd shaped her. The same Master who had set my body ablaze, climbed inside my soul, and stolen a piece of my heart. I positioned the figurine on the nightstand next to my bed so she would be the first vision I saw in the morning and the last at night.

My cell phone chimed, notifying me of a text. My heart nearly leapt from my chest as a stupid grin crawled across my face. Palming the device, I blinked. Reading the message, my hands began to shake as a ripple of dread snaked up my spine.

Unknown: A phone call would have been nice, bunny. I hope you liked the flowers. I'm waiting for your call. Don't disappoint me. Understood? Davis.

The blood in my veins turned to ice. "How did he get my number?" I wondered aloud. Frowning, my initial question didn't disturb me as much as the last line of his text. He actually presumed I was his sub again.

"No fucking way," I mumbled. It was time to nip this shit in the bud.

My fingers flew over the letters on the device as I delivered a message of my own.

Mellie Carson: I threw the flowers away. I'm not interested in pleasing or disappointing you, Davis. Don't waste your time waiting for my call. It's never going to happen. You don't get a second chance. We are through. Over. Finished. You made the choice—you have to deal with the consequences. Don't contact me again. Understood?

It took only a matter of seconds for his reply.

Unknown: It's over when I say it's over, slut. You don't get to decide what's a waste of my time or what isn't. You obviously don't remember a fucking thing I taught you. Don't worry. I'll retrain you with my belt. You don't get to shut me out, bunny. It's not up to you. I'm going to get you back, one way or the other. Count on it.

It was a good thing an ocean separated us, because a wave of anger washed over me so strong it threatened to drown me. Gripping the phone, I growled. The man was certifiably insane if he thought for one second I'd subject myself to the farce he called Dominance.

"You let me know if he contacts you again. Understood?"

Joshua's directive echoed in my brain as I automatically reached for my phone. Pausing to calculate time zones, I scrolled to his number, hesitant to place the call. I sucked in a deep breath, stared at his number, and eventually pressed *call*.

He picked up on the third ring. "What a fantastic surprise, little one." From his tone, I visualized his smile, and my heart skipped a beat. The fear calmed instantly. "Did you make it safe and sound?"

"Yes. I'm here at the castle, all settled in. How's it going with you?"

There was a long pause. So long I wondered if I'd lost the connection.

"What's wrong, Mellie?"

"W-what makes you think something's wrong?" I stammered.

"You might be halfway around the damn world, but I can feel and hear it in your voice. Tell me what's wrong."

"Davis somehow got my number," I confessed.

"What? How?" His voice turned hard and cold.

"I don't know. He sent me a couple of messages."

"Let me guess, he wants you back, right?"

"Yes."

Joshua blew out an angry sigh. "I'll take care of it, little one. You just focus on doing your job. I don't want you worrying about that dipshitiot."

I couldn't help but laugh. "A dip what?"

"Dipshitiot. It's a combination of dip shit and idiot," he chuckled. "Although Kerr might need a whole classification all his own, like dipshitiothole."

I flopped back on the bed, giggling. Joshua was amazing. He knew exactly how to wipe away my worries and insecurities, and make me laugh while doing it. No other man before him had possessed that kind of magic.

"It feels longer than a day," I whispered softly.

"I know," he murmured. "I'm in my studio. I come here when I need to think."

"What are you thinking about?" I urged.

"You. Me. Life," he replied cryptically.

"And what thoughts are running through that handsome head of yours?"

"Oh, they're not running through my head, little one. They're running through my hands."

I turned and looked at the statue. A lump of emotion swelled in my throat. I swallowed tightly and blinked the tears from my eyes. I should have realized from the start that Joshua filtered his emotions through his hands, not his words.

My brain flashed in a slide of the pieces displayed at Christian's gallery. I could clearly see the depths of Joshua's pain, the whimsy of his dreams, and the ache of his desires. It was as if he'd sliced open his chest, granting the world a glimpse of his loving and wounded heart. Yet, no one knew. No one but me.

"What are you working on?"

"It's a surprise," he chuckled.

"That's not fair." I grinned. "You have to give me a hint."

"Do I now? Seems you lost your submission somewhere over the ocean, girl."

He wanted to project a stern Dominant tone, but I sensed the grin on his face.

"No, I didn't, but I'm going to have to wear my Domme hat for the next three weeks. I'm just warming it up."

"Not with me you're not," he laughed.

A shiver raced up my spine. I pictured myself on my knees before him and remembered how right it felt.

"Of course not, Master Stephen," I purred.

A low moan rippled over the phone. "You're begging for it, aren't you, pet?"

"Hmmm, maybe just a little?"

"Be careful, or you might end up with a whole lot more than you bargained for."

"I sure hope so."

"I miss you."

Not half as much as I miss you.

I wasn't entirely sure he meant to say the words aloud. He cleared his throat as if his confession left him too exposed. "Get some sleep, little one. Don't worry about Kerr. I'll make sure he doesn't contact you again."

"Yes, Sir." I didn't want our conversation to end. "Oh, if you do bodily harm to him, would you send me the pictures, please?"

"I think there's a malevolent side of you I haven't seen yet, little one."

"Not really. I just like seeing karma in action, that's all."

He laughed. "If it comes to that, I'll be sure to have eight by ten glossies in hand when you get back. Sweet dreams, my girl."

His tender voice was like a gentle caress across my cheek.

"Yes, Sir. Good night."

"Good night."

I hung up feeling better, but worse. Glad Davis would be dealt with, but teeming with frustration that I was an ocean away when all I wanted was to be in Joshua's arms or his bed.

After a long, hot shower, I climbed into the big, empty bed and pulled the extra pillow to my chest. Pretending it was Joshua, just as I had the first night we'd met, I closed my eyes and crashed.

The alarm on my phone buzzed before the sun was up. I tossed back the covers and stumbled to the bathroom, mentally readying myself for a full and hectic day. Most of the morning was spent with Dixie discussing what renovations could realistically be accomplished. Hayes hovered, nodding in approval or wrinkling his nose. By afternoon, I was on the phone ordering wall covering, decorative tile, fabrics, and paint, keeping my fingers crossed none of the items needed were on backorder. The rest of the day I spent lining up a small army of carpenters, electricians, masons, and plumbers. Thankfully, I'd contracted with many of the workers on past projects. I knew they were fast, efficient, and possessed a work ethic I admired.

There were times it felt as if I were herding chickens, but by nightfall, I'd convinced myself the job could be accomplished in time. Thoughts of Joshua popped in my head throughout the day. Even when I was up to my ass in alligators, I'd think about him and smile.

Days passed into weeks, and my ache for the Dominant artist across the pond never waned. Neither did the messages from Davis.

His texts grew vile and vindictive. He'd been livid that I'd "sic'd" Joshua on him, and Walker vowed to get even. I had no idea what delusional planet the man had taken up residence on, but his obsession with me sprouted an anxiety that grew stronger with each repulsive message.

Joshua and I talked or texted almost daily, but still, I didn't bother to tell him about Davis' persistent and threatening messages. Deep down, I knew it was wrong, but I didn't want to sully what precious time I had with Joshua discussing a man who had no meaning in my life anymore. Besides, I was a big girl. I could take care of Davis on my own. Yes, his threats were unnerving, but deep down I knew he was nothing but a bully, gutless and spineless. Fueled by anger for giving him the power to control my life for eight fucking years, I planned to have a nice, long face-to-face with Walker. By the time I was through, I intended to have the bastard backed into a corner, sucking his thumb and crying.

The nights were long and lonely, and my never-ending longing to be with Joshua stole my sleep. Running on fumes, fatigue morphed into frustration, and I became cranky, resenting my choice of taking the job instead of staying in Chicago. But I concealed my bitterness and kept my nose to the grindstone.

It seemed like months, but the day finally came when I led Hayes and Dixie through the dining hall for a final walk-through. Mentally holding my breath, I crossed my fingers that the elegant room met their expectations. Hayes examined the craftsmanship, as always, while Dixie oohed and ahhed.

"Oh Mellie, it's all bright as a button." She beamed before leaning in close. "This is going to knock their knickers off. They say knickers here, not panties. Crazy language they have here in this country. Oh, and don't ever call your butt your fanny. It means something completely different in these parts. I found that out the hard way." Dixie blushed, then issued a wave of her hand.

"I'll be sure to call it my butt," I laughed.

"You and Hayes go tend to the bill. I'm going to check with cook. We're having dinner right here in the dining hall tonight. I want to break this new prairie dog in proper." Dixie beamed.

All through dinner I couldn't wait to get back to my room. I was anxious to collapse into bed, not only because I was exhausted, but because it would bring me one day closer to Joshua. Barring any flight delays, I'd arrive back home in Phoenix late tomorrow night, which was actually that night. Time zones confused me, but jet lag was a bitch. If all went as planned, I'd be in Chicago by Wednesday at the latest.

Just as I settled into bed, my cell phone rang. I couldn't help but smile. I knew Joshua had been counting the days too.

I snatched it up, not bothering to look at the screen, and pressed the device to my ear. "Did you call to talk dirty to me?" I giggled.

There was a long pause before the sound of a man clearing his throat wiped the smile from my face. Bolting upright in bed, my heart pounded in my chest. *Please don't let this be a client.*

"No, ma'am, I didn't." I could tell the man was trying not to laugh, but his next words were delivered in a slow, somber tone. "This is Detective Pruett with the Phoenix Police Department. Am I speaking to Melinda Carson?"

"Yes," I replied in a small, worried voice.

"Ma'am, I'm at your house—"

"My house? Why?"

"I'm sorry to inform you that you've been a victim of some rather extensive vandalism."

"Vandalism? What's happened? How?" I screeched. My heart thundered in my ears as I tried to wrap my head around the news.

"Someone spray painted the words, uh, 'slut' and 'whore' on your garage doors. The big picture window on the front of your house has been smashed. It's strange, maybe the perp got scared away, but from what we can tell, there's no sign of entry. They cut your alarm system and umm…"

"Um what?" I cried. "You mean there's more?"

"Yes, ma'am." The officer paused. "Someone hung a dead rabbit at your front door."

"A dead rabbit?"

The air left my lungs in a whoosh. My blood turned to ice as Davis Walker's words echoed in my brain. *'It's been a long time,* bunny. *A phone call would have been nice,* bunny. *Don't think I'm going to let you shut me out,* bunny.' Shades of 'Fatal Attraction' rolled through my brain. At least the son of a bitch didn't put the poor rabbit in a pot on my stove and burn the damn house down.

My entire body trembled as I blinked back the black splotches swimming behind my eyes. Sucking in a ragged breath, I exhaled in an attempt to calm myself. How did Davis find out where I lived? Why in the world would he fly all the way to Phoenix to fuck with my house? Was he trying to punish me for not giving him a second chance? Yes, Davis Walker had changed all right, changed into a raving madman.

"Do you have any idea who might be responsible for this? Because I have to tell you, I've seen enough of these things. This was personal, ma'am."

"That fucking bastard," I railed. "Yes, I know exactly who did it."

"Good. I need to get a statement from you. How quickly can you get here?"

Releasing a humorless chuckle, I closed my eyes. "About sixteen hours, give or take a few. I'm in the United Kingdom at the moment."

"Oh," he replied, sounding both surprised and disgruntled. "Hell."

I convinced the detective to take my statement over the phone. I supplied him with as much information as I had on Davis Walker, but I kept his association to Genesis to myself. I needed to talk to Mika before spouting out details of his club to the police. Pruett asked when I'd last seen Davis. I fibbed a little and said that I'd run into him while visiting friends in Chicago. After reciting the contents of Davis' text messages, Pruett promised to contact the Chicago PD. That was about the time my neighbor Chad showed up to see what the commotion was about. Using Pruett's phone, Chad offered to clean up the mess and get my security system back up and running. I thanked him profusely, vowing to pay him back as soon as I got home, but Chad seemed far more concerned about the safety of his family and me than the money.

Strung out, I paced, packed, and tried to find other ways to deplete my nervous energy, but nothing worked. Trying to force sleep didn't either. Staring at the clock, the minutes dragged into hours. Finally, I sat up and reached for the phone. Joshua would be pissed that I'd kept him in the dark, but I wanted to hear his calm, reassuring voice. My need for his comfort outweighed the lecture I was sure to receive.

"Mellie? It's three in the morning there. What's wrong?"

The man didn't even say hello. His first instinct was to find out why I was awake at the ass crack of dawn. Joshua's unwavering concern was the perfect balm for my turmoil.

"Please don't be mad. I wasn't trying to keep things from you. It's just that I didn't want to waste what time we had. I mean, hearing your voice was more important than…I swear, never in a million did I think—"

"Stop," he commanded. Hearing the tenor of his potent Dom voice, I snapped my mouth shut, closed my eyes, and winced. "Take a deep breath and relax. Tell me what you've been keeping from me, little one."

I followed his instructions and took several calming breaths. "Davis," I stated flatly.

"What about him? He hasn't been back to the club since I told him to leave you alone. He said he didn't know what I was talking about, but I didn't believe him. He's still bothering you?"

"Yes. But it's escalated. He's gone from bullying, to threatening, and now he's vandalized my house." I exhaled a heavy breath as panic bubbled inside me again. "Joshua, he killed a bunny and hung him on my porch."

Cringing, I pulled the phone from my ear as Joshua erupted with a string of curses, damning Davis Walker like a well-seasoned sailor.

"I want you to tell me every fucking detail, girl. Don't you dare hold anything back, do you understand?"

His bark was vicious, and if he found Davis before the cops did, I was certain they'd never find the asshole's body. Filling Joshua in on all the details only served to piss him off more. I felt like a kid caught feeding peas to the dog under the dinner table. I didn't expect my confession would earn a tiara and a dozen roses, or Joshua turning into Rambo. But he did.

"Give me your flight information from LaGuardia to Phoenix," he instructed.

"Wh—" I bit the question off. It was not the time to question the man. Pulling out my itinerary, I rattled off my arrival and departure times.

"I'll meet you in New York in a few hours, little one."

"But you can't," I blurted out.

"I can and I will," he challenged. "You are out of your pretty little mind if you think I'm going to let you waltz back into your house alone after what's happened."

"But what if it wasn't Davis?" I began.

"Of course, it was Davis, *bunny*," Joshua spat the nickname Davis had pinned me. "He hung Thumper from a noose, for fuck's sake. It's as good as leaving his damn business card on the welcome mat. I'm meeting you in New York, and it's not up for discussion. And I'm going to be stuck to you like glue twenty-four-seven until you're ready to come back to Chicago."

"But the airfare is going to cost you a small fortune," I exhaled.

Grateful for his chivalry, I didn't see a need for him to shell out a ton of money or play bodyguard. Yes, I was desperate to see him, but it rankled he thought me so weak and helpless that I needed protection to walk inside my own home.

Joshua let out a snort rife with sarcasm.

"Have you forgotten how we met, Mellie? Surely, you don't think I'm so strapped for cash that I can't buy a couple of fucking airline tickets, do you? As I recall, *you* were the one who paid Christian over seven figures procuring my art for Abbas. I think I can manage a few thousand dollars for some fucking plane tickets." He paused briefly and exhaled a heavy sigh. "Look, if I've flipped one of your independent triggers, I'm sorry, but right now, I honestly don't give a shit. I refuse to allow you to go home alone. If you don't want *my* company, fine. I'll call Dylan. He's been like a fucking disapproving father since we hooked up. He, Nick, and Savannah can accompany you back home. But you are *not* going alone. Do I make myself clear?"

Anger surged like a short fuse on a stick of dynamite.

"If it were any clearer, I'd have your pig-headed declaration tattooed on my fucking forehead," I snapped. Almost instantly, I regretted my outburst. "Shit."

I closed my eyes and bit back a scream. Joshua had gone silent on the other end of the line. He was either contemplating hanging up on me, or seething so vehemently he didn't trust himself to speak.

"I'm sorry, Joshua. I didn't mean that. Well, I did, but not out loud. Yes, I want to see you. I've missed you so much it hurts. I'm so damn exhausted I don't know which end is up. My head hurts. My eyes burn and instead of coming home to rush to you, I have to deal with the mess Davis left behind. I'm scared to death he's going to do something even more violent and stupid, but I gave that prick eight years of fear; I refuse to give him a second more."

Joshua didn't utter a word. It rubbed me raw, so raw it burned.

"Say something ‚please?"

"I want to take you to bed, wrap you in my arms, and stroke my fingers over your beautiful face while you sleep beside me for days."

His voice was a low and alluring, sensual whisper. I quivered.

"Then I'm going to slide you beneath me. Savor the feel of your sinful cunt as it ripples and milks my aching dick while I bite your hard, ripe candy nipples as you whimper beneath me. And I'm not going to stop until your screams are worn to nothing but strained cries of silence; then I'm going to take you again, and again."

"Oh, godddddd," I moaned.

"Spread your legs, bare your cunt, and stroke your clit for me, little one," he purred into my ear.

Wedging the phone against my shoulder, I slid my hands below the covers. Spreading my legs, I tugged my nightgown up over my hips. Jerking, I gasped as my cold fingertips fluttered over my wet, hot folds. I circled my clit while dipping deep inside my slick, soft center.

"Tell me how *my* fingers feel on your tight little cunt, girl. They're not your hands, they're mine."

"Wet. Hot. Soft," I murmured, finding it hard to concentrate on his question.

"Yes, you're burned into my brain. I can feel you, too. Smell your spicy, sweet scent…taste your tart nectar sliding over my tongue. Rub your fingers all around that pretty little cunt for me, girl. Imagine it's my tongue gliding past your swollen folds, lapping up all that sweet cream spilling from you. You're slick and oozing aren't you, my pet?"

"Yesssss," I hissed.

"Dip your fingers in deep. That's my tongue dragging in and out of your pussy, making all your nerve endings tingle and sing."

I moaned softly.

"That's it. Feel that sizzling arc of fire slide up your spine? The sexy kitten noises you make when I touch you still echo in my ears. Fuck. The moaning music you make has my dick so hard. Deeper, little one, roll your fingers as you slide all the way in. Can you feel my tongue rasping over your walls? Feel me drinking down your silky syrup as it slides over my taste buds?"

I had no trouble imagining my fingers being his persuasive tongue. Strangled whimpers of need burned in the back of my throat.

"Harder, little one. My tongue is fucking you so deeply. Feel me stabbing inside you…flicking side to side against your velvety walls? Sink your hands into my hair wile I snake my tongue deeper and deeper inside your fluttering cunt."

With each erotic word, his voice grew rougher, harsher. I envisioned his fist wrapped around his turgid cock, stroking ruthlessly as he fed my fantasy.

"Faster, little one. Fuck that juicy little cunt for me."

With a whimper, I did as he instructed. Soaring to the cusp of bliss, I clung to the edge, waiting for his permission to plummet over and shatter.

"Now pull your fingers out. Now!" he bellowed.

"Noooo," I wailed.

"Do it. Pull them out."

Begrudgingly, I drew my hands from beneath the covers and exhaled a huge sigh of frustration.

"Good girl. Now paint your lips with your juices, baby. Coat them nice and thick. Breathe in deep. Can you smell your essence?"

"Yes," I groaned as I coated my lips with my own warm cream.

"I can too. My lips and chin are covered in your glossy warmth. Now lick your lips, let my tongue inside your mouth as I kiss the heady spice from you. Can you taste yourself on my tongue, precious?"

"Yes," I hissed. "Please, I need more."

"Drive three fingers into your cunt. Stretch yourself for me. Rub your clit with your other hand," he demanded with a bellicose growl.

"That's my cock filling you, my fingers strumming your swollen little nub. Go to the edge, little one. Ride my dick hard and fast."

Whimpering and moaning, I did as he commanded. I could hear his heavy breathing in the phone, practically feel his warm breath upon my neck.

"Louder," he bellowed. "I want to hear your hunger, girl."

Hurtled to the crest, I cried out, "Pleaseee."

"Stop," he thundered. "Remove your fingers and place your hands above the covers."

"What?" I wailed. "Nooooo."

"I said stop, girl. Put your hands on the outside of your blankets this instant."

Howling in frustration, I withdrew my fingers. My whole body quaked with need.

"Please, let me come," I begged.

"No. You don't get to come tonight, little one. You may not get to come tomorrow night either."

"Why are you doing this to me?" Sounding like a petulant child, I clenched my jaw in anger.

"You tell me why," Joshua whispered.

Frustration bubbled into a cauldron of fury. "Oh, I get it. You're punishing me."

"You bet your sweet ass I am," he chuckled.

"You can't do this. I told you the reason why I kept Davis' threats from you. But I guess that doesn't count for anything when you've got your big, bad Dom pants on, does it?"

"Careful, little one. Watch your tone."

Joshua's warning dripped with such a patronizing tone I balled my hands into fists. So infuriated, I wished he was in the room so I could punch him…hard.

"Fuck my tone and fuck you. Don't bother coming to New York. I'll call Sanna. Dylan can pick me up and escort me back to Phoenix. With all the shit I've got to deal with, the last thing I need is some son of a bitch trying to mind fuck me. Goodbye."

I disconnected the call, covered my face with the pillow, and screamed long and hard.

Chapter Ten

Disembarking the plane at LaGuardia, my heart ached. Sanna and her Masters would be waiting for me. After I'd calmed down from my furious explosion with Joshua, I called Dylan and asked for their help. I should have felt a spark of excitement at seeing my sister and feeling her loving arms around me again, but I didn't. The only arms I wanted wrapped around me, comforting and protecting me, were Joshua's. But he wouldn't be there. No, I'd let my pride and temper fuck that up royally.

Tears stung my eyes, and I swallowed the lump of sadness burning my throat as I walked up the ramp and into the crowded terminal. Scanning the faces of strangers, I couldn't find Sanna, Dylan, or Nick.

Maybe their flight was late.

Trudging toward the digital display of arrivals and departures, I searched for their flight and frowned. They'd landed thirty-five minutes ahead of me.

"They're not coming to meet you, little one. I am."

Joshua's calm, deep voice blanketed me from behind. I spun around, my belongings sagging to the floor. A muffled cry of relief and remorse vibrated over my lips as I stepped into his open arms. Holding him tightly, I tried not to cry as I breathed in his familiar scent and absorbed the strength of his warm body. Thank goodness he was a tenacious, hard-headed man.

"I'm sorry. I'm so sorry," I whispered as I clung to him in a desperate hug.

I knew I'd pay a high price for my behavior over the phone, but trailing my fingers through his soft hair and being enveloped in his warm embrace was worth any punishment he wanted to give.

"I've got you, girl. I know you're scared, but everything's going to be okay," Joshua murmured as he held me tight.

"I'm so sorry I acted like such a bitch to you."

"We'll talk about that after we get Davis and your house sorted out."

"But…" I shook my head. "I need to apologize to you. I shouldn't have lashed out like that."

Joshua inched back, cupped my cheeks, and smirked. "I said we'll discuss it later. We have to catch our flight, but first, I need this."

Slanting his lips over mine, Joshua drowned me in a blistering kiss suffused with so much passion I grew dizzy. Wrapped in his strong, warm arms, contentment settled through me.

"There, I'm much better now," Joshua smiled.

He bent and lifted my computer bag from the floor and slung it over his shoulder, then handed me my purse. When he wrapped a possessive arm around my waist, my head swam in the clouds as we hurried to our departure gate.

After take-off, Joshua raised the armrest, unbuckled my seat belt, and stretched out in first class. He pulled a blanket from the seat pouch in front of him, and draped it around me before pulling me across his lap. Nestled against his sturdy chest, I wrapped my arms around him and issued a sigh of contentment.

"You're exhausted. Sleep, little one," he instructed with a soft kiss to my forehead.

"I am. Thank you," I replied with a weary smile.

Snuggled tight against his hard chest, I closed my eyes. Joshua provided me with the medicine I so desperately needed: compassion, strength, and understanding. I focused on his soft, even breaths as the tempo lulled me to sleep.

The feel of his long fingers threading through my hair rousted me from the darkness.

"Wake up, my sleeping beauty. We're getting ready to land."

"Mmm," I purred. "I don't want to. I want to stay wrapped in your arms forever."

He issued a low chuckle. "That can be arranged, little one."

Peeking up at him from beneath my lashes, the sincerity of his statement reflected in his eyes. It was both heartwarming and crushing. In a perfect world, we'd be in Chicago, tangled in the sheets until this manic connection binding us died. But in the real world, the stirring fantasy could never exist. Mentally adhering bandages to the bleeding wounds impaling my heart, I sat up as we prepared to land and steeled myself to face the ugliness Davis Walker had left in his wake.

After retrieving both my luggage and car, I felt Joshua's stare searing my flesh as I drove down the interstate toward my house.

"You're making it hard for me to concentrate on the road. You know that, right?"

"I'm not doing anything, little one," he smirked.

"Yes, you are. You're undressing me with those gorgeous eyes of yours."

"Perhaps, but I'm not following through with my thoughts. Not yet."

Carnal images flitted through my brain, and my body quivered. Reaching over, Joshua rolled his finger and thumb around my straining nipple.

"What were you thinking that got my sweet berry buds so nice and hard?"

Glancing over, I shot him a sultry smile. "I'll show you when we get home."

Joshua tossed back his head and laughed. "No, little one. You'll show me if I *let* you."

"There's always a catch, isn't there?" I pursed my lips in a fake pout.

"Not when you finally learn to behave yourself," he smirked. "Don't worry, I'll get you straightened out...against the wall, on the bed beneath me, or over my knee."

"Stop. You're going to make me wreck the car," I laughed nervously. My imagination didn't need his encouragement, it did just fine on its own.

Eager to get home to live out the scenarios making my girl parts wet and tingling, I finally pulled into my driveway. Pressing the garage door opener, I frowned when nothing happened.

"That's weird. Maybe I need a new battery for the remote," I mumbled.

Glancing around, Joshua held out his hand. "Turn off the engine and give me your keys."

Curious about what he was up to, I did as he asked and followed him to the back of the car as he opened the trunk. Zipping open his suitcase, Joshua withdrew a metal lock box. After punching in several numbers, he unlocked the case, and pulled out a pistol.

"You brought a gun?"

"Of course, I did," he replied, tucking it into the waistband of his pants. "If Davis is unstable enough to kill animals, he's capable of doing anything. I'm not taking any chances with you, Mellie. I will not lose you, too."

Joshua paused, pinched his lips together, then nodded toward the house.

"Come on, we'll get the luggage later. Let's go inside first. Stay behind me, understood?"

"You're scaring me," I whispered.

"You should be scared. Nobody's been able to locate him back home. He's not been at work; his neighbors haven't seen him. He's vanished."

"How do you know he's not been at work, or his house?"

"I called. His secretary said he was out of the office but offered to take a message. I asked her when he'd be back. She was evasive, but I got the feeling she didn't know where he was. Of course, she might have been holding back after I sidestepped her trying to screen my call. Ian's been doing some surveillance at his house for me."

"Maybe he's out of town working."

"Oh, he's out of town working all right—working on stalking you."

Something felt wrong, but I couldn't put my finger on it. Davis wouldn't throw away his career to terrorize me. His title as senior manager with the pharmaceutical company he'd been with for years meant more to him than anything in the world. He wouldn't mess that up for something so petty as revenge.

When Joshua unlocked my front door, a heavy sense of foreboding filled me. Dropping my gaze, I noticed drops of blood on my porch. An icy chill slithered up my spine. Pushing the door open wide, I followed him into the foyer. Standing still and silent, I listened for movement inside the house, but it was as quiet as a morgue. Shadows filled the recesses past the entryway. Reaching up, I brushed my palm over the three light switches, but none of the lights came on. My electricity was out.

"Back outside," Joshua instructed as he gripped my elbow and pulled me back out the door.

He yanked out his phone, and I watched as he dialed nine-one-one.

"What are you doing?"

"I'm calling the cops. I want them to do a sweep of your house. I'd do it myself, but if something happened to me, there'd be no one to protect you."

"Joshua, don't you think you're..."

"Hello, yes. I'd like to report a possible break-in." Pausing for a moment, he arched his brows. "What's your address?"

I rattled it off, then cast a wary glance back at the house. It no longer felt like the safe haven I'd once loved. The massive structure now seemed to hold a malignant, tainted aura. Anger spiked. Davis Walker had stolen my power, like a thief in the night. Pacing, I tried to keep the fury from consuming me. As if sensing my struggle, Joshua kept his distance but watched me like a hawk.

Four minutes later, the street was lined with patrol cars. Joshua stood by my side as several officers walked the perimeter of the house, while several more drew their weapons and stormed inside.

A man in a dark, tailored suit approached wearing a tight smile. "Ms. Carson?"

"Yes?"

"Hi. I'm Detective Pruett. We talked on the phone yesterday."

"Oh yes. It's nice to meet you." I forced a polite smile.

"I think the ballsy bastard came back. Well, someone did. He cut your electricity along the wall of the foundation in the back. The power company is on their way to fix it."

"Great." I sighed in disgust.

"Look, I'm not telling you how to live your life, but until we get this son of a bitch locked up, I don't think it's a good idea for you to stay here." The detective raised his gaze to Joshua. "I'm not implying you can't protect her, sir, but Ms. Carson has a full-blown, very brazen stalker on her tail."

"I'm glad we're on the same page," Joshua interjected.

Turning toward me, the detective continued, "I'm worried. The fact you're with another man might set this fuck-knuckle on an even more unpredictable path."

The foundation of my independence and self-reliance cracked, crumbling like dust beneath my feet. Not since losing my parents had I felt so helpless and angry. I may have been powerless over my mom and dad being from ripped from my life, but I sure as hell wasn't about to roll over and let Davis Walker strip my pride a second time.

"That prick hasn't seen rage yet," I hissed.

"Mellie," Joshua warned. "Think with your head and not your heart for a minute. Detective Pruett has had a lot more experience dealing with this kind of thing than we do. I think it would be wise to take his advice."

"I know that. But what am I supposed to do? Just walk away from my house, my life, my freedom because some dipshi—"

"Dipshitiot," Joshua smirked.

"Thank you. Some dipshitiot thinks he owns me again?"

"No, ma'am," Pruett chuckled. "I'm simply suggesting you two take a vacation. Go someplace tropical, sit on the beach, sip drinks with little umbrellas in them, and get the hell out of Phoenix until we arrest this joker."

"I have a business to run out of there," I railed, pointing toward my house.

"We'll be glad to escort you back inside so you can gather up whatever you need."

"How the hell am I supposed to fit my whole house into a couple of suitcases?" I hissed.

Strung out and on the verge of hysterics, I wanted to snag Joshua's gun and hunt Davis Walker down. Put a bullet in his head to end this surreal nightmare.

"I know it's not ideal," the detective commiserated.

"Fine. I'll do it," I snipped.

"Thank you, sweetheart," Joshua whispered. Pulling out a business card, he handed it to Pruett. "Here's my number if you need to reach us. As soon as she gets her things, we'll be heading back to Chicago tonight."

"Davis Walker's from Chicago. I don't think it's wise to take—"

"She'll be safe. Trust me. That prick won't get anywhere near her," Joshua informed him with stony reassurance. His brittle veneer softened as he turned toward me. "Go inside and get what you need. I've got a couple calls to make. I'll be in to help you shortly."

I nodded with a heavy sigh. As Pruett and two other officers followed me toward the house, I glanced over my shoulder.

"Ian, it's me. We're gonna need a lot more help," Joshua said, phone pressed to his ear.

As I stepped through the front door, I wondered what Ian did for a living and why Joshua was asking for his help. It would be nice if the dude was a hit man. That idea thrilled me entirely too much.

Tearing into the files in my office, I filled two briefcases with contracts and contacts. The entire time I fluctuated between rage and fear, unsure what I wanted to do most...scream or cry. Being forced from the comfort of my own home and having the safety it had always provided yanked out from under me. Giving up wasn't in my vocabulary, yet that's exactly what I was being forced to do.

With the waning sun spilling in through my bedroom windows, I stuffed my clothes into a couple of suitcases. Darting a glance at the three strange men monitoring me, I nixed the idea of snagging my vibrator. With a huff, I opened my panty drawer, then immediately recoiled in horror as a scream tore from my throat.

Ropes of thick, white come glazed my undergarments. My stomach rolled, and the room spun. The motherfucker had jacked off all over my panties. By the looks of his revolting calling card, I knew he'd done it recently.

"Mellie!" Joshua's cry echoed up the staircase. "Mellie. Dammit, where are you?"

Backing out of the room, shaking like a leaf, I gripped my arms against my chest. Violated and repulsed, I turned to run, but Joshua was there and clutched me to his chest. Panting from racing up the stairs and probably the surge of adrenaline from my scream, he hugged me tightly.

"He jacked-off on my panties," I explained with a quiver of disgust in my voice.

"Shouldn't your men be going door to door? Ask her neighbors if they saw something?" Joshua demanded.

"I don't need you telling me how to do my job, Mr. Lars. That's being done as we speak. It's procedure." Sucking in a deep breath, Pruett's tone softened. "Look, I want to nail this prick just as badly as you do. This fucker is pissing me off."

"You and me both. Look, I need you to escort Mellie downstairs and get her a drink or something while I finish loading her stuff in the car. She doesn't need to be here in case he's left anymore surprises." In true Dominant form, Joshua directed the detective in a tone implying negotiation was out of the question.

"I can do that." Pruett nodded.

"Thank you. I'll meet you both down there in a minute."

As he handed me off to Pruett, Joshua tucked the strap of my purse over my shoulder and assured me he'd be right down. I didn't want to leave him. He was my lifeline, my rock. Drowning in foreign emotions, I felt crushed and defeated. I didn't know how to fight the hammers that kept chiseling at my control. Panicked and needy contradicted every aspect I'd aligned in my life. There didn't seem to be a tourniquet big enough to stop the timid and indecisive blood gushing within me.

Pruett led me down the stairs and into the family room. Seated on the couch, I waited anxiously for Joshua to appear.

"Do you have any alcohol? Something to help settle your nerves?"

I wanted to laugh. Horse tranquilizers wouldn't be enough to calm my tattered nerves. Numbly, I pointed to the liquor cabinet on the far side of the room. There wasn't much to choose from, only had a bottle of citrus vodka and a bit of amaretto. Pruett carried the vodka to the kitchen, and I found myself alone for the first time since arriving home. The hairs on the back of my neck stood on end as an indescribable feeling of being watched filled me. Clutching my arms around me, I searched for any sign of the vaporous ghosts that had me on edge.

My cell phone chimed, and I jolted. The damn thing sounded like a gong in the stillness of the room. Digging the device from my purse, my hand trembled as I read the message.

Unknown: I'm coming to see you bunny, just as soon as you get those fucking pigs out of MY house. Do it now, or you'll be sorry.

My woman's intuition had been dead on. Davis *was* watching me. I set my phone on my lap and scanned the walnut bookshelves, looking for a camera or anything out of the ordinary. Nothing looked amiss. Unsure where he was watching me from, I realized it didn't matter. The prick had taunted me for the last time. His harassment superseded all fear and rekindled my anger. Squaring my shoulders, I raised my head, then lifted my fist and extended my middle finger.

"Fuck you, you son of a bitch. If you want me, come get me. I'm right here. Either shut up or man up, you fucking pussy."

"Mellie? What are you doing?" Joshua demanded from the doorway.

My phone chimed again, and I snatched it up to read the bastard's new message.

Unknown: That's going to cost you, cunt.

Immediately, it chimed again.

Unknown: Oh, good. Lover boy is there with you. Perfect. I think I'll let you keep him for a little while. I have plans for that prick.

Joshua snatched the phone from my hand. Reading the messages, he quickly put two and two together. Sliding my phone into his shirt pocket, he slowly turned as he glanced around the room. Cupping his hand, he taunted Davis with a motioned that said 'bring it.'

"Come on, coward. Let's see what you've got. When I'm through with you, cocksucker, you'll wish you'd never been born."

Anger surged off Joshua like flames. Pulling me up from the couch, he wrapped a protective arm around me and headed toward the door. Detective Pruett rounded the corner from the kitchen, his expression wrinkled in confusion.

"What about her drink?" he asked, striding up next to us.

Joshua grabbed the glass and hurled it across the room. As it shattered against the fireplace, glass, ice, and vodka rained down over the carpet.

"You either find that fucker, or I will," he snarled. "Get a team in here to sweep for bugs; her house is infested. Walker is listening to every word and watching every move we make."

"Fuck. Get her out of here," Pruett growled before storming toward the front door.

"Come on, baby. I've got your things in the car. Let's go," Joshua whispered.

My phone dinged once again, but he ignored it and led me out of the house and into the passenger seat of my car. Once behind the wheel, Joshua leaned over and fastened my seatbelt before flipping open my purse and grabbing my keys.

"Are you going to read what he sent?"

"No. All I want to do right now is get you someplace safe."

"Are we going back to Chicago?"

"Yes. But Davis isn't going to find you. Trust me," Joshua vowed as he turned the key in the ignition.

I placed my hand on his. "I do trust you. I know you'll keep me safe."

He softened, and a satisfied smile spread over his face.

"You bet your sexy ass I will."

He handed me back my phone. "Here, call Savannah. She's worried. Tell her we'll be home in a few days."

"Days?"

"We're driving to Chicago. Davis will be expecting us to fly. If we're lucky, Chicago PD will find him at the airport long before we leave the state. We're going home."

Home. The way he said the word filled me with warmth.

Staring at the blank screen of my cell phone, I didn't want to look at the unread message, but the conviction laced in Joshua's oath gave me strength and courage.

Unknown: That's right, fuck face. Bring her back home to ME. To a REAL man, you pansy assed prick.

"Joshua, Davis knows we're headed to Chicago."

"Good. Now call Savannah, little one. Let her know she doesn't need to worry anymore."

Joshua peeled out of the driveway and raced up the street as I dialed up Sanna. The Bluetooth engaged and her fragile 'hello' came through the car speakers. As soon as she heard my voice, she burst into tears, and Dylan ended up taking the phone from her.

"Mellie, don't worry. We'll take good care of Sanna. She's just scared and worried about you."

"So am I. But I know we're going to be fine. Please tell her not to worry, Dylan."

"I will. Tell Joshua we've been in touch with Ian, and we're getting things squared away on this end."

"I'm right here on speaker phone," Joshua confirmed. "Thanks, I appreciate it."

"What do you mean?" I asked, utterly confused.

"I'll explain later," Joshua replied cryptically.

"No problem. Hey, Mellie, just stick close to him. He knows what he's doing."

I darted a look at the man sitting next to me. His expression was resolute. Glancing over at me, he smiled and nodded. "Damn straight, I do."

"Great. Be careful," Dylan warned. "We'll see you when you get here."

"Mel," Sanna cried. "I'll see you soon, right?"

What if I never got to see my baby sister again? The desperation in her voice was the last straw. My walls of bravery and resolve crumbled as reality and panic stormed through me and I burst into tears. Joshua gripped my hand, unable to hide the shock of seeing me fall completely apart.

"I'll see you soon, baby," I sobbed.

"Savannah, I'm bringing her back to you safe and sound. I promise," Joshua guaranteed with both conviction and compassion.

"Thank you, Sir. I love you, Mel," Sanna wailed.

"I love you too, baby." My voice cracked as tears spilled down my cheeks.

Joshua disconnected the call and pulled off the highway onto an exit ramp. Shoving the car in park, he pulled me into his arms and held me as I sobbed.

"That's it, baby. Let it all out. I'm so proud of how strong and brave you've been through all this shit. But, sweetheart, you don't have to be anymore. I've got you, and I'm not letting go."

Yes, he had me…all of me, from the tough and mouthy to the damaged and fragile, and everything in between. I trusted him with the pieces of my soul because he'd already proven he'd hold them like a priceless treasure, right in the palm of his hand. For the first time in my life, I wasn't afraid to share them, regardless of what the future had in store.

Bolstered by his unyielding compassion, I pulled myself together enough for us to get back on the road. Staring out the window, the sound of my sister's fear resonated in my head. I'd wasted too many years neglecting her, and after all that had transpired back at my house, I knew I'd never feel completely safe there again. I was ready to move to Chicago and find a place to call 'home'.

Turning my attention to Joshua's conversation with Pruett, I listened as he informed the detective we were driving back to Chicago, not flying. In charge and in command, Joshua suggested Pruett send some plain clothed officers at the airport. Davis knew our plan to head home. Hopefully, he assumed we'd fly back to Chicago. With my hand clenched in my lap, I nervously worried one thumb over the other as I listened to their conversation. Joshua threaded his fingers through mine before bringing my hand to his lips for a tender kiss.

"We were able to get an image off Melinda's neighbor's security system. I'm having it downloaded as we speak. I'll send it via e-mail as soon as it's done. We need a positive ID on this guy to speed things along. We captured a clear image of his face for a couple of seconds. I'm going to have our IT gurus blow up some still shots for you."

"We'll keep checking our phones. Thanks," Joshua replied.

"Stay in touch with me while you're on the road, okay?"

"Will do." Joshua ended the call, then frowned.

"What's wrong?"

"Pruett just told us to keep in touch while we were on the road. I hope to hell he wasn't inside your house when he said that. Kerr will know we're not flying."

"Surely, he's not that stupid, is he?"

"Let's hope not."

My stomach swirled in a churning mixture of anxiety and fear, while my brain spooled in a constant cycle of anger and fear.

Out of the corner of my eye, I saw Joshua glance my way. "I can feel the thoughts swirling in your pretty, little head. Talk to me, sweetheart."

A humorless chuckle rolled off my lips. "I don't even know where to start. Anger and fear don't mix well, so excuse me if I'm not singing songs about rainbows and butterflies."

"Spitting sarcasm isn't going to help either," Joshua smirked.

"I don't mean to be snarky. I'm just being honest."

"I do appreciate that." He grinned. "Even though your plate is full, I won't allow it to erase the lines between us."

His message was loud and clear. Joshua expected me to stay a proper submissive when my whole fucking life was coming apart at the seams. Even Penn & Teller couldn't pull that one off.

My phone chimed, alerting us of a message. Joshua glanced over as his jaw ticked in anger.

"You don't have to read any more of his fucking threats, little one."

"I know." I didn't. I didn't want to see what scathing shit Davis spewed, but I wasn't going to let him dictate another fraction of my life. Leaning over, I dug the phone from my purse and slid the device open.

Unknown: So, you and lover boy decided to drive home. Perfect. Wanna bet I can figure out what route you're taking? Watch out, bunny. You never know where I might show up, maybe even in your hotel room along the way. Don't worry. I'll let lover boy watch me fuck you before I slit his throat and yours.

Trembling, I turned off the phone and shoved it back in my purse.

"Baby, you've turned deathly white."

"If Davis gets his way, it'll be my permanent color."

"Did he physically threaten you?"

"Both of us. He wants to kill both of us now." I closed my eyes. "Oh, and Pruett must have been inside the house when you talked to him, because Davis has figured out we're driving back to Chicago."

"That stupid son of a bitch," Joshua cursed as he punched the phone icon on the dashboard, syncing up his own Bluetooth. The first call he made was to Mika. Joshua didn't bother asking, he demanded the dungeon owner contact someone named Landes and have a restraining order drawn up on my behalf.

"You got it," Mika inhaled deep. "Between Nick, Dylan, and Ian, my damn phone's been ringing off the hook. You two get your asses back here safely. We'll handle the rest."

Before I could ask about the plans everyone seemed to know about, except me, Joshua called Ian. He informed his ménage buddy that Davis "just took a massive shit in his kennel."

"That's actually a good thing," Ian chuckled. It chaffed that he found humor in the whole craptastic mess. "Did he threaten to kill you two in a public place?"

"No," I replied. "He suggested he *might* be waiting for us at a hotel along the way so he could slit our throats."

Joshua issued a low growl.

"Dammit. The prick's smart. If he continues with the threats, try to see if you can get him to admit he'd like to kill you and everyone around you, like at a mall or a beauty salon—somewhere public. I'm not saying bait him, just lead him if you can."

"What good will that do?" Joshua asked, clearly irritated.

"That makes him a terrorist, man," Ian answered with glee. "He'll find himself in a federal shit storm. With enough charges, he could spend a lot of years behind bars."

"I don't want her encouraging him. Not. At. All," Joshua stated emphatically.

"You need to lighten up, man," Ian warned. "You know damn good and well we're going to keep her hidden away nice and safe."

"I know that. But I won't use her as bait. Not for you or anyone else."

"Okay, just forget I mentioned it. We don't have to go that route," Ian tried to soothe Joshua, but anger continued to roll off his body.

I placed my hand on his thigh in hopes it might relax him. It took several long seconds before I felt some of the tension leave his muscles.

"Who all is going to be there?" Joshua asked.

"Me, of course, and a couple guys from my team. Drake has arranged for Trev to stay with Mika and Julianna. I guess Savannah came unglued and topped all over the place, refusing to stay behind. So, she'll be there, too with Dylan and Nick—wearing a nice red ass, I'm sure," Ian chuckled.

"Coming where?" I asked.

"To the cabin," Ian replied.

"What cabin?"

"Ahh, I haven't had a chance to talk to her about that yet, bro," Joshua sighed.

"Oh, my bad. Sorry, man."

"No problem, I'll get to it soon." Joshua glanced my way with half a smirk.

"What else are you keeping from me?" I demanded in a sharp, accusatory tone.

"Well, well. Look at the time," Ian snorted. "I'll let you two work this out. I gotta run. Talk to you later. Bye."

Joshua hung up and shook his head. "Pussy." He chuckled.

"Well?" I asked impatiently.

Joshua laughed even harder. "That's the wrong way to start this conversation, little one. Would you like to start again?" He lifted his brows in an egotistical arch as he tore his eyes off the road for a split second.

"Can't we just be two regular people and have a normal conversation?"

"I'm not a two-sided coin, little one. What you see is what you get. With everything that's happened, I'm sure it's easier for you to wear your tough-girl armor. I get that. But it's my job to keep you in your place."

I hung my head and scrubbed my hands over my face. It was easier for me to confront things head on when presented with a challenge. Yes, I'd given the man my trust and submission; it filled me with a sense of completeness, but Joshua wanted me to mesh both the fragile and the strong? It couldn't be done. They were two totally separate entities within me.

I sucked in a calming breath and pulled out the submissive inside. "Would you please tell me about the cabin, Master Stephen?" I asked, trying oh so hard not to grit my teeth.

His chest expanded, and a warm smile tugged his lips. "I'd love to, little one, after we get some food."

Joshua signaled, taking the exit ramp, and pulled into a truck stop. Seated at a booth, I asked him again about the cabin.

"We'll talk about it in the car, Mellie." He smiled.

I opened my mouth to speak then snapped it shut. Tossing my head back, I stared at the ceiling and counted to ten. In my peripheral vision, Joshua smiled and studied the menu.

And the lesson for today, ladies and gentlemen, is...patience.

He had me so furious I wanted to scream. And I still hadn't figured out a way to pilot my own destiny while kneeling at his feet.

What are you whining about? You can have both, you're just too scared. Scared to let go of that stranglehold you have on your pride. What more does the man have to do to prove he's not going to let you down? Okay, so he's thumped his chest a few times. He even got a little snippy once, but you asked for it. How many times have you lost control? The scales are tipped, but not in your favor. He wants to help you, not only with your submission, but also save your life. Look at him sitting there. None of the fuck-buddies you've had would go out of their way to keep you alive like Joshua. If you trust him to save your life, for shit's sake, trust him to save your heart. Or are you nothing but a coward?

Tuning out the annoying voice in my head—the same one that had done a complete one-eighty since I met Joshua—I closed my eyes. Too exhausted and confused to sort it out, I simply wanted peace of mind for five damn minutes.

"Is there a winner of that war going on inside your gorgeous head, Mellie?"

Stop lying to him. But more importantly, stop lying to yourself.

"Yes, Sir. You are." Gazing into his eyes, I found that peace of mind, and I welcomed his penetrating stare without reservation.

"Hmmm," he murmured. "'Bout damn time. I like it. I like it a lot."

"Me, too…I think," I whispered.

Joshua cleared his throat. "Good. I'm glad we're on the same page. Now to answer your questions, Ian has a cabin an hour or so from Chicago. I've gone there with him several times. It's surrounded by six acres of woods and secluded."

"You've gone with him alone?" The question popped out of my mouth before I had a chance to bite it back. I had no right to ask, but the little green-eyed monster within wanted to know.

"Most of the time, he and I went to get away from the city, to hunt and fish and sometimes we brought along a sub to share," he replied directly.

"And exactly why are we going there now?"

"Because it's away from Chicago, and like I said, very secluded. It's where we intend to hide you until this shit with Walker is over."

"But why the entourage? I mean, why are Sanna, Dylan, Nick, Ian, and everyone coming, too?"

"Because they're our friends, our family. They want to be there to help make sure nothing happens to you, or me."

"How long are you planning on keeping me there?" I frowned. My question sounded accusatory. "That came out wrong. You know what I mean."

"As long as it takes. Until Davis is arrested," he replied resolutely.

"But all those people have jobs. Dylan and Nick can't be away from their company for an indefinite amount of time, and I'm dying to know what Ian does for a living, but they're not going to be able to stay forever, and neither are we."

"Well, unfortunately until Davis is caught, you're going to have to turn down any jobs that require you to travel."

"I can't do that," I gasped.

Joshua raised his hands. "Think about it for a minute before you lose your cool. Okay?"

Dammit, why did he have to use that calm, soothing tone? Why did he always have to stay in such irritating control all the time? *'I'm not a two-sided coin, little one. What you see is what you get.'* His words echoed in my brain. That was why.

"Yes, I understand. It wouldn't be safe for me to go prancing all over the world with some deranged dipshitiot after me."

Joshua laughed. "Exactly. But getting back to your original question, Dylan and Nick can work from the cabin, and if they have to go back to Chicago, then they'll go. No one is being forced to stay at the cabin, Mellie, not even you. But they're there because they want to be. They want to keep you safe."

After taking a drink of water, he continued. "As for your curiosity about Ian, he used to be a cop, but now he does private investigations and bodyguards a few musicians, actors, and an occasional political candidate or two."

"Seriously?" I blinked. "He looks like a banker or a stockbroker."

Joshua laughed. "His unassuming guise is what makes him so successful. But don't let him fool you. He can take a man three times his size down in seconds. Let's just say you definitely want Ian on your side."

"So, we're all just going to hang out at the cabin until Davis is arrested? That's the plan?"

"Yes, unless you have a better one?"

"No." I frowned. "It just seems way over the top. I mean, I know he threatened to kill us, but don't you think this is all a bit...excessive?"

Joshua sobered. "We've only known each other a short time, Mellie, but you mean a whole lot to me. I don't want to lose another woman who's touched my heart."

His confession would normally have sent me zinging out the door like a supersonic jet, but there was no way to deny it; he'd touched my heart, too.

I heard my sister's voice in my head. *"It's okay to let someone in.*

It's okay to take a chance, because it's so worth it. I could keel over and die tomorrow, but I'd go happy. I have these two incredible, wonderful men in my life who fill me full of all the things I'd been missing. The joy outweighs the risk by so much, it's incomprehensible."

The joy, completeness, and unconditional acceptance I'd found with Joshua in the short time I'd known him brought new meaning to Sanna's words. I didn't know what the crazy connection we shared meant, but it meant something. Maybe not love, but definitely something.

"You mean a lot to me too, Joshua."

A contented smile settled over his face. "Look, I know things are a mess right now, but later when it's all straightened out, do you think you might ever consider moving to Chicago?"

"To Chicago, or in with you?" I asked, watching his expression closely.

"To Chicago, first. The rest, we'll take one day at a time and see what happens," he clarified with a slight smile.

Four weeks ago, I would have responded adamantly, *'No'*. Although I was swimming in uncharted waters, Joshua suddenly didn't seem an imposing shark—at least not at the moment. It was flattering, and a wee bit scary, he'd given conscious thought to a relationship with me. Sanna was dying for me to be closer to her. If I lived in the same city, we wouldn't miss out on so much of each other's lives. Besides, if I lived closer, maybe I could make up for running away from her like I did.

"Yes, I've thought about it a time or two. Sanna wants me to move. She's made that crystal clear. After my last visit, I realize how much time I stole from the two of us."

"Don't. Don't live with regrets." He shook his head. "Learn the lessons life has to teach and do your best to move on."

"Is that what you've done? After Veronica and Camille were taken from you?"

Joshua's expression turned stony. I'd never brought up his wife or daughter before. I wasn't sure if he was going to shut me out or open up. Honesty and communication had to be a two-way street if he wanted me to consider pulling up roots and moving to Chicago.

Joshua didn't answer my question. He simply looked down at our empty plates, plucked up the check, then pulled out his wallet. Tossing some money on the table, he stood and extended his hand.

"We'll talk in the car."

Back on the road, he wrapped his hand in mine. The air felt heavy, and I swallowed tightly, worried I'd touched on a topic too painful for him to discuss.

"Veronica and I were high school sweethearts. She was an amazing woman, wife, sub, and mother. Aside from my parents, there wasn't another person on the planet who encouraged me to follow my dreams the way she did. I won't lie and say we had a perfect marriage—there is no such thing. Everyone has their ups and downs, but our ups surpassed our downs ninety percent of the time."

I sat quietly, strumming my thumb over his and listening as he opened up about his past.

"We never formally joined any lifestyle groups. Hell, I didn't even know Genesis existed until after she was gone, but we invented our own power exchange, I guess you could say. Our desires were polar opposite. She was a natural born sub, and me?" He shrugged. "A Dom. I haven't let anyone touch me below the surface since she died, until you."

Staring out at the road, lost in memories, he fell silent for several long seconds.

"Surviving isn't easy, but I can't wrap my head around how you cope and survive after losing little Camille."

Joshua swallowed tightly. I swore tears welled in his eyes. "I'm sorry, Mellie. I'm not ready to talk about her yet. I don't know that I'll ever be."

I trailed my fingers over the side of his face. "You don't have to. It's okay."

Blinking rapidly, he cleared his throat.

"I owe you an explanation for what happened that night in my room at the club. The night I lost my mind and my control," he scoffed softly. "When you brought out the amazing submissive inside you and begged to please me...begged me to use you hard?"

"Yes," I whispered.

"I haven't had a submissive draw out my Dominance in such a profound way since Veronica died." Silently, I drew his hand to my lips and placed a soft kiss upon the back of it. "I'm so fucking sorry I lost it that night and hurt you. I could sit here and make excuses for my behavior till the sun comes up, but I'm not going to do that to you, or to us. I've thought a lot about that night. I realized I hadn't totally come to terms with losing my wife and daughter, or that level of Dominance."

"I did it on purpose," I softly confessed. He darted a glance at me with a quizzical expression. "I didn't want you holding back on me. I wanted all of you and your Dominance. That's why I begged so hard, and it was beautiful. You were beautiful."

"Thank you for telling me that, little one. It helps ease my guilt." He gave my hand a squeeze before he continued. "I hadn't realized that I'd not dealt with the past until it came up and grabbed me by the throat. You took me out at the knees, totally blindsided me, Mellie. The flashback was brutal. I tried so hard to shove all those feelings back in place." He darted a bittersweet smile my way. "I never expected to feel whole again."

"You feel guilty that you couldn't save them, don't you?"

"I did." He nodded. "But not anymore. Veronica wouldn't want me putting a tourniquet on my heart or my Dominance. She'd want me keep living my life to the fullest. I want that, too, with you. Want all of it with you. Not just a few days. Not a week here or there. I want to be the Dominant part of your life—in every sense of the word."

Gripped by his profound declaration, no tendrils of fear or sinister panic assaulted. Before I could second-guess my timing, I turned toward Joshua and inhaled a steady breath.

"I've decided to move to Chicago."

Snapping his head my direction, he blinked. "Just like that?"

I giggled. "Yes. I'm either a fool or I've lost my mind, but yes. I've tried to convince myself this connection we share won't last. I still don't know if it will, but when I was in England, all I could think about was coming back to you. I couldn't erase you from my mind. It was even hard for me to totally focus on work. It's never been like that before. I'm tired of fighting this crazy wire that runs between us."

This time he was the one who drew my hand to *his* lips.

"So, would it freak you out completely if I told you I've fallen pretty hard for you?"

My heart literally skipped a beat. "I-I. Yes. Yes, it would."

"Fair enough. I'll save that for a later conversation." He shrugged with a wolfish grin.

"Good idea," I mumbled, swallowing tightly.

Several silent minutes passed as Joshua's claim swirled through my head like a tornado. I cared for him deeply, but was it love? I'd never been in love with someone before. Infatuated, yes. But it usually wore off in a few days. Weeks had passed, and it still hadn't worn off with Joshua. Time would tell.

Reaching Albuquerque a little past midnight, Joshua pulled into a resort. When we checked in, he requested the penthouse suite. Too exhausted to squabble over his extravagant choice, I remained quiet. I wasn't going to argue if he wanted to pamper me.

After ordering champagne and strawberries from room service, Joshua filled the massive spa tub. Slowly stripping me bare, he kissed my shoulders, neck, and breasts before clutching me to his hard body and claiming my mouth. His forceful control made my head swim and my heart soar. Mentally and physically wiped out, I held onto him, grateful he'd been the one by my side through the most craptastic and magnificent day of my life. While I had no desire to re-live the terror Davis Walker orchestrated, I'd take Joshua opening up and sharing pieces of his heart with me any day.

Joshua led me to the tub. After easing down into the swirling hot water, I watched him unbutton his shirt and peel it off. Dropping my gaze, I stared at his taut, lean muscles, the wiry blond hair between his flat brown nipples, and his washboard abs. My mind filled with memories of the perfection I had found beneath his powerful body. It was as if I'd waited a lifetime for the man, and in many ways I had.

"Please," I whispered boldly.

"What is it you want?"

"To touch you," I murmured as he knelt by the side of the tub.

A broad smile adorned his face. "Is that all you want?"

"For starters," I purred as I raked my nails through the hair on his chest before flattening my palm against his hot flesh.

Leaning in, I rested my head on his shoulder before pressing my lips to his skin. I licked at his salty flesh as I skimmed a hand up to cup his nape.

"Get in with me," I murmured.

His body shook softly in a silent chuckle. "Giving orders, are we?"

"No, Sir. I—"

"I'm teasing you, girl. I'm waiting on room service. They should be here any minute."

"Call them back, tell them to either hurry up or forget it," I replied with a playful pout.

"Didn't I teach you a lesson about patience at dinner?"

"Yes, but three weeks without you felt like three years."

There was a loud knock on the door.

"I'll be right back." Joshua grinned.

Moments later, he returned carrying a tray of plump ripe strawberries and a bottle of champagne chilling in a shimmering silver clawed bucket. I smiled as I watched him pop the cork, pour two glasses then set the plate of strawberries on the ledge at the back of the tub.

Sliding the leather belt from its buckle, Joshua toed off his shoes and socks then released his zipper. His hard and ready cock sprang free. *Finally, the wait was almost over.*

Hurry. Hurry.

Picking up his champagne in one hand, he fisted his thick erection with the other, edging closer to the side of the tub. As he stepped in, I eased back to give him room. Instead of joining me, he stepped in, then sat on the edge. Eye-level with his turgid cock, I licked my lips, antsy and impatient for his command.

Lowering the glass to my lips, he smiled. "Take a big sip but don't swallow. Hold it to the back of your throat."

Filling my mouth with the fizzing liquid, I tilted my head back as he instructed and parted my lips.

"Good girl."

A spark of satisfaction burned in my core as he circled his slick crest around my lips. Gazing into my eyes, he pressed inside my mouth. The cold bubbles tickled my tongue, and as I swirled it around his hot, throbbing flesh, Joshua let out a hiss of pleasure.

Setting the glass aside, he wrapped his fingers in my hair and clenched. The sting from my scalp raced down my spine, gathering over my clit.

Guiding my mouth up and down, I slid my tongue over the sensitive spot beneath the crest. He sucked in a gasp, issued a hoarse curse, and kept right on pushing my head up and down over his velvety steel. Pleasure played across his face and filled me with satisfaction that I could bring him such exquisite sensations. Filling my mouth over and again with both champagne and his cock, I basked in his guttural noises and rumbles of pleasure, but best of all were his raspy praises.

Sliding into the tub alongside me, he plucked a ripe strawberry from the tray beside the tub. Pinching off the stem, he tapped the tapered end to my lips. When I opened my mouth, he placed the fruit between my teeth then dipped his head, biting into it as he pressed his lips over mine. Tart, sweet juice exploded over my tongue as we feasted on the berry, sucking and slurping before he eased his body over mine. Surging inside me with a savage thrust, he skimmed his hands over my wet flesh, pinching and plucking my nipples as he swallowed my cries of pleasure. In an achingly slow rhythm, he thrust deep and dragged out, stretching me tight and full. A blissful burn spread over my swollen lips. It was the sweetest agony in the world.

"I missed you. Missed the way my body responds to you like this. Missed the feel of your touch, your scent, and the way you always scorch me to the bone," I gasped, freely conveying all the feelings within.

"Yes," he hissed. Arching his hips, he ground his crest over my g-spot. "Beg me to use you again, little one."

Staring at me expectantly, he wanted me to summon the beast. I searched for some glimmer of guarantee it wouldn't turn out like before, that his demons wouldn't resurface and drive a wedge between us again. After the rollercoaster events of the past twenty-four hours, I didn't think I'd be able to handle the magnitude he sought me to stir.

"Joshua…"

"It's okay, baby. I have to prove to you it'll be all right. Tell me, girl, do you want to please me?" He winked.

I stroked his face and slowly shook my head. "No," I murmured. His expression fell, dejected and lined with regret; I'd disarmed him with my reply. Drawing my thumb over his soft lips, I gazed at him, penetrating past his gloom. "I *need* to please you, Master. Take me wildly. Don't hold back. I ache to bring you joy."

His brows furrowed and his eyes narrowed as his nostrils flared. Yes, I'd poked the sleeping lion inside. Arching my hips to meet his, I urged him to unleash the beast and set it free.

"Again, little one," he demanded in a raspy, hungry whisper.

"Take me. Mark me. Own me, Master. Please," I purred.

An animalistic groan rumbled from deep in his chest. Joshua gripped my hips and hammered into my gripping cunt in an unrelenting frenzy. Water splashed between us, sloshing up and over the tub. Bending his head, Joshua sank his teeth into the tops of my breasts, biting and gnawing, marking me. Angry red welts dotted my alabaster flesh as he slammed into me, savage and untamed. My surrender soared, spellbound by his driving command.

"Who do you belong to?" he demanded.

"You, Master. I'm yours. All yours," I panted, bucking against his driving shaft.

His chest expanded, and a wild cry tore from his lips. Yanking me off his cock, Joshua jerked me out of the tub and hauled me to the sink. Dripping wet, he bent me over the vanity as he gripped my hair and pulled my head back in front of the mirror.

"Look at yourself, Mellie," he ordered as he spread my ass cheeks apart and slammed inside my cunt, claiming both my reflection and me. "Look how fucking gorgeous you are."

I slid a gaze over my lurching body, my breasts swaying with each driving thrust. My hard, cranberry-colored nipples were drawn up, wrinkled and hard. The outline of his teeth had branded into bright red welts and my face glowed in a flushed red hue. Staring into my eyes, I peered past the hunger and lust, catching sight of the woman who yearned for freedom, within. She looked stunning, peaceful, and serene.

"You can finally see her, can't you? Look at that striking submissive you had trapped inside you. She's mine now. All mine, isn't she, little one?"

"Yes," I moaned.

"Yes," he echoed. Scraping his teeth along my shoulder, he swiped his tongue up the column of my neck. Wrapping his lips around my ear lobe, he tugged and nipped. "I'm dying to claim all of her. Her joys, sorrows, and fears. Her triumphs and failures. Is that what you want me to do, girl?"

"Yes, Master. Yes."

Joshua hissed as he skimmed a palm between my shoulder blades, pressing me down upon the cool marble. Held hostage to his gaze in the mirror, he withdrew from inside me, keeping the crown of his cock nestled between my burning folds. His eyes narrowed, and his jaw ticked.

"You. Are. Mine. All of you. Mind. Body. Heart. Soul. Everything you are. Everything you'll ever be. Is. Mine." Snarling through clenched teeth, Joshua emphasized each vow with an arduous thrust.

Tears spilled from my eyes. My soul felt like it was disintegrating while yet morphing into someone or something else, tranquil and restored.

"Yours," I affirmed with a cry.

Sliding his finger to my pussy, Joshua strummed my throbbing clit, unraveling the thread of control I'd been clinging to. Clenching around his demanding thrusts, I tried to hold tight as the arcs of release spread through my limbs and up my spine.

Slamming himself to the hilt, Joshua stilled, seated inside me. I felt his cock jerk as he groaned out a command for me to 'come'.

A scream of deliverance ripped from my throat, fused with his, and echoed in my ears as I shattered. Leaning over me, Joshua sank his teeth into my shoulder, pinning me to the marble surface as he spilled inside my spasming core.

My legs felt like wet noodles, and I gripped the countertop for support while Joshua dried my shivering body. His reverent touch—a total dichotomy of the beastly way he'd claimed me—warmed my heart and moved me deeply.

"You're utterly amazing, little one," he praised as he wrapped a dry towel around me. "I didn't hurt you, did I?"

"No, Master. It was perfect," I whispered on a dreamy sigh.

Approval and pride lit his face as a smile played over his lips.

Drying himself off, we made our way through the sitting room and into the bedroom. Staring at the inviting bed, I all but drooled. Spent and ready for sleep, I dropped the towel and started to pull back the covers.

"Stop," Joshua issued in a firm command. "Kneel."

Dropping the fabric, I frowned and turned to stare at him. Joshua cocked his head and shot me a look warning it wouldn't be wise to challenge him. With a wistful glance at the bed, I knelt at his feet, lowering my head and eyes to the floor. Waiting several long seconds, Joshua finally sat on the edge of the bed.

"Look at me."

Raising my chin, I slid a gaze over his naked body before linking with his beautiful eyes. Power, satisfaction, and passion reflected there. A tiny smile tugged at my lips.

"We have some unfinished business to discuss, little one."

Still riding the lingering sparks of bliss, my brain couldn't find the path he was on. Drawing a blank, I issued a slight shake of my head and gently shrugged my shoulder.

"What were the last words you said to me on the phone in the UK?"

Chapter Eleven

S hit. He wanted to discuss that now? After the mind-blowing exchange we just had? Why did he want to rehash my ugly behavior now? Couldn't he wait and make me grovel in the morning?

Joshua chuckled. "You're as easy to read as a novel, sweet girl. Yes. We're going to discuss this now, then you can sleep."

I squared my shoulders and nodded. "I meant it when I told you before that I was sorry for being so rude and hanging up on you. I don't know what more I can say other than I'll never do it again."

"No, you won't, because I won't tolerate it." His even tone didn't hold a drop of anger or disappointment. "I denied your orgasm for a reason, but you chose not to accept it. Instead, you slammed up your walls and pushed me away, refusing to accept my Dominance."

"I know. I'm sorry, Sir."

"You now owe me two punishments, little one."

"Two?" I blinked. "So, you're not going to accept my apology?"

"Oh no, I accept your apology wholeheartedly. The problem I have is you didn't communicate with me—well, that and calling me a son of a bitch and hanging up on me. I didn't like that very much, either."

"I suppose asking for a postponement of my sentence to get some sleep is out of the question?"

"Absolutely." He smirked then patted his lap. "Climb up here and lay across my lap. Let's get this over with, so we can put this behind us and get some sleep."

Joshua's laid-back tone confused me. It lacked a level of disappointment and felt weirdly passive. Where was the anger...the censure? Punishment was supposed to come with a heavy dose of guilt, a need to make amends for displeasing the Dom. The way Joshua presented it felt almost as undeserving as the spankings I took at Genesis.

When I didn't move, Joshua silently shifted on the bed, watching me closely.

"Do you need to hear that I'm not pleased with you? That I'm annoyed by your lack of respect and I am disappointed in you?" Using that damn potent Dom voice, dripping with scorn, he narrowed his eyes.

Bingo. Yes, it was exactly what I needed, because almost instantly a black, oily sludge raced through my veins. Contrite and suffused in rejection, I rose from the floor and positioned myself over his knees.

"I'm sorry, Master," I whispered heartily as I glanced at him over my shoulder.

Joshua leaned over and kissed my cheek. "I know you are because you're willing to prove it to me, little one."

Straightening, he drew his hand into the air. I dropped my head. Clenching my eyes and squeezing my butt cheeks together, I waited for the pain.

He landed his hand with a stinging slap.

"Ouch," I groused. "That hurts."

Joshua chuckled. "Yes, it's supposed to. That's why it's called punishment."

"How many of these do I have to take?" I hissed.

"As many as I think you need. Stop complaining and count for me, girl."

Turning up the volume on his Dominant edict, a shiver rippled through me as he slapped my ass again, harder.

"Two," I yelped.

"No, that's one, sweetheart."

"But you already—"

"I can start from the beginning again if that's what you'd like?"

"One," I shouted.

Somewhere between swat fourteen or fifteen, I'd sailed away. The whispers passing over my lips ceased to be numbers. Instead, they'd faded into moans and whimpers. With Joshua's muscular arm banded around my waist and a decadent fire melting through my tissue, I lost myself in a buoyant void of peace.

I realized the spankings had stopped, replaced by the gentle caress of his hand over my blazing backside. I didn't know how long he'd held me before moving me onto the mattress; time had lost all meaning. Cold sheets fluttered over my skin, followed by his long, lean body pressed against my chest. I felt the reverberation of his voice as he threaded his fingers through my hair, but couldn't link meaning to his words. The synapses in my brain were fried. But I felt the approval in his tone, and that filled my heart with joy as the darkness carried me away.

The feel of waking in his arms the next morning was perfection, and a soft smile curled my lips as I snuggled closer. With my ear pressed to his chest, I listened to the strong, steady rhythm of his heartbeat and for a few blissful minutes, I forgot all about Davis, his threats, and our friends waiting at the cabin.

The sound of Joshua's cell phone ringing from far away in the suite broke my bliss. Remembering we'd abandoned our clothes in the bathroom the night before, I shifted to go get it, but Joshua cinched me tighter, refusing to let me move.

"Let it go. If it's important, they'll call back," he murmured. His eyes stayed closed and his face lax, as it had been in sleep.

"Mmm," I purred. "Marvelous idea."

Peeking up at him, he opened one eye and smiled. "I could get used to this."

"So could I."

"Oh really?" he asked as both eyes popped open in surprise. "What happened to the monoga-phobic woman I knew a few short weeks ago?"

"*You* happened to her."

"Works every time," he smirked.

"Ah," I gasped, mocking insult. "So, that makes me what? Another notch in your bedpost? Another nameless, faceless woman used to stroke your ego?"

"It's not my ego I like you stroking, little one. And you're certainly not a notch in my bedpost. You're mine, and I'm keeping you. Deal with it," he replied with a mock scowl.

"Hmmm," I pouted. "You make me feel like I'm a stray dog you want to take home."

"No, I'm not into puppy play, little one. Are you?"

"No! I like the way you make me pant, but I refuse to bark."

"I'll not make you bark, but I sure had you howling last night when I spanked your ass," he laughed. "Speaking of which, how's it feeling this morning? Sore?"

"I haven't rolled over yet. I'm afraid to."

A mischievous smile curled on his lips before he repositioned himself, tugging me beneath him. The warm sheet chaffed my tender tissue, but when he settled his powerful body over mine and his thick cock nudged my pussy, the discomfort vanished.

"How about now?" he whispered as he dipped his head and kissed my neck.

"Now works for me," I purred, spreading my legs open.

Joshua laughed, nipping his teeth upon my pulse point. "Minx. I was talking about your ass."

"You can have that whenever you want it, too, Master," I moaned.

Sliding my lips over his chest, I left a trail of soft kisses as I cupped his ass and ground my tingling pussy against his cock. Wedging a knee between my legs, Joshua spread me open farther before gripping his cock and aligning it against my opening. Just as he lifted his hips to slide inside me, his phone rang again.

"Fuck. Don't move," he muttered as he climbed off me and sprinted toward the bathroom.

Seconds later, he swaggered back in, phone pressed to his ear, and his hard erection all but begging for my lips. Even though he told me not to move, I couldn't resist toying with him. Sliding from the bed, I dropped to my knees, flashed him a devilish grin and opened my mouth.

Joshua narrowed his eyes and shot me an angry glare. Fisting his cock, he stepped in front of me, inching closer and closer to my waiting lips. As I leaned forward to gobble him up, he swayed back and shook his head. Dammit, he was going to make me sit and suffer, and wait for permission. I issued an inward growl.

"That's no problem. Send it to me, and I'll have her take a look."

I didn't know whom he was talking to, and at that particular moment, I didn't care. Rocking side to side on my knees, massaging my clit between my weeping folds, I stared at the clear bead of pre-come growing on his cock. Parting my lips, I slid my tongue over my bottom lip with a seductive tease.

"Sure, of course. I'll call you back with an answer."

His voice remained calm, but the sinful expression lining his face spoke volumes. Joshua's self-restraint was cracking beneath my brazen enticement. Drawing his lips together in a tight, angry line, he slapped his cock against my lips, sending the bead of pre-come landing on the tip of my nose. With an impish grin, I gathered it up with my finger and slid it over my tongue. Moaning softly, I closed my eyes and savored the taste.

"You too. I'll be in touch soon."

He didn't even say goodbye. Joshua simply ended the call, tossed his phone to the bed, then crossed his arms. He glared down at me, his nostrils flaring. "I have a belt, and I'm itching to use it on you, girl."

"I'm sorry, Sir, I couldn't help myself. You came back in the room all nice and hard and looking so damn sexy. I caved. A girl can only take so much temptation." I bit my lips together to stifle a grin.

"So, this is how it's going to be? You, constantly topping from the bottom, and trying to usurp my authority every chance you get?"

There it was, that harsh tone of disapproval. The smile fell from my face as I shook my head. "No, Sir. I was just having fun. I didn't mean to upset you."

"I'm not upset. I'm disappointed. Your spirit is unique, Mellie, and I never want you to lose it, but I specifically told you not to move.

We're not going to get very far if you insist on challenging me every step of the way, girl."

"I know, Sir. I'm sorry."

Inundated with remorse, I issued a heavy sigh. Joshua reached down and cupped my chin. Tilting my head back, he stared into my eyes as he brushed his thumb over my lips. A ghost of a smile tugged his lips, and his expression softened.

"You're not to beat yourself up over this, sweetheart. I'm simply setting ground rules, but I think I just found the key to unlock that gorgeous submissive inside you."

I couldn't help but notice the gleam of delight dancing in his eyes. Still, it didn't erase the guilt lingering within or the worry of repercussions to come.

"That was Pruett on the phone. He's sent over the surveillance footage from your neighbor. He wants you to look at it and ID Walker. Come on, hop up on the bed."

"Okay," I replied softly.

Helping me off the floor, Joshua snatched up his phone then sat next to me on the bed as he opened up the mail program. Staring at the screen, we watched a tall heavy-set man in dark clothing, sunglasses, and a baseball cap exit a black sedan. Giving a conspiratorial glance over his shoulder, the camera caught a surprisingly clear view of his face.

"What the…" I whispered. "That's not Davis."

"No. It's not. Who is he, Mellie?"

"I don't know. I've never seen that guy before in my life. Can you go back and pause or something?"

"Sure." Joshua rewound the video, stopping the feed and enlarging the image.

Staring at the man's round, fat cheeks and a bulbous nose, I shook my head. He looked nothing at all like Davis Walker. "I don't know who that man is. Why is he stalking me?"

"You're sure? He's not a disgruntled client or something?"

"I'm positive. I'd eat the cost of a job and start over before I'd let a client down." Perplexed, I gazed at the stranger's face, racking my brain for even a hint of recollection. There was none.

"Maybe Walker hired this guy to do his bidding. Maybe he didn't want to get his hands dirty."

"You mean, like a hit man?" I choked.

"I don't know. It's not Walker, and you don't recognize this guy. I'm just trying to find some logic here. Where's your purse?"

"Over there, next to my suitcase." I pointed across the room. "Why?"

"I want to see if you have any new messages, sweetheart," Joshua explained as he snagged my handbag before rejoining me on the bed.

Even with all his hateful and threatening messages, I never truly thought Davis Walker was crazy enough to follow through with any of them. But now, the idea he might have hired someone to do god knows what to me sent a harsher surge of fear careening through me.

"Joshua, I'm scared."

Turning, he pinned me with a sympathetic yet determined look. "No one is going to hurt you. Whoever this nut case is, he's going to have to kill me before he'll get to you."

Fear was lodged in my throat, and I trembled, but I gave him a resolute nod. Joshua leaned in and kissed me, then tugged the blanket from the bed and wrapped it around me. Standing, he pulled a pair of jeans from his suitcase and put them on. I numbly watched him as he turned on my phone and started reading my texts. With an angry expression, he flipped the device off and tucked it back in my purse.

"What did he say?"

"Nothing much, spewing shit about some welcome home torture he's planning for us." Joshua scrubbed a hand through his hair. "But since we're not going home, I'm glad we'll disappoint the prick."

I nodded mutely, questions and fears swirled in my brain.

"Come on, baby. You're still shaking. I'm going to start the shower for you, so you can relax while I make some more calls, okay?"

"Will you stay in the bathroom with me?"

My quivering voice drew a look of alarm to settle over Joshua's face.

I couldn't mask my fear. Riding a seesaw of one emotional high one minute and bottoming out the next, my self-confidence felt shredded. Stripped bare and made vulnerable by Walker's masterful manipulation, I feared he'd succeed in taking mine and Joshua's lives and every ounce of sanity before my torturous end.

With a slow, concerned nod, he took my hand and led me to the bathroom.

Stepping beneath the hot spray, my own bewildering emotions frightened me almost as much as Davis' threats. Grasping for something resembling normalcy, I reached down deep to find strong, capable Mellie beneath the sublime wings of my submission, but I couldn't find her anywhere. I was too mired in a worried sludge; even the warm water pelting me couldn't wash it away.

No matter how I strived to keep Davis from crafting me a victim, each new disturbing piece of information seemed to thwart my resolve and lock me in a foreign mental prison.

Joshua paced the room, making one call after the next. As if sensing my despondent mood, he paused at the shower doors and frowned.

"Don't you dare give that prick the power to steal your spunk, Mellie. If you do, the bastard wins."

He wanted me to fight Davis, to be strong and independent. But Joshua also wanted me to be pliant and submissive—for him. He didn't understand that I didn't work that way. I couldn't be both at the same time. Turning off my submission completely might be a deal breaker, and the thought of losing him through all this shit felt like a knife to the heart. But I couldn't steel myself and try to win the war with Davis unless I tossed away the sweet serenity Joshua had resurrected inside me. It was a no-win situation.

Leaning back against the tiles, I closed my eyes, wishing the water could melt my conflict away. Half listening to Joshua's conversation with Ian and halfway searching for ways to keep both sides of myself intact, I couldn't relax.

"Can you run the image I just sent through your face recognition software?"

Joshua's question bled through my brooding. Turning, I watched him pace. Tall and lean. Powerful and tender. He was the epitome of Dominance and protection.

Will you honestly be able to walk away from him? Turn your back on the light he's brought back to your life?

A single tear slipped down my cheek, and I quickly wiped it away. This wasn't the time or the place to mourn his loss. I had to pull up my bootstraps and ready myself to battle Davis while my heart was shattering.

"I understand about the sunglasses. Just see if you can get a bead on him. Okay, call me back if you do. Thanks."

As Joshua ended the call, I turned off the water, and stepped out of the shower. He took one look at me, and his brows furrowed in concern.

"What's wrong?" I wrapped a towel around me.

I wrapped a towel around me before tailing my wet hand over his cheek. "I'm sorry, Joshua. I can't do it. I just can't."

"Do what, baby?"

"I can't be a submissive to you anymore."

He recoiled as if I'd slapped him across the face. "Okay, hold on a second. I need you to explain that statement to me, little one."

"I can't do both. I can't be strong and tough and not fall apart, and yield to you like the submissive you want me to be. I can't do both. I can't switch those two pieces of me on and off—not without becoming a victim to Davis or failing you. I don't want to lose you in all this mess, but until it's over, I can't be your submissive." Even through the tears blurring my vision, I saw a tender smile spread over Joshua's lips.

"Oh baby. You're not going to lose me. When it comes to Davis, I'd rather see you spit and fight than see you lost and afraid like you are now." Wrapping his hand around my wrist, he placed my palm against his heart. "Let me save your submission for you, Mellie. I'll keep it right here, safe and sound, okay?"

"But you said—"

"I know what I said, but sweetheart, things have changed. I don't know who we're dealing with anymore. Ian's trying to find that out, and so is Pruett now. But if getting you through this emotionally whole means I have to deal with Mouthy-Mellie—" He shrugged. "So be it. Just don't call me a son of a bitch again, and everything will be fine."

"I won't," I sniffed. "I swear I won't."

"At least not out loud, you mean?"

I chuckled and nodded, then sobered. "I don't know if I'm really submissive, Joshua."

"Excuse me?" He blinked. "Did you not see the same woman I did in the mirror last night?"

"Yes, but that's different. I mean, I saw that side of myself, but the other side of me wasn't even in the same room last night. There are tons of subs out there that are strong *and* compliant. Why can't I be more like them?"

"Because everyone is different. Don't compare yourself to others, girl. Remember the analogy about the shoes?"

I nodded, wiping my tears.

"You still haven't broken them back in yet. It's too soon. I told you they were going to feel uncomfortable, remember?" He smiled as I nodded once more. "I'm not going to let you toss them back in the closet and slam the door, Mellie. I'm just letting you go barefoot again so you can feel a firm foundation under your sexy feet. Understand?"

Choking out a sob of relief, I wrapped my arms around his neck and clung to him.

"Shhh. Don't cry, baby. I'm not going to let you leave me. We're going to get through this together, I promise." His conviction was like a balm to my soul.

Joshua wasn't going to let me shut him out. He wasn't going to let me get lost or tangled in the strings I still hadn't figured out how to unravel. No, he had every intention of being by my side, to guide and lean on when I needed him, to protect and care for me through the dark and through the light.

Strumming his fingers up and down my spine, he feathered kisses over my head. As he held me tight, I realized somewhere along the way, I'd fallen in love with him. But ironically there was no panic, no stranglehold of fear, just an overwhelming warmth surrounding and filling my heart. Why wasn't I freaking out?

Because you've searched for him your whole life, you've just been too stubborn to admit it. Wanting—or God forbid—needing a man made the mighty Melinda Carson inadequate. Joshua strengthens you; you finally understand that now. Your irrational fear of commitment wasn't about losing someone close to you again. Deep down you knew that you'd never be whole until you found that one perfect person. All the men before him were nothing but stepping stones leading you to the mountain. Joshua is your mountain, Mellie, and you damn well know it.

That little voice inside my head was right.

Every man I'd dated wanted to change something about me. That's why it was so easy for me to walk away from them, but not Joshua Lars, aka Master Stephen. No, he accepted me—imperfections and all—without forcing me to fit into some preconceived mold. He wanted to cherish my submission, nurture it and help it grow, not force it down my throat until I choked. Only a true Dom would put the emotional welfare of his submissive before his own needs.

Joshua had accused me of blindsiding him, but it was crystal clear, he'd done the very same to me. Leaning back from his embrace, I sniffed and issued a tiny, trembling smile. "Thank you. I don't know what I'd do without you."

"You'd do what you always do, princess. Kick ass and take names. So, put your boots back on. I have a feeling I'm going to enjoy the show."

Something about his unabashed glee kicked my suspicions into high gear. "You're not going to keep a little black book of transgressions and punish me for the things I do or say later, are you?"

He laughed. "Now, would I do something that devious?"

"In a heartbeat." I grinned.

"No, little one, I'm not. You find the headspace you need to cope. I'll get your sexy ass back on the straight and narrow soon."

"Okay. I'll do my best to behave, but no guarantees."

"I didn't expect any." He kissed my forehead and winked before his expression turned somber. "I need to call Pruett back. While you get dressed, I'll hit the shower. We'll grab breakfast on the way out of town. We need to keep moving."

On the road again, Joshua held my hand as I kept my focus off Davis and let my mind flutter through all the ways Joshua had touched my heart. The miles stretched into hours, interrupted only for bathroom breaks, fuel stops, drive-through fast foods, and an occasional switch of driver duty. Though, we'd received numerous phone calls, and made even more, there was no news. Ian wasn't able to come up with anything from the image Joshua had sent him. The sunglasses he'd worn resulted in inconclusive matches. Ian was sorting through a mountain of 'maybes' that would take days instead of hours, and even then, there was no guarantee of a match.

When I spoke with Sanna, she sounded a bit calmer, but I could tell she was a nervous wreck. I needed to wrap her in my arms before she'd be convinced I was perfectly safe. James and his fellow officers had been scouring the city, both on and off duty, searching for Davis, but had no new leads as to his whereabouts. I tried to tell myself that no news was good news, but I wasn't doing a very convincing job of it. The closer we got to Chicago, the higher my anxiety rose.

After two days on the road, Joshua stopped outside Joliet to refuel and grab some lunch. An hour and a half later, he turned onto a gravel road surrounded by a dense forest, and squeezed my hand.

"We're almost there, little one."

"Good. I don't want to have to get back in this car for a week." I laughed, relieved and happy to see my family again.

As we pulled up to the massive lodge, I blinked. In my head I'd pictured a small rustic cabin; instead, I stared at a huge majestic and luxurious mansion. The tall, thick trees surrounding it resembled an impenetrable fortress. I knew now why Joshua had brought me here.

As soon as he put the car in gear, the front door burst open and Sanna rushed off the porch and down the stairs. She hopped impatiently next to my window with tears in her eyes, and my chin quivered as I ripped off my seatbelt and jumped from the car.

Yanking her into my arms, I held her tight.

"Oh Mel," she sobbed. "I've been so damn worried about you."

"It's okay, baby. I'm here. Joshua took real good care of me, and got me here safe and sound," I murmured as I held onto her for dear life.

"Savannah, you and Mellie get inside," Dylan barked from the porch. "We'll unload the car."

I felt my sister tense as she let go of me and gripped my hand.

Scowling, I watched as Dylan bounded down the stairs, a long rifle slung over his shoulder, and joined Joshua as he opened the trunk.

"What's he so pissy about? Is he mad at me for causing such a mess?" I whispered to Sanna.

"No, and you didn't start this. That prick-faced Davis Walker did," Sanna replied, leaning in close to my ear. "Dylan's gone off the deep end. He's in soldier mode. I don't like it, and I'm worried about him. He doesn't want me going outside, and acts like snipers are hiding in the trees, surrounding the place or something. Nick and Drake are the only sane ones here right now."

She rolled her eyes and shook her head before shooting a quick glance Dylan's way.

"Savannah," Dylan warned as he narrowed his eyes.

"We're going, Sir," she called back sweetly. Tugging my hand, she ran toward the lodge. I almost tripped trying to keep up with her.

Drake and Nick stood at the doorway, armed with guns, and gave me a quick welcoming hug. I couldn't miss the way they scanned the perimeter, watching as Dylan and Joshua unloaded our belongings from the trunk.

Once inside, Sanna took me on a tour of the lodge. When we reached the kitchen, she grinned and waved her and at a regular drip-style coffee maker.

"The minute I saw that, I thought of you."

I started to laugh, but something inside me cracked and sobs came out instead.

"Oh, Mel. Mel, don't cry." Enveloped in my sister's arms, the dam burst open wider. "You're here now, and we're all going to keep you safe. That rat-faced bastard isn't going to hurt you."

Pulling back, she forced a smile. "Trust me. My badass Master, Commander Dylan Thomas out there, won't let a fly's fart inside these walls."

Choking on a sob, I nodded. "I won't die and leave you alone, Sanna. I swear."

"No. You won't. I won't let you."

Both of us were crying when Joshua entered the kitchen. He took one look at us and shook his head. Ian strolled in behind him and smirked.

"On second thought, let's grab the beers and head out to the sunroom. There's a little too much uncontrollable estrogen in this room," Ian chuckled.

"Where's your compassion, man?" Joshua chided with a sour expression. "Go ahead, I'll meet you there in a few."

"Ah, I see how it is. You've not only lost your heart but your sense of humor, too. You're so fucked, man." Ian chuckled as he tossed Joshua a beer and sauntered out of the kitchen.

"I don't find anything funny about beautiful women crying, asshole," Joshua called out to his friend before casting a frown toward Savannah and me. "Come on, you two. You're killing me here. Dry those eyes before you two end up getting something to cry about."

"Holy shit, he just said what Dad used to say when we were little," Sanna laughed.

I covered my hand over my mouth and giggled.

"Oh, fuck me. So that's the thanks I get for trying to console you two?" Joshua grumbled with a grin. "I'll be with Ian if you need me."

"Oops," Sanna squeaked with a wide grin.

Joshua issued her a playful wink. "Since you got my girl to smile again, Savannah, I won't narc you out for your language to your Masters, *this* time."

"Thank you, Sir. You just saved my backside. Dylan's head is in a strange place."

"I can tell," Joshua exhaled deeply. "Don't worry. Nick will keep him grounded, girl."

Savannah issued a pensive nod as Joshua turned and walked away. Looking back at me, she nibbled on her bottom lip. "What do the messages that Davis sent you say? I know they're bad, but nobody will tell me what they are. I don't think they wanted me worrying more."

Plucking my phone from my purse, I turned it on and clenched my teeth. There were several new texts, and I had to force myself to read them.

Unknown: It won't be long now, bunny. My little funhouse is all set up ready and waiting for you and that so-called Master you're spreading your legs for.

Unknown: Tell me, cunt. Why are you letting that prick ass motherfucker sweat and grunt all over you? I'm a better lover and you fucking well know it. I've got a knife and I can't wait to scrape his worthless seed out of our pussy. Keep him off you from now on bitch. When I'm through with him, he won't be able to fuck you again.

"No. No," I whispered as I stood shaking.

Unknown: Where are you, bunny? Don't make me come looking for you. You won't like what I'll have to do to you if I have to hunt you down, you miserable cunt.

Unknown: Hiding on me, slut? Wrong choice, bunny. I'm coming for you.

I cast a glance at Sanna, who'd gone ghostly white. Turning on her heel, she began screaming for Dylan at the top of her lungs.

"Sanna. No," I hissed.

Within seconds, every male in the house pounded into the kitchen, guns ready and eyes wild. Body tensed and poised to kill, Dylan stepped up and gripped Savannah to his chest.

"What is it, kitten?"

"Davis…Mel's phone…he's crazy. Davis is a lunatic. He's going to take a knife and—"

"We turned your phone off for a reason, Mellie," Joshua scowled. "Give it to me. Everyone you need to talk to is right here."

"You can't keep shielding me from his threats," I hissed, shoving the device back into my purse.

"Mel," Sanna whispered.

"No," I snapped. "Look, I'm not going to—"

"Stop," Joshua interrupted. "Giving me your phone isn't a sign of weakness, Mellie. Yes. I want to shield you from his vile threats, but allowing me to do that isn't an act of submission."

"You promised me I could do, act, and say what I needed to, remember?" I countered.

"And you still can. I'm not asking you as your Dom, I'm asking you as a friend. Give me your phone, so you don't have to subject yourself to any more anxiety."

The other Doms in the room stared at Joshua as if he'd grown three heads. "Since when did you turn to the vanilla side?" Ian asked in absolute disbelief.

"It's complicated," Joshua replied with an unhappy expression. "Until we sort this shit out, Mellie is her own woman. It's the only way she feels she can keep Davis from taking her control."

Drake smiled. "You're a wise man, Joshua."

"No, I'm just willing to do whatever it takes to make sure she comes through this unscathed, mentally and emotionally." Turning his attention back to me, Joshua held out his hand and waited.

When I made no move to give it to him, he sighed. "Fine. If you need to keep control of your phone, then do it, but as a favor to me, don't read any more messages unless I'm with you. Is that a good enough compromise for you, Mellie? If not, I'll be more than happy to draw some hard limits. Are we clear?"

His scolding was like sandpaper chafing my pride, and its burn warred with my melting heart. Joshua went to such lengths—laying aside his pure Dominant nature—to ensure I kept my wits about me. I shot him a sharp nod of my head.

Ian let out a low whistle. "Somebody make some popcorn; this is going to be fun as fuck to watch."

Drake's big body shook in silent laughter and an unladylike growl rumbled in the back of my throat.

"Why don't we go upstairs and unpack?" Joshua suggested, trying to redirect my mounting ire.

"Fine," I replied in a clipped tone as I flashed a sarcastic smile at Ian.

"Second door on the right at the top of the stairs," Dylan instructed. "Your room is flanked between us and Ian, and Drake is right across the hall."

"Isn't that cozy," I flippantly interjected, still irked Ian ridiculed my need for control. "I'm all warm and fuzzy."

"Mellie," Joshua warned as Dylan bristled and moved in close.

Cupping my chin, Dylan zoned in on my eyes. Compassion and anger swirled in his aqua blue pools. "You should be. Ian and I are both expert marksmen. It might be what keeps your smart-ass alive."

And didn't that make me feel like a total raging bitch?

"I'm sorry, everyone," I exhaled on a heavy sigh. "I know you all are here to help me and I'm acting like a spoiled child."

"It's okay, Mel," Sanna whispered. "You've earned the right to. After reading the stuff Davis is sending you, I don't know how you're still keeping it together."

I gave Sanna a little shrug. Gratitude warmed me as I scanned the faces of those who had put their lives on hold to come and protect me. I paused on Joshua and smiled.

"I'm getting by with a little help from my friends."

"Good girl." Dylan nodded solemnly. "Just keep your shit wired tight. We've got the rest."

"I'll do my best."

Joshua guided me out of the kitchen while everyone grabbed a suitcase and my boxes of files before we headed upstairs. Once inside the room, I smiled. It was massive with a king-sized four-poster bed along the west wall. Tall, wide windows lined the north side of the room. The sheers had been pulled, concealing the forest outside.

Dylan stepped up next to me as I inched the creamy fabric open and glanced outside. "Keep away from the windows as much as you can. Ian will close the hurricane shutters at dusk."

"Okay." I nodded then stepped back as the fabric fell back into place.

"You two get unpacked. Dylan and I are going to start dinner soon," Nick informed us as he paused and darted a look at Joshua and me. "Glad you both made it here safely."

"Me too. Thank you, both of you, for taking such good care of Sanna." My chin began to quiver as I looked at both Nick and Dylan. Biting back my tears, I inhaled a deep breath. "I'm sorry I never told you two that before. You're the loves of her life and everything she's ever needed to be complete."

"She needs you too, girl," Nick reminded with a soft smile.

But I left her. Guilt spooled, playing the same worn-out tapes that had sung in my psyche for years.

Ian's cell phone rang. All heads turned expectantly as he answered with an unusually serious tone.

"Fantastic," he smiled. "Give me a sec. I'm heading to the office now to pull it up."

My brows tugged together as Ian turned and walked out of the room. Dropping my purse on the bed, I followed him back down the stairs and into a large study. The relaxing room had been overrun with computers and printers all linked by coils of power cords snaking across the floor.

Ian slid into a tall leather chair before rolling up to a large desk and pounding on a keyboard. Peering over his shoulder, he gave me a cursory glance before opening a document.

Side-by-side images of the unknown stranger appeared on the screen. One was the picture Pruett had e-mailed to Joshua, the other a mug shot. The facial features were identical. I didn't need to see behind the sunglasses of the original image to know it was the same man.

Ian scrolled down further, and we both scanned the information his source had provided. The man stalking me was Gordon Tideway. Forty-seven, six-foot-one, 285 pounds, brown hair, hazel eyes. His address was in a sketchy part of Chicago, and he had a long list of breaking and entering charges, as well as several for vandalism. He'd served a short stint in the Cook County jail for assault with a deadly weapon in his early twenties. Gripping the back of Ian's chair, I continued to read. Tideway had spent the past seven years in Statesville Correctional Center—a maximum security prison in Joliet—for statutory rape, extortion, and murder for hire. He'd been released just sixty days ago and was currently on parole.

Chapter Twelve

My heart hammered in my ears as I shook like a sapling in a hurricane. Glancing up from the monitor, I locked eyes with Joshua. Neither of us said a word. He simply strode into the room, pulled me away from Ian's chair and led me to a long leather couch.

"Hey, Drake. Do you mind getting Mellie a drink, please?"

"Not that Scotch shit. Vodka. I'll take vodka if there's any around."

"Sure thing."

With a concerned nod, the big, tattooed Dom poured me a healthy shot of vodka as everyone filtered into the study. Slamming back the alcohol, I exhaled as the burn warmed the back of my throat.

"Thanks."

After reciting Gordon Tideway's extensive criminal career, Ian steepled his fingers to his lips, sat back in his chair, and frowned. "No doubt if he discovers our location, he'll be armed. I know Savannah doesn't know how to shoot, but do you?" Ian looked at me, and I shook my head.

"Okay. Here's how this is going to go. Since I'm ninety-nine-point-nine percent sure Gordon is the same guy from your neighbor's surveillance footage, neither you nor Savannah will go anywhere alone." Ian glanced at the other men assembled. "From here on out, nobody steps foot outside, at least not without an armed escort. We're locking this place up tighter than a virgin's ass. Got it?"

"When are your guys coming to the cabin?" Joshua asked, tension rolling off his frame.

"Tomorrow morning. They're bringing provisions to last till... whenever," Ian explained.

"I'm going to go grab a nap. I'll take the first watch," Drake announced with a grim nod. "Keep a plate of dinner warming in the oven for me, will you?"

"Will do," Nick assured him.

"Okay, for now everyone go about your business and try to relax. We need to stay frosty but not to the point of being ready for a guest shot on Wild Kingdom. Try to think of this as a vacation."

"With deadly weapons," I mumbled, trying to keep it together and not uncoil like a damn spring.

"Yeah," Ian chuckled. "Keep your weapons handy. I'm going to get in touch with James. If we're lucky, Chicago PD will have both Walker and Tideway locked up before dinner is over."

I didn't share Ian's confidence. The level of anxiety thickening the air only increased my fears. Rubbing the tight muscles at the back of my neck, my temples throbbed with a massive headache.

"We still need to unpack," I reminded Joshua, anxious to get away from the oppressive weight squeezing in on me.

"I'll take care of it. You need to lie down for a bit and rest." He softly smiled. "Come on."

"Let me know if you need anything, okay?" Sanna asked as I bent and kissed her cheek on the way out the door.

"You know I will, sis. All I need is for you to relax, too. Okay?"

The confident nod she gave me didn't mask the fear in her eyes.

Once inside our room, Joshua sat on the edge of the bed. Tugging me onto his lap, he smoothed a hand over my hair. "How are you holding up?"

Instinctively, I wanted to say 'fine', but we both knew it would be a lie. "I'm okay at the moment. Not sure how I'll be five minutes or five seconds from now. How about you?"

"Well, this isn't how I normally spend my days. The pay's lousy." He cracked a smile. "But the fringe benefits are spectacular."

Gliding his capable fingers into my hair, he gripped my mane before pulling me to his lips. Dominant to the nth degree, his move pulverized the capable ground beneath my feet and sent my sub soaring. The sudden change of control sent me pitching and yawing. Like a ship lost in a blinding squall, I couldn't find my emotional balance.

Tensing, I tore from his kiss and reached back, clasping his wrist. "Wait."

"Mellie, I can't cordon off the Dominant in me. I can restrain some of it, but I can't just shut it off. You can't expect me to be something I'm not."

"You can't expect the same from me," I countered.

"No, but I'm not wired to submit to you or anyone else."

No. Joshua's DNA wasn't structured to sit passively by and/or cater to someone else's demands. By asking him to take my independence head on, without a feather of opposition, I was really asking him to submit to me.

I issued a heavy sigh and rubbed my pounding forehead.

"We've discussed this, little one. Use that internal armor of yours as much as you need to and if you have to toss on your Domme hat, then do it. I've already promised to stick by your side, and that's what I intend to do. By. Your. Side. I won't kneel at your feet. And I won't try to stifle my natural urges, either. I need you to realize that I'm willing to deflect all that beautiful tenacity you toss my way, because I want you to feel secure. Whatever it takes. Trust me. There'll come a time when I'll command you out of your comfort zone, but it's definitely not now."

Dammit. The man was understanding to a fault. It was one of the things I admired most about him, until now. I didn't want him being tolerant or supportive. I wanted to argue and cuss and fight, to slam a stake in the ground and draw a safe perimeter around me.

You want to throw a fit like a five-year-old because he's not letting you have your way. The man only knows how to nurture in a specific way...Dominance. You can't tell him to stop who and what he is any more than you can tell him to stop breathing. Instead of fighting his comfort, take it. You're going to need it before this shit is through.

Leaning in, he gave me a tender kiss, conveying he understood my agitation. Scooping me into his arms like a child, Joshua stood and turned, settling onto the bed.

"Close your eyes and rest. I'll join you as soon as I unpack." I opened my mouth with an offer to help poised on my tongue, but he pressed his finger to my lips. "Don't argue with me about this. Save it for the important stuff."

I shot him a derisive smirk, then nodded in resignation. Closing my eyes, I listened as he moved around the room. Comforted simply by his presence, I wrapped it around me like a blanket and drifted to sleep.

I woke to the sound of snoring in my ear. Listening to his masculine music, a grin spread over my mouth. Cupping my hand to his cheek, I pressed my lips to his. Joshua let out a loud snort and jerked. I couldn't help but giggle.

"Sorry. I didn't mean to wake you, but I couldn't resist."

He grinned. "Is that so? Well then, I guess you'll understand if I can't resist this then."

Pulling me beneath him, he bestowed a tingling kiss. A low, satisfied moan rumbled deep in his chest as he sucked my tongue into his mouth, devouring me in demand. My body responded to his animalistic claim and rapidly growing erection pressed against my clit. I writhed beneath him, hungry for more.

"Make love to me, Joshua. Please."

"My way?" he asked in a gravely tone.

"Any way you want," I purred.

As if waving a red cape in front of a bull, Joshua stripped me bare in seconds flat. Tearing at his own clothing, he settled his hot, naked flesh over mine before ebbing his lips down my body. Kissing, licking, and nipping at my flesh, he worked his way to my aching pussy. Cupping his hands around my knees, he spread my legs before plunging his tongue inside me. I jolted at the wicked sensation, and Joshua gripped my thighs, holding me as I relaxed and rocked against his masterful mouth.

Consuming me in a frenzied fury, he filled me with his fingers, driving my wicked delight higher. Peaking like a spire, Joshua coaxed me to fracture hard beneath a rolling wave of bliss. As my tunnel contracted and quivered, he slid up my torso and drove inside me with a feral grunt.

Gazing into my eyes, he dragged his cock from within me, only to rock back in with a forceful thrust. Driving in and out of my sucking cunt, Joshua coaxed one orgasm after another, until I was soaked in sweat, boneless, and spent. When he rubbed his thumb over my clit, I shook my head.

"No more. I can't take anymore," I whimpered, satiated and drained.

A gratified smirk curled on his lip before that familiar tautness lined his features. Bucking against me in quick, feral thrusts, he chased his own pleasure with a muffled groan.

Dropping onto his elbows, he lay atop me panting like an Olympic sprinter. A tiny knock came from the other side of the door.

"Just a minute," I called out.

Joshua hadn't yet managed to catch his breath, but he groaned at the inopportune timing of our visitor.

Nick laughed from the other side of the portal. "You lucky fuck. Okay, well, dinner's ready when you two can get your clothes back on and come down."

"We'll be there in a few." I grinned, trying not to giggle.

Joshua slowly eased from inside me, then pulled me out of bed. "Shower then food."

Sitting at the table with wet hair and a sated smile I couldn't seem to wipe away, we ate and talked. Steering clear of the topic that had brought us together, I noticed Ian had closed the windows beneath thick hurricane shutters. The motive for our 'vacation' could be brushed under the rug, but such a visible reminder couldn't be ignored.

Drake ambled down the stairs. Scrubbing a hand over his face, he blinked then squinted against the bright lights. "I couldn't sleep with all the mouthwatering aromas filling my room."

Grabbing a plate, he filled it and settled into the vacant chair at the end of the table. Spearing a chunk of potato with his fork, he raised his head and looked at me. "You hanging in there, Mellie?"

"Yes, Sir. I'm doing just fine." Pausing, I gathered my words, praying they'd come out right. "I can't thank you all enough for everything you're doing for me. In essence, you're putting your lives on the line for Joshua and me. This isn't exactly where any of us want to be, or the circumstances we want to be in, but I'm grateful for what you're all doing for me…for us."

"Mellie, there's nothing on this planet that would stop me from keeping you safe. Not just because you're Sanna's sister, but because fuck-knuckles like Kerr give us all a bad name," Dylan announced with grim determination. "Let's just hope James calls back with good news."

"James has news?" I asked.

"Maybe," Ian interjected with a hint of apprehension. "Chicago PD might have a lead on Gordon. We're waiting to see if it pans out or not."

"Why didn't you tell me that when we came down to eat?" I challenged.

"Because we don't know anything yet, Mellie," Nick replied in a quiet, calm voice.

Sanna forced down the food in her mouth and set her fork down. The color drained from her face, and for a minute I thought she might pass out. Dylan snatched the glass of water from in front of her plate and pressed it to her lips as he leaned in close to her ear. I couldn't hear what he said, but she nodded and took a sip.

"Try to calm down," Joshua instructed. "No one is trying to keep things from you. If Ian has information, he'll share it with all of us. You need to trust him. He knows what he's doing."

Trust. Such a simple word that to me meant taking a massive fucking risk.

With my appetite gone, I pushed my plate aside just as Ian's cell phone rang.

"Would you put the call on speaker phone if it's about this mess?" I asked. "Please?"

Glancing at the screen, Ian nodded. "It's James." Enabling the device so we all could hear, he set the phone down in the middle of the table. "Everyone can hear you, James. What information do you have?"

A humorless chuckle emitted from the phone. "Well, two weeks suspension and a meeting with Internal Affairs when it's done."

"What? Why?" Sanna gasped.

"Captain caught me sniffing around where I shouldn't have been."

"And where was that?" Ian asked with an amused grin.

"Gordon's parole records and eavesdropping when I was talking to the guys I sent over to check out his last known address."

"Let me guess," Dylan piped up. "Your captain didn't instruct you to put your own personal APB out on Tideway, did he?"

"It must have slipped my mind," James replied with a cynical snort. "Anyway, I figured y'all could use some reinforcements to hold down the fort up there, so I'm on my way to join you. It'll be a lot more fun than sitting around watching TV. I might be officially off the case, but unofficially? Well, let's just say I've got a bunch of friends looking for these pricks. They'll find 'em; they just know to be more careful than I was."

"Well, shit," Ian groused. "Look, if your meeting with Internal Affairs goes south, I'll hire you, bro."

"Thanks, man. Since this is the third time the captain's busted me for pretty much the same shit, there's a good possibility you'll be getting my resume real fucking soon."

"James, I'm sorry I got you into trouble," I moaned.

"You didn't, gorgeous, I did. Trust me. It wouldn't break my heart if I got canned. I'd rather work for Ian. He doesn't have a lot of rules to follow. I think I'd like that kind of freedom."

"When do you think you'll be getting here?" Ian asked with a wide smile.

"In about an hour or so. I need to grab some gear. Oh, but I did find out something," James remembered. "Tideway missed his meeting with his parole officer last week. He's also not supposed to leave the state, so Mellie's neighbor's video is enough to land his slimy ass back in a cell. My captain was kind enough to tell me he'd see what he could do about it, after busting my balls for twenty minutes."

"Hopefully, that'll be enough to lock him away for a while. Call me when you get here. We'll escort you in," Ian advised.

"Aww, now you're making me feel like fucking rock star. I could get used to that."

"Don't let it go to your head, asshole. And watch your six."

"Ten-four," James confirmed. "Hey, I know Dylan and Nick are cooking up there. Save me some dinner."

"Then you better get your scrawny ass up here before I eat it all," Drake taunted.

"Dammit," James grumbled. "I forgot you were there, Drake. You'd better not eat it all, or I'll kick your big ass."

"Better bring a fucking army then, son," Drake taunted with a grin.

James laughed. "I'm on my way."

After dinner, Sanna and I cleaned up the kitchen. Nick and Joshua kept watchful eyes on us. I knew how animals in the zoo felt. Joining the others gathered around the massive river rock fireplace in the great room, Sanna eased to the carpet between Dylan and Nick's feet. With a courageous breath, I followed her lead and knelt by Joshua's feet. I didn't want to analyze my outward show of submission; it just felt right.

Glancing down at me, Joshua's eyes widened in surprise before his nostrils flared and he sucked in a deep breath. Pride was written all over his face.

"Easy, tiger," Ian chuckled, sitting in a big leather chair across from us. "I've got some rope if you want to tie her to the coffee table."

"Don't tempt me," Joshua warned with a wicked grin.

"I'm not trying to bust your balls. Well, not too much, but you're the one that's tied up in knots, man," Ian laughed. Dropping his gaze to me, he cocked his head. "Explain something to me, Mellie. Are you one of those subs that only want to submit in the bedroom or something? I don't get that. I never have. Help me understand that. What am I missing?"

I exhaled a heavy sigh. "I wish I understood it, but I don't, at least not fully. No, I don't want to keep it exclusively confined to the bedroom, but I can't get the divided parts of my brain to come together. One side is strong, the other is weak."

"Excuse me?" Savannah squawked with a look of surprise.

"I don't mean you, sis," I exhaled with a suffering sigh. "I'm talking about me."

Ian blinked as Drake shook his head and let out a snort.

"What?" I challenged sarcastically.

"Mellie, Mellie, Mellie. If you think submission is weak, you've never really submitted. I think you're equating compliance with weakness," Ian stated in disbelief.

"Well, in a way, it is. I mean, all you really have to do is try to make your Master happy. It's not hard."

"Oh, sis. Do you honestly think I'm some kind of damn doormat?" Sanna huffed.

"No," I cried.

"It takes a hell of a lot of strength to hand over every part of your body, mind, and soul. If you think that's easy, you've never fully submitted before."

I frowned. Was she right? I hated the fact she had me questioning my own beliefs, but what I hated more was the look of pity in her eyes.

"Dude," Ian exclaimed as he stared slack-jawed at Joshua. "Are you hearing this? Did you know she felt that way?"

"Not outright," Joshua smirked. "But I suspected as much."

Bristling, I clenched my jaw. Ian was mocking me. What an asshole.

"Tell us about the other side," Drake urged.

With a disgruntled frown, I pondered whether to answer any more questions. I didn't want to hand Ian any more ammo to scorn me with. As if sensing my reluctance, he cursed under his breath.

"I'm sorry, Mellie. I'm a natural born smart-ass. I honestly wasn't trying to hurt your feelings or make fun of you. I was just giving Joshua some shit, and my lack of sensitivity toward you backfired in my face. I'm sorry, girl. I really am." By his remorseful expression, he meant it. "Please, carry on."

Pursing my lips, I nodded. "There's another part of me that's strong and independent. I've achieved a lot of success with my business and keep my life on track when I'm in charge. I do what I want, when I want, without having to answer to anyone."

"But you have submissive longings, right?" Drake asked.

"Yes. But I can't combine the two sides of me. I won't sit here weak and defenseless with Walker or Tideway out there ready to strike. That just makes me a victim."

"So, why are you sitting at *Master* Stephen's feet?" he pressed, emphasizing Joshua's alter ego.

"B-because it feels right. At least for now, just not all the time." I shook my head, confused by the Dom's questions and my own frustration at trying to sort out my jumbled emotions.

"But, Mel," Sanna interjected. "The sub has all the power. Even when you submit, you're still in control."

Nick chuckled. "Don't let all that power go to your head, precious."

Sanna grinned. "Never, Master."

"There," Ian exclaimed as he pointed to Nick and Sanna. "That's a perfect example, right there."

"What?" I asked confused.

"Ian," Joshua interrupted. "Can I have a word with you in the kitchen?"

"Sure." The other Dom shrugged.

Watching the two men saunter off, anxiety spiked, but in a totally different way. Joshua was brewing something, and it wasn't another pot of coffee.

"Why such a pensive expression, girl?" Drake asked with a tiny smile.

"Oh, gee. I can't imagine," I scoffed, drawing a frown from the big Dom.

"I know you've been in the lifestyle before, and obviously, Kerr was as inept then as he is now. But surely, you remember disrespecting a Dom can get you into serious trouble."

Drake's disapproval saturated me like cold winter rain. My snarky comeback wasn't earning me any submissive brownie points. They simply made me look like an unmanaged brat.

"I'm sorry, Sir." The apology rolled off my tongue without an inkling of thought.

A knowing smile curled on Drake's lips as he nodded in forgiveness.

"Whatever they're cooking up isn't important," Nick noted with concern. "The lesson attached to it is."

"It might be the push you need, sis." Sanna grinned.

"What's wrong about going at my own pace?"

Drake chuckled. "Because setting your own speed means you're only submitting to yourself, sweetheart. If you'd been trained properly, you'd know that."

I wanted to argue with him, but I couldn't. It made sense. I didn't solve my dilemma, though. Meshing the two opposing sides seemed a daunting task in my mind. I knew there was a submissive side of me. I simply didn't know if I could give her free rein and not lose part of me in the process. Before I could dissect my feelings further, Ian and Joshua strolled back in the room. Their serious Dom expressions worried me.

Oh shit, this isn't going to be good.

Joshua didn't smile as he stopped and bent, cupping my chin in his warm palm. Focusing on his tender touch, I tried to calm the dread crawling under my skin.

"We're going to try a little experiment, a test, if you will," Joshua began to explain. His expression softened slightly, but expectation pinged off him like a live wire, charged and hissing. "Ian and I are going to prove to you that your inner sub will respond to the Dom and not the man."

"Are you up for a challenge, Mellie?" Ian didn't bother disguising his dare. If he was blindly pushing buttons, he'd hit a winner on the first try, thus tossing down the gauntlet. I couldn't just let it lay there. Squaring my shoulders, I stuck out my chin.

"I never turn down a challenge," I replied with a tight, combative sneer.

"Mellie," Joshua warned. He had to have felt the tension spike within me. "Put your hackles down, girl. This is an exercise to help enlighten you. No one is backing you into a corner. Understood?"

He and Ian wanted to open the doorways of my submission, but why? Joshua had already seen it numerous times. Darting a quick gaze around the room, I was met with a myriad of expressions. Drake looked intrigued, Nick curious, Sanna concerned, Dylan suspicious, Ian expectant, and Joshua hopeful.

"Yes," I responded hesitantly.

Lifting his hand from my chin, he stood. "Good. Now stand and strip."

"Excuse me?" I choked.

Sanna's gasp of surprise barely registered in my brain, I was so stunned. "Master Stephen, I don't think—"

"Kitten, you will remain quiet, or we'll take you upstairs," Nick warned with a scowl.

Sanna pinched her lips together in a tight, angry line. Anger flashed in her dark eyes before she cast them toward the floor. The room was totally silent. Anticipation, razor sharp, sang in the air.

"I won't repeat myself. Do it," Joshua demanded in an unusually harsh tone. And dammit, why did it turn me on so much?

He wanted me to strip. Okay. No big deal, or at least, I wanted to convince myself it wasn't. Lots of men had seen me naked—so had my sister, that didn't bother me. Hanging out in my birthday suit in front of her Masters? That wasn't what skeeved me out either. They'd seen my bare ass cheeks at Genesis. Pondering the real reason I balked at Joshua's request, I realized it was the unknown. The lack of control over what he intended to do was what kept me resting on my heels and refusing to follow his command.

Coward. Sanna went to bat for you and got duly chastised for it, too. You owe her the satisfaction of not backing down.

"Fine," I countered with a huff. Scrambling off the floor, I stripped, quickly, hoping no one noticed my trembling fingers. But as Joshua danced his gaze over my nude and trembling body, I knew I'd outed myself.

Smiling, he brushed his hands over my shoulders and down my arms. "The other part of this exercise involves the realization that you can be both strong and submissive. It takes strength and courage to be vulnerable. Let's see how strong you really are, little one. Do as Ian tells you. Make me proud."

My heart felt as if might explode from my chest. He was passing me off to another Dom. A Dom he'd shared women with no less. I couldn't do it. I couldn't let Ian touch or fondle me, not with Joshua right there watching, as well as the other Doms *and* my sister. Panic paraded through me. My cheeks blazed in embarrassment. I had to put a stop to this awkward and embarrassing little test.

"Her safeword is 'fantasy,'" Joshua casually offered up, as if divulging my favorite color or flavor of ice cream.

"I was just about to ask. Thanks, bro." Ian took a step closer. Our eyes locked in a war of wills. A slow smile tugged the corners of his mouth. "You may no longer speak until given permission, unless it's your safeword. If you are willing to proceed, nod your head, please."

With a sour expression, I jerked my head and bit my tongue to keep from lashing out at him.

"Hmmm, this might be harder than I thought," Ian smirked. "Stand in front of the fireplace facing us, girl. I want you to cast your eyes toward the floor and kneel like a proper submissive."

Shooting daggers Joshua's way, I stomped my way to the designated spot, but I didn't kneel or lower my gaze. Defiantly looking past Ian, I stared at my sister. Peeking up at me, I saw pride and unwavering support glimmering in Sanna's dark eyes.

Smiling internally, I gave her a slight nod before snapping my head toward Joshua, who squatted down next to Drake's chair, talking quietly with the big man. How long was he going to allow this stupid charade to continue?

As long as it takes. You're the one who opened your fat mouth and accepted Ian's challenge. Big mistake. Huge.

"Look at me," Ian instructed. When I did, he flashed me a tight, controlled smile. "Are you refusing my instructions, girl? Or just trying my patience?"

Holy hell. Where had Ian been hiding that badass Dom-tude of his?

"What exactly is it that you two are aiming for here?" Dylan asked, rising to his feet and pinning Joshua with a disapproving glare. "I meant both physical and mental pain when I told you not to hurt her."

Joshua stood as if squaring off for a knockdown, drag-out.

"I'm not aiming to do either, Dylan. If you'll sit back down and watch, I think you'll understand." Joshua's voice was brittle and sharp.

It was the same tone he'd used when Davis Walker interrupted our session at Genesis. A cold shiver raced down my spine.

The Dominant stare-off lasted several uncomfortable seconds before Dylan gave a curt nod and sat back down.

"Continue, Ian," Joshua instructed in an icy command.

When Ian snapped his fingers, I zipped my focus back to him. "Follow all my instructions, or safeword out. I won't remind you again."

Ian wanted to test my will—poke at my self-restraint? Oh, buddy, bring it on. I wasn't about to go down without a fight.

With a loud huff of annoyance, I eased to my knees onto the thick pile carpet. Darting a contemptuous look Joshua's way, I could see a fire of pride and desire dance in his eyes. Blood pooled and throbbed behind my clit. Just looking at the man's feral hunger and approval turned me on like a damn light switch. My pussy started to weep. There was something fundamentally wrong with me. Trying to ignore the sexual need flickering inside me, I cast my eyes toward the floor.

"You look gorgeous in that pose, Mellie," Ian praised quietly before his tenor took on that cutting Dominant edge. "I want you stand again for me. Close your eyes and count to ten. Center yourself for me, girl. Let that sweet submission flow through your veins. Then I want you to kneel again for me."

Slowly rising to my feet, I did as he instructed. Inhaling a deep breath, I mentally started counting to ten. A soothing sense of peace began to settle through me.

"Yes," Ian whispered. "So beautiful. Handing over your hypnotizing power is a glorious sight to see. Fall at my feet and kneel before me, girl. Release your inhibitions. I want to see every inch of it. Feel your control in the air, fill my lungs as you hand your submission over to me."

Gliding back to the floor upon my knees, that familiar feeling of liberated bliss warmed my chest and spread through my limbs. I didn't try to push it away or deny its existence. Instead, I welcomed his invisible hands wrapping around me, molding and protecting my vulnerabilities…my surrender.

"This is your strength, Mellie. Your power. Your control. I see it.

He sees it. Your Master is watching you, girl. This priceless gift you give him is what feeds his soul and makes him whole. Nourish him, little one. Give him life and strength."

Ian's words were barely above a whisper, but the weight of each phrase pressed around me, blanketing me in contentment. I sensed movement in front of me. The tops of Joshua's shoes appeared in my periphery, and it took all the strength I possessed not to raise my head.

"I can smell your hot cunt from here, girl," Ian murmured.

Mortified, I gasped softly, wanting nothing more than to melt into the carpet and disappear.

"Your body responds to its natural calling. It's your head that's blocking your path, sweet girl. Spread your thighs, little one. Spread them nice and wide. Show your Master your courage and strength," Ian directed.

Terrified, Ian would want to touch me to feel how wet I'd become, I swallowed tightly and tried to force myself to comply. A swell of panic overtook me. Snapping my head up, a pained expression tugged at my brows.

"I'm not having sex with him," I boldly declared, looking Joshua in the eye.

He simply smiled as Ian squatted in close next to me. When he gently brushed my hair over my shoulder, I tensed and fought the urge to pull back.

"I have no desire to claim your pussy or ass, Mellie," Ian began in a reassuring timbre. "This lesson isn't about sex; it's about power and control, submission and freedom. It's about giving *everything* inside you over to your Master. All your fears, your pain, your insecurities, along with all your strengths and weaknesses. It's about trusting someone with the very essence of your being; that they'll not only keep them safe but make you whole in the process. Master Stephen is going to keep you safe. And if you let him, he'll also make you whole."

"Submission isn't weakness, little one. It takes a hell of a lot more courage and strength to hand over your power than it does to keep it locked in your fist with a death grip," Joshua expounded, picking up where Ian left off, like a tag-team match. "Freedom is found within, little one. You know it, and I know it. When you give me the power to make all the decisions for you, to bind you with my mind and body, what happens inside you?"

"I come alive," I whispered.

"You do a hell of a lot more than that, baby. You soar. You fly away in such pure and peaceful beauty, I want to beat my chest and howl. Do you have any idea how fucking empowering that is to me?" I shook my head. "It's priceless. Because you *let* me take you there. Tell me, who holds the power, little one? Who owns the control for all that?"

Something strange and unexpected swelled inside me, and the pieces aligned with clarity. I'd professed for days that I wouldn't let Davis steal my power, when I'd done nothing more than allow him to make me feel like a victim. Joshua's words made me realize I'd had the control to wipe the vile sludge from my being. I had the power with Walker, but I also had the power to give the amazing man in front of me the control to fulfill my fantasies.

"I do," I whispered, still pondering his words.

"Damn right, you do. And that power comes from both, Mouthy-Mellie and submissive Mellie. There is no division. They're one and the same. One beautiful collection of sass and sweet, not fragmented pieces of strong and weak. There's not a weak bone in your body, girl. You're mighty and powerful, and…fuck, the heady rush I get when you give all that to me. It's indescribable." Joshua's tone was filled with wonderment. "When you beg to please me, you're finding the strength to cast aside your fears and uncertainty and open up your entire soul to me, little one. And when something blocks your path, you grab hold of it with the same courageous strength and kick your way clear to charge right on through. Strength comes in many forms, sweetheart, and you, my beautiful sub, are powerful beyond compare."

"Spread your thighs, girl," Ian whispered. "Show your Master your strength and let him guide you. Give him what's inside your heart, your body, and your soul."

Shards of fire and ice swirled inside me, intertwining and sifting together in a hazy smoke of power. Floating through my limbs, meshing and melding, growing and surging with such force I thought it might burst from me at the seams.

Tears prickled the backs of my eyes, and I spread my legs. Joshua brushed his knuckles along the insides of my thighs, leaving a path of tingles in his wake.

"You're so fucking gorgeous, little one," Joshua growled. "Spread them wider. You're stronger than this. Show me how strong you really are. Give me all your sweet control. I want it. Need to taste it on your flesh, feel it breathe and glow beneath my hands, wrap it around my heart and give it back to you tenfold. Let me have it, little one. Let me make you whole. I need your love, baby, as much as you need mine."

Joshua needed to satisfy his desires, but his words conveyed more than Dominance. He was ready to open up and let someone inside him again…me. For the first time in my adult life, I ached to be loved—and give love—as deeply in return. Spreading my legs to the point of pain, I wanted to give Joshua my power, my control, and my love. I knew unequivocally that he'd never use me and toss me away. Knew he'd never purposely hurt me.

For years, I'd kept my heart isolated, crippled with the fear of abandonment. After my parents had left me, and Davis had left me, I convinced myself the only way to keep from being hurt again was to throw away my submission and let bold, fearless Mellie take charge.

But I'd been wrong. Dead wrong to deny the pieces of my soul Joshua had resurrected.

Tears of salvation and joy spilled down my cheeks, dripping onto my breasts. Raising my head, I stared into Joshua's loving eyes. I no longer needed to wear a mask or surround myself in armor. This gorgeous, compassionate, caring man was worth the risk of losing it, losing all of me.

Leaning in, Joshua dropped his head to my breasts. Sipping the droplets between his lips, he steered clear of my nipples. His restraint was clear. The lesson he sought to teach me was clear. This wasn't a sexual awakening—it was an emotional and spiritual rebirth. He'd reached inside my soul and saved my submission, like he'd promised.

Sobbing, I raised my hands up to him. "I need you, too, Master."

"Oh, baby," Joshua whispered as he wrapped his arms around me and hugged me to his chest.

"Fucking gorgeous. Well done, girl," Ian whispered as he bent in and pressed a kiss at my temple.

The sound of Joshua's heartbeat echoed in my ear, and in the distance I could hear Sanna softly crying. Sliding my arms around Joshua's neck, I clung to him with all my might. As he stood, he slid a strong arm beneath my knees. Lifting me, he cradled me and carried me toward the stairs. The sound of Ian's cell phone made me flinch, but Joshua didn't stop, didn't pause; he didn't even look back. Instead, he ascended the stairs and carried me to our room. Kicking the door closed behind him, he laid me down in the center of our bed.

Wiping away my tears, I watched as he tore off his clothes and climbed into bed. Embracing me in his sweet, blissful heat, Joshua peppered my face with gentle kisses.

"I'm so proud of you, little one. Words can't describe how in awe I am of you right now. Watching you struggle so mightily and transform as the puzzle pieces finally came together was the most gorgeous and amazing thing I've ever witnessed." Joshua beamed in a combination of satisfaction, happiness, and pride.

"It's funny how self-preservation forces you to compartmentalize and cordon yourself off from pain."

Joshua nodded. "Yes, I know exactly what you mean. I'd done the same until I met you. I meant what I said when I told you that you blindsided me."

"You've done the very same to me," I softly chuckled. "You brought the mighty Mellie Carson down, but more than that, you found a way to reinvent her."

"I've not yet started to do all the things I want with you, little one." He dipped his head and claimed my lips in a soulful kiss. Slowly pulling back from me, he frowned.

"What's wrong?" I asked nervously.

"When you move to Chicago, I want you to move in with me, Mellie."

"Whoa." I laughed nervously. "But you said we'd start off with me having my own place and see how it went. Remember?"

"I've changed my mind." His smile spread so wide I thought his lips would split.

"I think you're pressing your luck a bit, mister, don't you?" I teased with an impish grin.

He laughed and shook his head. The smile slowly faded from his lips as he gazed into my eyes. "No. Pressing my luck would be telling you that I'm ready to start a family again, and I want it with you."

"Y-you do?" I whispered.

Tears filled my eyes once more as I realized the importance of his words. He'd healed. Somewhere along the way, Joshua had not only put his wife to rest, but little Camille as well. Overwhelmed by his revelation, I could only sob and nod as I wrapped my arm around his neck as he buried his face against my neck.

"Yes. I miss being a father…a husband," he murmured, his voice thick with emotion. "I want you, Mellie. I ache to feed your submission, spar with your feisty spirit, spend my days and nights with you, and watch you grow ripe with our child. I've never wanted anything as much as I do you."

As his words echoed in my brain, a sense of completeness seeped deep into my bones. Nothing had ever felt so right. I sighed.

"Yes," I whispered softly in his ear.

Rising up, Joshua stared at me in surprise. I wiped the trail his tears had left before lifting my head from the pillow and kissing him deeply.

"My beautiful little fantasy," he whispered in awe.

Suddenly, the bedroom door swung open with a bang. Both Joshua and I jumped as Ian raced into the room.

His grimace from interrupting us quickly vanished, replaced by excitement. "Sorry for barging in, you two need to get your clothes on and get downstairs. James got here a few minutes ago. You're gonna want to hear this."

Chapter Thirteen

"Did they find Tideway?" I asked Ian.

"Better. James just got a call from a friend at the precinct. Chicago PD picked up Davis Walker at his house about forty-five minutes ago."

A huge smile spread over my lips as relief flooded my veins. "We can go home now."

Joshua shook his head. "Not until they pick up Tideway, baby."

"James will fill you in when you get downstairs," Ian promised, then rushed back out.

"I would love to be in the room when they interrogate him." A flash of retribution zipped through my veins as Joshua eased off me and stood. Rolling out of bed behind him, we quickly redressed.

"I'd rather have a two-by-four and five minutes alone with the prick," he sneered.

Back downstairs, Sanna wore a knowing grin. I gave her a wink and blew her a kiss as Joshua sat on the couch and pulled me into his lap. James sat across from us in one of the big leather chairs talking on his cell phone as we silently listened to the one-sided conversation.

"Did he have a burner phone on him? Well, shit. That's not the news I wanted to hear." With a disgruntled expression, James shook his head. "Let me know if he gives up any info about Tideway."

Joshua combed his fingers through my hair in a calming touch as James ended his call and sighed.

"Walker's attorney showed up demanding the captain charge Davis with something or let him go. He cooperated fully while our guys checked his alibi. Several people corroborate Davis had, in fact, been in China on business for the past two weeks. So, my captain had to let him go. Davis handed over his cell phone, and there wasn't a damn thing on it. No messages of any kind to Mellie, even in his deleted files. Of course he could have wiped them off, but right now, the motherfucker has an iron-clad alibi."

"Dammit," I whispered as I scrubbed my fingertips on my forehead. "Did they ask him about Tideway?"

"Yep, and Davis claims he's never heard of the guy. My buddy Tommy, who I was just on the phone with, shares an apartment with one of the detectives. They're looking under every rock and sewer lid for anything that ties Davis to Tideway, but they haven't found a damn thing yet." James exhaled a heavy sigh. "I really thought this house of cards would fold once they brought in Walker, but I was wrong. I'm sorry, Mellie."

"It's not your fault. I appreciate everything that you're doing, James. I really do." With a weary sigh, I painted on a smile. "Well, I guess we'll be staying here for a little bit longer then. Anyone up for a game of 'go fish'?"

Turning his head, James scowled at Drake. "Speaking of fish, where's my food?"

"You're lucky I like you. It's in the oven, asswipe," Drake chuckled.

"Yes," James hissed, tossing a fist pump in the air before racing toward the kitchen. He quickly returned with a heaping plate of food and devoured it in minutes flat. Patting his belly, he grinned. "Dylan and Nick, you two need to open a damn restaurant. I'd come in every day."

"I agree." I nodded with a grin. "Of course, anyone who cooks for me is sent from heaven."

"No, the hours are too long. Besides, we'd rather spend our time cooking up ways to heat Savannah up." Nick let out a low, raspy chuckle.

"Can't argue that reason," James agreed. "Speaking of bed, I need to get my stuff out of the car."

"I'll go with you," Ian offered, grabbing his gun before following James.

Pulling the sturdy wooden door open, James lunged back. "What the fuck?"

My heart skipped a beat as I tried to peer between their muscular bodies, worried another dead rabbit had been hung on the porch.

Pushing past him, Ian stuck his head outside, peering to the left first, then to the right. Fear lined his face. "Son of a bitch," he spat, reaching for his phone.

"What's going on?" Dylan demanded, racing toward the door.

"Fire. The whole fucking woods are on fire, and it's moving this way," James relayed.

Joshua set me on the floor, stood, and gripped my hand as we all clustered around the portal. A smoky haze filled the night sky while a flickering red and orange glow crept toward us on the horizon like a slithering snake of destruction. Surrounded by trees, I prayed the fire wasn't edging in on us from the back of the lodge as well. The distant crackle of dry, dead timber being consumed sent a chill up my spine. Red, twinkling embers whipped through the air, landing in the nearby trees and on the fringes of the manicured lawn.

James pushed us back and slammed the door as Ian frantically alerted the fire officials. Joshua slid his arm around my waist as we numbly stared at one another, unsure of what we needed to do.

Shoving his phone into his pocket, Ian studied us with a worried expression. "We're pretty remote out here, so it's going to take the volunteer fire department a while to get to us. We should start saturating the ground around the place with the garden hoses, make a fire line as best we can until they get here. Hell, we might even have to evacuate. I just don't know yet."

"We need to think about this for a minute. The fire may have been set on purpose to flush us out of the lodge and into the open. We might play into Tideway's hands if he's behind this." Joshua voiced the same worries rolling around in my own head—and likely the others, too.

"I'd say there's a real good chance of that. Dylan and I did some recon over the past couple days. We didn't come across any campers, and it hasn't rained in a week up here, so we know lightning didn't start it." Ian's suspicious tone made me tremble.

Slinging his rifle over his shoulder, Dylan stomped across the room, stopping at the bottom of the stairs. Turning, he pinned Sanna with a stern look. "Stay glued to Nick, kitten." Then, with a tortured expression, he stared at Nick. "Keep her safe, bro. I'm going up on the roof to see if I can get a bead on anyone with my scope. I'll be back in a few."

"With my life, man," Nick vowed. "Keep the target off your back. Got it?"

Dylan gave a solemn nod.

"I'll go with you. Two eyes are better than one," James announced. Nodding at the rifle in Drake's hand, he grinned. "Mind if I borrow that?"

"Help yourself. I'll get another. There's plenty more," the big Dom assured, handing James his gun.

"I'm going with you two. I want to see how close this damn fire is," Ian stated. "You all sit tight. I'll be back in a few. I need to figure out if we're going to chance going outside or not."

As the three men raced up the stairs, Drake ambled over to a pile of duffle bags heaped in the corner. Nick and Joshua led Sanna and me back to the couch, both eyeing their handguns poised on the coffee table and at the ready. Drake retrieved another big rifle and paced. I reached out, gripping Sanna's hand in mine.

"We're going to be fine," I said with a tight smile, uncertain who I was trying to convince, her or me.

"I know," she replied with a resolute nod, and fear in her eyes.

The others had been on the roof only a few brief minutes, but it seemed like hours. Joshua did his best to calm my riotous nerves, massaging the back of my neck, but I couldn't keep my mind from looping with worst-case scenarios. Was someone actually lurking outside waiting for us to abandon our sanctuary so they could pick us off one by one? Or was our only physical threat the raging fire crawling in around us?

Not knowing what we were truly up against was nerve racking, and the palpable vibe emanating off the four of us seated on the couch told me I wasn't alone. Drake's incessant pacing, pausing now and then to peer up the staircase, didn't help either. I wanted to scream for the burly Dom to sit the hell down, but there was enough tension in the room. I didn't need to add any fuel to the proverbial fire.

Suddenly, the entire lodge shook with a deafening boom. Sanna and I screamed as we clutched one another in terror. Launching to their feet, Nick and Joshua snatched up their guns. Eyes wild, they swiveled their heads back and forth, searching for signs of danger in the room. The sound of breaking glass from somewhere on the second floor filtered down the staircase, only to be drowned out by thunderous footsteps echoing from the roof overhead.

"What the fuck?" Drake barked.

We could hear the men above us shouting, but couldn't make out what they were saying.

"What *was* that?" Sanna gasped.

"It sounded like an explosion," Joshua replied.

A gunshot rang out, followed by yet another, and a muffled cry of terror peeled from my throat. Sanna squeezed me tighter as more shouts and heavy footfalls reverberated through the lodge. A cacophony of chaos had erupted above us.

Joshua knelt down in front of me, fear dancing in his gorgeous eyes. "Don't get split up from me. Don't leave my sight. Understood?"

"I won't, I promise," I swore as fear surged through my veins. "Joshua, I'm scared."

"Don't be." He shook his head. "I'll keep you safe. If I have to fight the devil himself, I will, because I'm not going to lose another woman I love."

"You…you love me?" I whispered.

Flashing me that incredible heart-melting smile of his, Joshua grunted. "You bet your sexy little ass I do."

My heart galloped in a combination of bliss and fear. Dazed by his admission, I remembered what my little voice had told me: *"You've searched for him your whole life. Deep down, you knew you'd never be whole until you found that perfect person."*

Releasing Sanna, I wrapped my arms around Joshua's neck and kissed him, pouring the depths of my heart and soul into it. As I pulled away, the three words I'd never spoken to a man, besides my father, sat poised on the tip of my tongue.

Ian bounded into the room, his eyes wide and his expression grim. Skidding to a halt on the polished wooden floor at the base of the stairs, he sucked in a quick breath. "Somebody just blew up Mellie's car."

"That was my car?" I screeched.

"Yeah," Ian nodded hastily. "But Dylan clipped the guy good as he ran back into the trees. Come on. Grab some flashlights out of the bags. We need to track him down. Hopefully, all we'll find is a fucking dead body."

Drake, Nick, and Joshua nodded before Ian glanced at Sanna and me. "You two run upstairs and start packing. The fire's getting too close for comfort. Throw what you can in your suitcases and line them up by the door. As soon as we find this fucknut, we'll be back to start loading the cars. Dylan and James are still on the roof. Holler if you need them."

"Keep the doors locked," Nick instructed Sanna before he kissed her hard.

"I'll be right back, little one. You stay safe," Joshua ordered. For once, I didn't argue.

"You too," I urged. Joshua gave me a quick, forceful kiss, then Sanna, and I watched them rush out the front door.

Following behind them, I locked the deadbolt and pulled Sanna to my side. "Come on. Let's get our stuff packed up so we're all ready to go when they come back."

"So, do you?" she asked with a cheesy grin.

"Do I what?"

"Love him, too?" She rolled her eyes and shook her head, mocking my question.

I grinned. "Yeah, I do."

"I knew it. I knew it," she squealed. "Can I say it now?"

"Say what?" I asked as we walked up the stairs.

"I told you sooooooo," she giggled.

"Shut up," I laughed, then gave her a quick kiss before we each dashed into our rooms.

Tossing clothes into our suitcases like a wild woman, I couldn't help but grin.

"So, that means you are moving to Chicago, right?" Sanna called from the other room.

"Looks like it," I laughed.

"Fuck yeah," she screamed.

I just laughed. Even though we were probably surrounded by fire and going to have to run for our lives, I knew the guys would find Tideway's body and this surreal nightmare would be over. Joshua and I could begin a new journey in our lives together.

I heard a thud, followed by a howl as Sanna let out a curse.

"You okay?" I hollered out as fear slammed the joy from me.

"Yeah, just stubbed my toe," she growled.

I sighed with relief and finished filling the suitcases. After packing the last bag, I lifted a box in one arm and gripped a suitcase in my hand before heading down the stairs. Lining them up by the door, as Ian had instructed, I turned, ready to go back up for more, when a strange noise at the back door caught my attention. It was a quiet tapping sound. Cautiously, I eased closer toward the door, trying to peer through the small crack in the hurricane shutter, but could only see darkness. There was another tap, and I flinched.

"Mel. Mel. Open up," Sanna whispered in a frantic tone.

Gripping the knob, she called to me again.

"Mel. Hurry, open the damn door," she whispered, her tone more desperate than before.

Leaning in close to the crack, I frowned. "Sanna? What the hell are you doing outside? I thought you were upstairs?"

"Shhh," she instructed. "I climbed out the window, Mel. He's inside the lodge. Open the door and get out. We'll hide in the forest until the guys get back."

Inside the lodge!

I whipped a terrified glance over my shoulder, praying Tideway wasn't sneaking up behind me to slit my throat on Davis' behalf. Thankfully, he wasn't...at least, not yet. My mind whirled. I needed to stay with Sanna, find a safe place away from the fire, and hide.

"Mel," she hissed. "Hurry."

Nervously fumbling with the locks, I yanked opened the door, but Sanna was gone. My heart thundered in my chest. Had Tideway followed her out the window? Had he discovered her tapping on the door? Had my questions bought him precious seconds to capture Sanna instead of me?

Seized with gut-wrenching panic, I raced onto the back porch. Turning to the left, I frantically called for Sanna in a terse whisper. Spinning around, I jumped, then froze as a figure dressed in black raised a gun to my head. Edging back slowly, we both stepped into the light that poured onto the porch from the open kitchen doorway. It was a woman with her hair tucked beneath a black ski cap, but instantly, I recognized the face.

Carnation.

"Don't make a fucking sound, Mel," she warned in a voice that mimicked Sanna's, perfectly. I blinked in surprise as my heart leapt to my throat. "Lace your hands behind your head and don't move."

My whole body vibrated in a petrified quiver. "Why are you doing this? What do you want?"

"I said don't make a sound, cunt," she snarled with an evil hiss. "I told you that you'd be sorry if I had to hunt you down, didn't I, *bunny?*"

What. The. Fuck? I'd thought Davis had been stalking me. But all along, it had been Carnation. She'd slashed Joshua's tires. She'd probably hired Tideway to smash up my house and plant the cameras and microphones. She'd been the one sending me all the threatening texts. The bitch was certifiably insane, one hundred and ten percent bat-shit crazy, but how did she know about my connection with Davis?

"Surprise," she giggled with a demonic grin. Sliding the barrel of the gun to my temple, she stepped in behind me. "Now shut the fuck up before I blow your brains out right here. Walk to the end of the porch and turn the corner. Don't even think about running, or I'll kill you right now."

My mind swirled with questions. How had she found out about Joshua and me? What could I do to buy myself some time? The barrel of the gun pressed hard against my head, making it impossible for me to focus on anything other than fear.

Had Carnation sent the flowers or had they truly been from Davis? I needed to get that damn gun off the back of my head so I could think. I could stumble and fall, cry out maybe. Glancing up, I inwardly cursed. The fascia covering the porch shielded the two of us from being seen by Dylan and James. Coupled with the darkness, I would be dead long before either man figured out what was going on.

Moving at a snail's pace, I tried to think of a way to draw attention to the bat-shit bitch without ending up in the morgue. Turning the corner, advancing along the west side of the lodge, she whispered for me to stop as she jabbed the gun against my scalp. Flicking on a tiny flashlight, Carnation shone a faint beam on a set of stairs leading to a storm shelter or an underground root cellar.

"Go down the steps and get inside. Not a fucking peep, whore," Carnation hissed in a seething tone.

My head screamed 'no', but my body obeyed. Praying somehow one of the men would catch a glimpse of the tiny light, I quickly scanned the horizon. My hope dwindled. I couldn't see anything but the glow of the encroaching fire. The guys were out there somewhere, blinded within the thick forest of trees. Help wasn't coming.

Stepping into the musty smelling room with the gun to my head, Carnation eased the door shut behind us. Shining the tiny penlight around the earthen room, she handed me a battery-operated camping lantern and ordered me to turn it on.

As light flooded the room, she ripped off the stocking cap and shook out her long, blonde curls while staring at me with a venomous look.

"Down on your knees. You've had a lot of practice in that position now, haven't you?" she chortled with a derisive sneer.

As I crouched and knelt on the hard dirt floor, Carnation raced in toward me, slamming the gun against the side of my head with a brutal blow. Pain exploded through my brain as I fought the swelling blackness devouring my vision. Blinking rapidly, I tried to clear the spots as I attempted to rise back up, but Carnation stomped a heavy boot into the small of my back, pinning me to the dark soil of the floor.

Gripping my wrist, she twisted one arm behind my back. Fight or flight took over, and I struggled to rip my arm from her grip. She landed another agonizing blow to the back of my head, and the darkness won me over.

Slowly rising from the inky chasm, I blinked against the bright light. I didn't know how long I'd been unconscious, but as I tried to move, I discovered I was lying on the ground with my hands bound behind my back.

"You've caused me a lot of trouble and a shit load of money, bitch," Carnation railed, fisting a handful of white zip ties. I knew then what she'd used to bind my wrists. "Do you have any idea how much it costs to hire a damn hit man? I should have let him blow your brains out, instead of ordering him to fuck with you for a little while."

"Why do you want to hurt me?" I murmured. "Who are you?"

"Don't play dumb with me, you fucking bitch. You know exactly who I am, just like I know who you are," she sneered. "I was sitting in my car outside the church that day of the stupid wedding. I saw him all over you in the parking lot. And I know you fucked him at the club. I still have a good friend at Genesis. She told me all about the scene Master Kerr made when *my* Master took pity on you and spanked your pathetic ass. I also know you fucked him that night. I would have thought Master Stephen had better taste, but obviously, he'll fuck any hole. So I had to slash his tires," she boasted.

She'd been watching Joshua and me. She had a spy inside the club watching us, too.

"When I asked my friend to cozy up to Kerr, I found out that *my* Master Stephen had told him to leave you alone. Poor Master Kerr was dumbfounded and still pissed that Mika had asked him to leave that night. Stupid prick. Kerr thought you were playing games with him. That's when I hatched my plot to get rid of you." The terrifying gleam in her eyes made my blood turn to ice. "When my friend told me she was sad Kerr was leaving the country on business, it made my job that much easier."

"You could have come to me and told me you still loved him. I would have stepped aside," I lied.

Carnation snorted with a sarcastic scoff. "As long as you're alive, he'll always want you. He doesn't love you. He's never loved anyone but me. You know that, right? He loves me, and he always will."

Agree with her. Play along with her irrational rambling. Buy yourself some time.

"You're right. Joshua doesn't love me, and I don't love him. We're only friends," I fibbed.

"Who the fuck is Joshua?" she snarled. "I'm talking about *my* Master…Master Stephen."

"Oh, right," I whispered as my head screamed in pain.

"Hmph, I must have hit you harder than I thought. Are you trying to pull some psychological mumbo-jumbo on me, whore? It won't work. A couple dozen shrinks have already tried. I'm not crazy." She paused and narrowed her eyes. "You think I'm crazy, don't you? Just like all those other fucking bitch subs at Genesis. They always talked about me behind my back. They thought they were better than me. But I'll show them. Master Stephen will take me back, and he'll force that weasel-prick Mika to reinstate my membership. I'll be back, dammit. Even if I have to kill them all."

"In your fucking dreams," I murmured. Fuzzy and sick to my stomach, I wasn't sure if I'd actually said the words aloud or simply thought them.

Carnation gripped a fist in my hair and yanked my head back. I cried out in pain as she kicked me in the ribs. I grunted, biting back a howl of agony.

"My dreams are none of your fucking business, whore. Let me tell you something. You've spread your legs for *my* Master for the last time. I'm going to cut your nasty cunt out and shove it down your throat. Now shut the hell up. My fun with you is just getting started," she cackled in a dry, brittle whisper.

"How did you find us here?" I whispered, hoping I could keep her talking long enough that someone would find me.

She chuckled. "Might as well tell you the truth. You'll be taking it to the grave, anyway. My Master Stephen used to bring me here sometimes with Ian," she preened. "I was special enough that he wanted to share me. Show the other less fortunate Doms what a special girl I was. Ian loves me, too. Don't think he doesn't."

I wanted to gag. She was beyond delusional. Outside, I could hear voices calling my name. *Oh, thank heavens. They're looking for me.*

"Fuck," Carnation hissed. "That didn't take as long as I'd hoped. Be quiet now, *bunny,* or I'll have to slit your throat."

Snatching a knife off a long wooden workbench, Carnation squatted down near my face.

"How did you like my texts? Pretty convincing, huh?" she snickered. "It was fun and so damn easy. I played you like a damn fiddle. All this time you thought it was your old Master after your ass. That's fucking classic. Sorry, bitch, but Kerr doesn't want you anymore, and neither do I. Looks like you're going to have to die, bunny. You're in my way."

The more Carnation confessed, the faster the pieces snapped into place. She was obsessed with Joshua. And in her twisted, totally fucked-up mind, she truly thought he would take her back. I wasn't about to argue with her.

Pulling a blue bandana from her pants pocket, she tried to shove the cotton cloth into my mouth. Clenching my jaws, I jerked my head back. A fresh wave of pain crashed through my brain, but I refused to open my mouth.

Landing a fist to my cheekbone, then another, she cursed me under her breath. White lights exploded behind my eyes. I cried out, but my wail was instantly muffled as she crammed the bandana inside my mouth. Pressing her knee against my lips, she peeled off a strip of duct tape. Where the roll had come from, I didn't know.

My vision faded in and out, and I fought the urge to vomit as she slapped the adhesive over my mouth. I knew I was going to die in the cold, musty room. I just didn't know when or how. I prayed she wouldn't make me suffer long, that she'd put a bullet in my head before she beat me to a bloody pulp or dismembered my body.

Why hadn't I told Joshua that I loved him when I had the chance? How was he going to survive losing two women that he loved? Would he ever risk his heart again? Tears stung my eyes and made the throbbing in my head expand with a gut-churning spike.

Sanna's frantic cries for me grew loud. I groaned as I raised my head off the floor and looked toward the door.

"Do you want sissy to come in and play with us?" Carnation asked in a manic whisper.

Grunting, I shook my head no. My brain felt like it was lined with spikes, and my movement sent the barbs piercing inward with an agonizing stab.

"Oh, but I'd like for little Sanna baby to have just as much fun as you are. Wouldn't you?"

A pitiful moan burned in the back of my throat, and I shook my head more adamantly, sending shards of white-hot pain piercing inside my brain.

Long minutes later, I heard Joshua call my name in a tone dripping with so much panic my heart shattered. He called out again. His voice was louder, more demanding. I didn't want to die. Not here. Not now. I'd finally found the man who made me complete. Fate wouldn't be cruel enough to take me now, would it?

"We don't want him playing with us," Carnation whispered. "If he knew what I was doing to you, he might not want me back. He can't find us, because I won't be able to finish what I started. And I've been looking forward to making you suffer for a long, long time." The sound of her vile, hissed cackle made my skin crawl.

Joshua screamed my name again. He was close, so close it sounded as if he were in the room. I knew Carnation would make me pay, and might very well kill me on the spot, but I had to do something to draw Joshua's attention.

As the mentally unstable bitch stared pensively at the door, I drew my leg back and kicked her in the shin as hard as I could. She let out a scream that intensified the ringing in my ears. Then, as if realizing her mistake, she slapped a hand over her mouth and lunged toward me. My life would be over in a matter of seconds.

The weathered, worn door exploded with a deafening crack as Joshua burst into the room, gun drawn and pointed. A look of absolute shock registered on his face when he realized he was aiming his weapon at his former sub. As she raised her gun and pointed it at my head, Joshua fired. Carnation sailed backward with a shriek of pain that crashed through my thundering head.

Loud footsteps running overhead mixed with the cacophony echoing in my ears. Closing my eyes, I tried to combat the pain vibrating in my head.

"Down here," Joshua yelled.

The agony inside my skull grew unbearable. With a whimper, I faded into the darkness.

"Come on, baby, wake up. Please come back to me," Joshua's poignant plea coaxed me toward the surface.

Opening my eyes, I tried to blink the blurry fog away. The light from the room felt like daggers, stabbing unmercifully into my skull. Squinting, I saw Joshua sitting next to me on the couch. A tiny smile of relief tugged his lips, but his eyes still wore a veil of fear. Leaning over the back of the leather divan, Sanna gazed at me as tears spilled down her cheeks. She softly caressed her hand over mine. Briefly closing my eyes, I savored her loving touch before realizing something cold and wet lay pressed around my head.

"Did you kill her?" I asked Joshua, licking my lips.

"No," he murmured. His tone was contrite.

I raised a hand toward my throbbing head, but Joshua tenderly drew it back down. Static buzzed in my ears as commotion and chaos seemed to ripple all around me, making it hard to focus.

Glancing over Joshua's shoulder, I saw Carnation tied to a kitchen chair in the middle of the room. A silver strip of duct tape covered her mouth. Drake pressed a thick pad of gauze to her blood-stained shoulder as she jerked and thrashed, fighting his attempt to offer first-aid.

A part of me wanted him to let her bleed out, while another part of me felt nothing but pity for the twisted and demented girl. Locking gazes with me, Carnation stopped struggling and shot me a hateful glare. Turning her attention on Joshua, she stared at his back; longing and rejection filled her tormented eyes.

A few feet away, a heavyset man lay face down on the floor, hogtied and silenced with another strip of tape. White gauze had been wrapped around his thigh. Blood seeped into a bright red circle, marking the spot where Dylan had shot him. *Tideway.* As if resigned to his fate, he didn't struggle against his awkward position, but the malevolent evil in his dark eyes promised retribution.

Anger chiseled Nick's features. He looked deadly standing guard—gun aimed at the stalker, ready to blow him away if given half a chance. A shiver raced up my spine.

"Can we go home now?" I asked.

"Soon, baby. Soon," Sanna cooed.

It seemed Dylan had appeared out of nowhere. As he crouched next to my head, he set something on the floor and leaned in close to my face. Lifting each of my eyelids, he flashed a small light into my eyes, and I winced.

"How's the head, sweetheart?" he asked in a soft, concerned tone.

"Hurts," I affirmed. "Can we go home now?"

"Baby, I told you already, soon," Sanna sniffed and shot Dylan a worried look.

"She's asked the same question before?" he quizzed my sister, who nodded. "Concussion. Don't be alarmed if she asks it again, kitten."

I didn't remember repeating myself, but my thoughts felt scattered like confetti in the breeze. I could pluck them out but couldn't hold on to them.

"This is going to be a little cold, and it might sting. I'm going to put some Betadine solution on your head. You've got a couple pretty good lacerations there, sweetheart," Dylan explained as he pulled the cold, wet compress off my head.

Alarmed at the amount of blood saturating the thick squares of gauze, I gasped.

"It's all right, baby. Head wounds bleed a lot." Joshua's soothing words contradicted the tension vibrating from his body. "Dylan is trying to minimize the risk of infection. Let him work on you, okay?"

"Okay."

Dylan trickled the cold solution over my scalp, and I hissed as the liquid stung my open lesions.

The front door opened, and James rushed in, followed by two white-shirted paramedics with Ian close behind. Quickly darting a glance at Tideway and Carnation, incapacitated and guarded by two men toting large rifles, the first-aid responders exchanged a nervous glance.

"Check her out first," Ian instructed as he herded the two men my way. "She's a victim of the other two."

"I'm not a victim," I corrected softly as Dylan stood and stepped aside. "I'm a survivor."

Joshua grinned, a true grin that lit up his face and reached his eyes. "That you are, my love. That you are."

"Can we go home now?" I asked.

"Oh, Mellie," Sanna moaned. "Do something for her. Fix her. I want my sister back," she instructed the paramedics as fat tears streamed down her cheeks.

Dylan stepped around the couch, pulling her into his arms as she broke down in pitiful sobs.

"I'm right here, sis. I'm fine," I confirmed, wondering why she was coming so unhinged. "I got a couple bumps on the head, but I'm fine."

"You will be, little one," Joshua assured.

Two more paramedics, several firefighters, and a couple of police officers paraded through the front door. Joshua stood as the men in white slowly helped me sit up. I closed my eyes. There was too much motion in the room. It made my stomach churn and my head spin.

"Mellie?" Joshua softly called to me. Lifting my heavy lids, I peered up at him, all tall, handsome, and strong…and all mine. "I'm right here if you need me, sweetheart."

"I'll always need you," I promised with a tiny smile before closing my eyes again.

Listening to the conversations going on around me was hard, but I garnered bits and pieces of them. The fire had been contained and was purposefully set, but the lodge was no longer in danger. Someone had removed the duct tape over Carnation and Tideway's mouths as they both responded 'yes' after being Mirandized.

One of the paramedics told Joshua I needed to go to the hospital, but Tideway's and Carnation's gunshot wounds took precedence over my concussion. A derisive string of curses erupted from my sister's mouth. Neither Dylan nor Nick reprimanded her, but a few soft chuckles resounded in the room. Even Joshua chuckled as he cradled me in his arms. Peeking up, I watched Sanna storm across the room, going toe-to-toe with a paramedics as she demanded I be transported in one of the ambulances. A tiny smile curled on my lips. We were indeed cut from the same cloth.

Several minutes later, I lay nuzzled in Joshua's arms, but this time in the back seat of Nick's truck as he drove us back to Chicago, to the hospital. Dylan peered over his shoulder in the passenger's seat, watching me with a worried expression and gazing lovingly at Sanna as she sat next to me skimming her hand up and down my leg. Ian, James, and Drake had remained behind to finish answering the sheriff's questions and to lock up the lodge.

"Hey, Mel," Sanna grinned with a mischievous twinkle in her eyes. "We're going home now."

~

Two days later, I sat in Joshua's massive bed—loopy on pain meds and looking like I'd been in a cage match with a gorilla—as he spoon-fed me some soup Sanna had brought over earlier. Joshua had pampered me non-stop since I'd been released from the hospital the day before. My heart swelled at the adoration brimming in his eyes and the care he gave tirelessly.

It was time. Time to tell him the things I thought I'd be taking to my grave in that dank, cold cellar.

"There's something I need to say to you," I said nervously.

His brows furrowed slightly. "Okay. Tell me."

Swallowing tightly, a quivering smile fluttered on my lips. "I love you."

A look of bewilderment and amazement lined his face as the spoon slipped from his fingers and landed in the blow with a clatter.

A giggle seeped from the back of my throat as a stunned smile tugged Joshua's lips, growing wider and brighter. He placed the soup on the nightstand, then carefully dragged me onto his lap. Gently cupping his masterful hands around my cheeks, he stared at me… studying the contours of my face along with every freckle and pore.

Leaning in, he brushed his lips to mine. "It's about damn time, little one," he whispered against my mouth. "I love you, too."

Sliding toward the center of the bed, he drew the covers over us and held me in his arms. Neither of us said anything for a long time; we simply savored the strange and newly fortified connection that bound us to each other.

When nighttime came, he helped me into a long silk robe and carried me down the stairs, out of the loft and to the rose garden behind Christian's gallery—the place where it all began. Seated on the padded bench, Joshua slung his arm around my waist as we stared up at the stars.

"When you were in England, I came here every night," he confessed.

The thought of him coming to this special place night after night took my breath away.

"You did?"

"Yes. I'd spend hours in my studio working—"

"You still haven't shown me your surprise," I interrupted.

"Tomorrow, little one. I'll let you see it tomorrow." He grinned.

"I'm sorry, go on,"

"Working with my hands wasn't enough to process everything," he began again. "I came here to remember the touch of your skin, the taste of your lips and how you sweet you smelled."

His expression turned solemn. I knew there was more he wanted to say, but he struggled with the words, or the courage to say them.

"I also came here to talk to Veronica and Camille, to tell them goodbye, and to let them go."

A fat tear slipped down my cheek as I leaned in and rested my head on his shoulder.

"I meant what I said at the lodge. I want to start a new chapter of my life with you, Mellie. And now that Carnation and Tideway are locked up, I need to know if you really, truly want the same. I love you, and I know you love me, but we're not young and naïve. We both know that sometimes love isn't enough."

Sitting up, I stared at him. He was worried I didn't need him anymore. Or that I didn't love him enough to make the necessary sacrifices and changes in my life for him...for us. How could he think such a thing?

Umm, maybe because your track record isn't the greatest, and even though you've turned over a new leaf, maybe he wants a guarantee you're not going to flip back out and float away on the wind. He wants a commitment, dumbass. You know, that thing you swore you'd never give any man? Seriously, do you blame him?

"I didn't keep you by my side as an emotional safety net, Joshua. I stayed with you because I wanted you and needed you, far beyond the circumstances we were forced into. I still do. I meant it when I said I love you." Joy flashed in his eyes. "I want to start a new chapter, too. With you. Change and grow, so we can live happily ever after. I might be your fantasy, but you're my fairy tale."

"I thought girls grew into women, and reality conquered their childish fantasies," he quipped with a knowing grin.

I chuckled, wondering how he'd remembered the words I'd said to him that night. But maybe they'd been branded in his soul, just as every moment I'd spent with him had been branded into mine.

"They do, but if the girl is smart, she'll save one dream, just in case fairy tales do come true."

"I knew you were a wise woman," he whispered as he brushed another kiss over my lips. Closing my eyes, I welcomed the tingling sensation and the profound sense of peace that filled me. I finally knew what love and submission felt like. It was exactly what I'd always dreamed it would be.

Bright and early the next morning, as Joshua snored in my ear, I bit back a giggle and kissed him awake.

"Mmm," he rumbled as he pulled me in closer, warming me with his lean body.

"It's tomorrow. You know what that means. Come on. You promised you'd show me," I reminded him with an excited lilt in my voice.

Popping one eye open, he looked at me and frowned. "It's not going anywhere, little one."

"I know, but I can't wait any longer."

He chuckled. "I can't wait to see you on Christmas morning, little one. You're so cute." With a mock scowl, he shook his head. "But you need long hours of patience training. If I was a stern and hard-nosed Master, I'd make you wait until tonight."

"But you won't, because you love me, and you know it will make me happy to see it now."

Joshua closed his eye and shook his head. "I've created a monster," he murmured with a grin.

Hoping a different tactic might work, I slid my tongue over his nipple. "Come on, Master Stephen, pleaseeeee."

Opening both eyes, he looked down at me and scowled in earnest. "Don't even play that shit, girl. I won't have you manipulating my Dominance to get what you want. Topping from the bottom isn't going to get you anything but a sore, red ass. Understood?"

His reprimand bordered on stirring my guilt and enticing my submission, both of which flickered to life in a heated rush, and I sobered.

Satisfied he'd made his point, Joshua leaned over me, studying my face. "The swelling's gone down a little bit around your eye, but the bruising is getting brighter. There are some green tinges spreading out from the purple area and the blood in your sclera isn't as dark."

"Marvelous." I pouted. "So, you're saying I look like a mixture of Barney and Kermit with a raging case of pink eye?"

"Not at all. You look like the woman I love." With a tiny smirk, he arched his brows. "I believe you woke me up to *ask* me something, little one?"

There it was, the not-so-subtle lesson he wanted me to learn. *Communication.*

"Yes, Sir. May we please go up to your studio so I can see the surprise you've been working on?"

"Indeed, we can, since you asked so sweetly." He smiled. "After we've had some coffee."

I frowned. "I guess tempting you with my body falls under the topping from the bottom category, right?"

"Yes, it does. But there'll be no sex, at least not for a little while. We need to give your brain time to heal, girl."

"Then why do they call it sexual healing?" I challenged with a sly grin.

Joshua laughed. "I fucking love you."

Easing out from the covers, he stood and extended his hand.

"Coffee? Really?" I asked, curling my lips in a melodramatic pout.

"Yes," he replied in that nipple-hardening Dominant tone.

Our simple cup of coffee turned into a huge breakfast. Tempering my impatience as we ate, I leaned back and sipped my coffee while Joshua chomped on his last bite of pancakes. With a wicked grin, he turned and glanced at the dirty pans and mixing bowls lining the countertops of the big kitchen and sighed.

"I suppose the dishes can wait," he teased.

"Yes, they can. I'll even help you clean up…after."

"After? After what, little one?"

"Arrggghh," I groaned, then flashed him a knowing smile. "After you decide if I can see the surprise in your studio now or not, Master."

"Now you're catching on. I think I've made you wait long enough." He laughed. "Come on, girl. It's time."

I jumped from my chair and a sharp blade of pain pierced my skull. Quickly sitting back down, I gripped my hands around my head and groaned.

"I think you need to go lie back down," Joshua whispered as he rushed to my side.

"No, I just need to stop acting on impulse and take it slow."

Halfway up from the first floor, Joshua lifted me into his arms and carried me the rest of the way. Once on the third floor, he eased me to my feet and told me to close my eyes. I bit back the urge to argue, since I'd barely gotten a glimpse of his studio, and did as he instructed.

As he led me through what felt like a maze, my anticipation built. When he pulled me to a stop, my excitement swelled.

"Open your eyes, Mellie," he whispered.

When I did, a soft gasp cooled my throat. On a tall pedestal before me sat the sculpture of a beautiful four-poster bed, painstakingly carved and glazed in a rich masculine chocolate color. A woman lay bound and naked upon an intricately etched blanket.

A slow smile tugged my lips as I realized it was an exact replica of

Joshua's bed. The piece appeared to be about the size of my computer bag: about a half a foot long, maybe a foot or so wide, and about six or seven inches tall.

She lay on her back with her wrists bound in long, braided rope, stretching her arms open wide, while her long, slender legs remained free. One knee was bent, and I followed the smooth ivory flesh to find her toes pointed and slightly tucked behind the calf of her other leg, resting on the bed. Her right hip thrust forward as if frozen in time while she writhed in ecstasy. Her shoulder blades pressed against the blanket, thrusting her full breasts and beaded nipples outward in silent supplication for her Master's tongue, lips, and teeth. She looked so lifelike and real, I almost expected her to move and to moan.

"Oh, wow," I murmured.

"Look closer, little one," Joshua urged as he pointed toward her face.

Moving in closer, I gazed at her features. It was me, from the top of her head to the tiny scar on her chin, the one I got when I wiped out on my skateboard the summer I turned ten. Awestruck, I blinked and leaned in even closer. My heart skittered in my chest as I stared at the expression poised on her face. It was hauntingly identical to the overwhelming serenity I'd witnessed the night Joshua pressed me over the marble vanity and brought me face to face with the submissive inside me.

The woman on the bed was me—soaring in sexual splendor, lost in submissive bliss. Her hooded lids, heavy in seduction, partially concealed her glassy, unfocused gaze. Long, billowing curls spilled over the pillow, fanning across her delicate shoulders. Her swollen lips glistened—as if freshly kissed—parted and pursed in a silent cry to please. Though I couldn't visibly see it, or tangibly touch it, a palpable energy emanated from the flawless figure. She was readily handing over her soul to the Master who owned and controlled her.

I couldn't hold back my tears as I gazed at the vision of unadulterated submission.

"It's…It's…beautiful," I sobbed.

"It's you, my love. It's the way I see you. The way I've always seen you in my dreams and in my fantasies."

"Oh, Master." Wrapping my arms around him, I wept.

My heart, mind, body, and soul had been swept away—a feat I had thought impossible—by this remarkable man. Joshua Lars had made good on his promise. He'd taken my discarded submission, sculpted it beneath his masterful hands, and brought it back to life.

Thank you for reading *Arouse Me.* I hope you enjoyed Joshua and Mellie's journey as he helped her rediscovered her submission. If you did, I'd love for you to leave a review and recommend this book to *all* your friends.

And if you'd like to be the first to hear about my upcoming releases and read exclusive excerpts, please sign up for my **newsletter**. Oh, and if you want to let your hair down, get a little rowdy, and grab some freebies, join my private Facebook group **Jenna Jacob's Jezebels**. I'd love to see you there!

What's happening next at Club Genesis? Take a peek...

IGNITE ME

He seduced me with his kiss...while his boss blew my mind with his touch.

IGNITE ME
Club Genesis – Chicago, Book 5

IGNITE ME

He singed me with his kiss…while his boss fanned the flames with his touch.

I'm ER nurse **Liz Johansson**. When a hate-crime victim becomes my patient, I meet his concerned friends, sinfully hot **James Bartlett** and his equally gorgeous boss **Ian Stone**. Both men loom so tall, dark, and lethal, they pique my forbidden fantasies. I couldn't decide if I was more attracted to one or the other—not that it mattered. They'd never notice me.

But they did.

Even more shocking, they told me I didn't have to choose. Was I the kind of woman to take two lovers at once? I'd never thought so.

Until they proved I could.

As desire soars and ecstasy beckons, I must find a way to cast my inhibitions and shame aside and surrender while these masterful men ...*Ignite Me*.

Previously published as *Seduced by My Doms*.

Here's a sneak peek of *IGNITE ME*...

"Is there a full moon tonight, or what? This is beyond crazy," I mumbled, striding to the nurses' station and sidling up next to Cindy, my best friend and supervisor.

Without taking her dark eyes off the patient chart in her hand, she nodded. "It's balls to the wall, that's for sure. Oh, and pull up your thong, Liz. Dr. Reynolds just informed me, EMS is en route again. E.T.A. is six minutes."

The Emergency Room of Highland Park Hospital, where Cindy and I worked, had been filled to capacity since my shift began at noon. The entire unit had been slammed with patients from a six-car pileup on the interstate. Cindy and I hadn't had time to utter more than a few words all night, and with the waiting room still packed, that wasn't likely to change.

"Somebody needs to take away the baton from whoever's leading this parade." I grumbled, waiting for the printer to spit out discharge papers for a six-year-old with tonsillitis.

"They will, in two more hours, at shift change." Cindy laughed, then quickly sobered. "Hey, if you'll keep an eye on my patients in two, six, seven, and fourteen, I'll take the guy coming in."

Cindy's offer, though benign, spiked my suspicion. She never passed off her patients, and the concern lining her face made me even more wary. Cindy was hiding something from me, and I aimed to find out what.

"Who are they bringing in, the Pope?" I joked.

"No. A bunch of drunk frat boys decided to beat the shit out of some guy."

"Piece of cake. Let me drop off these discharge papers to my patient in twelve, and I'll prep the trauma room," I offered. "My guy in three is being admitted, and my woman from eight is down in x-ray. They're so swamped, she won't be back for another hour or so."

"I said I'd take the new arrival."

Cindy's tone was unusually short, and I shot her my best *bitch, please* look.

"I'm sorry," she apologized with a heavy sigh. "Just cover my patients, okay? I'll take them back as soon as I can."

"Why do you suddenly think I'm not qualified to handle the patient coming in?" My voice held a bitter edge as I scowled at my bestie. "An hour ago, I was sopping up blood from a dude who'd nearly cut off his leg with a chainsaw. I think I can handle a guy who's been in a fight. Unless you question my abilities, in which case, I find your lack of confidence insulting."

"It's not that you can't handle it, Liz. It's that I don't *want* you to."

"Why not?" I countered.

She wrapped a gentle hand around my elbow. Her dark eyes swam in a pool of compassion. "Baby, you're an amazing trauma nurse. I've never once questioned your skills. They're impeccable. This isn't about the job. It's about *you*. I love you, and I don't want you dealing with what's coming through that door. Can't we just leave it at that?"

"No, we can't. What is it you're trying to protect me from? I'm thirty-one years old. I've been a nurse longer than most of the doctors on rotation here."

She exhaled a heavy sigh as a look of resignation settled over the delicate bones of her slender face. "The guy they're bringing in is gay. He told the cops a bunch of homophobic assholes beat him up. He's in pretty bad shape."

My heart lurched to my throat. Swallowing tightly, I tried to detach my personal emotions from my professional duties. Digging deep, I squared my shoulders. "I appreciate your concern, but you don't need to coddle me. Just let me do my job, okay?"

As I turned on my heel to walk away, Cindy gripped my arm tighter. "Liz, you've been through hell and back, after Dayne…" She closed her eyes and let out a heavy sigh.

"Ended his own life? Yes, I know." Simply saying the words

brought a rush of anguish so bitter and hot I clenched my jaw to keep from howling.

"Take my patients. Please. Let me deal with the beating victim."

I shook my head. "No. I need to do this. I *have* to. For Dayne's sake, as well as my own."

Cindy frowned in defeat. "If the ghosts get too real, come find me. I'll take over for you. Understood?"

With a weak smile, I nodded. "Don't worry. They won't."

The double doors swung wide. "Bay one," Cindy called out as the paramedics wheeled in a thin, young man covered in blood.

As the trauma team raced into the room, Cindy and I ran in behind them. In a familiar and well-choreographed ballet, we moved around each other seamlessly, each knowing precisely what role we played.

After easing the patient from the gurney to the bed, Dr. Reynolds and I began assessing the man's injuries while two fellow nurses cut off his clothes. Cindy's fingers flew over the keys of her tablet as a paramedic read from the run sheet. Multi-tasking, I continued my own evaluation while making note of the man's vitals en route. Trying to stay focused on helping him, I noticed the patches of blond hair—not covered in blood—were the same color of sun-bleached wheat as Dayne's. So were the man's aqua blue eyes.

Don't go there. This isn't the time or place to mourn Dayne.

Running an IV, I took a new set of vitals, watching as Reynolds poked and prodded, checking for internal injuries. The patient's face was swollen and bloodied. He had a large contusion on his forehead and a deep laceration over his right eyebrow. Blood oozed from his nose and lips, and he had a gash above his ear that looked to be about eight centimeters long. The chicken-shit bastards had tried to beat the poor guy to death by the looks of him.

Doctor Reynolds pressed his fingers under the young man's rib cage, causing him to scream in agony.

"Hang in there, sweetheart," I assured him in a calm voice. "We're going to fix you up. Tell me your name."

"Ever," he murmured.

I gently lifted his top lip, split and bleeding, to discover both his front teeth missing, as well as badly bleeding gums and a deep laceration on the side of his tongue. It was a wonder he hadn't choked to death before the paramedics arrived.

"Evan?" I asked, leaning in close.

"Trevor," he sobbed. "I want *Daddy*."

"You just relax, Trevor. We'll call your dad as soon as we can, honey. My name is Liz, and that's Dr. Reynolds." I nodded toward the physician who scowled as he listened to Trevor's chest. "What's your last name, Trevor?"

"Ham...mond," he mumbled, then sniffed.

Coaxing as much medical history as I could from him, I jotted his answers on the bed sheet with a surgical marker. Concerned when he couldn't remember his address or social security number, I suspected concussion, but thankfully, he wasn't throwing up or losing consciousness. Both a plus.

"I know this isn't the kind of party you planned for your Thursday night," I teased, trying to put him at ease. "We're going to give you an IV cocktail that will take the pain away just as soon as we can. Do you like tequila or vodka?"

He tried to smile but winced instead. I gently patted his shoulder. "Don't worry, you just lie back, relax, and let us take care of you, okay?"

Trevor gave a brave nod as he stared up at me with hauntingly familiar blue eyes.

"You're going to be just fine." I forced a reassuring smile.

Being unable to administer a narcotic to take the edge off his discomfort made my heart ache. But until the extent of his injuries had been determined, I couldn't give him so much as an aspirin.

"I want a fast scan of his belly and chest x-rays," Reynolds ordered, as I fit an oxygen mask over Trevor's nose and mouth.

Popping the stethoscope into my ears, I listened to his chest while another nurse slid a portable x-ray machine alongside Trevor's bed. I knew his right lung had collapsed. Turning as the lab tech squeezed in next to me, I prepped a chest tube for the doctor.

Reynolds held the finished chest x-ray up to the light, studying the black and white image. Narrowing my eyes, I could make out three broken ribs on the right and one on the left. Handing off the readied chest tube to the doctor, I issued an inward curse. Though Trevor needed the procedure, inflating a patient's lung was horrifically painful. It seemed sadistic to make the poor man suffer more torture.

"I'm going to fix you up so you can breathe better, son," Dr. Reynolds announced. "There'll be a sting and some pressure, but I'll be quick."

Sting and pressure, my ass, I scoffed internally. Clasping Trevor's hand in mine, I gave a gentle squeeze. As if sensing the procedure was going to hurt, he gripped my hand firmly and closed his eyes.

Trevor issued a soft whimper as Reynolds made the initial incision. But when he pressed the large tube between the soft tissue of the rib cage, Trevor's eyes flew open wide. A brutal cry of agony ripped from the back of his throat. He sucked in a huge gasp of air. I did as well, not realizing I'd been holding my breath. Watching Trevor's chest inflate and continue to rise and fall evenly, I bit back a sigh of relief.

"It's all over. You did good," I praised, smoothing my fingers over an unbloodied patch of his hair. I watched as the tortured expression slowly melted from his face.

"Daddy," he whimpered.

"Yes. Let's try to reach your dad."

I glanced over my shoulder as Monica—the social worker whose job it was to notify next of kin—popped into the room as if she'd read my mind. Hurrying over to the bed, the short, round, fifty-something Hispanic woman's brow furrowed as she regarded Trevor with compassion.

"Who can I call for you and let them know you're here?"

"Daddy," Trevor moaned. "Call Daddy."

"What's your father's name and phone number?" Monica asked, pen and paper in hand.

"Not my dad," Trevor exhaled on a bleak sigh. "My Daddy."

Monica looked confused.

"Is Daddy your life partner?" I asked.

"Yes."

"Ah." Monica nodded in understanding. "What's his phone number, honey?"

Trevor paused a moment, then slowly slurred out the numbers.

Monica jotted them down before hurrying out of the room, to make the call.

Nurses hovered, cleaning up Trevor's wounds as the fast scan—an ultrasound—of his abdomen and spleen was administered. Dr. Reynolds studied the display screen as I helped sponge the blood from Trevor's hands and face. He needed stitches in the gash over his eyebrow, but I was more concerned about the unhappy expression lining Reynolds' face.

"I don't like the looks of that," he announced grimly. "There's tissue disruption and blood around the spleen. I'll call upstairs and order a CT. Make sure he gets up there as soon as his airway is stable."

"Will do," I replied.

Monica breezed back into the room. A trace of anxiety reflected on her face. "Trevor, no one answered the number you gave me. Is there a different one I can reach Daddy at?"

"No," he replied miserably. "He... lef his phone ah house. We were habing dinner wiff Ika. Call M...Mika."

"What's Mika's number?" she asked patiently.

"Dunno. Cell phone in pock'o my jeans."

Digging through the bag of Trevor's shredded clothing, I plucked the device free. The screen was shattered. I couldn't read anything beneath the web of fractured glass. Monica frowned in concern.

"Your phone's broken," she said sympathetically. "What's Mika's last name? I'll call directory assistance."

Trevor's shoulders sagged. He looked defeated and drained...with good reason.

"Juss call jeni sisss," he whispered.

"Jenny? You have a sister named Jenny?" I asked, leaning in close.

"No," he moaned. "Cluv Genesis."

"Club Genesis?" Monica repeated.

"Yeah." With a weary nod, Trevor closed his eyes.

"I'll call right now," she promised before scurrying out of the room, nearly colliding into another nurse, Judy, who seemed unusually frantic.

"Dr. Reynolds? EMS just pulled up. We've got another one. Critical," she announced.

"Who dropped the ball and didn't bother to let us know they were en route?" he barked. "For the love of... Give it to Glendale."

"He's working a code blue two doors over," Judy informed him.

"Son of a bitch," the doctor muttered under his breath.

Ripping off his gloves, Reynolds angrily tossed them into the trash. Storming out of the room, he called over his shoulder, "Take this one up to CT stat and let me know the minute he comes back."

"Will do," I assured, but the doctor was already gone.

Noting Trevor's blood pressure and oxygen saturation level, I felt confident his airway was stable. A second later, Cindy darted back in.

"CAT lab is ready," she announced. "Is he good to go?"

I nodded affirmatively before she helped me prep Trevor for transport. After they wheeled him out the door, I grabbed a cup of coffee at the nurses' station as the last of my original patients walked out.

Plopping into the chair next to Monica, she ended a call on her cell phone and picked up the landline at the desk. "Sorry, but I've had back-to-back calls from ICU," she explained. "I'm just now calling the bar to try to find Trevor's Daddy."

Nodding, I took a sip of coffee and nearly spit the bitter brew out. Wrinkling my nose, I tossed the cup in the trash as Monica punched in a phone number. Just then, her cell rang. With a groan, she went to hang up the landline. Lifting the receiver from her hand, I motioned for her to take the call on her cell.

"Thank you," she mouthed as she stood and hurried out the door.

Finally, on the sixth ring, someone picked up at the bar.

"Genesis. James speaking. Can I help you?"

The man's rich, buttery voice spilled like syrup down my spine. It was almost as if he'd caressed me with his hands. My stomach tightened, my pussy twitched, my heart rate quickened, and my nipples drew tight. Every neglected hormone in my body zipped to life. For a minute, I thought Monica had mistakenly dialed 1-800-Studs-R-Us.

It took a long moment for the man's question to glide past my sexual impulses and register in my brain. *Could he help me? Hell yes. If he fucked as good as he sounded, he could help me for days, weeks, months. Maybe even years.* Biting back a moan, I cleared my throat, subduing my visceral reaction to his erotic voice.

"Um, yes. Hello."

"Hello," he repeated with a hint of humor in his tone. "Is this your first time calling Genesis?"

Why would he ask that? Aside from his strange question, I noticed there wasn't any loud music or rowdy patrons yelling in the background.

"As a matter of fact, it is. My name is Liz—"

"You don't have to use your real name, sweetheart. But since you probably just did, rest assured, we grant total anonymity here."

Anonymity? For what?

"Ah...okay." I grew more confused by the second. Frowning, I dismissed his strange behavior and focused on finding Trevor's partner. "I'm an emergency room nurse at Highland Park Hospital. I'm calling for a young man by the name of Trevor Hammond. Do you know him?"

"Yes. What's happened to him? Where's Drake? Is he with him?" James barked out his questions without giving me a chance to answer. That didn't bother me. What did was the command in his tone, slicing with such potency I trembled.

What the hell is wrong with me?

"I don't know who Drake is, but Trevor arrived alone. I'm trying to reach someone he refers to as Daddy. Do you know—"

"Drake is Daddy. Um...he goes by Drake, but his real name is Moses. Trevor's the only one who calls him Daddy," James explained hurriedly. "What's happened to Trevor?"

"I'm sorry. That's confident—"

"Answer me," James barked in demand. "I need information to give to Drake."

"I'm sorry, but—"

"If you're going to start spewing HIPPA crap, save it," he growled. "On second thought, fuck it. *I'll* call Drake."

"Wait," I shouted before James could hang up. "We've tried to reach him on his cell, but Trevor said he left it at home. He also said he and Drake were having dinner with someone named Mika. Do you know how I can reach him?"

"Well, at least I know Trev is alive if he's fucking talking," James drawled sarcastically. "Tell me what happened to him."

"I can't do that," I replied, desperately clinging to the last of my civility. Subconsciously, I knew James was lashing out in fear. Still, it didn't mean I had to take it. "I'm trying to explain to you that I need to contact—"

"Lady, I'm a cop," James snarled. "Tell me what happened to Trevor. What's his condition? I know you've taken his vitals, dammit."

The man's ruthless tone should have pissed me off, but for some crazy reason, my girl parts started throbbing…and weeping. James' voice and his caveman demeanor turned me on. I squeezed my thighs together to try to smother the flames.

"Listen," I began, masking my girls-gone-wild libido in a slow, icy tone. "I need to notify Trevor's next of kin. Do you think you can calm down long enough to help me with that or not?"

"Oh, lady. You do *not* want to go there with me. Not like that," James warned.

The threat in his voice was unmistakable, and damn if it didn't add gasoline to the mystifying fire sizzling and crackling inside me.

Or what? I wanted to ask. Was he going to show up at the hospital, turn me over his knee, and spank my ass? The thought sent lightning arcing between my legs.

IGNITE ME
Club Genesis – Chicago, Book 5

CLUB GENESIS - CHICAGO
Awaken Me
Consume Me
Seize Me
Arouse Me
Ignite Me
Entice Me
Expose Me

Bare Me
Unravel Me
Command Me
Tame Me
Tempt Me

Looking for more sizzLing BDSM stories? Check this one out…

THE BRINK
The Unbroken Series: Raine Falling, Book 3

One Woman. Two adversaries. A dangerous web…

As rivals Liam O'Neill and Macen Hammerman work together to demolish the walls around Raine Kendall's wounded heart, Liam's ex-wife returns—with a shocking secret that threatens to destroy their new bonds. He leaves Raine in Hammer's care so he can expose his former flame's scheme...but the longer he's away, the more he worries Hammer will claim Raine for his own.

Though Hammer does his best to protect Raine from the threats to their budding happily-ever-after, when she discovers their subterfuge, it rekindles her insecurities. For her sake, the men resolve to bury the destructive past once and for all, but Liam's ex discovers his weakness and aligns herself with a monster who will do anything for a pound of Raine's flesh. With her life hanging in the balance, will Liam and Hammer banish their animosity in time to save the woman they both love?

ABOUT THE AUTHOR

USA Today Bestselling author **Jenna Jacob** paints a canvas of passion, romance, and humor as her alpha men and the feisty women who love them unravel their souls, heal their scars, and find a happy-ever-after kind of love. Heart-tugging, captivating, and steamy, her words will leave you breathless and craving more.

A mom of four grown children, Jenna, her husband Sean, and their furry babies reside in Kansas. Though she spent over thirty years in accounting, Jenna isn't your typical bean counter. She's brassy, sassy, and loves to laugh, but is humbly thrilled to be living her dream as a full-time author. When she's not slamming coffee while pounding out emotional stories, you can find her reading, listening to music, cooking, camping, or enjoying the open road on the back of a Harley.

CONNECT WITH JENNA
Website - E-Mail - Newsletter
Jezebels Facebook Party Page

ALSO BY JENNA JACOB

CLUB GENESIS - CHICAGO

Awaken Me

Consume Me

Seize Me

Arouse Me

Ignite Me

Entice Me

Expose Me

Bare Me

Unravel Me

Command Me

Tame Me

Tempt Me

CLUB GENESIS - DALLAS

Forbidden Obsession

BAD BOYS OF ROCK

Rock Me

Rock Me Longer - Includes Rock Me Free

Rock Me Harder

Rock Me Slower

Rock Me Faster

Rock Me Deeper

COWBOYS OF HAVEN

The Cowboy's Second Chance At Love

The Cowboy's Thirty-Day Fling

The Cowboy's Cougar

The Cowboy's Surprise Vegas Baby

BRIDES OF HAVEN

The Cowboy's Baby Bargain

The Cowboy's Virgin Baby Momma - Includes Baby Bargain

The Cowboy's Million Dollar Baby Bride

The Cowboy's Virgin Buckle Bunny

The Cowboy's Big Sexy Wedding

THE UNBROKEN SERIES - RAINE FALLING

The Broken

The Betrayal

The Break

The Brink

The Bond

THE UNBROKEN SERIES - HEAVENLY RISING

The Choice

The Chase

The Confession

The Commitment

STAND ALONES

Small Town Second Chance

Innocent Uncaged

Made in United States
Orlando, FL
18 January 2025